KC KEAN

THE SAVAGE SIX

SAVAGE HOPE

www.authorkckean.com
Published by Featherstone Publishing Ltd

Cover Designer - Dark Imaginarium Art
Formatting Designer - Featherstone Publishing Ltd
Editor - Encompass Editing Service
Proofreader - Sassi Edits

ISBN: 978-1-915203-52-6

To Trauma,
Go fuck yourself.

Much love,
This bitch.

1

P

TEN YEARS OLD

"Are you excited, Honey?"

My fingers curl into the fabric of my birthday dress as I rub my lips nervously. My mother and father smile down at me, making me feel all warm and fuzzy inside.

I shrug, my shoulders moving just a little and my mother's smile weakens as she leans closer, running her thumb over my cheek in comfort. It eases the sharp pain in my chest a little, but I still can't bring myself to feel the excitement they're waiting for.

"It's going to be okay, Darling," my father says, crouching in front of me, his eyes still warm behind his thick-rimmed glasses. "We're right here with you—every step of the way. It's simply a pin prick this morning, and then in a few days, we'll find your blood connection."

My bottom lip wobbles as tears gather in my eyes, the storm rattling in my chest, growing with every breath until I can't contain it anymore. "But I don't want to die."

There, I said it.

I let the dam break open and the truth reveals itself. The soft smile on my mother's face confirms my outburst isn't a surprise as the sweeping of her thumb continues.

My hands are clenched in my dress. The soft silver color that matches my hair is a crumpled mess, but I can't let go. Speaking the words hasn't calmed the pain and worry simmering inside of me; it only burns brighter now that the words have escaped my lips.

"You're not going to die," she soothes, tucking a loose curl of hair behind my ear as I sniffle. "I'm right here. I didn't die, neither did your father."

They're standing right in front of me, but that doesn't change what I know. It doesn't change the truth. "But Georgia said it's a blood curse, that I can't control until I'm twenty-one, and if I haven't by the time I turn twenty-two, I'm going to die. We're *all* going to die." My sobs turn into a wail and my eyelids clamp shut, refusing to see the truth that I know will flash in my parents' eyes.

It's not just Georgia, either. We learned all about it in school this week. The teachers spoke of it too. They weren't quite as blunt as Georgia was, but still, a darkness seeped into their gaze.

"Darling, open your eyes." I scrunch them tighter, feeling the tears track down my face, but my father pushes on. "I need you to look at me so I know you truly hear me."

Lips press against my temple, and my mother's hand on my cheek is gone. Despite my hesitation, I pry my eyes open and settle my stare on my father. I look at him, just like he wants, but this time, I *really* look at him. It feels like the first time I'm genuinely taking note of the man I love so much.

His brown hair is a mess from the constant fidgeting of his fingers swiping through it throughout the day; a nervous habit he's always had. His blue eyes are piercing, made brighter by the glasses that frame them. His nose is sharp, his lips wide, and the dots of freckles across his cheeks makes him look younger than I guess he is. An old band t-shirt is hidden behind a worn black blazer and his tattered jeans fall over a pair of frayed sneakers.

I hope I don't get my sense of style from him when I'm older—assuming I get to be older.

The reminder sends another pang of panic down my spine, but it's quickly quelled by my father's hands wrapping around my wrists as he brings my attention back to his face.

"I won't lie to you, Darling, what they say is true, but not yet, not now. Today is all about testing your blood so we can find out who was born at the exact same time as you, who your blood kin is. The curse doesn't take effect until you're twenty-one. There is time. Lots and lots of time."

My face crumples as I shake my head. "Why do we have to know now if it doesn't matter until then?"

Why scare me now?

Why tell me at all?

"Because it's important for both families to work together to ensure you both remain safe."

I rear back, looking over my father's shoulder to where my mother stands. Her hands are clenched together, nerves flourishing into the air around her as she nibbles at her bottom lip. Her flowery dress blows gently in the wind, the small cardigan over her shoulders providing little more than an extra thin layer of protection against the autumn weather. Her hair is as silver as mine, and our eyes are the same shade of blue, too, but the smile plastered on her face doesn't resemble me at all.

I don't think I'm going to smile again.

Ever.

"Why do we want to keep them safe too if only one of us can survive?"

It doesn't make sense to me. Not even a little. They've talked about it all week at school, and I know the people inside the medical center a few steps away are waiting to take my blood so they have the results, but why?

My parents seem excited about it, encouraging even, but it doesn't make sense.

"Because until you turn twenty-one, if something happens to one of you, it happens to both of you."

"If something happens?"

My father glances over his shoulder, looking to my mother for help. She offers me her hand, and I take it, basking in the warmth of her touch as she pulls me into her side. "If they were to die before then, you would too, and vice versa, so it's important for us to protect you both at all costs."

Horror blossoms in my veins as I gape at my mother.

"B-but you said I wasn't going to die yet!" I

tremble beneath the weight of her words, and she nods.

"And you won't. Not when we can protect you. This is a good thing, Honey. I promise."

Two words, and my confidence in her grows. They have a particular way of calming the storm inside of me. Guided by trust, I let their words wash over me, drawing the power of them into my bones as I exhale slowly.

I promise.

Two simple words, and I shake the tremors that threaten to make me explode.

With my free hand, I wipe the tears from my face and push my hair back, while my other hand clings to my mother as though my life depends on it.

Seemingly, it does.

"Just a pinprick?" I ask, glancing at my father, who remains crouched beside me, and he nods.

"Just a pinprick," he repeats, digging a hand into his pocket to reveal a flash of gold. "Hold on to this; it will always protect you, okay?"

He holds out a gold coin and I watch in awe as it shimmers under the sun. Taking it from his grasp, I bring it closer, noting the pattern on one side of it. It's etched so delicately it's not easy to make out at first, but it almost looks as though it's the face of a joker. A silly hat with bells on the ends and a long face, just like the ones we've read about in books, from times when blood curses didn't hold us all captive.

Turning it over in my hand, initials adorn the other side and nothing else.

T.M.O.G.

"Now, are we ready to get this part over with so we can move on to the birthday party for the princess herself?" my father asks, drawing my attention back to him, and I nod, slipping the coin into the small pocket sewn into my dress.

If anything is going to make this better, it's cake.

My eyes are fixated on the Band-Aid wrapped around my finger. There had been a single drop of blood left on the very tip of my finger when they were done. The red stain spread across the fabric of the bandage, making it look so much worse than it was. Father says I won't even know it's there in the morning.

It wasn't exciting, but it wasn't disastrous, either. It was just a nurse with some kind of device that pricked the end of my finger and did…something.

I've always known I had a blood kin—we all do

—everyone in my class at least, but until today it had always been some kind of faraway idea that I never really even thought about. Now, someone is out there going through what I am going through, and come tomorrow, we'll officially know of one another.

What's that going to feel like?

As an only child, the prospect of a blood kin instinctively fills me with excitement and questions of whether they will like me or not, maybe even become a friend, but reality quickly rears its ugly head and I know the likelihood of that happening is slim.

We have eleven years. Eleven years where we will both exist before the curse takes effect. Only one can survive. No one has told me the details of how it is decided, but my fate is known. My fate is confirmed. There's nothing I can do about it.

"Where is the birthday girl hiding?" My mother's sing-song voice pulls me from my thoughts and my hiding spot.

Leaving the safety of my treehouse behind, I hurry over the long grass to where she stands at the kitchen door. My father is a step behind her, and I spy the flickering candles on the cake behind them.

Genuine happiness spreads through my chest for the first time today, leaving a wide smile on my face. Eager to blow out the little balls of fire, I move to sprint into the house, but my mother plants her hand on my shoulder, stopping me in my tracks.

"Hold up, birthday girl. You have a gift to open first."

Turning to her with wide eyes, I spy the wrapped box in her hand. The silver bow holding it in place is soft against my touch, but the wonder it brings quickly fades when I tear the gift open.

The contents almost tumble to the ground, but my mother catches them just in time. I'm too busy staring in awe at the two golden bangles in her grasp to do anything but appreciate how they sparkle.

"Aren't you going to put them on, Darling?" my father asks, nodding for me to do just that.

My mother slips one onto each wrist and I gape in wonder at the new jewelry. It seems one too many times dipping into my mother's jewelry box has gifted me my own today.

"Thank you," I breathe, still in a state of disbelief.

Best. Birthday. Ever.

As soon as I think about it, my gaze drops back to my fingertip and my thoughts darken.

Maybe not the best *birthday ever.*

My mother must catch the shift in me because

she's eye level with me a moment later, my hands in hers as she looks at the bandage. "Do you want to see a magic trick?" she asks, making my eyebrows crinkle in confusion, but I still nod. "Okay, but you can't treat me any differently when you see how fabulous I am, alright?" she adds with a wink, and a small chuckle tumbles from my mouth.

"Okay," I agree, completely distracted and caught up in her smile.

She undoes the Band-Aid, revealing the tiniest pin-prick on the tip of my finger. "Ready?" she asks, and I nod, even though I have no idea what she's doing. The quietest whisper slips from her lips, so soft I have no idea what she's saying, but when she strokes her thumb over my fingertip, a warmth spreads across my skin. I gape in confusion, but her touch is gone a moment later, and so is my pin-prick mark.

"Now, do you want to make a wish, Honey?" she murmurs, pointing at the pink cake decorated with a rose in the center.

I glance between her and my finger but the flickering of the candles draws my attention away, and with my new bangles for company, I hurry to the table. My gaze is fixed on the flames like my mother didn't just do…whatever that was. I hear my parents sing *Happy Birthday* to me, but the words are a dull, distant drone as I watch the fire dance. It's only when my father plants a hand on my shoulder and tells me to make a wish that I remember what I'm supposed to do.

I plant my hands on either side of the cake, leaning forward as I decide on a wish for this year.

I had initially planned to wish for jewelry, but after today, after my gift, I know that's not where my wish needs to go.

There's only one wish I want to be granted.

Taking a deep breath, I extinguish the flames as I scream my wish as loud as I can in my head.

I wish to survive the blood curse.

Overcome with fear, I can't sleep.

The unknown future leaves me feeling helpless. Questions swirl in my mind, and I worry that my dreams will be haunted by what might happen, keeping me awake, staring at the ceiling.

I've tried distracting myself, counting sheep, even closing my eyes and praying for sleep, but nothing seems to be working. The only sense of comfort I have found is from my father's coin pressed tightly against my palm. Occasionally, I rub my thumb over the face, imprinting the engraving to memory, but mostly, I hold it in fear of losing it.

I can hear my father's snores through the wall. It's almost comforting, but a sense of loneliness clings to me like a second skin.

Closing my eyes for the fiftieth time, I will sleep to come. I've counted to eighty-seven before I sense slumber lurking like a shadow in the corners of my mind. Trying to remain calm, I keep counting, and the weight of my eyes grows heavy.

It's happening, it's finally happening.

The remaining tension leaves my body as the promise of darkness washes over me, and that's when a bang rings out in the distance.

My eyes dart open, my body stiff as I peer around my room, searching for the source of the noise, but all I'm greeted with is the pitch-black of the late hour. Straining my ears, I listen for something else, *anything* else, but when nothing comes, I try to relax again.

Taking a deep breath, I settle into the mattress, letting my eyelids fall closed. The second my eyelashes grace my cheeks, another bang echoes around me, only this time, it's closer. *Much* closer.

I jolt in the bed, sitting up straight as my eyes dart to the door.

It's not the shadows that greet me this time.

It's a man.

Two.

Three.

Four.

Five.

I gulp, panic flooding my limbs as I stare in horror at the looming figures in my doorway.

The man at the front takes a step toward me, and it's as if the movement sets off a trigger inside of me. I scream.

My lungs burn, my throat raw as an almighty cry parts my lips.

I have no idea if my parents can hear me. I can only hope. All I know is that I set the men in my room into motion the moment I shriek.

Fingers coil around my arms and legs as I'm torn from my bed. I panic, freezing in place as I scream and cry, but I just can't fight them off. The noise doesn't seem to bother them as they march me from the room.

My general cries become pleas for my mother and father, but I still find myself outside in the cold night air, growing no closer to them as a black van waits on our driveway.

Reality kicks in and understanding dawns on me.

I have to fight. I have to.

Swinging my arms and legs against their hold, I catch them by surprise and manage to slip my right arm free. My hand is balled and ready, with my coin still pressed tightly against the palm of my hand, but before I can attempt a feeble swing, a white cloth is pressed against my mouth.

My vision blurs.

My mind goes quiet.

My screams become muffled.

For the first time tonight, the darkness truly takes me, and my last thought plays on a loop in my mind, wondering if this is what death feels like.

2

P

TEN YEARS OLD

Everything hurts.

My legs, my arms, my back, my tummy…all of it.

Even my eyelids feel like they're sealed shut. Confusion makes me frown, and as I try to wiggle my fingers, I feel the weight of something in my palm.

Already aware of the impression it leaves on my hand, I know it's my father's coin. The one he gave me to be brave. My brain plays catch up to the recent memories floating in my thoughts; my birthday, and I'm overwhelmed with a stark reminder of how it ended.

The bad men.

The black van.

Panic has my eyes opening wide. Light bursts

against my pupils, making it impossible to see anything for a moment, but when my gaze does come into focus, I wish it hadn't.

It wasn't a dream—the men, the van—it was all real.

The four walls that surround me now don't offer a sliver of likeness to my bedroom. The ceiling is pure white. Whiter than white. Blinding. There's a small square window above my head, black bars standing scarily in the opening.

Gulping, I tilt my head down, noting the black windowless door on the other side of the room. The handle is steel, thick, and robust, as if it's wearing a giant neon sign advertising just how heavy it is.

The room is bleak and bare.

A steel two-drawer cabinet sits in the far corner, and there's a bed beneath me. The mattress is hard and reminds me of lying on the rocks by the river back home. However, there are no trickling sounds of flowing water or the rustling leaves in the distance. It's just quiet, and scary, and…not home.

My daisy-patterned pajamas are still in place, and my toes are cold from the lack of a blanket. A shadow casts over me from my left and I tilt my face to find a woman sitting poised beside me.

She instantly reminds me of the headmaster from school. Her hair is combed back, curling into a bun at her nape, with not a strand out of place. Her nose is pointed and narrow and her eyes are practically slits as she glares at me. Her cheeks are hollow and her collar bone pokes out beneath a white, silk shirt that cuffs at her wrists. She laces her manicured fingers together in her lap as she clears her throat.

"Name."

I blink at her. No answer comes, and her eyes somehow manage to narrow further.

"Name," she repeats expectantly, but I can only gape at her.

Name? I don't remember.

"Excellent," she breathes, more to herself than anything. "Welcome, P. This is where you will be staying now. My name is Mrs. Bealish, and I am the owner of the Florentine School for Blood Kins."

"Staying?" The word rasps from my lips as she stands.

Florentine School for Blood Kins? None of this makes any sense.

She nods, leaning over me to grasp my wrists. The bite of my new bangles dig into my flesh, growing warm as she mutters a few words under her breath. I gasp, the heat growing hotter and hotter, before she releases her hold on me and takes a step back.

"W-what was that?" I ask, peering down at the bangles, but they don't look any different.

Slow, measured steps clink around the room as she makes her way to the bottom of my bed. "I will be frank with you, P. There is no use for lies in these walls." She glances at the window behind me before she fixes her eyes on me again. "You are here because good money has been paid for it to be so. Your blood kin has parents who are more than well off. Parents who are willing to do whatever is necessary to protect their child, and that means ensuring you are safe from harm."

I was already safe from harm…wasn't I?

"This is your new home now. You will learn here, you will eat here, you will sleep here."

"But my parents," I whisper, my face heating with emotion as tears brim in my eyes.

"We leave this world alone, P; we might as well live in it alone too," she retorts, completely dismissing my concern for my parents. The pain in my chest grows tighter than ever and I can't breathe.

Nothing makes sense. Not a single ounce of it. Is this the bad dream I was frightened of? Is this the answer to my birthday wish? Because it definitely doesn't feel like it.

"I want to go home," I say, my voice tight with

urgency as I try to shuffle off the bed, but I'm pinned in place and unable to move. My arms feel heavy at my sides and my legs are straight and frozen. Her eyes bore into mine, showing not an ounce of sympathy, empathy, or sorrow.

A sigh parts her lips as she shakes her head. "It will be easier for all of us if you figure it out sooner rather than later. This is your home. The quicker you get used to it, the better."

I shake my head from side to side, irritated that this is the only thing I seem able to do. "Please, I just want to go home," I beg, tears streaking down my face once again as despair settles in my gut.

"It seems you're opting to take the challenging route. I understand. We will sedate you for the remainder of the day, and tomorrow, we will begin again. Classes take place with or without you. The education we offer is not mandatory, but a kindness despite the harsh reality of your future."

The coin in my hand burns against my palm as I cling to the thought of my parents, of my home, but the more I think about them, the more blurred my vision becomes.

Not from tears of pain but lack of memory.

A scowl etches between my eyes as I stare at Mrs. Bealish. "M-my parents?"

The corner of her mouth lifts in amusement as

she nods, but instead of leaning closer to comfort me, she steps back toward the door. "Your memories are fading. Eventually, all you will know is Florentine." Her hand curls around the door handle and the sound of the latch echoes around the room a moment later. I brace for the impact of it closing behind her, but it's her final words that make me flinch instead. "It's for the best, really, because even if you did remember, it's not like they could come and find you. Death tends to be the obstacle even the most devoted parents can't overcome."

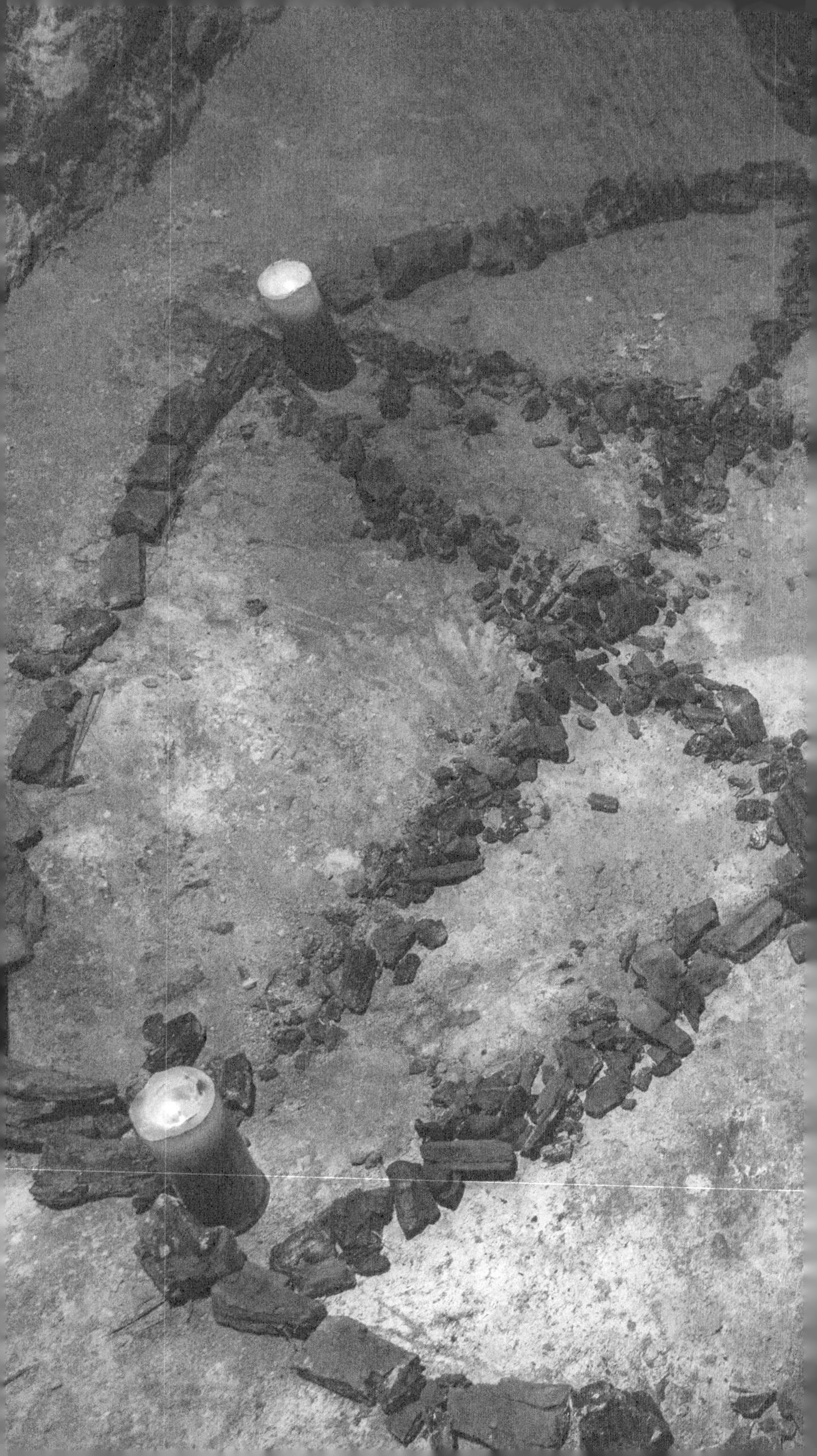

3

—

P

TWELVE YEARS OLD

The cold chill in the air brings no promise or hope for what the day may bring.

It's dark, eery, and full of sadness that seeps deep into the bone, leaving you helpless to the sensation. I wish I wasn't familiar with this feeling that now ripples through my veins, holding me captive, just like it always does.

Looking up at the dark clouds, I wish for something to happen. Anything. But it's no surprise when nothing comes.

I rub my lips together, wrapping my arms around my legs as I pray for the world to fade around me, revealing its true self. I remember very little of any time before here, nothing of importance, but the sweet scent of flowers that dance in the meadow remains.

As soon as the old memory floods my body, my right hand dives into my blazer pocket, curling around the familiar coin that has become my lifeline in this place. I could draw a replica of the face etched into it with my eyes closed by now. It brings me peace and solace, even though I have no idea where it came from. Despite that, it's my prized possession.

I wonder if the sun will shine tomorrow. It feels like forever since I've seen it. It would be nice, especially since tomorrow brings the brightness of what should be an exciting birthday. My first step into my teens.

Thirteen.

Thirteen and alone, with no understanding, no answers, and nothing but the cold embrace this place continues to provide.

The only fun thing that comes with your birthday here is the extra hour you get to play outside with one other person. I only get to experience it on my birthday since no one else chooses me on theirs, but that extra hour is what I live for.

What else is there to live for?

I've fought, I've kicked, I've screamed, but it seems I'm now the product of my surroundings.

Glancing around the concrete playground, I spy

the usual people. We're all out here at the same time, from ages ten to eighteen. People have either formed friendships or claimed a spot on the asphalt for themselves. I'm the latter. I like to be alone so I can think and observe.

It's always a wonder where the older kids are. They don't need to kill us until we're twenty-one after all, but no one knows where they go once they turn eighteen. They're just not here anymore.

The teachers here are as nameless as we are.

I'm P. Just P.

That's all I've been since I woke up in that lonely bed almost three years ago. I don't know if it stands for anything—the P—I just know it serves its purpose in addressing me when required. I don't even know if I stand for anything.

All I know is I'm supposed to wither away here until the time comes when they can kill me.

Death.

Five little letters making one word that holds such power and I have no control over it.

Laughter comes from my right, pulling me from the darkness that claims my thoughts. I turn to where two girls are skipping rope. The sound of their joy swirls in my stomach, the same noise threatening to bubble out of me, but the heaviness that weighs on me quickly quells any levity I may have been on the verge of expressing and I see them for what they are.

They're only eleven. They don't know where they come from, just like me, but at least they can manage to find some joy here. It's more than I've ever been able to do. Maybe I let the darkness seep in too soon, maybe I let life ruin me before I really got a chance to live it, but I don't recall ever making a sound like that. I don't recall laughter. I don't recall anything but impending doom.

"Are you always going to sit there and just watch the world go by, P?"

Drawn to my left, I find a friend. No, not a friend, maybe a frenemy? Either way, she gives me her usual stare, with her hand on her hip, eyebrow cocked, and her eyes narrowed.

She's S. Just S.

We're the same age, and she arrived a few weeks after I did, I think. She still lives life like those eleven year olds, oblivious to the fact that everything we do is pointless.

In her eyes we should be full of life, full of laughter, and full of joy despite our circumstances. But why bother wasting such energy? We may be the same age, but my darkness is just a little bit older.

I refuse to see the world her way, she refuses to see it mine, and now here we are.

As she gives me one of her usual looks, I brace for the rest of the speech that usually comes with her statement. Every day we're allowed thirty minutes to come outside.

She spends it gossiping and smiling at everyone and anyone, prancing from one group to another, while I claim my spot on the asphalt and give off enough bad energy to ensure everyone else leaves me alone.

When it's clear she's not going to walk away until she's gotten a response, I sigh. "I'm doing what I always do best, S: keeping this spot warm. What more do you want?" I turn my attention away from her, hoping she'll take the hint and go about her way.

Unfortunately, even if she does, there's not very far for her to go. This place is small. Really small. I can see all four corners of the playground from my small patch of concrete, despite everyone out here.

Apart from my room, which hasn't changed since the day I arrived, there is a small dining area for us to eat, where we aren't given a single choice on what we would like. Outside, the four corners are filled with pieces of rope the girls are playing with, a battered ball for the boys, and a slab of asphalt beneath us.

There's no joy on these grounds, in those walls, even in the air outside with the thick, dark clouds that consistently loom above us. The classroom, however, stands as a stark contrast to the rest of our drab world, a flash of color in an otherwise monochromatic reality. Part of me wonders why they even bother trying to teach us, but here we are, learning what they want us to within the confines of another square room.

There is chalk in there, though.

Pinks, yellows, and blues.

Not that we get to use them; they're just for the teacher. All we are allowed to do is sit straight and listen without making a single sound.

That doesn't help with the way I see or feel the world.

S clears her throat, making it clear she's not done lecturing me, but she's cut off by the whoosh of a ball heading our way. It slams against the ground an inch away from where I sit, and I manage to catch it before it bounces into my face.

My gaze darts toward the boys who were playing with it and they instantly shrink at the sight of the frown on my face. The question of whether to give them a piece of my mind or not holds me captive for a few moments. But as I steeple my fingers on the worn leather, I decide to give them a free pass this time. Maybe it's because my birthday is tomorrow. Maybe it's because there is still a flicker of hope somewhere deep inside of me. Or maybe I just don't have the energy to waste on them today.

Bouncing the ball back toward them, I decide not to wait for another chance of it coming back my way. So I stand, wiping my hands down my black pants before heading toward the door.

"Wow, P, that was almost…nice of you," S murmurs, making me roll my eyes as she continues to follow after me.

I don't know who gave her the power to tell me what I can and can't do, but here I am, living with the results of it anyway.

As I approach the steps that lead into the school, the whistle blows, calling time on our very small break. Instinctively, I fall into line with everyone around me. The noise is gone, the laughter quieting, and all that surrounds us is the whipping of the wind, the dark clouds overhead, and the heavy wooden door that leads us back to our doom.

"Call out your numbers," Mr. Thompson orders, and the line begins.

"One."

"Two."

"Three."

"Four."

"Five."

"Six."

"Seven."

"Eight."

"Nine."

"Ten."

"Eleven," I call in tune with everybody else as my shoulders release the tension coiling through my body.

The numbers don't stop until D speaks, calling number forty-eight.

Forty eight.

It doesn't seem like a big number, but for this cramped place, it's the fullest we've ever been.

Thirty girls and eighteen boys.

That's what makes up the school. Today, at least. Who knows when a new arrival will come or when one will leave? The choice isn't ours. We're just here at their will, molding into the students they insist we be.

We're a product of our surroundings. The words play in my head like a mantra, like it should have meaning, like it hurts, like it brings some kind of understanding to what any of this is, but it's none of those things.

My parents are gone, whoever they were, and part of me is grateful for the fact that I can't remember. I can't imagine the pain I would possibly feel if I was missing someone too. No thanks.

What I'm not grateful for, is that somebody else had the opportunity to turn my life into this. Somebody had more power than me. Somebody was able to bring me here against my will, harm my family, and erase my future.

I never want anybody to have that kind of power over me ever again. Except it's not that easy, and that fact is confirmed when the teacher claps his hands, summoning our attention. "As you enter the halls, Mrs. Stephens will hand each of you a journal and pen. You will now enjoy the art of journaling every evening before dinner. No exceptions. The pens are powered to offer an endless supply of ink so no alternatives are to be used. Anyone who fails to journal will miss the following day's break session."

I gulp, soaking in the information he quickly fires at us as the panic of losing our only sense of freedom rattles in my thoughts.

Marching into the corridor, Mrs. Stephens hands out a brown leather journal to each of us, along with a thick black pen.

Another action out of my control, another breath I can't take for myself.

Stomping through the halls, our footsteps echo around us. The sound offers no comfort as we make our way to our rooms. One by one, we step behind the metal doors that hold us even more imprisoned in this cramped, small school. When door number eleven comes into view, I step inside and let it click shut behind me. With a heavy sigh, I lean back against the metal, blinking back any emotion that threatens to come to the surface.

I am numb.

I am pain free.

I am merely in existence.

I wonder if I've always been this sad. I wonder if I've always been this cold. I wonder if this is who I was before I came here. But nothing really makes any sense for me to know the right answer to that. All I know is these four walls, the same four teachers, and the same daily routine that greets me the moment I open my eyes and clings to me until I close them once again.

There's no break, there's no joy, there are no

weekends. There's just seven days a week of the same thing: wake up, wash, brush your teeth, join the breakfast line, school, lunch, school, break, back to the rooms, food, back to rooms, sleep.

Peering down at the new belongings I've been given, I try to figure out the negatives to it. There's always something in their favor, but I can't see their angle on this one just yet. Not that it matters. It's not worth risking going against their wishes if it might cost me my break time.

Pushing off the door, I trudge to the bed, flopping down on the stiff mattress with a groan. I don't know whose idea this was, to create such a space, but thinking about it on a deeper level always brings out a fire in my gut. It tells me to push back, to fight against it, but the most present thought in my mind is to succumb to it.

If I was weak enough to let this happen to me, I'm not gonna be able to stop anything else.

Now, I'm nothing but a creature of their design.

Now, it doesn't matter what comes my way, we already know the ending.

There's no point, no hope, no dawn to bring any kind of light to such a twisted situation.

All they're doing is prolonging the inevitable.

Turning to the journal once again, I open it up

to the first page, running my fingertip over the lined sheets, before I scribble across the top line the only thing I can think of.

I just wish they could kill me now and save me from having to live this way.

4

P

Dear Diary,

Lame.

I'm P, and I'm...sad? Lonely? Broken?

I don't know what I am, I just know I'm here even though I wish I wasn't.

If I knew of a way to get the hell out of here I would. Hands down. Don't even have to ask me twice, but unfortunately, I'm not so lucky. None of us here are lucky.

Maybe I should take comfort in the fact that I'm not alone in the matter, but finding the ability to connect with anyone here feels impossible. The only thing we have in common is the fact that we're all here waiting to die. What am I going to ask someone? Oh, hey, do you feel sadness deep inside, like an overwhelming swell of waves crashing against your strength again and again and again? They would likely laugh in my face, I'd rather avoid any and all interactions than deal with embarrassment.

It seems these pages are the only form of expression I have, so I'm pushing through the discomfort of writing my thoughts. At least this way, I feel like someone is listening to me.

It's my birthday today.

Happy Fourteenth Birthday to me!

Still not dead. Still lost in the cycle of this damn place. Still no purpose.

But...maybe for my fourteenth birthday, I could possibly try to...smile? Be happy? It doesn't feel possible, but I guess trying does no harm.

There are fifteen of us in total in our class. Each with our own initial. It's fine for the most part, unless we happen to cross paths with someone in a younger year with the same initial, then it becomes even more regimented and they call out our age too. Thankfully, there's only one other P at Florentine's. He's a boy, a year older than me, and he sneers every time I'm close, like I chose the initial I'm called by.

Mostly everyone in my year seems nice enough. Not that I care to get to know them any better. S, however, she seems to leave me no choice.

S says I need to focus on what is possible instead of everything that isn't. I'm still undecided whether I like her enough to appreciate her opinion. She doesn't act sad and lonely or scared, so I keep my mouth shut. I guess the sound of her voice isn't completely irritating.

For now.

Either way, I'm choosing her as my... companion to spend the extra hour outside with me today because a part of me thinks it's better than being alone.

P x

Dear Diary,

I hate Mrs. Stephens.

I'm not sure if she hates me more than I hate her, but the feeling is definitely mutual.

She's just...mean.

She made V, a quiet girl who sits at the back of the class, read out a passage today about blood kins. I guess the knowledge about the blood curse that hangs over us is a part of our memories they allow us to keep, but the news keeps changing and evolving.

The law has now changed.

Blood kins may not know of each other until their twenty-first birthdays. We may be isolated like this, but not know of each other until a time declared by someone else.

V started crying, but Mrs. Stephens wouldn't take over. She made her read it.

I almost started crying too.

I don't remember anything from home anymore, but I remember the knowledge that you were supposed to learn who your blood kin was so you could protect each other, like siblings, until the blood curse came to fruition.

Apparently not.

Mrs. Stephens enjoyed the pain in the classroom today. She practically sparkled with it.

One day she's going to enjoy bringing us to our end. I just know it.

P x

Dear Diary,

(I guess it's a little less lame today.)

There's a weird sensation in my stomach and I need to write about it.

I'm still sad, but maybe only ninety-nine percent of the time? I don't know, the loneliness clings to me like a second skin still, like I'm sure it always will, but actually spending time with someone seems to be... helping? There, I said it, I admitted it, but don't you dare tell anyone.

S drives me insane most of the time, talking and talking and talking, but it distracts away from the pain I guess. When she turns to me and smiles, I feel almost obliged to do it in return, and sometimes, only sometimes, does it linger a little longer than necessary too. As if it's actually meant to be there on my face.

On top of all that, and while we're on the topic of S, it's her birthday today. Even though it's a day to celebrate her, I felt the butterflies in my tummy too when she chose me to be the one to enjoy the extra hour outside with her.

Me.

I. WAS. CHOSEN.

We didn't do anything different than usual,

but I did wish her a Happy Birthday. I think there were tears in her eyes, but she waved them away before I could be sure, and she was back to her bubbly self again.

Maybe she is my friend; maybe what she says about being positive is something I should listen to, but there's no way in hell I could be as positive as she is.

I'm too negative at the core.

Who knows? Not me.

I know I'll still be here tomorrow. Maybe I could try.

P x

Dear Diary,

(Almost not lame at all.)

Trying to be nice is more complex than it sounds. I'll leave that to S. She sits with me now, claiming the spot beside me on the asphalt, and instead of drifting off in my head, I watch the rest of the school around me.

People watching is her favorite thing to do, but the way she chatters about the boys tells me there's only certain people she's interested in spying on. Yes, spying on, because she's always trying to teach me how to do it as unsuspectingly as possible.

Sometimes, we watch the guys play football, throwing some weird shaped ball between one another. While she's ogling them all, I spy the younger girls skipping in the corner, or observe the other stragglers sticking to the edges of the playground with their heads down, closed off from everyone.

That would usually be me too, but I must admit, it's much more fun to see the world as it passes me by. It's going to rush right past me whether I like it or not, maybe S is right, maybe there's no harm in enjoying something about each day instead of wallowing.

Although, wallowing is my safe place. I'm excellent at that.

If I was getting marked on it, I would definitely come out with A's instead of the B's and C's I'm actually achieving in my classes.

I may be here, waiting for my death, but at least it isn't coming today.

P x

Dear Diary,

Sixteen.

One word, one number, and a whole world of a difference.

Something about the number makes it feel sweet and special as I now get to declare that's how old I am, but I'm acutely aware of the gloom hovering closer in my life.

Two more years, and then I'll disappear to wherever the eighteen-year-olds go.

I don't want that.

As much as I despise it here, at least it's familiar.

Like the last few years, I chose S to celebrate today, even though she insisted I should have asked T.

T.

A. Guy.

He watches me on the playground. I track him too.

If he catches the ball? He looks my way. If he throws the ball far? He looks my way.

S says he's making sure he has my attention.

I don't know where else I'm meant to look.

He's cute, I suppose, but there's no way I'm asking him. Nothing in my gut is urging me to do that, so I'm sticking to what I know. I don't need anyone else—just myself. Maybe S too, but I can't tell her that.

P x

Dear Diary,

HE. ASKED. ME.

It was awkward. I gaped at him for a solid five minutes before I remembered to speak. He had a weird grin on his face, a smolder. S insists it has something to do with his eyes too, but I didn't pay enough attention.

I was ready to say no, I didn't want to give him the wrong idea, but the thought of the extra hour…changed my mind. His birthday is tomorrow, so at least I've got tonight to prepare myself.

S says he's going to want to kiss me, maybe even more, but that's ridiculous. I've heard the stories. I've seen couples kissing on the playground, and it makes my nose crinkle in disgust every time.

Get. A. Room. Losers.

None of that is for me.

No thanks.

P x

Dear Diary,

He kissed me.

K.I.S.S.

And I think I kissed him back?

Dammit.

The control I insisted I had was gone. It was nice, I guess? I'm not desperate to do it again, but it did things to my body. Things I'm not ready to talk about.

I'm more mad that I have to admit that S was right. She always is.

I just hope he doesn't think we're doing that on the playground tomorrow too.

Although...maybe...

P x

Dear Diary,

I just...I don't know what just happened.

I was heading back from the shower block as always, but instead of Mrs. Stephens guiding us today, it was Mr. Deakin, who usually handles the year below us.

He ignored us for the most part, which is fine

by me. Although, he doesn't seem to sneer at everyone like Mrs. Stephens does.

Anyways, none of that matters, what matters is what I saw...or what I think I saw on the way back.

I don't even know what to say or how to say it.

Dammit.

~~She... I... Well...~~

On the way back, we were walking past Mrs. Stephens classroom. Mr. Deakin told us to wait against the far wall while he spoke to her. He was taking ages, and I mean ages, and I was starting to get cold, so I... well... I gave up waiting, but I didn't leave altogether, I'm not dumb, I just... went to knock on the classroom door, which was open I might add, but before I could hit the wood with my fist, my gaze locked with Mrs. Stephens at the other end of the classroom... and... well... She snarled at me, told me to get back in line. Which is fine, really, she's said worse, but it's the way she flicked her hand almost dismissively. I jumped back a step, but more because a second later the classroom door was swinging in my direction.

There it was.

Slammed shut in my face.
But no one was close to it.
Not that I saw.
Mrs. Stephens and Mr. Deakin were in a heated discussion at her desk.
It doesn't make sense.
No one else in the line knew what I was talking about.
I don't know what it was, maybe the wind, but it didn't feel like the wind.
Maybe I'm going insane in this place.
Yeah, that's it. It makes total sense.
Here I am, signing out while still sound of mind.
I hope.
P x

Dear Diary,
Seventeen.
The final countdown is here.
I don't feel any joy at all for this birthday.
None.
Not when I spend my thirty minutes every day doing the same thing, chatting with S for twenty-five of them and kissing T in the

corner for the last five.
I'm not the only one; S has a boyfriend, his name is, B.
T isn't my boyfriend.
I don't think he's even my friend. There's no talking, just kissing, but he inched his hand to my breast today, squeezing gently around my tiny B cups, and I liked it.
I also chose him for my birthday today. We didn't do anything else, but I'm starting to think I want to. Everybody else is, and for the first time in my life, I'm intrigued and curious by what they're doing around me...
Maybe for his birthday?
P x

Dear Diary,
~~I... Well he... I just... He just...~~
I couldn't do it.
Sex.
How do three little letters make up such a tiny word that holds such huge meaning? Whoever came up with it needs to reassess themselves. That's what I told S too, but she was too busy correcting me on the fact it

stands for sexual intercourse. That just makes it worse.

His hand slipped under my skirt, teasing the hem of my panties, and I just...I couldn't. I'm sure I'm the only one missing out at this stage, but the idea of it, right there, on the asphalt, only solidified that it wasn't for me. Not when there's always a teacher supervising. I don't need an audience to embarrass myself any further.

I wasn't happy, but it wasn't about him. I don't think he's ever going to speak to me again, and I think I can live with that. What's one more person to leave in the pile that keeps on growing?

Disappointment threads through my veins tonight, mostly at myself, but no matter what, I know I made a decision for myself, one that was right in the moment, and there's strength in that. Strength that won't matter when I'm dead, but at least it mattered today.

P x

Dear Diary,

I hate it here.
No I don't.
I just hate him.
No I don't.
I loathe him.
That's a lie.
I actually hate that I don't feel any anger, maybe just more disappointment?
It seems since I haven't been putting out, T has been looking elsewhere. Multiple elsewheres, if we're being honest, but that's beside the point.
Anyone in our age group has been a target, except me and S, since she's still got a boyfriend.
I'm not sad, or mad, I'm almost...relieved. But lonely. Definitely lonely.
I didn't want to kiss him anymore, and I definitely didn't want his hands on me, but he could have at least said goodbye or something? Maybe, I don't know.
Despite how much I don't miss it, I miss the feeling of being connected to someone.
The reality is, I didn't give him what he wanted and he left.
I wonder if there's something I don't remember from my childhood that played a

significant part on my behalf that brought me here. Maybe it wasn't just because my blood kin's family had more money, maybe my family couldn't deal with me. Maybe I deserve this.

I'm still talking with S, but I see the look in her eyes, the one that confirms I'm slipping back to my old ways, but solitude has only ever been my savior.

Besides, the clock is ticking. In six months, everything is going to change again.

I may as well distance myself now because people will only slip between my grasp whether I like it or not.

The truth of where the eighteen year olds go will soon be information I'm privy to, but for the first time in the seven and a half years I've been here, I don't want to find out.

P x

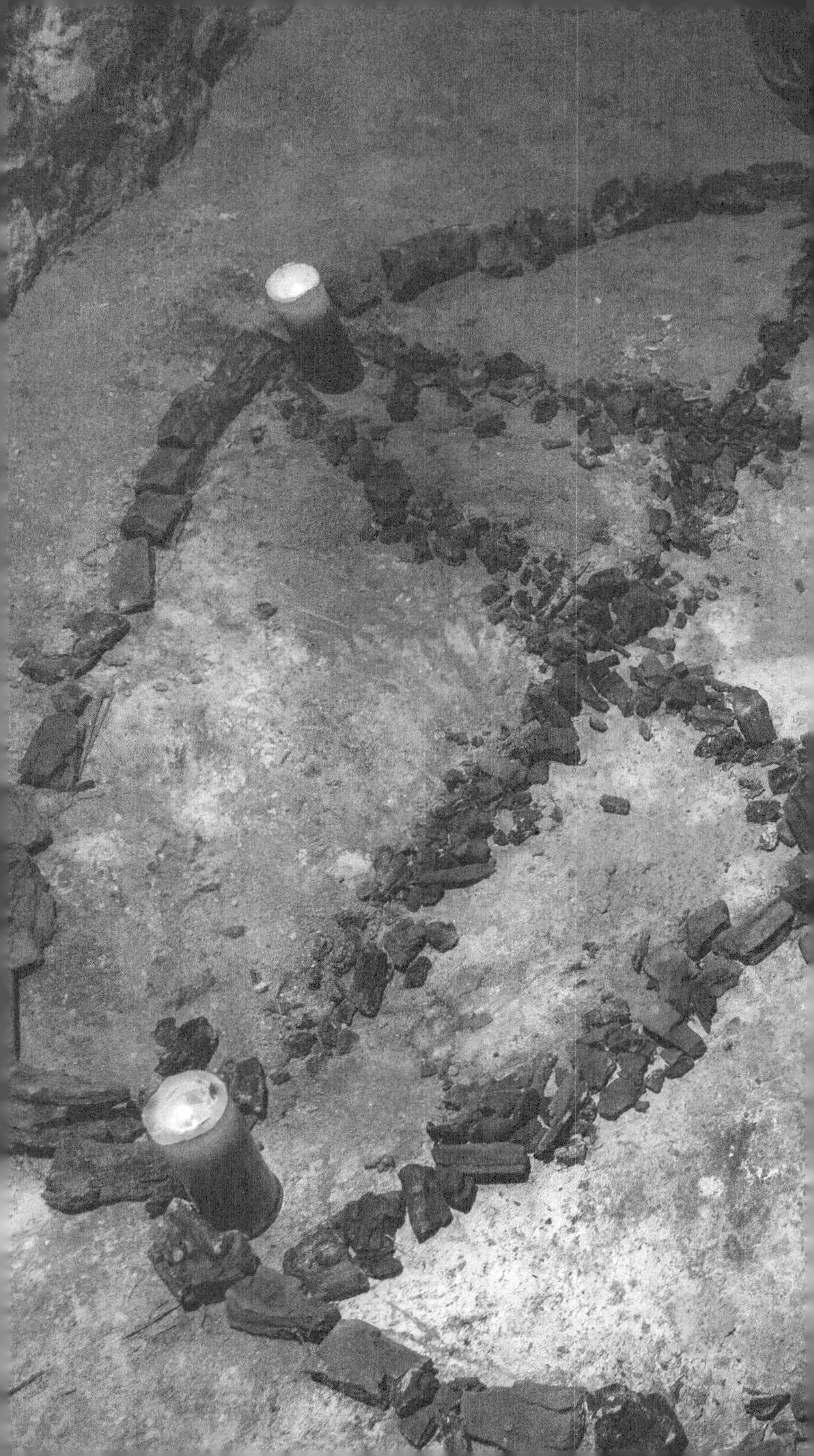

5

P

NOW

I almost don't recognize the person looking back at me in the mirror. Time seems to be moving in a distorted way and all I can do is watch it pass me by. My all-black uniform suits my mood and the hollowness in my eyes makes my silver hair feel out of place as it frames my gaunt face.

I've always wondered why I was blessed with silver hair, a color that feels brighter, cheerful, and happy. Yet I'm here feeling none of those things.

Running my hands over the front of my blazer, I sigh, taking a step back from the mirror. There's no use worrying over things I can't change.

"Come on, P, otherwise we're going to be late," S shouts from the doorway, and I roll my eyes. We're never late. We don't have that far to go. But that doesn't matter to her. She likes to be early. And despite my cooling attitude towards her, she still tries every morning.

I turn to her with a half attempt at a smile, one that makes her lips widen with hope, showing her teeth. Following her out the door, we make our way down the hallway, where the line is already forming for everyone to head to class.

I skipped breakfast today, I didn't want to eat. I don't want to eat most days. The impending doom of where my life is going leaves me helpless to the spiral that consumes me. Food is the last thing on my mind.

Sometimes I wish my mind worked differently. Sometimes I wish I was set on taking control of whatever meager remains of my life I can get my hands on. Like gorging on pizza or singing and dancing like I'm happy, but I can't fight the inevitable that has taken root inside of me.

The sound of someone clearing their throat behind me makes my spine stiffen, but I try to push past it and turn around to find the culprit at hand. T, with his megawatt smile back in place as he beams down at me and a flash of hope in his eyes.

I grit my teeth in a way that probably looks like a smile but feels anything but.

"Hey, P, what are you doing today on your break?" he asks, rocking back on his heels.

Dammit. Here we go again.

It seems now that T has made his way through the handful of girls of our age or in the year below us, he is circling back around to me.

No. Nope. No way.

I'm nowhere near interested, not even a little. He can take his ass and he can see himself out. I don't say that, though. I get the feeling that if I did, Mrs. Stephens would overhear me, and I'd somehow be the one in trouble. Instead, I roll my shoulders back and I meet him dead in the eyes.

"I'm already busy at break, T. I'll be busy for tomorrow's break, the break after, and all the breaks until we're done here. But thanks." I turn around, my hair whipping around my shoulders as I do, but a hand curls around my upper arm, threatening to turn me back to him.

Thankfully, Mrs. Stephens comes into view, standing at the head of the group, looking down her nose through the glasses perched precariously at the end as she assesses everyone.

"Follow me," she orders, leading the usual drill line to her classroom. The creak of the door as we pass over the threshold hasn't changed in at least eighteen months, but nobody seems to want to do anything about it. As I step into the room, I spot my usual seat that's been my home every day for almost eight years.

My steps waver under the weight of my reality, which grows thicker every day.

The end is coming, and nobody wants to talk about it.

The end is coming, and girls laugh beside me.

The end is coming, and guys like T still want to try and dip their tiny dicks in anything that they can. I guess that makes sense, if it's something you're into, but I don't really know how I want to spend the last of my days. All I know is I don't want to spend them near him.

As I take my seat, S taps on my shoulder, drawing my attention to my right, where she gives me a pointed look from her spot beside me.

"You didn't have to be so mean, P," she whispers, her eyes trailing to where I know T sits. I hold back my eye roll this time, curling my fingers so my nails press into my palms, biting back the snark I want to give her, but she doesn't deserve my aggression. She doesn't deserve my irritation, either, but her lack of understanding always brings it to the surface.

"I wasn't being mean, I was just being me," I grumble before turning toward the chalkboard. Instead of engaging in any further conversation with her, I focus on the pastel colors that swarm across the black background. I hear the usual sound of my bangles jingle against the desk as I link my fingers together in front of me. Instinctively, I want to dig into my pocket and pull out my coin, but I fight against it. I can't pull it out here, and I can't let anyone see how weak and vulnerable I can be. Not when I've worked so hard on being aloof and unfazed. There are some things that are just meant for me to know and others to never find out.

We're under scrutiny here at all times. Everyone knows everything about everyone, and I refuse to be any more of a statistic than I already am.

I can sense S still looking at me. She's always got more to say, but I have no interest in hearing it. Her boyfriend has remained at her side this entire time and is also best friends with T. That's not my issue. I don't want to be with the guy. It was nothing more than physical anyway.

Thankfully, I'm saved again by Mrs. Stephens, who makes her way from the door to the chalkboard, her high heels echoing on the wooden floor with every step she takes until she reaches her desk. I expect her to pull her seat and take her spot, as she always does with her fingers laced together on the desk, but this time, she doesn't. She pauses behind her chair, curling her fingers into the worn leather as she assesses everyone in the classroom.

I instantly feel the shift, the distance, the awkwardness that has never been here before. There is something in her eyes I haven't seen either; something wicked, somewhat relieved, and possibly a hint of…shame? I can't be sure, that's not something I've ever recognized on her face before.

Truthfully, I know if they ever made teachers in hell, that's exactly where she came from. She's cut-throat, she's fierce, she has no bend, she's strict, completely black and white, and we must fall into step or feel the blaze of her fury. I've felt the wrath from this woman one too many times, but I've never seen this side of her before.

A silence dances over the room as she passes her gaze around us a second time, and my palms begin to sweat as anticipation coils through my veins. Chancing a glance around the room, nobody else seems to be picking up on the weird vibe that's making the air so thick I can barely breathe.

Reluctantly turning my attention back to Mrs. Stephens, I find her gaze set solely on me, like she is waiting to have my full attention before she opens her mouth.

"Good morning, class. Today is going to open and proceed a little differently than usual," she starts, and the dread swirling in my stomach intensifies.

She's calm, way too calm. Her voice is almost melodic, as sweet as a lullaby, and I don't believe it for a second.

"Instead of coming to you today with our usual classes, we celebrate the eldest person in the class reaching their eighteenth birthday," she states, her gaze turning to the quiet short girl in the back of the class. V. Her hair is jet black, her eyes even blacker.

She immediately recoils at the attention she gets from around the room, likely wishing everyone was looking anywhere but at her, and I can't help but acknowledge and understand that feeling. I've never spoken to V. She's owned her spot on the asphalt just as much as I've owned mine. We've never even exchanged a smile. But now, as I look at her, a sense of guilt consumes me as I consider the fact that I could have done more to make this person feel... better? But I quickly suppress it, because actually, that's not my job. No one's here to make me feel safe or comfortable. Well, maybe S, but I think that's more for her savior complex and less to do with me.

The truth is, I can't save anyone from the path we're on. If I could, I would be helping myself first.

"Everybody, please join me in wishing V a Happy Birthday."

A chorus of Happy Birthdays murmur through the room, making V's cheeks burn bright with embarrassment before everyone turns back to Mrs. Stephens.

The crooked smile on her face only seems to amplify, making my concern grow stronger.

"Now that that's over, the fifteen of you are all progressing together, as each of you will come across your significant birthday over the course of the next six months. I'm sure you've always wondered where everybody goes when they leave here, so I suppose it's time you find out." Her announcement descends over the room with the weight I can only assume she intended.

Panic now seeps into every cell in my body, clogging my throat, leaving me gasping for breath.

I was right. I don't want to know. *I don't want to know.* She needs to stop talking right now, please, right now.

My toes curl in my shoes, my nails slip back to my palms, so harsh I'm certain I'm going to break the skin.

"Mrs. Stephens, what do you mean?" The tremble in S's voice is clear, but I can't turn to look at her. It will only make my spiral deepen.

If Mrs. Stephens notices it, she pays me no mind. Instead, she beams, spreading her arms out wide as she proceeds with the speech she's pieced together for us today. "Well, today is the day you finally get to figure out what progression looks like. Today is the day you leave this school."

Gasps ring out around me, the panic I feel inside floods the room as others drown in it too, and this time, I know it's not just me. I've never been the only one worried about it, but they have always done a much better job at hiding it than me.

S reaches for my hand, bending her fingers tightly around mine, and I feel the tremble that I heard in her voice. I clench my eyes tightly shut for a brief second before I pry them open and turn to her. When our gazes collide, her fear is on full display.

"It's nothing to fear. Really, you should be thankful for the new law that was enforced last year. Otherwise, you wouldn't be enjoying this as much. I would be, but that's out of my control," Mrs. Stephens explains, a villainous snicker rattling from her lips. "Now, we must do what is deemed right, and that means your journey here has come to an end."

I squeeze S's hand right back, trying to swallow

past the lump bulging in my throat, but it’s impossible.

“Mrs. Stephens, we can't go anywhere.”

“It's not time.”

“This can’t be possible!”

Students shout out around the room and I watch as the teacher's eyes darken.

“It's not time? Of course it is time,” she snaps, irritation flashing across her face, but the way the corner of her mouth tilts up confirms she loves any opportunity to raise her voice, and this is one of them.

“But we're supposed to be twenty-one, that’s when the blood kin curse changes,” T grunts, running his fingers through his hair as he sits stiff in his seat two rows in front of me.

“Ah, this is the part I enjoy,” Mrs. Stephens practically sings as she walks around her desk to perch against it. Her fingers curl around the wood as she gleams at each of us and the room falls into silence, waiting for whatever bomb she’s about to drop.

My bones tense as I gape at the woman holding everyone captive.

“What you must know about a blood kin, is that they are supernatural beings.”

My pulse thrums in my ears as I watch her lips

move without understanding a single word that slips past them.

That's not possible.

Supernatural?

We're not supernatural.

If we were, we wouldn't be held captive. Would we?

"We're not—"

"But. You. Are," she bites, snapping her fingers. Darkness fills the space as the classroom devolves into chaos. Horror burns through my limbs. She's enjoying this control, this dominance, far too much "Not only are you descendants of supernaturals, but you're not the age you believe you are either."

What the hell?

"The first two years you are here, you will not fully remember. Think about it now. Think about it clearly. Remind me of the first memories you have at the school. You see, it's all an illusion to keep you safe. Really, you should be thankful that we took the courtesy of keeping you calm as you edge closer to the almighty year of your life." Standing, she runs her hands over her skirt, a light illuminating her from above so all I can see is her snarling face. "So, to be clear, it's not V's eighteenth birthday today, it's her twentieth."

"What? That's not possible," someone calls out, but the darkness means I can't pinpoint who.

"So, without further ado, let's celebrate today as if it's the day you leave and the day I finally get to see the back of you all."

But where are we going? What are we doing?

"Thank you for giving me the pleasure of making you all comfortable for travel," she states, and I shake my head in disbelief, finally finding my tongue.

"What does that even mean?" I blurt, and she snickers, baring her teeth as her head tilts back for a moment.

"It means sleep tight, my children, for you will have many challenges ahead of you."

6

P

A warmth floods my veins, tingling through my limbs as my eyelids pinch and light flickers through. With a twitch in my finger and a shiver down my spine, I startle awake. My eyes are wide, feasting on the new surroundings I find myself in, but it offers nothing in the way of an answer.

We're moving. A coach, I presume. I'm fastened into my seat as if I did it myself, along with the other students who were present in the class with Mrs. Stephens before the world went dark.

Pressed against the window, I look to my left to see S groggily coming to, a frown pinching her eyebrows together as she glances around our new confines. Turning away from her, I focus on everything I can, from the air conditioning blowing above, to the murmured whispers coming from farther down the bus, and the rumble of the engine beneath us, but none of it tells me where we are or where we're going.

A sharp inhale to my left startles me, and I turn to see S's boyfriend sitting across the aisle with T beside him, but I quickly dart my attention away from them. They look just as confused as I feel.

My mind begins to race a mile a minute as panic kicks in and I scramble, patting at my chest and legs until I stuff my hand into my blazer pocket and find the familiar piece of metal that I'm searching for. Straining my fist around the coin, I press it into my palm tighter than ever, the imprint burning into my soul.

I don't care where we go as long as I have this with me.

Taking a deep breath, I turn my attention to the window, hoping to find something outside that may help me understand what's going on, but I have no idea where we are. Not a single clue. The road moves under us and there's no one else in sight as the sun looks ready to set in the distance.

Pinching the bridge of my nose as I take another measured breath, I turn back to the inside of the bus, hoping a second glance around the space may offer me something new, but it seems everyone else is seeking the same information. We're all glancing around and not one of us has an answer.

It's weird, though. Everyone is so focused on observing their surroundings, no one's actually causing a scene. There's no shouting, no screaming, no raging. Just a sense of bewilderment that grows with every set of eyes that opens.

Brushing a loose curl back out of my face, I clear my throat just as S speaks.

"What's going on, P?" she asks, and my lips twist. Staring into her eyes, I find the familiar storm of panic I've seen in my own reflection countless times.

My lips twist. I don't even know what to say. Nervously rubbing them together, I shrug. "I don't know, S," I admit, hating the taste of it on my tongue. I don't think I've ever acknowledged a lack of insight before, but there's no use lying.

I guess there's a first time for everything.

S nods, the uncertainty and anxiety obvious in the rigid set of her shoulders and ticking of her jaw in time to my own.

Easing my hold on my coin, I lace my fingers together in my lap and focus on the bracelets that cradle my wrists. I don't remember a time when they weren't there. They've been welded in place for as long as I can remember, and along with the coin, they feel like a piece of…home. I don't know why, there's just something about them that feels like a part of me.

"Are you okay, P?" T asks, and I internally recoil at his intrusion to my thoughts. I try my best to suppress the snark and hold back the eye roll threatening to take over as I manage a grumble.

"I'm fine."

I don't bother to look in his direction as a hand curls around my upper arm. I know it's S, probably with a disapproving look on her face, but when I peer at her out of the corner of my eye, it's a soft smile of comfort that I receive instead.

Weird.

"So, supernatural, huh?" S's boyfriend, B, says with his eyebrows raised. They're so high, they almost touch his hairline.

I shrug. "It doesn't seem possible." The words fall flat. There's no wonder, no curiosity, no anything. Right now, I need to figure out what's going on instead of believing such dramatics from a woman who has done nothing but cause mayhem in my life.

T scoffs from the other side of B, forcing himself back into the conversation once again. "It looks pretty possible to me," he states all matter of factly, and this time I can't hide the eye roll.

"For Mrs. Stephens, sure, but us..." My words trail off as I shake my head.

"She's right, wouldn't we know something like that by now?" S asks, and I internally thank her for seeing the same level of sense as I do.

If we thought we were in the midst of the unknown before, that is nothing compared to what we face now. The uncertainty is scary, and the feeling of being lost in a deep, dark forest without a ray of sunlight feels very daunting.

As I glance back out the window, all I can think is that the concrete is gone, the plain halls and four walls are gone, and all that lies before us are rolling hills, winding roads, and an uncertain future.

I don't know what's more daunting: the surety that Mrs. Stephens was going to comprise the entirety of my memories of my time on this planet, or the promise of an unknown future stretching before me like a great, dark cave with no end in sight.

"I'm scared, P," S murmurs, leaning into me as she whispers.

"We're going to be fine," I promise, attempting to comfort her with a small squeeze in return. I don't think we've ever been this close before, and

I'm not usually the consoling type, but it looks like she needs it. There's a part of me that understands that she needs some form of comfort, I guess we all do, but the last thing I want is for anyone to start overreacting and making this situation spiral into something bigger.

We have to remain level headed and focused, otherwise we're never going to be able to help ourselves.

I gasp as I consider my own thoughts.

Was that…hope?

No.

I wipe a hand down my face, hiding my scoff. Definitely not hope. Not from me—*never* from me.

"It doesn't feel like it's gonna be fine, P," S murmurs, resting her cheek on my shoulder.

"I know it doesn't," I murmur in an attempt to soothe her. "But we will be. We have to be," I insist, the positive words foreign on my tongue.

B leans across the aisle, running his hand over her thigh in comfort as he tries to encourage her too. "We've made it this far."

S scoffs, bolting upright in her seat as she turns to glare at him.

"That's because they were protecting us," she bites as I gape at her.

Her outburst is a surprise, one that I would

expect from myself more than her, but it seems there's a side of this girl that we haven't seen yet—a side that might actually be interesting.

She's right, though. They were protecting us. Not for us, but for *them*. The buyers. But the reality is, we have no recollection of our time before Florentine's. Whatever we're rolling into, we don't have the upper hand. Not even a little.

Pursing my lips, I face the window as the murmurs grow louder, running up and down the bus. I go to stand, but my butt is practically welded to the seat. Even though I can move freely while I'm seated, that's about all the freedom I have. As the ability to stand seems to fail me, I shift from side to side, trying to see what's going on, but I come up just as empty as ever, until I hear someone shouting from the front of the bus.

"The sign. Look at the sign!"

I turn to the window so fast that I almost snap my neck, but it's worth it when a giant wooden carved sign comes into view a moment later. The engraved words leave a sinking feeling in my gut.

Trinity Falls Academy.

Fuck.

We're going from one hell hole to another?

I didn't sign up for this.

"What is that? Why are we here?" S asks, her

eyes frantic as her breaths meld into short pants. Her gaze fixes on me, but all I can do is shrug as my mouth sets into a thin line. I'm in the same position as she is, I don't have a single clue.

Sighing, I pinch the bridge of my nose again for good measure. It works wonders on making me focus instead of letting the anger that coils through my chest burst free. I jolt when the bus seems to roll over a bump in the road, looking up just in time to see us pass through a set of wrought iron gates.

As we turn the bend, my breathing accelerates, matching S's as a tall, Gothic-style building comes into view; turrets, pointed roofs, arched windows, and a sense of dread greets us.

Subconsciously, my hand finds its way to S's, tightening around hers, searching for a sense of support. I can't decide if it's more for her or for me. I guess I can, but the denial is real.

Turning to look into her wide eyes, I swallow past the lump in my throat. "I guess we're about to find out."

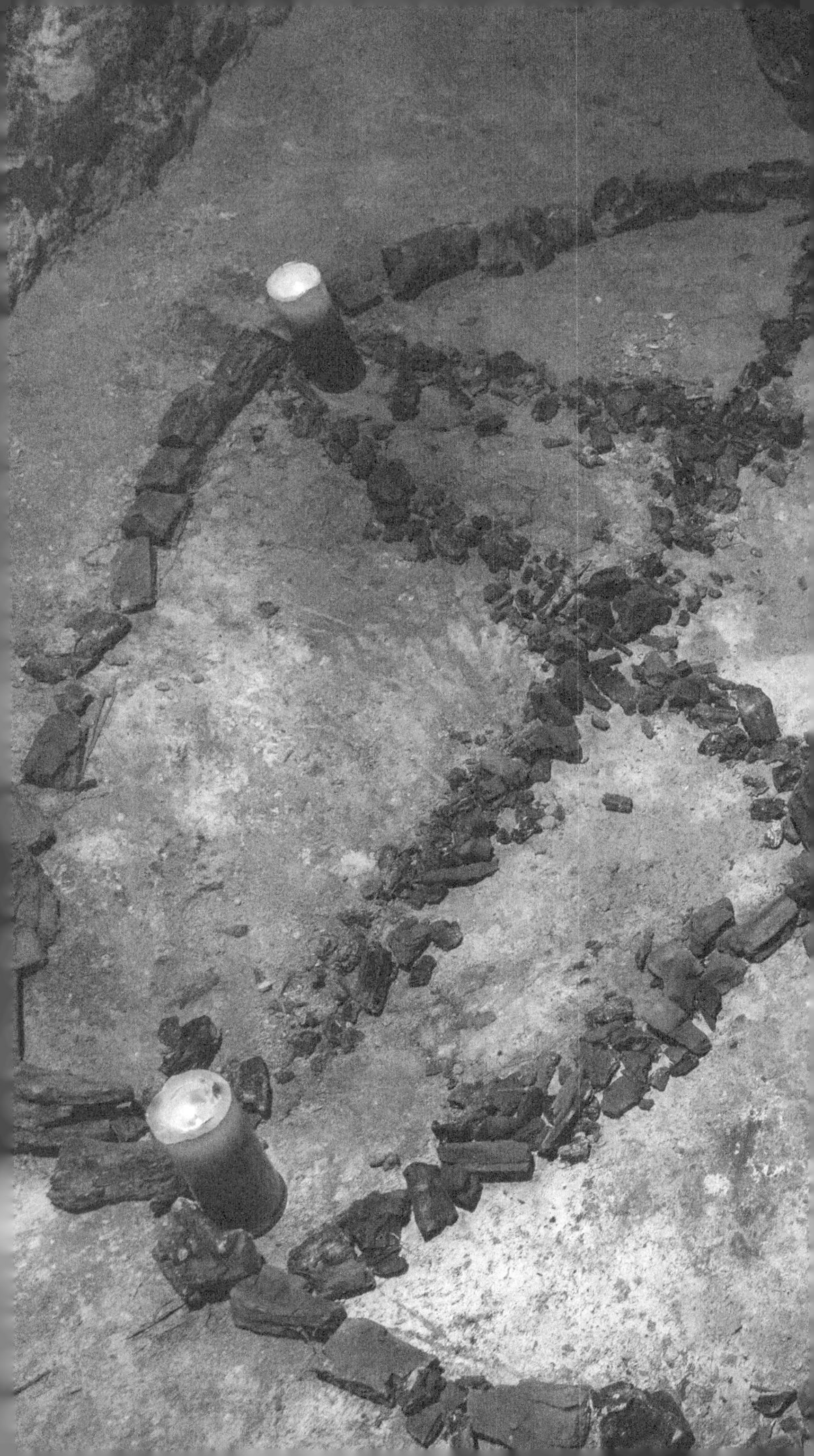

7

P

The coach lurches to a stop and anxious whispers seem to slither through the small space, chased by an undeniable sense of excitement, but I don't get the sense of thrill that others seem to be basking in right now. If I give myself a moment to think about it, I'd consider myself in a state of fight or flight, torn between what to do.

Run or stay.

It's a weird feeling. I've never really acknowledged the option to run before, to fight for myself, but in a place like this, I don't see my chances of escape being any greater than compared to Florentine's.

I can accept the fact that I've spent so long trapped in the 'mental' freeze zone,' that when things come my way, I accept them, but now, sitting here in a state of uncertainty, I feel like there's something I should be doing. I think.

A sudden sensation ripples through my body, tingling down my spine. I don't know how I came to know it, but I immediately sense the relief flooding through my veins and I know I can stand. Jumping to my feet, S is right beside me, eyes wide and staring deep into mine as we hear the sound of the door opening at the front of the bus.

Without a word, everyone is escorted off one by one. When it gets to our row, I let S lead the way, but I hold back. My feet seem rooted to the spot, my mind swirling with ideas, but it's as if she senses my uncertainty, and before she even takes a single step, she reaches for my hand and tugs me along behind her.

It looks like there's no choice but to face it head on, even if I don't want to. It seems I spend a lot of time doing things I don't want to do. I can't assume being at this place is going to be any different.

S's hold on me tightens as she rushes down the steps, pulling me along with her, and I feel like I'm choking on my breath as unfamiliar asphalt comes into view. I run my tongue over my bottom lip as I stare down at my feet. A shiver runs down my spine as an eeriness whispers in the gentle breeze around me. It's strange to feel stronger sensations than I would at Florentine's. I've lived my life on repeat inside that glorified cardboard box, and now I feel triggered even more than usual. I thought it didn't get worse than that. Was I wrong?

Taking a deep breath, I lift my gaze, gaping at my new surroundings. I can see for miles from here. Hills after hills after hills, in every direction. They all roll into one another. The grass is as green as emeralds. The sky is as blue as sapphires. And the asphalt beneath my Florentine-issued school shoes is as deep as onyx.

It's a far cry from the playground we're all familiar with.

Taking in my fellow Florentine students, it's clear I'm not the only one gaping in wonder. I feel a burst of...something, in my gut, burning bright for the briefest moment before reality washes over me and trepidation claims me. Now I'm balanced on bated breath, waiting for the other shoe to drop and a dark truth to spring itself on me.

As if sensing the rolling questions swirling in my brain, the creak of a door rings in my ears, drawing my attention to the entrance of what I can only presume is Trinity Falls Academy, as the sign stated. A man steps out in a fitted suit. The navy matches the color of his eyes, while his black hair is peppered with speckles of gray. The smile on his face is wide, pride etched into every feature on his face as another bubble of excitement swirls among my peers.

I can't decide if I want to feel it with them. Was that the sensation I quickly squashed only moments ago? Excitement is something I've seen in others many times, but it's such a foreign feeling I don't think I could even identify it if I tried.

Bringing my attention back to the man approaching, I watch as he comes to a stop in front of us and everyone grows quiet, waiting for him to speak.

"Good morning, children of Florentine. It is so wonderful to have you joining us today. My name is Professor Whitmore, and I am the headmaster of this fine establishment. I'm aware that, as many have before you, you will have questions today, questions that will take more time to answer than we have sunlight remaining, but I promise you, by the end of the week, you will be more than familiar with how we operate here."

Clearing his throat, his eyes meet mine as he laces his fingers together in front of him. "You are, quite politely, the runts of the litter," he states, his eyes moving on to the rest of the group as I gape at him, shocked at his choice of words. Any attempt at a response is lost as I reel in the turmoil of his description of us. "But you're here now, and that is what matters. We are Trinity Falls Academy, home to wolves, witches, vampires and humans alike. I'm sure Mrs. Stephens filled you in on the possibilities your futures now hold, so our goal today is to get you familiar with who you truly are and set you on the path to make the most of this new and exciting life you've been given."

His words are filled with possibility, sending a ripple of glee through our small group. I don't feel any glee, though, all I feel is a sense of horror.

If what he's saying is true, then Mrs. Stephens was telling the truth. If that wasn't shock enough, the words being spoken send me over the edge.

Supernatural? Wolves? Witches? Vampires.

How? Why? What?

I shake my head, disbelief clawing at my insides as I struggle to breathe.

I don't want any of this. Whatever this sick, twisted joke is about, I don't want any of it.

On top of all that, the reality is clear. This man is aware of what has been happening to us. He stands before us unashamed in the fact that nothing was done to help us. It's not even a thought to him, I can sense it.

Orphaned, ripped to nothing, drained of our memories, and he wants me to jump for joy at the news he's providing. Apparently, I should be ecstatic, but in all actuality, I'm in absolute disbelief. This isn't exciting.

This is a new path that is sure to be riddled with new hurdles. A new school and new rules inside a new set of walls whose sole purpose is to contain me. I'm going from one prison to the next.

S squeezes my arm, bouncing on the balls of her feet, her eyes shining bright as they meet mine. This is one time in our lives that she is one hundred percent not going to receive any positivity from me. I'm too stuck wondering what this all means.

I may have hated it, but at least I was familiar with how Florentine worked. From the lessons to the hierarchy, it all made sense. Not only is all of this unknown, but what do they want from us? Our lives? Haven't they already taken enough?

"At Trinity Falls Academy your eyes will be opened to a much broader spectrum. For my witches, you will learn how to become one with your magic, hopefully finding a coven for yourselves along the way. Our wolves fall into packs, running free in the night when the full moon shines, finding a true part of yourself that you hadn't found before. Vampires, the friendships, abilities, and new skills that will be available to you are nothing that you will have experienced before. For those that are actually humans here, do not stress that you are one of the fatal few humans that are unfortunately a descendant of the blood kin curse along with my supernaturals. The rest of the human world lives without knowledge of our existence, and as such, it will be a blessing for you to gain such knowledge. It is with tremendous pride that I assure you it is my responsibility, as the law states, to ensure that an equal platform is provided for everybody. It is our utmost intention to give you a level playing field. There are many things that await you on the other side of those doors. So please, take a moment, take a deep breath, and be prepared to say goodbye to the old version of yourselves, because once we enter, there is no turning back. There is no yesterday. There is only hope that over the next twelve months you can grasp the opportunities we put in front of you and give yourself a chance to survive the blood curse."

"What's the point in any of this? If people paid for us to be hidden away and protected, they can surely just pay to ensure we fail here," V shouts from the back of the group, gaining everyone's attention as I too turn to her with wide eyes, silently applauding her.

Professor Whitmore chuckles, the sound grating at my brain. "Of course, I understand your concerns, but the law dictates equal rights, and the law is bound into the very being of our existence." He tilts his head at V before glancing around the entire group. "It is believed that any family who interferes over the course of the next two years of your life may find the blood curse runs deeper than they know, for their fate may take a dark turn come their child's twenty-second birthday if they don't follow the rules."

I bite back a scoff. He seems confident in what he's saying, but it sounds like a lot of what ifs and assumptions to me, when what we really need right now is plain black and white. We're being ripped from one home and stuffed into another. Again. Only this time, we might be privileged enough to remember the transition and what we're leaving behind.

Silence greets us when no one else raises any cause for concern, but I'm internally thankful that V seems to be on the same wavelength as me.

Professor Whitmore throws his arms out wide as his smile grows further, although it doesn't seem to quite meet his eyes. "Please, Florentine students, follow me, and explore the adventures your future now holds."

It feels like a well practiced line, but it seems to do the trick as everyone starts to move, including V, who does stutter for a moment, but eventually falls into line. I watch as they all move. S is now curled under B's arm, and I don't even remember when she let go of me. I'm left with my feet rooted to the ground. My heart racing wildly in my chest.

"I'm assuming you're going to follow, Miss?" Whitmore's words are polite, but the tone is clear. Meeting his gaze, I realize he's already by the door.

I rub my lips together, summoning the courage to open my mouth. "What is all of this for?" I ask. So few words for such a big question, but I can't seem to move without a little more understanding. A simple question, yet endless possible responses. My fear of the unknown holds me in place as something deep inside me screams for an answer.

When the professor smiles this time, it meets his eyes, the gleam genuine as he nods in my direction. "This is your chance to survive. The question is, are you going to take it?"

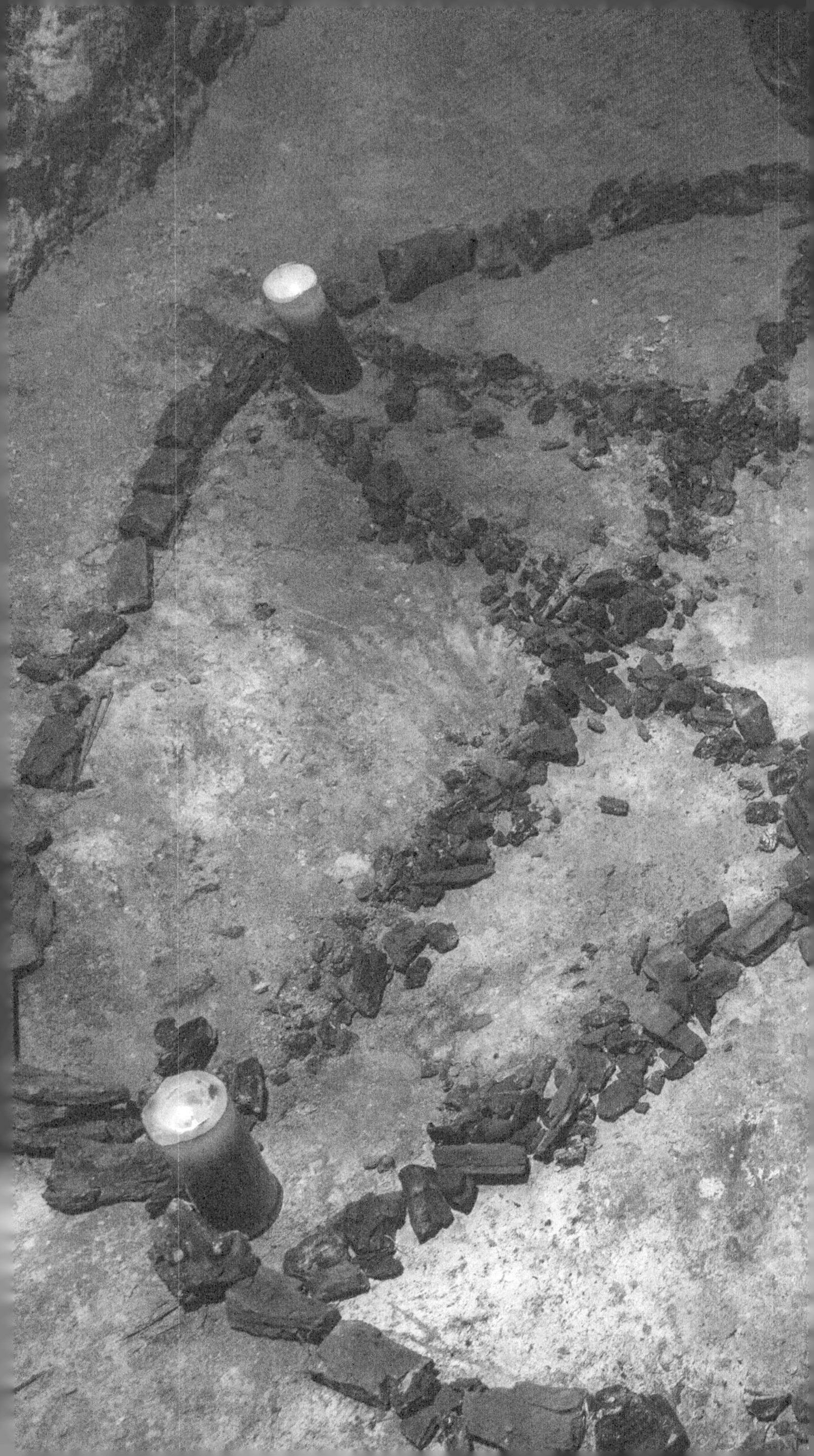

8

P

Stepping through the arched doorway and into the academy, I find it impossible to inhale a full breath of air. His words fuel my ability to put one foot in front of the other. It's the only way I can explain it. It definitely doesn't help that what greets me, steals what remains of my breath as my eyes dart around the grandeur that surrounds me.

I don't know where to look first.

Intricately detailed gray marble floors are framed with sparkling black tiles leading off in every direction. The pattern proceeds up both sets of stairs that run parallel to one another until they meet at the balcony that overlooks the entire foyer. Dark wooden beams and huge panes of glass decorate the upper floor, trailing down the staircases, but as I tilt my head back, it's the black and gold chandelier that hangs from the ceiling that captures my attention.

I can hear the lilt in Professor Whitmore's voice as he addresses our group, pointing out every little detail of the space, but I'm struggling to take it in. He's talking, but his words aren't registering in my mind as I soak in the sights before me.

Curling my hands in front of me, I look down at my feet, panicking over the dirt that lines the bottom of my shoes. It's not even dirt, barely dust, but I'm acutely aware of it and the mess I could leave in my wake.

I'm out of place here, I'm certain.

It takes all of my strength to push down the nausea that churns in my stomach as I focus on trying to keep up with the group, but my wandering eyes make it far more difficult than it should.

"This way will lead to the dining facilities, and the right will lead to the Grand Hall, where we will be visiting once we have finished our tour," Whitmore explains, the sounds coming from his mouth finally registering in my brain as I follow his direction. "There are lots of exciting things to come in there, but telling you would spoil the surprise," he foretells with a teasing smile before pointing toward the staircase as if he hadn't said anything at all. "The staircases lead to a multitude of classrooms, which I'm sure you will have the privilege of attending come tomorrow. For now, though, let us follow the pathway leading out to the lawn, shall we?" he offers, turning without a backward glance, and everyone follows after him.

Myself included.

A set of double doors sit invitingly at the other end of the open space, a replica of the ones we first entered. Only, when they open, with no one present to turn the door handle, a shiver runs down my spine. It's quickly eradicated by the brightness that filters into the room, offering a warm glow to bask in.

Stone steps lead down to the lawn Whitmore mentioned, and once again my gaze flicks around the space, trying to take it all in at once.

"Our sprawling lawn is where most gather to enjoy recreational activities in their spare time. The buildings off in the distance house the dormitories, to which you will be assigned later today."

Everyone seems to be hanging off his every word, but I opt to tune him out, focusing on the people that fill the space around us.

It has to be the largest lawn I've ever seen in my life.

Maybe. Possibly.

I don't really know.

I just remember the four corners of Florentine's barren playground and a fleeting memory of the meadows from my past, but that could just be a figment of my imagination at this stage.

This space is…it's something. My mind swells with a sense of abundance I've never felt before. As if the possibilities are endless; *my* possibilities are endless. Like I could be free. As if I'm not alone. *We're* not alone.

There are people everywhere and I'm overwhelmed by the sound of laughter coming from every direction. Excited murmurs stir within my group, and a tingle flickers through my fingertips as I close my eyes and focus on the sound of the gentle breeze rustling through the trees to the left. I'm sure S is basking in the positive vibes that echo around us.

Forcing my eyes back open, I focus on the lawn again. To my left, in front of the tree line, are multiple benches filled with girls and boys mingling amongst each other. Some are eating, some are huddled in close, whispering among themselves, while others are laughing and joking around. It's all so foreign, and probably perfectly normal.

Straight ahead, people are lying on the grass, staring up at the clouds, while to the right is a group of guys playing around, running with a football.

Not like they did at Florentine's, though. There are actual white posts set up and people calling out orders, and is that…

A wolf. There's a freaking wolf. More than one. Multiple. Holy crap.

A dozen wolves prowl along the football field, some listening to the people shouting out instructions while others seem to trail around the perimeter.

The taste of excitement ripples on my tongue as my stomach churns with something more than just fear for the first time I can remember. Mrs. Stephens wasn't lying. Professor Whitmore wasn't lying. I can see them with my own eyes.

So does that mean there are vampires and witches mixed among them as well?

Holy fuck.

I think I might pass out.

Taking a deep breath, I note the smell in the air is rich with flowers, and a sense of hope combined with a desire for wisdom that I've yet to learn. It's impossible not to feel out of my depth given the fact that I have zero knowledge of what is going on here, but there is a part of me, a teeny, tiny part of me, that is intrigued.

I hear Professor Whitmore's voice grow quieter, and when I turn to follow the sound, I find him trailing to the right with everyone else a step behind him. S is sandwiched between B and T, but I'm frozen, my shoes nestled on the grass as wonder dances along my skin, threatening to send my emotions into overdrive.

How can Professor Whitmore expect us to carry on looking at everything this place has to offer when it's already so much to digest. Tilting my head to the sky, I force my eyes to remain open as I take a deep breath. I count the seconds I inhale, and I count the seconds I exhale, repeating the motion again and again, slowly parting my lips as I let the warmth wash over my body.

I've barely been here five minutes and I've already experienced more emotions and feelings than my entire time at Florentine's. It leaves me torn between excitement and panic. As if the fight or flight has morphed into sink or swim and I can't decide which is the right option. One is definitely easier than the other, but that doesn't always make it the correct answer.

Explaining it is impossible.

"Watch out!" Someone hollers, their voice growing closer. It's the only warning I get before a force like a pickup truck collides with my right side. I grunt, my body stiffening as I brace for further impact, but when I find myself flat on my back, the grass tickling my fingertips, it's not as painful as I expect.

Blinking, my breath lodges in my throat when I find what had plowed into me hovering a few inches from my face.

Not a man, not a woman. Not a human at all.

A wolf.

I'm surprised and speechless, but if I think the wolf is a shock, watching them shift in front of my very eyes is something else entirely. Their fur turns to flesh, animal to man, and I peer up at a face so ridiculously handsome, it must be another part of a dream. Regardless, the rest of the academy blurs into the background. All I can see is him, all I can hear is the ringing of my pulse in my ears, all I can smell is a woodsy scent that is definitely coming from him, and it takes all I have not to reach out and run my fingertips over his cheek.

Tousled brown hair sweeps across his forehead, his eyes a piercing blue as they burn into mine. Caught up in him, my gaze trails down, noting his shoulders are tense as he braces himself over me, fists coiled on either side of my face. Taut muscles travel down into what looks like a six-pack, when realization washes over me and heat rises to my cheeks.

I'm pinned to the floor by a guy, but not just any

guy. I'm pinned to a manicured lawn by the most attractive guy I've ever seen.

His abs disappear where his body meets mine, and I become acutely aware of the fact that the limb pressed against my right thigh is not, in fact, his leg, but his third appendage. It leaves me dizzy.

Quickly returning my eyes to his face, I find a light-hearted grin plastered from ear to ear.

Busted.

He knows I was checking him out. The fact is written all over his face. There's no use denying it, not when I can tell he's enjoying it.

"You're new," he states as I gape at him. The only words I'm able to find feel embarrassingly sharp, but they tumble from my lips nonetheless.

"And you're naked."

He scoffs, the sound turning into a snicker as he glances back to where the football players are, before his focus finds its way back to me. My eyes don't even dare look away from his face, too captivated by his proximity to willingly acknowledge we're not alone.

"Florentine's?"

I gulp at his assessment, unable to decipher whether it's said with disdain or amusement. His facial features give nothing away.

"Would that be a good thing or a bad thing?" I

ask, unsure where the confidence to speak is coming from as the darkness threatens to seep back into my bones.

Why am I trembling in anticipation for his answer like my world hangs in the balance?

He shakes his head, his hair flopping with the motion. "I'll take that as a yes. I just find it amusing that you are more focused on the fact that I'm naked, and not the reality that I'm a wolf. A verity that I'm pretty sure Florentine's have no knowledge of until they get here. Which was, what? Twenty minutes ago?"

My cheeks burn hotter under his assessment as he remains pressed against me, dick and all.

"The wolf is new, too," I manage to rasp, and he snickers once again, only this time, his eyes seem to soften.

"You could be a wolf," he states, as if the words falling from his lips don't hold so much weight. I'm not ready to delve further into this just yet.

"And you could be getting up now," I murmur, glancing over his shoulder to avoid the shift in his eyes.

Instead of standing as I hoped, his hand reaches for my face, his fingers curling around my chin as he tilts my head back, forcing me to meet his gaze. "Where's the fun in that?" he asks, the words raspier than necessary. The glimmer in his eyes makes it profusely clear that he knows the effect he's having on me right now.

"Fun. What's that like?" I retort, quirking my eyebrow at him, and his smile grows wider.

I don't know what's gotten into me, but I need to put as much distance between me and this guy as I possibly can right now.

"You're amusing. Say thank you and I'll leave you be."

My eyebrows narrow. "Thank you?"

He scoffs like my question is ridiculous. "For saving you," he explains, and I gape at him.

"You knocked me to the ground. Why am I thanking you?"

He scoffs again, the sound seemingly familiar from his lips already. "It was either that or a knock to the head from the ball. What would you prefer?"

Neither is on the tip of my tongue, but something about our intimate position makes it impossible for me to lie. Despite the desire that seems to ripple through me at his proximity, I need this to be over sooner rather than later, so I bite back the snark that plays on my tongue and clear my throat instead.

"Thank you," I rush, watching as something flashes across his face. I can't decide whether he's disappointed or had enough of me, but either way, he stands, offering me his hand.

I take it without wasting a moment to consider if it's a good idea or not, and he yanks me to my feet. He remains completely unfazed by the fact that he has no clothes on.

"Aren't you going to cover yourself?" I ask, glancing around at the audience we seem to have garnered. Not that I think any of them care much about my presence, but the spectacle he's putting on has definitely caught the eyes of quite a few girls here, possibly some of the guys too.

Definitely some of the guys, and I don't blame them.

"Cover a masterpiece like this? That's diabolical. I was made to be appreciated. I can't deny the people what they want."

Once again, I'm left gaping at him, his ego growing larger than should be possible.

S's voice cuts through the air, breaking the stare off between us. "P, you're holding up the tour again," she hollers, making my cheeks grow pinker as the blush spreads down my throat.

Pressing my lips together, I turn away from him, unable to stop myself from eyeing the dick that was pressed against my leg, and I gulp. Rushing toward S, I stop halfway, unable to deny myself another glance at him in his full naked glory.

He picks up a football that was lying right by where I was flattened and tosses it toward his teammates with a force that has to be…well, inhuman. As if sensing my stare, he turns to face me fully before walking backward toward his group. With a wink and a salute, he turns, and I'm forced to refocus on Professor Whitmore again.

Hurrying to catch up with the others, I exhale harshly, trying to rid the disbelief from my mind. Everyone is staring at me, T included, but I act like I didn't just partake in such a spectacle.

Instead, I shake out my hands, roll my shoulders back, and fix my attention on the professor. I need to pretend that didn't happen. Without pause, Whitmore continues the tour, while I'm left lost in my own mind, floating through this thing that's supposedly my life.

I might not have a single clue about what's going on, but I can't deny that I'm more intrigued with every passing moment that I'm here.

9

P

Sitting on a long wooden bench, in another unfamiliar setting, I still can't grasp how I ended up here. I mean, I know they told us why, mostly, but it still doesn't feel like it should be happening. Just a few hours ago I was fully resigned to the fact that I was going to live the rest of my life in that cold gray box they called a school then die an unsung death.

S sits beside me, the usual procession of B followed by T on the other side of her, as I stare down at the full plate of food before me. Gone are the plastic trays and the food that can only be described as slop, with the rare occasion of pizza, if we were lucky, and in its place is bone china, steel cutlery, and steak. I don't recall ever having steak before, but I'm not exactly in a position to turn down new experiences, and the moment I bring it to my lips, I can't stop shoveling it into my mouth like a Neanderthal.

Acutely aware of my actions, I take a deep breath and start timing myself between each bite. To occupy myself from demolishing it in one go, I take my time looking around the room as I count. The room is massive, rectangular in shape, with long dining tables occupying most of the floor and matching benches on either side. There are eight in total, each with a runner down the middle in one of four colors.

Bronze, silver, gold, and onyx.

Something tells me the colors mean something, but I'm not entirely sure.

Chandeliers hang in rows along the ceiling, every single one of them black like the entryway, which is through the double doors to our right. I assume the kitchen is located along the left wall since there's a long, narrow opening revealing white chef hats on the other side. Other than that, everything is focused around the food on the table. Cute floral centerpieces dot the table top, and even the unoccupied spaces have cutlery and bone china ready and waiting.

It's just us right now. Whitmore left a while ago, promising to be back soon, but he's yet to return. As the murmurs and whispers among us grow louder, and fill with more excitement, I can't help but feel the usual tendrils of impending doom lurking at the edges of my awareness.

I hope it's just my penchant for overreacting and not the truth of what's waiting for us. Because there is a part of me, a small, almost insignificant part, that is filled with the one word I've always disassociated myself from: hope.

I promised myself on the bus that I didn't feel it. I've promised myself throughout the entire tour that it wasn't an emotion I was familiar with. Yet, as I sit here, in my head, it's the one word I can't escape.

It's impossible to wrap my mind around it. I can't begin to fully understand the opportunities that we may have inside these new walls, but the part of me that's always dipped in gloom is waiting for this charade to drop and the truth to reveal itself.

Sighing, I distract myself with another fork full of food, biting back a groan at the deliciousness.

S places her cutlery down on her empty plate beside me and I turn to her. The moment I do, her eyes find mine, and I brace for the barrage of questions I can see swirling in them.

"Who is that guy, P?"

Well, damn, that's not what I was anticipating. I

was expecting her to ask me things about the academy, things I wouldn't have answers to. And I guess she did. The reality is, I don't have any answers about him either.

Besides, it's not really a topic I'm open to discussing.

"What guy?" I ask, opting to look away from her before she sees the lie in my eyes. Stabbing another piece of steak, I hope to completely distract away from the conversation, but before I can bring my fork to my lips, she speaks again.

"Don't 'what guy' me. The naked one," she insists, and when I turn to her, the pointed look I'm anticipating is firmly in place as her eyes narrow.

All I can do is gape at her for a moment, just as I gaped at the naked guy.

"I don't actually know," I admit when I finally find the words, and a sense of disappointment swirls through me.

How have I had his naked body pressed against mine, yet I don't even know his name?

Why am I disappointed by that? I've never cared to know a guy's name before. Hell, I've never even had a name of my own that I can remember.

I don't think it's possible for this day to get any stranger.

"He was hot," S says, shaking her shoulders

with a shiver of excitement as she wiggles her eyebrows while B grumbles from the other side of her.

"I'm sitting right here, babe," he sings, his tone teasing, and S rolls her eyes dramatically, turning to him with a sigh.

"And I love you, B, but even you can't deny it." She turns to face him fully, and even though I can't see her face, I know the look she's giving him. Practically the same pointed one she just gave me.

He sighs, a wistful smile on his face. "That's true," he admits before taking a bite of the burger he opted to have, while grunts from the other side of him echo around me.

"He shouldn't have been pressing himself all over you like that," T snaps, eyebrows pinched with agitation, and it only seems to make me more irritated with him.

I want to push him on why he thinks it's even necessary for him to have an opinion on the situation, but instead, I take a deep breath, avoiding his gaze as I mutter, "Thanks for the insight, T."

I know he's not done. I know he's not finished expressing whatever negative opinion he's formed, and even from the corner of my eyes, I can see his lips part as his eyes burn into the side of my face. "P, we don't—"

I open my mouth, ready to cut him off, but the snap of a clap does the job for me. I lean back in my seat with relief as I turn toward the sound, along with everyone else. Professor Whitmore is standing at the double doors, his smile somehow wider than the first time I saw him.

"Please, Florentines, it is time for the housing ceremony," he announces, and my eyebrows gather in confusion.

"Housing ceremony?" someone farther down the table hollers, and his grin seems to gleam even brighter.

"I'll explain more once you're in the Grand Hall," he states, spreading his arms out wide at his sides. "Please, follow me."

Looking down at the few forkfuls still left on my plate, I internally berate myself for eating so slowly. Placing my cutlery down, I stand, and S links her arm through mine, seemingly deciding that we're going to continue the tour together. I'm unwilling to admit I could use the support for whatever lies ahead, so I keep my mouth shut and fall into step as we make our way toward the double doors leading out into the marbled entryway that we visited earlier. Whitmore continues across the distance through the matching doors on the other side, and I vaguely recall him pointing out the room as the Grand Hall earlier, despite my lack of attention.

As we follow him inside, panic starts to coil in my veins when I find what I assume is every student of Trinity Falls Academy gathered and awaiting our arrival.

I feel like a lamb being led to slaughter. Or a convicted criminal taking their penultimate steps to the electric chair.

I feel so far out of my comfort zone that I am certain nothing good will come of this. It cannot be possible.

Professor Whitmore guides us to our seats and we shuffle down the front rows that have been left empty, presumably for us. I'd say I'm thankful, but I'm definitely not. The back of my head burns from the attention directed our way from every set of eyes in the hall. But instead of focusing on it, I clench my hands in my lap and train my eyes forward to where the stage sits as everybody else filters in.

I take a look around the space the best I can without fully turning around. I know there are rows and rows of velvet-padded seats in the same array of colors that were splattered through the dining hall.

Bronze, silver, gold, and onyx.

They fill the majority of the space reserved for the students, while the stage in front of me is lined with a handful of ornate throne-looking things along the back. There's also a microphone up front and a table with some kind of silver cup in the center.

Red satin drapes hang around the room, framing arched windows that are detailed with small, square panes of glass. There's something opulent about the room, just like there's something grand about everything else here. I guess it's in the name, but in comparison to the entryway, it feels older in here, unmodernized with the dark wood and beams lining the ceiling. As if you were to carve into the wood, it'd have a story or two to tell you.

Before I can wander any further down the rabbit hole, my thoughts are interrupted by Professor Whitmore. "Good afternoon, students of Trinity Falls Academy. It brings me great pleasure, as it does every year, to introduce the children of Florentine's school." He pauses as if a clap is going to come, but thankfully, nothing does. "New students, Trinity Falls Academy is split into four quadrants. I've mentioned them to you previously, but as a refresher, it is based on the supernatural ability, or lack thereof."

I cringe at the use of the word 'lack' as my heart

ricochets in my chest, knowing full well I'm going to be someone in the more *lacking* category.

"Witches, wolves, vampires, and humans," he declares, and a round of applause sounds from behind us, along with wolf whistles and cheers as each group is mentioned. And I can't help but think that there are humans in this room unaffected by the terms he's using. That must be a good sign, right?

Whitmore basks in the euphoria until the noise simmers down for him to continue. "Everyone here is cursed by blood, and among this crowd is the knowledge that your blood kin is here too."

The room falls deathly silent as my heart all but stops in my chest. My breath lodges so tightly in my throat, I'm certain death is here as I repeat his words in my mind. My blood kin.

My. Blood. Kin.

Goosebumps ripple over my skin as panic and horror make my vision grow spotty. Do they know who *I* am? Can I find out who *they* are? What would I do if I did?

As if sensing my thoughts, Whitmore's eyes find mine in the crowd. "No one will know in advance. Only on the rightful day, when it is your time, will you know who your blood kin is. I should also bring it to your attention that, as you stepped into the academy, a sigil will have taken root. It masks every student present with the inability to provide their specific birth details. Now, I know what your first concern is, birthdays, and of course, we're still going to celebrate them. They're just going to take place a little differently from now on. Not that you have many more to celebrate here, but in that instance, we will celebrate birthdays as a whole for each month. On the fifteenth of every month, anyone born in that month shall be celebrated. Yes, that may help narrow down who your blood kin could be, but it will still leave an element hidden. This is a priority because deep down, above all else, the fact still remains that the blood curse does not change. If one of you dies, both of you die."

I think I'm going to be sick. Every word out of his mouth makes my fate more and more real.

"Until the right time, of course, it is our aim to provide everyone with the opportunity to survive, and the first step we must take in offering this is giving the Florentine students a chance to experience the housing chalice," he continues, like he's not breaking my soul.

Murmurs echo around the room once again, leaving me just as curious as before. A housing chalice? What does that even mean? I glance down the line to my left and right, noting the similar expression on everyone's faces, but not one of us asks.

There's no need, not when the look on Whitmore's face tells us it's clear he's going to continue. And with his next words, he leaves me breathless. "Not only will it offer you the acknowledgement of potential supernatural blood in your veins, but it will also allow one of the sigils placed on you to release from your body. Not the one protecting your connection to your blood kin, but one from many years ago. The one that contains the secret of your name."

10

P

My name?

My freaking name!

His words collide in my mind repeatedly, making it impossible for me to process them. My breath turns to pants as my face heats and I track his every move.

Professor Whitmore is far too level-headed to be dropping bombshells like that; his shoulders are relaxed, his smile is one of ease, and his entire demeanor makes it clear he's having a good time. The sparkle in his eyes is the only thing making it abundantly obvious that he's enjoying this.

He must get some pleasure out of telling every set of new students that there's information up for grabs. Information that we should already have, but the way he's dangling it like a carrot in front of my face, damn, the semantics don't even matter.

A shriek from my left startles me from my thoughts as the room comes back to life around me. The shocked moment of silence has been shattered, and as the weight of surprise lifts from my shoulders, it takes a little of the brain fog with it.

Apparently, there's a sigil on me, hiding my name, just like everyone else from Florentine's. I don't even know what a sigil is, or what it might look like, but if I were to take a guess, I would say that it had something to do with magic.

The prospect of learning my name has me more than ready to jump through the hoops that Professor Whitmore may place before us.

Hope.

That word is deep, nestled straight in my soul, and I'm powerless to it. I am powerless to the knowledge that I may learn something about myself today.

"Now, if we would all like to get to the good part, shall we begin going through the list in alphabetical order? We'll have each Florentine student join me on stage when their name is called, and then you will join your appointed faction within the academy," Whitmore explains, clapping his hands together excitedly. The moment his hands collide, the other students join in, cheers rippling through the hall as a few of my fellow Florentine students clap along too.

A woman appears on the stage, handing Whitmore a rolled-up piece of paper before scurrying back off the stage. Professor Whitmore instantly refers to the parchment now in his hands, unfurling it to reveal the first initial on the list of the fifteen new students, myself included.

"B, please," he summons, and my gaze whips to the other side of S. B's eyes are wide, his jaw slack, and his knuckles white as they lay curled into fists in his lap. He nods slowly, rising from his seat, likely aware that all eyes are set on him now. He takes the steps cautiously, meeting Whitmore at the center of the stage, and the professor guides him to the table I noted earlier.

"Now, let me quickly explain how this works while, unfortunately, using you as an example, B," Whitmore states, a warm smile on his face as B nods nervously. "This chalice is filled with enchanted water. You must scoop both hands into the liquid and bring it to your lips. In doing so, the sigil will reveal your supernatural ability, and the chalice shall call out your name. Do you have any questions?"

B shakes his head warily, staring down at the

chalice before him, and I think my heart is going to explode in my chest.

Slowly, without any further prompt, B does as he's asked. His hands scoop into the water. The tremble is noticeable from where I sit, and I watch with intense rapture as he brings the liquid to his lips. The moment it reaches his mouth, his head jerks back, his eyelids closing as another booming voice rings through the air.

"Benjamin Flasker."

I gasp, disbelief curling through my stomach as the truth falls free. I don't know where the source of the sound is coming from, but it's there.

Benjamin.

Benjamin.

I tilt my head as I look at him with fresh eyes. It actually suits him. A shy smile teases the corner of my mouth as I play his name on my tongue, and the second the whispered word leaves my lips, a thought comes to mind.

B.

B equals Benjamin.

Would that mean P stands for a name that begins with a P?

Have we had the initial for our true name this whole time? I guess I'm going to find out when my time comes.

"It seems, Benjamin, you are indeed a human cursed by blood," Whitmore states, pointing toward a shimmering symbol glowing on the chalice. It looks like the outline of a pair of hands, but my focus quickly whips back to B, I mean Benjamin, watching as he stares at Whitmore with confusion morphing his features. "I understand the disappointment, Benjamin, but please join the humans on the far right; they are now your quads."

Applause comes from the group Whitmore indicates, encouraging B to head in that direction, despite how reluctant he seems. His steps are slow and almost sad as he loses everyone's attention before he makes it even halfway. Seems we're all just as desperate to move on to the next person.

One after another, I watch more of my peers approach the stage and repeat the process. There's an array of wolves, vampires, witches, and a few more humans called out. I get lost as more and more repeat the method until the one letter I've been waiting for with bated breath comes.

"P."

The desire to hear it quickly dwindles to nothing as my excitement is replaced by a clawing panic. My limbs tremble, my eyes unable to focus as I rise from my seat and carefully make my way to where Professor Whitmore stands.

I don't think I can take it. I don't think I can bring myself to know. It feels like I'm going to self-combust. But despite the inner turmoil, I reach the chalice in the center of the table and look to Whitmore for guidance.

Can I trust him? No.

Should I be expecting him to lead me? Definitely not.

Is he the only option I have for direction? Yes.

Dammit.

With a single nod from the professor, I feel every nerve-ending zap through my body as I dip my hands into the water and bring the liquid to my lips. A tingling sensation courses through my veins and my head tilts back as my eyelids slam closed.

A gasp falls from my lips, my body bracing for impact, when the crackle of the booming voice echoes in the air around me.

"Polaris Beauchamp."

Emotion gets the better of me as I hear a word that refers to me yet holds a meaning I'm not yet familiar with.

Polaris.

Polaris Beauchamp.

That's me.

Blinking my eyes open, I turn to Professor

Whitmore, ready to hear my supernatural fate as I feel everyone's eyes on me.

"My dear, you are a witch." I look down to where he points to the glowing light on the chalice to see a star illuminated. "Join your quadrant," he commands, pointing toward the cheering crowd, and I gulp as I follow his line of sight. It's impossible to process what any of this actually means, and as I feel myself start to sink, my eyes draw to the left, settling on a familiar face and a cocksure grin that has been haunting me since I first collided with them.

He knows he has my attention. He winks like before, but I quickly shake my head and turn away, only to see a row of ridiculously hot guys flanking both sides of him.

Wolves.

It seems they're a soft spot for me already.

Shaking off the distraction, I turn my attention to my new group and approach them. Just like with everyone else, by the time I reach them, no one's paying me any attention anymore. I take a seat at the back, and a few actually turn to smile at me. I hope I return the sentiment, but something in their eyes tells me I'm coming across as cold and distant as ever.

There's no time for me to delve further into

overanalyzing because S is called to join Whitmore on the stage. Excitement coils in my stomach as I watch her swoop her hands into the liquid, bringing it to her lips before the familiar booming voice rings in the air.

"Sian Gloom."

Tears instantly stream down her face, her disbelief evident as Professor Whitmore points to the chalice. "Sian, you are a vampire." He points to the glowing symbol that looks like it's shaped like a teardrop, perhaps a drop of blood.

A vampire.

It's going to take me forever to wrap my head around the fact that I'm apparently a witch and my not-friend is a vampire. This is bizarre. *Too* bizarre. But if a blood curse is possible, I guess all of this is too. "Welcome to Trinity Falls Academy; please join your quad," Whitmore adds, smirking in amusement at how slack Sian's jaw is. Nervously tucking her hair behind her ears, Sian joins the group sitting center.

T is called up next, and despite my irritation towards him, I gape at the announcement of his name.

"Terence, you are a vampire."

I'm still reeling from all of this new information when the final person takes the stage.

V.

I watch in awe as she cups the water, and her name is echoed around the room.

Veronica.

"Welcome, Veronica, you are a wolf. Please join your pack."

The glowing symbol looks like a crescent moon this time, but it quickly dims as the whole room beams with pride, the chants and cheers echoing so loudly I almost need to cover my ears. A few of the witches around me, both boys and girls, lean in close, rubbing a hand down my arm, cheering, patting me on the back like I've done something miraculous, but all I've done is find out way too late in life who I truly am. As if the disadvantage of time doesn't matter.

Professor Whitmore lifts his hands in the air to bring everyone's attention back to him as he speaks. "Florentines, welcome to Trinity Falls Academy. Please follow your guides back to your houses, where everything you need will be waiting for you in your rooms. If you have any questions, please ask those around you. If not, lessons will begin tomorrow, and the professors will be able to offer support as needed. But please, more than anything, get some rest. Tomorrow is a new day, and work must begin immediately."

SURROUNDED BY MY FELLOW WITCHES, we cut through the path that leads through the immaculate lawn area, trailing toward four buildings that stand powerfully tall in the distance. As we draw closer, following the perfectly manicured shrubs and flower beds, I can't help but notice the only real difference between the four buildings are their colors.

The first one shimmers in a metallic bronze, a sight to behold as it looms ahead. The second stands just as strong in a startling silver, the light reflecting off the windows only making it seem brighter. The next is washed in gold from roof to floor, regal among the buildings, while the fourth and final building stands dark and dangerous, dripping in onyx. Just looking at it sets me on edge.

"Ours is the first one on the left," the girl beside me states, and I nod in acknowledgment. "Whenever in doubt, always look for the sand. That's where you'll find us," she adds, and I nod like it makes total sense to me, but it doesn't, even though she seems to be very sure of her words.

I have no idea what her name is, but she's taken it upon herself to walk beside me, pointing out things along the way. It doesn't take long for the pathway to reach a fork, branching off in four directions, each one leading to a different building as the textures begin to change.

That's when I see it.

The path shifts from perfectly paved stone to a winding sand trail.

Follow the sand.

I don't have a moment to take a deep breath or prepare myself for entering another new space. Instead, I'm hustled inside to find a substantial communal area. Sofas and chairs line the walls. There are coffee tables, a television in the corner, and an open archway leading to a minimalistic kitchen area.

There's more here than I've ever seen before, and I watch in bewilderment as over half the group flops down into their familiar surroundings like it's no big deal.

It's definitely a big deal.

A commanding voice rings through the air as soon as the door clicks shut behind us. "All the new witches, please follow me. I'll guide you to your rooms," says the girl who was walking beside me on the way here.

I'm hesitant to question whether I should follow her anymore, but it seems I've let her lead me this far; going up another flight of stairs won't make much difference now.

She marches up the stairs, stopping halfway to turn to face us. "I'm Bryony, by the way. If you need anything, please ask. I'm always here to help. But for now, we need to focus on the fact that none of you have access to your magic yet, and you've got a lot to learn." Without another word, she turns away, ascending another flight of stairs with determined purpose guiding her footsteps.

Trailing after her, we reach the fourth floor before she finally stops. She sweeps her hand to the side to reveal a few doors behind her.

There are three of us, three new witches.

"Your names will be engraved on the doors. This will have happened the moment you touched the chalice back in the Grand Hall. Everything you need will be inside. I know you've recently eaten, but we will be leaving for a late supper in about two hours if you would like to join us." Without another word, she heads back down the stairs, leaving the three of us to look at each other. D and H. That's who they were back at Florentine's, but I wasn't paying enough attention to know what those initials stood for.

Instead of extending the awkwardness between us, I turn toward the doors Bryony signaled to, searching for my name. I find the words *Polaris*

Beauchamp engraved in cursive font across the plaque fixed to the second door.

Rubbing my lips together nervously, I take a deep breath before I wrap my fingers around the door handle and twist. The door falls open, stealing my breath as I prepare myself for whatever may follow.

Before I dare take a single step over the threshold, I stuff my hand into my pocket, curling it around my coin for comfort.

I need the strength it offers. More than before, more than usual, more than ever.

Pulling it out, I uncurl my fingers to see the imprint and rub my thumb along the face. Emotion clogs in my throat, but I try my best to tamp it down. Stuffing it back in my pocket, I head inside and startle when I see my few meager belongings on the bed in the center of the room. I don't move toward them, though. Instead, I take in the space surrounding me. There's not much in here, but it's a complete contrast to the room I had at Florentine's.

A double bed sits under a massive window sill, central to the wall ahead. There are nightstands on either side, a desk to the left, an oversized chair in the corner, and an armoire to my right, with a matching chest of drawers beside it.

There are a few piles of clothes on the bed that

weren't mine before I came here, and I take cautious steps toward everything littering my new sheets. Rubbing a hand at my chest nervously, I spy a folder nestled among the madness with the words "Trinity Falls Academy" scrawled across the front.

I'm definitely going to have to read that, but something else captures my attention and everything else around me drifts into nothing. Collapsing on the bed, I wrap my fingers around the familiar leather binding, grabbing the pen with excitement burning through me. I flip open the book, pressing the ink to the page, and the rest of the world drifts away.

Dear Diary,
Florentine's is no more, not for me, at least.
It seems I'm now a student at Trinity Falls
Academy. It seems I'm now a witch.
It seems I also have a name.
I don't know what's in store for me anymore,
and I definitely don't know what tomorrow
may bring, but there is one thing for sure
that I can no longer deny.
I don't want to die.
Not when there's a chance of survival.
No matter how small.
Polaris x

11

POLARIS

With my hands planted on the window sill, I track the movements of people outside, watching as they go about their lives while I stand here, still radiating with shock. The main academy building looms in the distance, a Gothic silhouette against the night, conveying a sense of grandeur that Florentine's could never imagine.

After scribbling in my diary, all I've been able to focus on is my breathing. My mind is wild, repeatedly recounting today's events as if I'm a character in a novel. It's like one of the many fables that were lined up in the classroom at Florentine's. It was a luxury for Mrs. Stephens to share a snippet of a story with us, and now here I am, experiencing my own whirlwind.

I'm not the only one, of course.

My mind wanders to S—I mean Sian. I hope she's doing okay. B, too, I guess; he looked devastated when he was declared human. I think he's lucky; at least we know how to be that. Well, a little, I guess.

Today has been…a lot, but I can't bring myself to feel disappointed about it. Am I out of my element? One million percent. Am I scared of what tomorrow may bring? Absolutely. But am I out of Florentine's grasp with a tiny seed of hope nestled in my chest? Yes.

It's weird to acknowledge that, seeing as I've isolated myself in here since the moment the bedroom door closed behind me, but it still feels different. Back at Florentine's, once the bedroom door was locked, I was left alone with the same four walls to entertain me. The window there was too high to see through, and the light that shone through the small square was always dim.

Now, it's like a whole new world. What I'm really unfamiliar with, and what I'm unsure I'll ever be able to relax with, is the noise vibrating through the rest of the building. As if sensing my thoughts, a bang echoes as a door is slammed, and I startle, but the quick procession of giggles that follows instantly helps to ease the tension radiating through my body.

Running my tongue over my bottom lip, I turn from the window and tiptoe toward the door. Curling my hand around the door handle, I slowly pull it open. My breath lodges in my throat as the hallway comes into view. Just as gently as I opened the door, I close it, but before the latch can catch, I whip it open as fast as I can, closing it just as quickly. I can't help but repeat the motion a few times, completely awed by the fact that my door is not locked by someone else.

I'm not trapped. I'm not a prisoner. Or maybe I am, just not in the physical sense that I was previously. The sense of freedom is present, even in the ability to just open my door whenever I please. Especially when the essence of the unknown still lingers. Outside these four walls, on the rest of the campus, I don't know how free I am, but it's still freer than before.

I hope. But, I'm locked in my brain, fearing a different type of prison awaits.

Another round of laughter dances through the air as I close the door, keeping it shut this time, acutely aware that there is definitely no soundproofing in this place. However, the noise and different vibe filling the space should not keep me up at night. I hope.

Pressing my back against the door, I take a deep

breath before shuffling over to the bed. The sheets are soft beneath me as I sit beside my new belongings. Like a hammer to the gut, a feeling washes over me, confirming the swirling thoughts in my mind.

I'm definitely not at Florentine's anymore.

Looking down at my laced fingers in my lap, the noise in my head quiets as if finally accepting a slice of my new reality. If my eyes were deceiving me, the red marks pinched all over my arm would confirm that I've double-checked with myself multiple times, and I'm right here in the flesh. There's no denying it: this is not a dream.

My stomach grumbles, reminding me that I declined to join everyone for food earlier, but I push past the gnawing. Hunger isn't a new sensation. If anything, it's almost comforting right now. It's the most familiar feeling I've had since we woke up on that coach.

In desperate need of a distraction, I prop my pillow against the headboard and get comfortable as I reach for the manual that's been left for me. Running my fingers over the leather casing, I take a deep breath, preparing myself for what lies inside. As if the words written in ink are about to change my life any more than it already has.

Gazing over the first page, I don't know where

to begin. Brushing my finger over the contents list, I scan each word with ferocity.

There are general rules, information about the house's layout, details about classes and timetables, opening times of facilities on campus, information about weekends and school days, and details about sigil magic. There's a lot, and as much as I'm sure there's some information that's more important than others, I decide to start on the first page, where it's safest.

When I flip the page over, a plastic case greets me. Nothing was listed on the previous page, which makes it feel even more daunting. Inside is a device—one I'm aware of but never had the luxury of having before.

A cell phone. A freaking cell phone.

As cool as this is, what do they expect me to do with it? I don't have anyone to call. I don't have anyone to update about my whereabouts.

There is no one.

It's just me.

Florentine's made sure of that.

The notion is sobering, and darkness threatens to seep through me, tainting my thoughts, but instead of allowing it to grasp me like it always does, I quickly turn the case over and move on to where the pages begin. I can circle back to the new addition later.

"General rules" is written in large block letters along the top of the next page, followed by bullet points that get straight to the point, outlining the rules that have been set by Trinity Falls Academy.

Number one: no killing.

Number two: no harmful acts toward others.

Number three: no using your abilities negatively.

Number four: no using other students as practice targets.

Number five: do not skip classes.

Number six: treat those how you would like to be treated.

Number seven: any illnesses must be reported to the student nurse to authorize absence.

Number eight: enjoy finding who you are.

Number nine: follow the guidelines on staying safe, especially around a full moon.

Number ten: Do not seek information about your blood kin. This will result in instant expulsion and imprisonment until your twenty-first birthday, when you will meet your ultimate end.

I scoff at the complete mash-up of rules listed. An unnerving fact lingers in my thoughts as I consider how many of these rules stem from people attacking or hurting one another. Hopefully, everyone will listen to these rules. The one about my blood kin leaves me worried, making my stomach twist, but it fills me with reassurance that they take it seriously.

I've faced disadvantages my entire life, especially since arriving at Florentine's. All I can do now is hope they adhere to this rule. There's that word again: *hope*. I despise how deeply entrenched in me it has become since coming here. I must keep that in check. I can't go putting all of my trust in a fickle word that could break me so easily.

Moving on, I have a layout of the witches' dorm with a key detailing the important rooms. It explains that bathrooms for both boys and girls are on the first floor, and each student has their own storage fully provided by the academy, named and ready. I should be able to find mine when I make my trip down there.

No wonder they put the newcomers on the fourth floor. I might have beautiful views out the window, but I have a treacherous walk to and from the bathroom. At least I can go when I want, which is another huge difference from Florentine's.

Everything else about the building is pretty self-explanatory. I've seen the communal areas already, and there's not much more I need to know. The map of the entire academy is much more daunting, and I know I'm going to need to use it to get around this place come morning.

No amount of staring at it now is going to help me absorb the information, so I move on to the details of my classes. Excitement churns in my gut like it's a familiar feeling. Yet, I've never felt it before today—just like hope.

Attempting to calm the butterflies in my stomach, I read the words aloud. "As a witch, your focus will be on potions, enchantments, and charms. Additionally, with all factions within the academy, you will also partake in curses, hunting, and both offensive and defensive skills. It is paramount that all information provided is of the highest quality. We take great care in ensuring an even playing field, offering you information that will not only help you to graduate the academy, but also prepare you for what may come after."

It sounds surreal and insane, but the prospect of a future beyond these brand-new walls doesn't seem fathomable right now. All I can do is appreciate that I'm no longer at Florentine's and the countdown I've been obsessing over in my head has the opportunity to be extended. Living until I'm twenty-two? Twenty-three? Thirty?

The prospect is enough to steal my breath. But

what's worse is the knowledge of what I would have to do to survive the curse that hums in my blood.

Shaking my head, I push the thought away and move on to the next page. It's filled with my schedule and the starting times for classes, the dining hall, and each professor's office hours. The idea of being able to speak to anyone outside of classes and the thirty-minute break feels bizarre and overwhelms my brain, so I focus on the details surrounding the dining hall. It opens two hours before the first class of the day and closes at midnight during the week, remaining open twenty-four hours over the weekend.

I could possibly go now, but after declining to go with the witches earlier, a trip on my own doesn't seem the best idea.

Scanning my eyes over the schedule again, I can see that my first class tomorrow will be for offensive and defensive skills class. I have no idea what I'm going to be walking into, and even though the thought leaves me a bit worried, it beats the mundane lessons I'm used to.

I turn the page again, eager to read every line, and find information detailing that school days will take place Monday through Friday, with all students enjoying the weekends to relax, practice at their own pace, and take in all that Trinity Falls Academy has to offer. If anyone wishes to leave campus, a pass may be authorized and issued by the office upon request. The possibility leaves me gaping, with tingles dancing up my arms. Not that I have anywhere to go, but the idea of it…wow.

As I continue down the page, it states that no uniform is required, and acceptable attire has been provided. Finally, I turn to the last page, and in dark letters, the headline reads, "Sigils."

I rub my lips together nervously, confusion layering over every other emotion I'm feeling right now as I read the passage that explains so much yet nothing all at once.

"There is a sigil hiding your magic. It has been placed on you with an item already attached to you. It will likely be an item from before your time at Florentine's. Though you may not recall, it will be impossible to remove by touch. Each item unlocks the sigil in a very different way, and we will work through this on an individual basis in the sigil class. What may work for one is unlikely to work for another, but we have learned from experience that magic unlocks the sigil when you discover something about yourself or who you are as a person. We look forward to spending each sigil class learning about your purpose in life."

My fingers tremble at the words and my eyes

lock on the familiar gold bands around my wrists—my bangles. I have never tried to remove them. I have never considered it, but I'm starkly aware that they're the only items I've never taken off since being at Florentine's. It may have been eight years ago when I arrived there. Well, ten if what Mrs. Stephens said is correct, but I know these bangles have been a part of me forever.

Toying with the metal, I know it's not worth considering whether they will come off. I already know they won't. What captivates me further as I look at them is the knowledge that wherever they came from was once home.

I've always known it, and I've always felt it in my gut every time I look at them and my coin.

Now I know it's the truth.

Part of me aches because progressing in my life means losing them. However, as long as I keep my coin, I can achieve anything.

I close the manual with a thud, exhausted by the knowledge that now resides in my mind. My fingers slip into my pocket, wrapping around the coin, and I draw strength from it as I always do.

Tonight, I may drown in the unknown, but come tomorrow, I will strive for the once unachievable.

12

POLARIS

My nerves threaten to get the best of me on what is officially my first day at Trinity Falls Academy. A day I didn't think was coming. A day I didn't know existed until yesterday. Yet here I am, exhausted to the bone but willing to try and see where this may lead.

I barely slept at all last night. The unfamiliar surroundings and the chaos from the past twenty-four hours kept me awake. Even when the building was nearly silent, my own breathing distracted me too much to let my eyelids fall closed. It was almost impossible to succumb to sleep. At one point, I considered using the newly issued cell phone to figure out how to contact Florentine's and have Professor Stephens use her magic on me to make me sleep again. But even I'm not that crazy. I don't think.

Instead, I tried to keep myself busy rather than lying in bed. The last thing I want to do is train my brain to think that the bed is just for lying awake at night, staring at the ceiling. I want to be able to slip beneath my new sheets and have my brain switch off from the outside world. It's just going to take a bit more training than I had hoped.

I did it at Florentine's; I can do it here too. I don't think I slept very well during the first month I was there. They may have tampered with my memories, but I remember the sleepless nights all too well.

I've managed to organize my clothes into the drawers and armoire, where I found a long mirror on the inside. Now, I stand here looking at my reflection.

I don't know who I am.

After rifling through all the clothes, I find myself faced with a choice I've never had before. Instead of the usual Florentine-issued uniform, I have options and I don't know what to wear. After a moment of careful consideration, I opt for a pair of slim black sweats, a short-sleeved, plain black t-shirt, and a gray jacket. I've got a choice of boots, flats, or sneakers available, all in my size, just like the clothes. I am still unsure how they knew this information about me, but I opt for the sneakers, choosing comfort over anything else as I prepare to walk these new halls. My silver hair falls around my face in loose curls since I managed to run a brush through the ends, but that's about all I've done. There's a hair tie on my wrist, just in case I need it, but the few cosmetic items lining the top drawer of my nightstand remain untouched.

Makeup? What am I supposed to do with that? I'd rather not make a fool of myself on my first day. Maybe ever.

Before I can delve deeper into examining my reflection and decide on another outfit change, a knock sounds from the other side of my bedroom door. Nerves threaten to steal my breath as I run my hands over my jacket. Attempting to take a deep breath, I cautiously approach the looming barrier that stands between me and whoever is knocking. I pry it open just a little, and I'm surprised to see Bryony.

For the first time, I take in her features. Her blonde hair is braided back off her face, and I'm relieved to see that she is also wearing a more casual outfit—a mauve pair of matching sweats and jacket, a white tee, and sneakers.

Her eyes track me, just as I assess her, like two

predators trying to decipher each other's intentions, until she clears her throat. "Are you joining us this time?" she asks, pointing toward the stairs as her gaze becomes expectant.

"Yeah," I manage with a nod, my heart pounding in my chest. I might not be the best at being friendly or positive, but I need to make some kind of connection with the others if I'm supposed to join a coven. I don't actually understand what that entails, but the one thing that kept me up more than anything else last night was the knowledge that I won't survive this place with my usual standoffish vibe. Well not that alone at least. I need to learn, and I need to learn fast, especially when everyone here is cursed too, only they have powers and abilities my sigil refuses to relinquish.

Aware I'm not actually moving, I take a step back, pointing behind me. "Let me just grab the manual," I rattle, my panic reaching new heights as she scoffs and grabs my arm before I can take a single step.

"You won't need that," she insists, and my eyebrows gather in confusion.

"But my schedule," I mutter as uncertainty gets the better of me.

She sighs, pulling me out of the doorway and leaving me no choice but to follow her. "You're with me all day, so I've got you. I know where we're supposed to be and when."

She slips her hand from my door as it clicks shut behind me, heading toward the stairs as I stare after her. Without a backward glance, she descends the stairs, and I finally remember how to move. As always, worries plague my thoughts, but I refuse to give in to them, tamping them down as I fall into step behind her.

The silence is deafening as I scramble to think of something to say. "Aren't you older than me?" I blurt, instantly cursing myself internally. The scathing look she gives me over her shoulder is answer enough.

"No, I'm twenty too. I've just been here longer than you. Everyone usually comes here when they're fourteen. It's just the Florentine students that arrive later," she states, and all I can do is nod.

We reach the bottom of the stairs to see a few other witches hovering around in the lounge area. I don't see D or H, but that doesn't matter. We weren't friendly before we got here. That's not going to change now.

Bryony doesn't wait around for me to follow her outside, but she does slow down to fall in step with me once I do. Following the pathway toward the main academy building, I tilt my head back, letting the early morning sun beam down on me. It's strange to see and feel it so early in the day, but I think it might be my new favorite sensation.

I remain quiet as we make our way to the dining hall. I am too busy gleaming under the sun and people-watching the other students filling the pathway with us to worry over the silence this time. There's so much chatter around us and so much electricity in the air that it's intoxicating.

As we near the main academy building, the smell of food reaches my nose and my stomach grumbles, tightening with need.

It is another reminder that I won't be eating crap like I would at Florentine's. When we step into the dining hall, I gaze in awe. Yesterday, I was here with my fellow Florentines, but now, almost at capacity, it's a completely different level of energy.

Taking Bryony's lead, I look at the same four long tables I noted yesterday. This time, they're filled with groups gathered together. The humans sit at the table on the far left of the room; a calmness surrounds them, suggesting they are humans, even though I can't figure out how or why I know that. I try to spy B among the mix, but there are too many people for me to single him out.

Bryony leads me to the next table, leaving the other two on the right side of the room either vampires or wolves. From my vantage point, I can't determine which is which as I take the open seat beside my new guide.

The spread of food lining the table distracts me from my observations, leaving me unsure where to begin. There is an array of hot and cold breakfast foods, including bacon, sausage, eggs, croissants, pancakes, fruit, cereals, and even donuts. I've seen a donut before; I've just never had the luxury of trying one. As I reach for the glazed treat, I notice Bryony staring at me from the corner of her eye.

Sitting back in my seat, I blindly reach for a water bottle as I turn to her.

"What?"

Blunt much? Maybe, but as much as I'm trying to be…nice, it doesn't change overnight, like I'm willingly going to idly walk around with her staring at me all day.

She tilts her head at me, a slight softness to the curl of her lips. "What is Florentine's like?" she asks, ultimately knocking the confidence from me with one simple question.

I instantly feel myself shut down, offering a meager shrug as I turn away from her, opting to bite into my donut. Trying to focus on the sickly-sweet dough in my mouth, I will her question to disappear from existence, but the burning sensation on the side of my face comes from her expectant look, one that seems already too familiar with her, and I sigh.

“That bad, huh?” she asks, reaching for a stack of pancakes and a small jug of what looks like maple syrup beside it.

I shrug again. “I’m sure you've had someone tell you the answers to that before,” I say, looking down at my plate.

“No, actually. Last year, there was only one witch, and he was an ass.”

I nod in acknowledgment as I look around the room before offering her the simplest answer I can. “It's nothing like this.”

That's all I can offer. That's all I can say to even try to summarize the differences between Florentine’s and here. Not without the pain in my chest intensifying and stealing what little strength I’ve mustered for the day.

It’s tempting to slip my hand into my pocket and feel the coin I know is there, but I refrain, too scared of losing it. Besides, I promised myself last night that come morning, I wouldn’t think about anything that happened before today. I'm certain that trauma will be lurking in the corner of my mind for the rest of my life, but it won't start today. Not when I have such little time left on

Earth. Letting it consume me is not on my to do list.

"Don't worry, you may feel out of your comfort zone right now, but you'll get there," she insists, tucking into a stack of pancakes as if she didn't just send me on an emotional roller coaster.

I hum in agreement. "I hope so."

Thankfully, a comfortable silence washes over us as we eat. I move from the donut to a plate of pancakes until my stomach is on the verge of exploding. Nausea threatens to claim me from all the sweetness, but I take a few small swigs of water to help it pass.

"We're about to drop you in the deep end. Are you ready?" Bryony asks. I gulp, watching her stand up, and follow suit before I can think better of it.

I can't decipher which emotion is most prominent within me; I'm a mixture of nerves and excitement, caution and hope, worry and exhilaration. Somehow, every single emotion morphs into one, leaving me jittery as we head toward the exit. As I near the end of our table, a familiar face at the end to the right catches my attention, and before I can think better of it, I close the distance, waving excitedly when I see S. I mean Sian.

"Hey," I breathe, taking note that this must be

the vampires' table, leaving the table on the other side of them to be the wolves. "Are you doing okay?" I ask, tilting my head at her as I come to a stop beside her chair, but the instant feeling in my gut twists with uncertainty. Her lips press together, her eyes darting anywhere but at me, and a sickly feeling settles in my stomach.

I'm waiting for some kind of interaction, but it seems she's reluctant to give me anything. I'm about to take a step away when her eyes finally meet mine again; her lips are pursed and her hands ball into fists in her lap.

"We're not friends, P. Don't come over here again," she grinds out through clenched teeth. Her tone is empty, her words are cold, and all I can do is gape at her.

A daunting realization washes over me as I consider that this is probably how I've made her feel the entire time we've known each other. Have I been this dismissive and cold? I thought that in a sea of all these people, we might see each other first, but it seems the pillar of joy I relied on so much no longer exists, and it's been less than twenty-four hours since we got here.

Worry gets the better of me as I consider whether something is wrong with her, refusing to accept the sudden distance between us. As my eyes glance across the table, I also find Terence. He's deep in conversation with the guy beside him, peering at me from the corner of his eye, but he doesn't turn, not like he usually does.

Whatever vibe I'm getting from Sian, I'm getting from Terence too.

The guy beside him, though, the one holding all of T's attention, is looking straight at me. My chest constricts as I will myself to turn away, but it's impossible.

He has jet-black hair, piercing blue eyes, and broad shoulders that create an all-encompassing aura that pulls you in deeply, but not in a good way. Definitely not in a good way. Even though he is sitting, I can already guess he would tower over me. Not that that's difficult to do, I'm only five foot five, but I know he would make me feel three feet tall at best. There's a curl to his lips, a fictitious smirk that makes me feel like I don't want to be the target of it.

He drinks me in just as much as I absorb him, and then I have the unfortunate opportunity of experiencing him open his mouth.

"Are you a vampire?" he asks, tilting his head as his eyes sparkle with a sense of dark mischief. I can't find my tongue, but I manage to shake my head, making his teeth appear in a fake smile. "You lost your friend when you had the misfortune of being announced as whatever the fuck you are. The moment you're not a vampire is the moment our ties are cut. Do yourself a favor and fuck off." His chair scrapes along the floor as he stands, the smile turning to a sneer on his face as his gaze goes from me to Sian. "Come now, Sian, we don't fraternize with the enemy," he adds for good measure, but there is no need. I already got the message. But it seems I'm not done experiencing the wrath of his tongue. "Especially not ones with dirty silver hair. It seems it's a good thing you don't remember your past because wherever the fuck that came from can't be anywhere good," he snarls before turning away and storming towards the exit.

His words cut deep, a jab at me unlike any I've heard before, and I feel like I might pass out. My breathing is ragged, my skin tingling with panic as my gaze snaps to T for a split second, but gone is the guy who has irritated me for as long as I can remember, and in his place stands the man now known as Terence. He tries to mimic the rude guy's walk as he saunters after him, and S quickly rushes to her feet, trailing after them.

Gaping in horror, I feel a hand on my arm and turn to find Bryony staring at me with a hint of sympathy in her eyes.

"Ignore Blaze. He's a cunt, and I don't use that

word lightly, but with him, it definitely freaking counts."

I nod, despite the ache in my chest and the lump in my throat. Since when have I become the enemy? Since when have I become a target?

Bryony waves a hand toward the exit and I move with her instantly, desperate to get out of here since I can feel a few people still staring my way after that little performance. With every step, I sink deeper and deeper into my head as I overanalyze whatever the hell that was. It's impossible not to replay the moment repeatedly, feeling my cheeks heat more and more with every flash of it in my mind.

It doesn't matter how many times I recount everything from start to finish, one reality remains: the people I thought I knew, the people I took for granted, are gone, just like everybody else I've known, and once again, there is nothing I can do about it.

This time, my hand slips into my pocket, the imprint embedding itself in my palm as I bite back the emotions threatening to consume me.

How am I supposed to survive the blood curse if I can barely survive breakfast?

13

POLARIS

Bryony tugs me up the stairs and down the corridors as we head to our first class, my mind foggy from the aftermath of my first encounter with my old friends since they were declared vampires. The word friend always felt weak before; now, it somehow holds no weight at all. I wonder if B has turned into an ass too?

I stumble over my feet as I'm dragged from my thoughts and launched back to reality as a familiar face comes into view. I can't bring myself to step over the threshold and enter the room as I gape at the man who knocked me to the ground yesterday.

A man. That's what he is. That's the ultimate difference I've surmised when comparing him to the guys I attended Florentine's with. Terence included.

He's fully dressed this time, in a pair of black

shorts and a matching tee, and I can't decide whether that's a good or bad thing. Seeing all of him yesterday—feeling all of him—was more fun than I care to admit.

My bubble of awe-inspired ogling quickly bursts when I look at his surroundings. He sits in the center seat in the back row, girls flanking either side of him, with another one perched on the desk as well. He's basking in their attention. It's like he was made for it, leaving me with the startling realization that I'm nothing more than a wisp in the wind as he dotes on them in return.

Of course, the first hot guy I have a reaction to is surrounded by all of the girls. It's the reality check I need. I'm not here to be distracted by anyone, not when the chance of survival burns so brightly in my future now.

Thankfully, Bryony tugs at my arm, pulling me from my one-way stare-off toward the middle row of seats. I grab the chair at the far left, and Bryony drops down beside me. If she notices my weird behavior, she doesn't mention it.

I take a shaky breath as I nervously look around the room. It's nothing like the classroom back at Florentine's. There is an array of posters all over the wall, a vibrant color scheme working its way around the room. Combined with the chatter, laughter, and joy that radiates from every corner, I'm left with a weird sensation.

No one made those kinds of noises in the classroom back there, mostly because if they did, they would likely receive some sort of punishment. But to experience it now, even though I'm not technically taking part, feels completely foreign.

The paint on the walls is a pale sage green. It's hidden deep among the posters, but it's there. It's a slight contrast to the darker wood furnishings that fill the room. Instead of a chalkboard with different-colored chalk splashed all across it, there's a whiteboard with a digital screen projected onto it.

As my gaze casts over the door, my breath shudders once more, only this time, it's from watching Sian and Terence walk into the room with Blaze right behind them. As if sensing the deathly glare the latter gives me the second he enters the room, Sian and Terence look anywhere but at me.

I quickly drop my gaze to my desk, heat burning at my cheeks as my fingers twist together nervously in my lap while nerves gnaw at my insides. I try as hard as possible not to sink into my sudden new surroundings, praying for the teacher to come and distract me. Instead, I feel tingles on the back of my neck, a sensation I know comes from someone staring intently at me.

I shouldn't look.

I know I shouldn't, yet it's impossible not to.

But when I turn around, I don't know who is causing the intense heat against my skin because it's not just one set of eyes I find. Quickly whipping my face forward again, I try to keep my breathing even.

'Mr. Hot Wolf, and he knows it' gave me half a glance but quickly dismissed me for the girls still vying for his attention, while the guys who fill in the rest of the row seemed a little more curious about the weird new girl. I think they're the same few guys he was sitting with yesterday, but I can't be certain. Not when I refuse to turn back and look again.

The spot that was generating the intense burning at the back of my neck came from the farthest seat on the right—the guy who seems to have labeled me his newest enemy.

Blaze.

He's a vampire, a thing I thought was nothing more than a myth up until twenty-four hours ago, and now here he is, already attempting to make my life as uncomfortable as possible, all because I was declared a witch. Isn't he aware that I didn't get a say in the matter?

I know I can keep my head down, stay out of everyone's sight, and I'll get through this just fine. I have to. Yet something tells me that he's going to enjoy sneering at me more than I'm going to enjoy hiding away from him as best as I possibly can.

"Good morning, class. Please take your seats. That means you at the back too, Bianca."

My gaze latches onto the professor as he strolls into the room with a tired smile on his face. My teeth sink into my bottom lip as I note his embarrassing comment to the girl, who I can only assume is the one sitting on the hot guy's table. My suspicion is confirmed a moment later as she saunters past me, muttering under her breath and taking the spot two seats in front of me.

"For those new here, I'm Professor Green, and I am the specialist in offensive and defensive skills." His smile widens with pride at the acknowledgment before he continues. "I won't waste any time today delving into past lessons. There's little that you have missed, but a small booklet will be sent to each of your rooms to summarize what we covered by the end of the day." He nods, more to himself than anything, as he doesn't seek confirmation from anyone. "Now, the main topic of why we're here, as mentioned, is to learn both offensive and defensive skills for us supernaturals in a world where the humans don't know we exist. Unless they're tainted by the blood curse, of course. Otherwise, we operate under the radar. Despite the secrecy in broad daylight and the effort it can sometimes take to remain hidden, it doesn't hide the intensity, the conflict, or the pain that lies among us. It just makes it harder for us to disguise it in the open."

I gape at him, trying to absorb every word coming out of his mouth, but it feels like he's talking too quickly for me to take it all in.

"Now, as I've just mentioned, the human world knows nothing about us, except for those with a blood kin. The humans who survive the blood kin curse later become supernatural hunters. Not by choice, really, not because anyone has really done anything wrong, but it's their way of offensively and defensively approaching the supernatural world as they move forward. Besides, it's not unknown to the supernatural world that some may…go a little rogue, and this is nature's way of restoring some balance in the rare instances that protection is needed."

"Why doesn't a vampire just compel them?" someone shouts, interrupting the professor, who rolls his eyes at the question.

Compel them?

"Because that would take away the rights of someone who survived the blood curse. They deserve to remember what they have faced and what they have endured. And it is also not a vampire's job to control that," Professor Green states before waving a dismissive hand and refocusing. "It's a natural order, just as everything else is."

All I can do is gape at him, my jaw refusing to close as his words go over my head, no matter how hard I try to gobble them up. Maybe if it wasn't such a confusing topic, I might be able to get a better grip on it, but none of it seems real.

"So, with that in mind, we are very aware that each supernatural faction has a different way of showing both offensive and defensive actions. For example, if we were to look at witches," he starts, and the mere mention of the word that suddenly clings to my name makes my heart stop in my chest as I stare at him with wide eyes, desperate to know more. "Their natural defensiveness is to form covens to help shore up their weaknesses. They spread their wings and join with others, creating collective groups where they're stronger defensively. There's always power in numbers in my opinion, especially when it can amplify your powers too."

I hope that's just a metaphor and there aren't any actual wings.

"In contrast to that, offensively, they are a force to be reckoned with. They work tirelessly with spells, enchantments, charms, and potions to ward off most things. They can also use particular abilities that others can't, and you will find that other supernaturals will lean on a witch's coven for aid. That is their strength among the supernaturals."

My pulse rings in my ears and his words carve themselves deep into my soul as I learn more about who I am meant to be. It doesn't feel as though those words fit me, not entirely, but something about them promises to give me strength like I've never felt before.

"Can anybody here give me an example of a wolf's offensive and defensive tactics?" Professor Green looks around the room, and his eyes settle on someone behind me. "Asher, please explain."

"Similar to the witches, I guess wolves form packs to create a defensive border. Our packs are our family, our friends, our ride or die. Nothing comes between you and your pack, not ever," he explains, his voice thick and rich as he speaks slowly, like he knows he's holding everyone's attention and enjoying it. "That's probably our defense, so our offensive is likely the fact that we can shift into said wolves from our human form, mostly at our own choice, except for under the full moon, which is out of our hands. With the shift comes abilities and strengths, along with the instinct to attack when threatened. That's why nobody messes with the wolves."

A scoff rings out at that statement, and all eyes in the room dart to the far corner where Blaze sits, a dark grin on his face.

"Please. That's bullshit."

"Mr. Williams, if you think you can explain the vampire's offensive and defensive tactics better, then please, go ahead," Professor Green encourages, and Blaze doesn't back down, sitting taller in his seat as he leans over his desk, casting a deathly glare over everyone in the room.

For a split second, I'm thankful it isn't just me, but I still can't stop myself from hiding my face before his eyes can find mine across the room.

"A vampire can compel you to do whatever they want. *I* can compel you to do whatever *I* want." I gulp as he reiterates his statement. "We don't have to deal with your bullshit going forward if we don't want to. We don't care to have a pack or a coven. We care about survival. That's our offensive, to strive for ourselves, to fight for ourselves, and to stand firm at all times. There's no need for us to be defensive, especially not like the witches, who always expect a bargain in order to offer their services. Nobody's interested in paying those prices. Definitely not a vampire."

I don't know why, but that added point feels directly aimed at me. My gaze snaps over my shoulder, finding his laser-sharp stare settled on mine, and I shrink in my seat.

Don't freaking look, Polaris. You're your own worst enemy right now. Internally, lecturing myself does nothing to quell the growing worry inside of me. Still, I silently shimmer with a hint of pride at the fact that I at least berated myself with my name instead of the lone initial I'm so familiar with.

The room remains silent, everyone hanging on his words until Bryony suddenly grunts from beside me. "Maybe, if you didn't piss the witches off to begin with, you might have more allies." There's a snark in her tone, a thunder crackling through her anger as her fingers curl into fists in her lap.

"I don't need allies," Blaze retorts. "That's the last thing I need in here," he adds, driving his point home. The look of disgust on his face is evident as I peer at him out of the corner of my eye, and I quickly turn around in my seat again to face the professor, who clears his throat.

"It's interesting to see how we all depict our factions and what that looks like to each of us. Although, I do believe that vampires may have an offensive and defensive side, Mr. Williams, but that's why I'm here. For you to learn and understand over the course of the next year." He strolls from around his desk, his demeanor calm and relaxed. I expect him to move on from the topic, but to my surprise, he proceeds to toy with the points already raised. "Let's say there's an emerging threat, if another faction were to attack you and your group, what would your responses be?" His eyes latch on to mine, and I already want the floor to open up before me. "How do you think you would react in response to an attack from a vampire, Polaris?"

The prospect of dying doesn't feel as intense as answering his question right now. More than that, how the hell does he know my name? Even more than that, is he a supernatural?

I gape at him as my mind swirls down a rabbit hole of questions that are completely unhelpful at the moment. My mouth is opening and closing like a goddamn fish as I struggle to think of what to say. When I do finally come up with something, it feels more than lacking, but the look on his face makes it obvious he isn't going to move until I've spoken.

"Right now, without any kind of abilities, since my magic sigil is still in place, I don't feel like I have any choice but to run."

"Never run."

Two words, one familiar voice. Yet it does not

comfort me; instead, it causes me to fight back an eye roll.

"Thank you for your insight, Lincoln, but you can't give an answer based on someone you don't know. Do you have a sigil in place? Have you just found out that you're a witch?" The professor blasts him with questions but gives him no opportunity to answer as I sink into my seat, hoping no one can see me. "You haven't walked a single day in her shoes. You can't determine her actions any more than she can determine yours. If I were to ask you what you would do if you were under attack from a vampire, I'm sure we all know you would use the highest offensive weapon you have against them and defend your pack. Is that good to assume, Lincoln?"

'Mr. Hot wolf, and he knows it,' has a name, it seems. Lincoln. But I don't get time to appreciate it as he scoffs in response to Professor Green's onslaught.

"Pretty much," he states, his tone far too husky for a guy that was just draped in half the female population of the class.

I am not attracted to him. I am not attracted to him. I am not…I'm a liar.

"But I guess that's more because I'm a wolf, and wolves don't run, not from anything," he states, and the burning sensation at the back of my head is definitely coming from him this time as my cheeks heat under the pressure.

Thanks, asshole.

His ego is back in full force, ready to rival Blaze's. I don't need any of this.

Biting back a sigh at the public embarrassment that has clung to me since the moment I left the witches' dorm this morning, I jolt as a hand curls around my arm, tugging my attention to my right, where I find Bryony looking at me. "Don't let him get to you. Don't let *any* of them get to you. You're right with your answer. All we have to do is get you to blend in with the witches and the other factions will pay no mind, I promise. The factions don't mix." Her words are firm, and I can't decide who she's trying to convince more, me or herself. I also can't decide why she cares, but that's not for me to figure out right now.

"They don't?" I clarify, like what she's saying makes sense, but when she shakes her head sharply, understanding washes over me.

"No, Polaris. Factions don't mix. Ever. And the quicker we get that target off your back, why ever the fuck it's there, the quicker we can get to teaching you about being a witch."

I offer a tight smile, falling back in my seat as the professor continues to speak. The swirling sensation in my gut is a mixture of emotions I can't decipher, but all I truly know is that I am relieved at the prospect of not being on their radar. Since the factions don't mix, the prospect of there already being a line drawn between me and so many people leaves a heavy pit in my stomach.

I should have known the moment I walked in that Lincoln was out of my league. Hearing his interjection just now only confirms it. I'm a witch, and it seems the vampires and the wolves don't think too highly of me for that fact alone.

The truth cuts through the hope that threatened to take root, and I quickly build my walls back up, isolating myself from the outside world once again.

It's safer in here. It always is.

14

POLARIS

The rest of the morning rolls into a blur of new surroundings, new textbooks, and new classrooms for every lesson. It's weird, no longer being caged to just the same familiar walls, and despite how overwhelming it feels, I want nothing more than to soak it all in. There have been no more deathly stares cast my way or what feels like public humiliation, but that's likely because I had classes specifically for witches, so there was no opportunity for it.

Bryony is right at my side as we stroll into the dining room and my anxiety instantly kicks up a notch. My eyes dart around the room, seeking out any threats, but I come up empty-handed as Bryony tugs at my arm.

"Let's get a drink first," she states, and I frown,

spying the water bottles already on the tables. "I don't want water," she insists as if sensing my thoughts, then she guides me to the right, where there's a drink station set up.

I watch as she fills a glass with a fizzy orange concoction and I follow suit, nervously filling my glass halfway in case it's gross. We head toward the same table as this morning, and I decide to keep my head down as we breeze past the vampire table. Settling into the seat beside Bryony, I take a tiny sip from my cup and hum in delight at the burst of orange that dances over my tongue. My eyelids fall to half-mast as I shiver at the deliciousness, but I quickly place the glass on the table so I don't proceed to make a fool out of myself.

I wonder how many people here have drank this stuff a million times. I wonder if they remember their first sip. I know I will for the rest of my life.

Turning my attention to the selection of food spread out on the table, I rub my lips together as I consider my options. It feels much harder than it was this morning when it was just breakfast foods to choose from. Now, there are various meats and accompaniments, carbohydrates, and vegetables, all with little labels. There are some that I've never heard of, nevermind tasted, but I shake off the uncertainty and reach for a plain chicken breast, mashed potatoes, and vegetables. I fill my plate with a small portion in case I don't like it, but the moment the mashed potatoes hit my tongue, I groan.

I need to stop embarrassing myself.

Keeping my gaze fixed on my plate, I will the heat in my cheeks to subside as my mind swirls with endless questions and wonder.

How am I ever supposed to be prepared for this change?

How am I supposed to ever fit in quickly, like I've been here the entire time?

How am I supposed to catch up?

How am I supposed to survive a single day, never mind the blood kin curse?

I'm sinking in worry, and to top it all off, deep down, I'm glad my magic is restricted by the sigil and untouchable right now. The thought of adding that to my plate on top of everything else would definitely send me to the brink of no return.

The chairs pull out across the table from me, and I spy D and H. They both remain huddled together, heads down, as they avoid eye contact with me, and I opt to stuff the forkful into my mouth to distract from the disappointment.

Thankfully, it's a comfortable silence that envelops the table as we eat, but I can't help but take in the whole atmosphere of the dining hall as I finish guzzling my new favorite thing in the entire world.

Orange soda.

Placing my empty glass on the table, I glance around the room again, and my eyes latch on to the wolves at the farthest end. Lincoln seems to capture my stare immediately, and I find him surrounded by girls once again. Dragging my eyes away from him, I look down the length of their table, and it becomes abundantly clear that wolves are just a different specimen of man altogether.

When I sense myself wandering down a rabbit hole of hot distractions that I don't want to get involved with, I turn my attention back to my plate. Once I'm done, I spy a bottle of water on the table and my stomach clenches in disgust. It doesn't look appetizing anymore—not in comparison to the soda.

Before I can change my mind or talk myself out of it, I stand. "I'm going to go and get another drink."

Bryony nods in acknowledgment and I quickly hurry down the length of the table, beelining straight for the soda machine. With my glass fully loaded with the addictive concoction once again, I turn back to the witches' table, but I only make it a meager three steps before I'm sent sailing through the air, clattering to the floor with a *thump*.

Glass shatters and orange liquid sprays everywhere as my palms ache from catching my fall and my knees burn from slamming against the floor. My pulse thumps in my ears, panic coating every inch of me, but through the sheer terror ringing in my ears, I hear a familiar voice.

"Maybe you should watch where you're going. You and that fucking silver hair are nothing but a beacon for disaster."

My cheeks burn and the backs of my eyelids are inflamed with unshed tears as I fight past the pain, both physically and mentally, and tilt my face to the right. Blaze is slouched in his seat, his foot extended in my direction, and his gaze is filled with a raw look of disdain.

How did I not see him there? More than that, how had I given him such an open opportunity to tear me down? Even *more* than that, why does he feel the need to attack me at all? Especially when it wastes such a valuable drink.

"Why don't you just fuck off, Blaze, and leave the new Florentines alone?" a guy grunts.

The voice is familiar. I think it might be Asher, the guy who spoke in the class earlier, but I can't bring myself to turn and look at him. Horror and embarrassment already engulf me, tinting my skin crimson from head to toe; I don't need to add anything else to that.

Acutely aware that I'm still on my hands and knees, not helping defuse the situation, I push up and stand, dusting myself off without lifting my chin from my chest. I can hear Blaze and, whom I assume is Asher, grunting back and forth between themselves, but it's impossible to decipher their words over my tight breath as I nearly hyperventilate.

Struggling to draw air into my lungs, the panic grows stronger, and all I can think about is the fact that the entire student body is probably watching my downfall, and I can't take it. Panic stole my breath like this once before, that I remember at least, but that was when my period started and I thought I was dying. This is something else entirely, and I can't just stand here and let it happen again, not with such a large audience.

My eyes lift, just a fraction, to find Terence frowning at me from his seat beside Blaze, while Sian looks down at her lap. It's the final push of the knife wedged between my ribcage, making black spots form in my vision, but before I collapse in a heap, I take off, running without a backward glance. I make my way through the few students standing between me and the door, and once I'm out in the corridor, I don't slow my pace. I keep going until I reach outside and the fresh air wraps around me. Even then, I struggle to slow down, my heart wrestling in my chest as I seek some form of shelter from the storm that's following me like a dark cloud fixed above my head.

I cut across the manicured lawn and through the trees that frame the edges before I stumble to a stop. What looks like a little maze made out of cropped hedges and arched vines sits nestled among the trees. A piece of serenity among the madness that ripples through the campus. I step through the arched vines without a second thought. I have no idea where I'm going, but I find my breathing calming, just a little, as I stumble to a stop at the center. Planting my hands on my knees, I keel over, praying the nausea subsides as I slowly start to catch my breath.

I know I'm gaining control when I can take in more detailed notes of my settings. I focus on that, letting my surroundings bring me back to reality. The shrubs stand about waist high, trimmed to perfection, with pretty pink flowers dotted through them. The ground beneath me is perfectly manicured, just like everywhere else, and the arched vines are laced with large white flowers that attract bees.

Pursing my lips, I attempt to stand tall and plant my hands on my hips, but I fail miserably and slump back down, my entire body giving out as I find myself flat on my back, the cropped grass tickling along my skin.

Looking up at the sky, the sun is muted by the full trees looming above, but watching them gently sway in the breeze seems to calm the fire roaring inside me. With every controlled breath, I start to feel the rest of my body come back to life, the numbness slowly seeping from my bones. With a pinch of clarity, as the flames slow their coiling through my veins, I settle on the emotions taking hold.

Panic.

Anxiety.

Get yourself together, Polaris. Get yourself together.

It doesn't matter what other people can do. They won't hurt me, not in any way that matters. I can survive stupid shit like this. I can survive Sian and Terence pretending I don't exist. I can survive no one speaking to me forever, Bryony included, because I'm sure it'll come to that after she sees the drama unraveling around me. But it doesn't matter; I can survive it all because I have to focus all of my energy on surviving the blood kin curse.

The pep talk seems to ease some of the tension that still lingers inside me, when a voice sounds in the near distance, causing me to freeze. It takes a second, but I quickly realize it's not me that they're speaking to. The air grows quiet again, and I consider peeking to see if they've left or not, when their raspy voice cuts through the air again.

"I know, I know. I'm just…today is the anniversary, okay? It's hard." I can feel the pain in his words and I hold my breath, scared to breathe and draw attention to myself. "I know you care," he continues, but the sigh that escapes his lungs ripples through the air. "I do. For sure. I will come and see you guys, I will, it's just…it's a lot right now. No…I know. I know. I get what you're saying, but—are you even listening to me, or are you just allowing me to speak as you wait your turn to carry on getting your point across like what I'm saying doesn't matter?"

My eyebrows gather as I listen, acutely aware that I'm eavesdropping on a conversation that has nothing to do with me, but it's intriguing, nonetheless. The way he's trying to stand up for himself, even if he's failing, is inspiring. I need to take a page out of his book.

Pressing up onto my elbows, my gaze follows the

direction of his voice, and I find a guy with his back to me, pacing in front of the arched vines. His head is dipped, his fingers pressing along the bridge of his nose as he seems to be struggling with something.

"I'm not going. I can't be there today. Tomorrow. I'll try tomorrow." He tilts his head back, looking up at the sky, defeat clinging to his features.

I can see him easily from here now.

Long brown hair is secured in a bun at the back of his head, with the sides shaved short. Deep brown eyes stare off into the distance as he stands tall, pain palpable in the air around him.

"Fine. I'll be there today," he grunts before ending the call, letting the cell phone fall to the ground with a thump, and I suddenly feel like I'm seeing a glimpse of his vulnerability that nobody should be witnessing right now.

Lowering myself back down, I press myself into the ground, trying to hide my presence as I hear him curse under his breath before the sound of a punch crushing against a hard surface, likely a tree, fills the space around us.

He exhales heavily, and a part of me wants to jump to my feet and comfort him, but something tells me that wouldn't be taken too well. Whoever he is, he doesn't look like a witch. Not from who I've seen at my table, and any approach from me is probably going to make the situation worse. I'm already covered in orange soda, my pride tarnished; I don't need this guy getting angry at me, too.

Instead, I beg for the ground to open up, but his voice cuts through the air, confirming I'm still where I shouldn't be.

"You can come out now. You're not exactly doing the best job at hiding."

My spine stiffens. This time, I know those words are for me, but I can't convince myself to move an inch.

Plastered to the ground, I hold my breath, willing him to leave, but he doesn't seem to take the hint.

"Is eavesdropping a habit of yours, or should I count myself lucky?" he asks. There doesn't seem to be any disappointment in his tone, just a sense of defeat and reluctance. Yet I still don't move.

I brace for impact, ready for him to charge over here and make a complete mockery of me, but to my surprise, he sighs, and the sound of his footsteps disappearing in the distance is all I hear.

I have no idea what that was, but I've already got enough of my own drama going on. I don't need to concern myself with anything else right now. I don't have a savior complex; I'm too selfishly trying to escape my own troubles to worry about someone else.

I just need to survive today, then I can figure out how to survive tomorrow. And eventually I need to figure out how I'm going to face the blood kin curse.

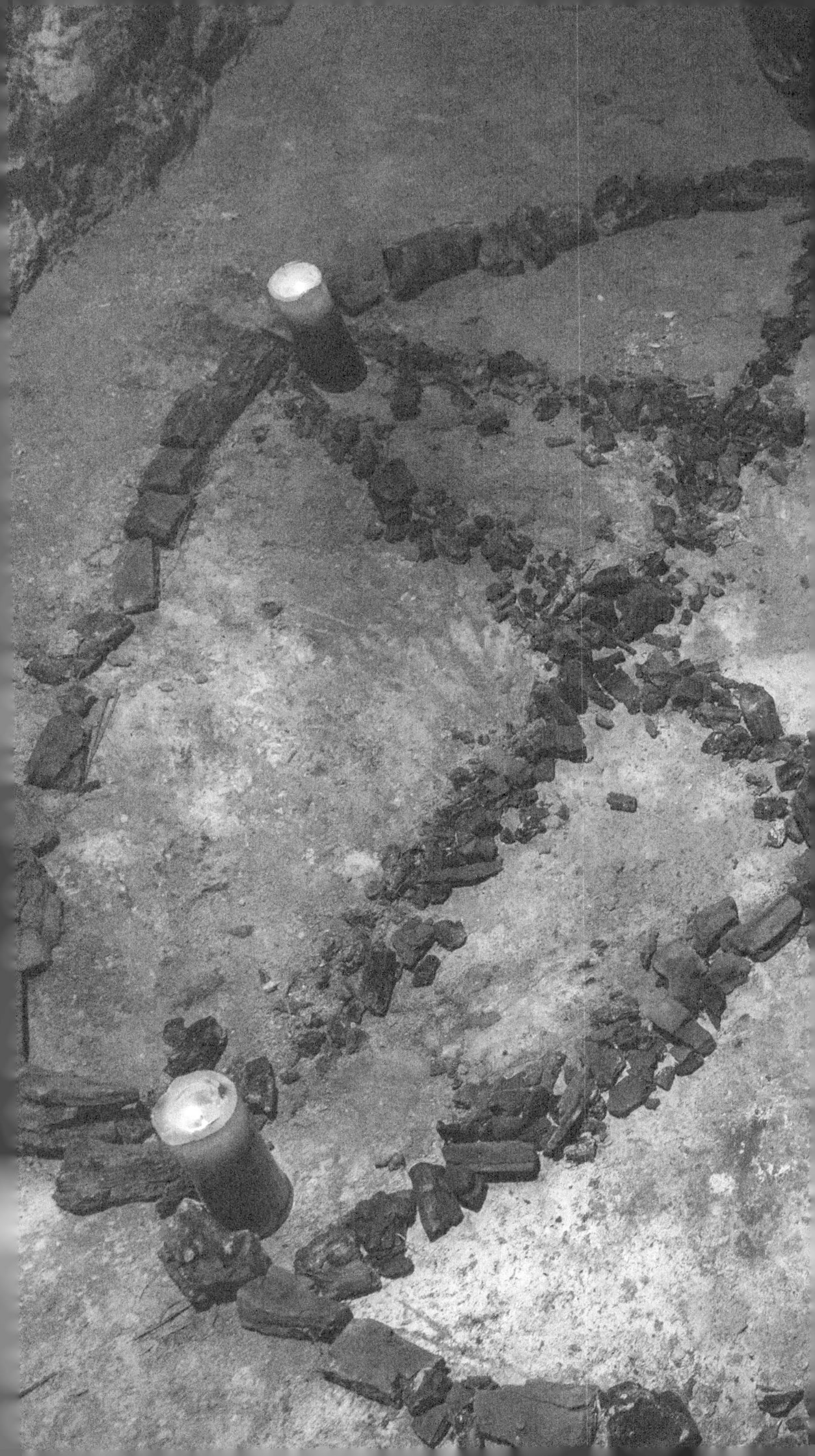

15

POLARIS

I don't know how I made it through the rest of the day, but somehow, I managed to pick myself up off the ground, walk myself back to the main academy building, and participate in the rest of the day's lessons.

Nobody said a word.

Not one.

I didn't even get a side look from anyone, even with my gray jacket still stained orange. It felt anticlimactic. I was expecting snickers and finger-pointing, but nothing came. More than that, no one really looked at me at all, as if it was a rule to ignore me, and as much as I appreciated the lack of incessant bullying, the itch that I had done something even worse clawed at me.

Bryony remained at my side, as silent as

everyone else had been, but as I stole a deep breath and re-entered the dining hall for dinner, I couldn't keep quiet anymore.

"Am I imagining the drama I endured at lunch?" I ask as we take our seats, only this time, we're at the far end of the table, as far away from the drama-seeking vampires as I can get. The wince on Bryony's face confirms I didn't make it all up, but it still doesn't ease the pit in my stomach. When she doesn't look at me, I push, knowing there's more I'm unaware of. "Bryony, please, you've got to help me out. I'm drenched in orange stains, I fled this damn room like my life depended on it, and no one—and I mean *no one*—has batted an eyelid at me since. Not a vampire. Not a wolf. Not a witch or a human. It's like it didn't happen, but I've still got the stains and the tension headache that proves I'm not making it up. What am I missing?"

My chest heaves with every breath, my eyes wide as I plead for her to help me out.

She looks at me from the corner of her eye first, the sigh parting her lips loud in my ears before she turns to look at me. She inches closer, and I do the same, my heart thundering as I wait to hear the secret she seems hesitant to share, but before she speaks, she glances around the room, making sure she can't be heard before she zones in on me again.

"You didn't hear this from me," she starts, and I shake my head profusely, even though I don't understand why it matters. Her tongue runs over her lip, her eyes casting over the room again before she leans in even closer. "The Alpha Pack wasn't too happy about Blaze's little stunt. I hadn't even realized you had escaped until they took over the room."

"Took over the room?" I repeat, eyebrows gathering in confusion, and she nods.

"One on each of the tables. They were furious."

One on each of the tables? Furious? I don't understand.

"They marched along the wood, barking out orders, making everyone swear to keep their mouths shut and heads down. If anyone is seen making fun of you or even looking at the mess on your jacket, then they would tear their fucking heads off."

I lean back, disbelief swirling in my mind. "That seems a bit dramatic."

"That's the Alpha Pack," she states with a shrug, as if it explains everything, yet I feel no wiser.

"Why would they do that?" I ask as she starts to choose her dinner, but I can't bring myself to reach for a plate with my mind still struggling to process all of this new information.

"Why does the Alpha Pack do anything?

They're insane. Some might call them savage, but sticking up for a witch isn't usually on their agenda. You should be honored," she says with a wink, and my eyes flare wide in shock.

Honored? I feel anything but.

I don't say that, though, dipping my chin to my chest as I take an easing breath before forcing myself to look at the food options. Reaching for a burger and fries, I also grab a bottle of water, refusing to go anywhere near the drink machine.

Bryony falls into a comfortable silence, eating her pizza while I nibble at my fries. The deliciousness is wasted on me as I drown my thoughts, overanalyzing every moment. More than anything, I'm acutely aware that I don't deserve her positivity and support, just as I didn't deserve S's back at Florentine's.

I'm lost in my head as I devour the burger, not really tasting it as I chew on autopilot. I'm ready to be done in here, head back to my room, and hide away for the rest of the night when a shadow casts over us from across the table.

He curls his hands over the back of a chair, not bothering to take a seat as his gaze settles on Bryony. "Are you guys coming to the wolf party tonight?" he asks, offering me a side glance, but it doesn't last long before his attention quickly shifts back to Bryony. He stares her down, and there's a sparkle in her eyes as she preens in her seat.

"Tonight?" she asks, cocking her brow at him, and he shrugs.

"The wolves don't care if it's a school night. We only need an hour's sleep to survive. Besides, it's a full moon, so the party won't run too late," he explains, leaning closer.

Instead of answering him, Bryony turns my way. "What do you say?"

I gape at her, my cheeks heating under her watchful stare as the guy observes us. Clearing my throat, I look down at my lap. "I've never been to a party before," I admit, and her eyes widen, her jaw falling slack as she nods.

"We should go," she says, returning her attention to the guy. "I'll be there. *We'll* be there," she insists, not waiting for my answer. But the guy seems happy with that, and he's gone in the next moment.

Nerves claw at me, threatening to manifest themselves in the form of a panic attack as I shake my head. "I don't think it's a good idea for me to go. I don't need to draw any more attention to myself," I insist, and she scoffs, waving a hand at me dismissively.

"You won't draw any attention. It's perfect."

I give her a skeptical look this time, pointing at my hair. “Have you seen the color of this? I stick out like a sore thumb. Blaze said it himself, and as much as some Alpha pack or whoever they are might have said something, I can’t imagine a world in which that man gives a shit about what someone else has to say,” I admit, hating the color of my hair now more than ever. All it seems to do is encourage painting a target on my head. For what? I don’t think I’ll ever know, but I don’t want to make things worse.

“Girl, just say the word, and we can dye it,” she offers, and my eyebrows furrow.

“Dye it?”

“Yeah. What color do you want?”

I gulp, staring at her with wide eyes as I struggle to comprehend what she's offering. I really need to catch myself up to speed with this place, figure out the finer details on how it works because all I seem to be doing is drowning in every damn word that comes out of anybody's mouth.

“I don't know,” I finally admit with a sheepish shrug. “I never thought it was a possibility.”

She tucks a loose tendril that’s fallen free from her braid behind her ear as she beams at me. “I love dyeing my hair,” she states, and I shake my head in disbelief.

"You're not naturally blonde?" I ask, and she scoffs again.

"Heck, no. So what do you say? Want to try?"

I sink my teeth into my bottom lip, at a complete loss of what to do. When it's clear she won't stop staring at me expectantly, I finally scramble for an answer. "Can I say yes to the hair without committing to the party?"

"You can try," she retorts with a smirk, and I know I'm not going to be able to talk my way out of it, but the idea of changing this beacon on my head is too alluring for me not to give it a chance.

Despite the barrage of emotions in my gut, I nod.

"Lead the way."

THE GIRL STARING BACK at me in the mirror is someone I have never seen before. The blue of my eyes somehow stands out more prominently now with a darker color framing my face, and I'm torn.

I feel a little excited, more than I care to admit, but I don't feel like my old self at all.

Along with my black hair that falls in loose waves around my face, I've learned everything I think there is to know about Bryony as she sprinkles me with her expertise.

She has three siblings, two older and one younger. The two older siblings both survived the blood curse, which makes her nervous, but she's a badass nonetheless. What she learned about me in return is…nothing. I have nothing to offer except the tendrils of darkness that Florentine's infused within me.

I've barely been here a whole day, and the trauma that threatens to rear its ugly head now that I'm out of the bubble is enough to floor me. It takes all of my strength to tamp it down.

Running my fingers through my hair, I look at my face. Maybe it's the mascara she put on my lashes that make my eyes pop more, or the blush on my cheeks, or the bronzer or highlighter. She used so much stuff that I don't think I look like the same person anymore.

Either way, I feel empowered tonight. I feel stronger than I've ever felt before. I don't feel weak, I don't feel panicked, I just feel…new.

A new me for a new place.

Is that possible?

It's not like anybody from Florentines is desperate to cling to the version of me that I was. Even if tonight is the only night I'll ever get to experience the freeing feeling it offers, it's better than to have never experienced it at all. Right?

"Girl, I've got the perfect outfit for you," Bryony states, running her hands over my new clothes hanging in the armoire beside me. She pins them against my chest, rifling through a few shirts before she settles on her decision. "Get ready here. I'll turn my back in the corner," she insists, giving me no room to decline, and there's a part of me that doesn't want to.

Sighing, I eye the clothes in my hands and focus on the fact that I'm going to attend my first party. I'm slightly worried about who else might be there, but that's a problem for later. Right now, I want to prolong this fuzzy, exciting feeling inside of me.

I slip into the denim jeans that fasten high up my waist, change out of my tee for a cropped silk top, and step into the black boots I was issued.

Staring at myself, a twinge of a smile curls at the corner of my lip, and no matter how hard I try to drop it, it only grows stronger. Instead of letting myself get too carried away with these changes, I clear my throat, looking at the back of Bryony's head as she stands in the corner, just like she said she would.

"Can I ask you a question?"

"Are you getting changed?" she retorts, and I smirk.

"I'm done."

She whips around, clapping her hands together excitedly as she beams at me. "Looking as hot as you do, you can ask me anything."

I roll my eyes at her, pretending I didn't hear the compliment as I step away from the mirror. "The Alpha Pack you mentioned before, who are they?" She mushes her lips together, biting back a smile as she taps the side of her nose. "You have to tell me," I insist when it's clear she's not going to say a word.

"Please, it's amusing to watch."

"What's amusing to watch?"

"Them protecting someone, and that *someone* having no idea. Especially when you're not a wolf."

I pout at her, planting my hands on my hips, hoping like hell I'm conveying a badass vibe like I want. "You're talking nonsense. If you don't tell me, someone will."

"Sure, good luck with that," she teases before she sweeps her hands over her body, muttering soft words under her breath, and I watch in complete awe as her clothes change.

Gone are the joggers and tee, and in their place is a tank top tucked into a mini skirt. Sandals now crisscross over her feet and a delicate anklet has settled itself on her right leg.

"What was that?" I finally manage when I find my tongue again, and she grins.

"When you figure out your magic, you'll notice you'll be able to do that and a lot more. It's my favorite part about magic. So much of my time is no longer wasted on mundane things. It's fun."

"Why didn't you use that on me?" I ask, bewildered at the amount of time we just spent putting me back together again.

"Because I love the process of hair and makeup. Besides, it's your first time. You deserved the real experience. Don't take that away from me."

I roll my eyes at her sass, and she gives me a pointed look. "Now, are you ready or not?"

"If I said not?" I retort, and she scoffs.

"Then I'd pretend I didn't hear you because... what have you got to lose, Polaris?" she asks, and I freeze in place, letting her words drift over me before I exhale slowly, the sensation somehow calming a little of my tension.

"Nothing. I have nothing to lose."

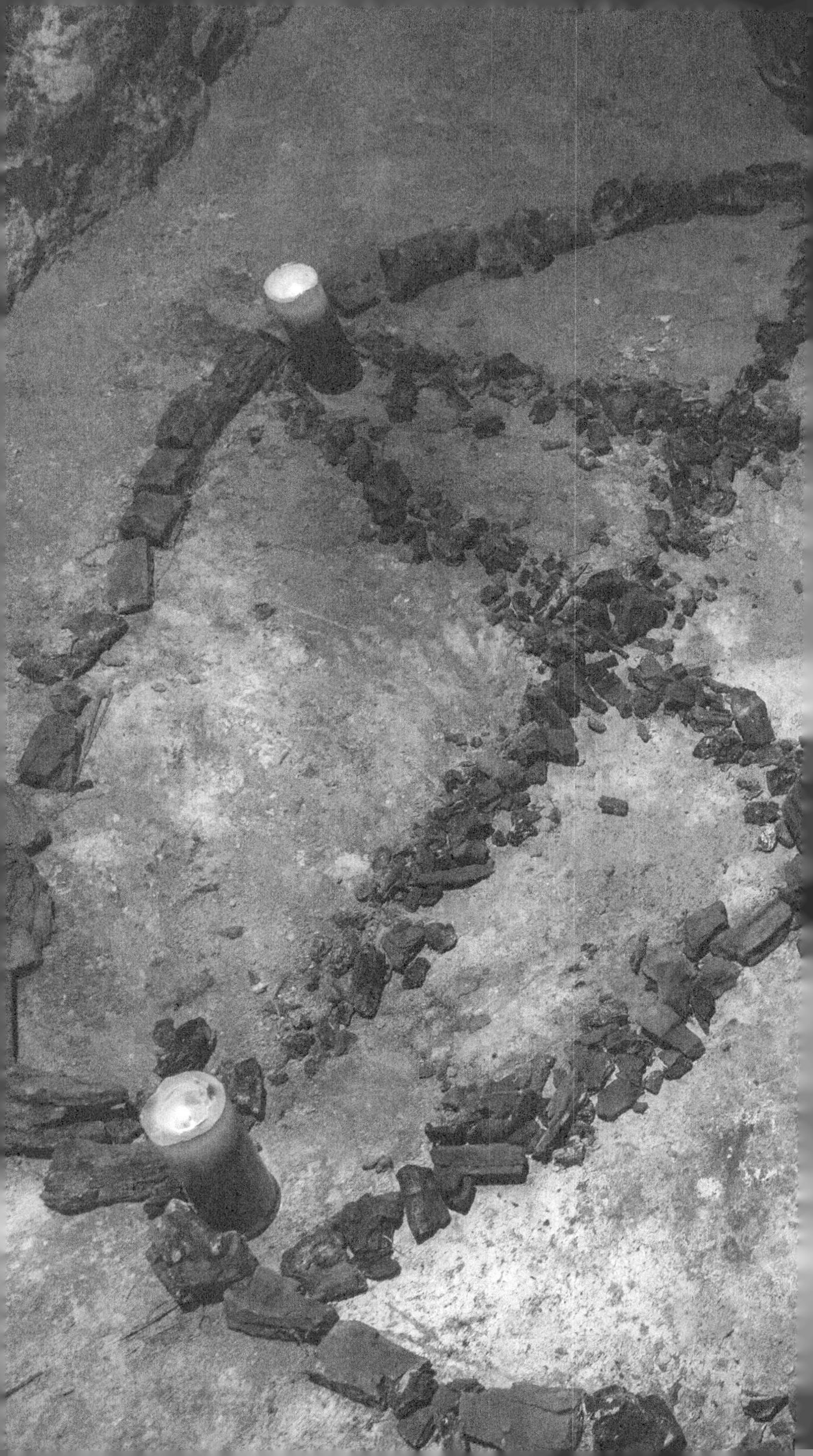

16

POLARIS

I was wrong.

There is something I could lose... my damn hearing. How is it possible to be out in the woods, a stone's throw from where I was earlier, hiding out from the world, yet feel like I'm in the pits of some music mosh pit or something?

There are bodies everywhere.

The music is loud, I can barely hear myself think, but I quickly learned that it's all part of some crazy magical mirage created by the witches to soundproof the area. You wouldn't know by looking, but Bryony explained it's from the sand drawn around the perimeter. And she was right. Before I stepped through the entry point, I didn't hear a thing. It was only when we crossed over the threshold that everything changed.

Follow the sand.

That's what she said to me yesterday. Now, seeing it in this form makes it clear what she meant when she said it. Following the sand will lead you to the witches, not just the witches' dorm, as I'd initially assumed.

Barely over the threshold, the music thumps around us, the ground shaking from the base as I gape at the array of bodies dancing, laughing, singing, and screaming. What holds my attention most is the fact that I can clearly see factions mingling amongst each other. There are no wolves in one corner and vampires in another. People I recognize dance together in the center of the space as if factions don't exist. It's not an impossible thought either; I didn't know they existed until yesterday. If I hadn't seen it for myself today, how it's a faction-eat-faction world here, I wouldn't believe it. Yet, humans, witches, wolves, and vampires are all willingly together.

I don't see Blaze in the mix, but that doesn't mean he isn't here. Hopefully, my black hair will deter him from me altogether.

Turning to Bryony, I clear my throat. "I thought everyone hated each other?" I shout over the music, and Bryony shrugs as she follows my line of sight.

"They do," she hollers back, making me frown.

"But I thought factions don't mix?" I retort, intrigued, but all she does is shrug again.

"They don't," she offers, but this time, she looks at me, and I raise my eyebrows. Thankfully, it encourages her to provide a little more explanation. She leans in so she doesn't have to shout so loud and murmurs in my ear. "A full moon wolf party is different. What happens at a full moon wolf party stays at a full moon wolf party," she says with a grin on her face as she leans back.

"If you say so," I murmur, more to myself than anything. I'm almost sure she didn't hear me, but the wink she offers confirms that she did.

Tilting my face at her, I can't help but question her more. "That looks like experience in your eyes."

She taps her nose, the same sign she used earlier to declare she won't spill any more details. "It stays at the full moon wolf party, remember?" She smirks before pointing off to the side. "Now, let's get a drink, and then we're dancing," she insists, wrapping her fingers around my arm and tugging me around the perimeter.

Any chance of refusal dies on my lips as the energy that booms around us seeps into my bones. I'm too intrigued and curious to leave now. That doesn't mean I have to partake. I need to talk her out of dancing, but being here, in general, doesn't seem too much of an issue.

Yet.

A corner of the space is set up with an array of drinks behind it. Neon lights curl to spell out the word "bar" in bright blue, followed by "free drinks" in hot pink.

I let Bryony do the ordering before she hands me a brown bottle. My nose crinkles instantly as I bring it to my nose, not appreciating the smell.

"What is that?"

"Beer," she states, a hint of confusion in her tone, and my nose crinkles further. "Wait, you haven't even had a beer?" The question is evident in her statement, and her jaw falls slack. I shake my head, looking down the neck of the bottle at the brown concoction inside.

"Not even a beer," I clarify before I can bring the bottle to my lips. She rips it from my hand before I can dare taste it, scowling at the bottle as though it's offended her.

"You're right. That definitely can't be the first alcoholic drink you ever taste." She turns back to the guy behind the bar, and his eyes are already settled on me.

"First drink?" he repeats, clearly having heard our conversation, and I can feel my cheeks heat.

I've never been more grateful for poor lighting in hopes that it hides my embarrassment.

He stares at me expectantly, waiting for confirmation, but I'm too locked onto his hazel eyes. They swirl with grit and fire, pain and fury, yet the softness he offers me feels almost unnatural. His blond hair is cropped, almost all the way, and his bulky frame is overwhelming. I'm not sure if his muscles have muscles, but the way his sleeves dig into his biceps only seems to confirm my suspicions.

Suddenly remembering that he's waiting for an answer, I feel my cheeks burn so much I'm sure they're going to burst into flames, so I quickly find his gaze and nod.

"Yes," I admit, already hating myself for the single word response, but he smiles at me. It's so short I could have imagined it, but the words that follow are more reassuring than they should be.

"Don't worry, I've got you," he says, his eyes darkening just a touch before he turns around to run his gaze over the bottles behind him. After a few seconds, he reaches for one high up. I watch him break the seal, twisting the cap and grabbing a tiny glass before pouring the liquid into it.

He places it on the bar between us, and all I can do is stare at it as Bryony leans closer. "That better not have been messed with," she states with a bite that could rival the growl of a wolf, and the guy steps back with his hands raised in surrender.

"You just watched me break the seal. That means nothing has been messed with," he grumbles, his nostrils flaring with irritation as my eyes flick between them both.

"Messed with?" I ask, scared that I don't want to know the answer when her eyes widen.

"Drugged," she clarified.

Horror seeps into my bones and I take an instinctive step back. I might not know much, but we at least learned about drugs at Florentine's. Before I can bolt, she grabs my arm, a soft laugh parting her lips as she attempts to offer me a reassuring smile.

"I think this experience is going to be way more intense than either of us anticipated," she says, tugging me back toward her. "All I'm saying is, he better not be a cunt. Now, a cunt is a guy like Blaze who thinks he's a gift from God when he's really a warden from hell," she explains, earning a snicker of agreement from me before she proceeds. "The other kind of a cunt is someone who will try to drug people to do things they may not want to. Okay?" She turns me to face her head-on now, hands planted on my shoulders as she stares into my eyes. "'No' is a whole sentence. 'No' is enough of an answer, but there are some dick for brains around these parts. You have to be focused at all times, Polaris."

"Polaris, that's a pretty name."

My gaze darts to the guy behind the bar as my lips press together. It's not embarrassment that tinges my cheeks pink this time, but I'm still thankful that the poor lighting hides it all the same.

"I don't think I want this drink," I mutter, unable to respond to his compliment as I push the little glass away, and Bryony scoffs.

"Oh, you want it. Not the drugs, but the high from the tequila."

The guy pulls another glass and pours a drink for Bryony too. Nerves tingle through my veins, but I reach for my glass anyway and Bryony clinks hers against mine before downing her own.

The familiar question reverberates through my mind. What do I have to lose?

The guy looks at me expectantly, and I feel myself on the verge of drinking him in instead of the liquid in the glass. I've already been stupid enough to react to some of the guys on campus. I can't keep distracting myself like that, so I quickly bring the glass to my lips and toss my head back.

Just like I watched Bryony, I slam the glass down on the bar as the liquor burns down my throat. I can't help but cough and splutter for what feels like an eternity before I turn a deathly glare to both of them.

"That's awful."

Bryony chucks her head back with a laugh while the guy grins at me. I feel his eyes raking up and down the length of my body as he speaks.

"It's tequila. It's strong as fuck, but better than a beer for your first taste."

Bryony cheers at that, grabbing my beer bottle off the table as she moves it toward me, but the guy interjects, sweeping it back behind the bar before I can reach it.

"Hold off on that for a while. Let the tequila take effect first. We don't want you comatose, not at your first full moon wolf party. We throw too many of these for you to bow out so soon," he says with a wink, and I smile, murmuring my thanks as Bryony sighs.

"Fine, party pooper, let's go dance instead."

Dammit.

My mouth falls slack, my refusal falling short as the guy pats the bar separating us.

"Nice meeting you, Polaris."

"Nice, meeting you too," I mutter helplessly in response.

"It's Wylder," he states as Bryony starts to tug me away, and I frown,

"Wylder?"

"The name that you're looking for. That's me. See you around, Polaris," he says with a megawatt grin, and I suddenly have no interest in following after Bryony.

Could he tell me more about the Alpha Pack?

I could ask, but just like every other moment since I arrived here, it's not my choice. Yanked onto the dance floor, I'm surrounded by a sea of bodies and the beat seems to vibrate through the ground, into my feet, through my legs, and into my hips, making them sway from side to side. I dance to music I've never heard before. I think it's more euphoric than the taste of the liquor that still burns my throat.

My eyelids close and the world shifts away as I feel the most exuberant vibe through my body. I have no idea how much time has passed—a minute, ten, an hour, a year?

That's extreme, but it feels like the best time of my life until my feet start to ache. I'm certain I can't shake my ass any longer. Prying my eyes open, I find Bryony dancing with the guy who invited her to the party earlier.

I wave a hand at her and she peers at me. "I'm

going to find somewhere to sit," I holler, and she moves to step away from the guy, but I wave my hand frantically. "Stay. I just need to sit," I insist before working my way through the sea of people once again.

I take a deep breath when I'm in a less crowded space and find the closest spot to sit. It's a fallen tree trunk, but it will do. Resting my elbows on my knees, I catch my breath as I watch the party unravel around me. Sweat beads at my forehead, sticking my hair to the back of my neck, but I can't fight the smile on my face.

It's freeing.

There's no stress out here, no issues, no inter-faction treachery.

Watching everybody mingle, dance, and have fun with one another is amazing, especially when I can't tell who is who because everyone is simply connected.

One word and my heart clenches.

Connected.

Everybody here has someone they're connected with on another level, like no one else. Everybody here faces the death penalty by the time we turn twenty-two at the hands of somebody else here, present right now. At this time, in two years, only half of us will remain.

That thought alone is sobering, but my brooding is halted as a guy sits down beside me.

"Hey, baby," he purrs, throwing his arm around my shoulders. "I don't like a girl like you looking so lonely. Why don't you join me in this beer?" His eyes are blown wide, a bottle extended my way, but I'm already shaking my head.

The fact doesn't seem to matter, though; he's still nudging the bottle into my hands.

Retreating as best as I can, I clear my throat. "I'm good, but thanks," I insist, hoping he'll take the hint. Instead, he drops his hand from my shoulder to the small of my back, running his fingers over my bare skin.

My hands curl into fists in my lap.

Is this a cunt like Bryony was talking about earlier?

Turning back to him, I keep my facial expressions neutral. "No, thank you," I state proudly, the words firm, but instead of removing his hand like I'm expecting, his fingers creep higher.

"Remove your hand from me, or I'll do it for you," I state, anger coiling through my veins like I've never felt before, but it only brings a smirk to his lips.

I have no idea where I just found the strength to stand my ground, and all he does is…smirk?

"Baby, I'm a vampire. I could lean in close and compel you to give me exactly what I want, and you'd have no say in it otherwise. Now, I don't mind how you take it, but I always prefer my subject willing."

My heart races in my chest. Bryony didn't mention this part when she described this kind of guy earlier. My eyes rake over him, figuring out where his weak points may be for me to attempt to hit him and run. With every second that passes, I become more and more aware of how naïve I am to even think I could manage that, when a hand lands on my arm, tugging me to my feet.

"There you are, Midnight. I've been looking all over for you." Lips press against my temple, stealing my breath as my skin heats.

The guy beside me quickly fumbles to his feet, panic washing over his features. "My bad, Linc. My bad. No harm, yeah?" the guy says, stumbling back a step as I'm locked in place, going from the embrace of one man to another, completely out of my comfort zone, as the new voice beside me grows darker.

"Yeah, your bad, man. Now fuck off."

17

LINCOLN

I have no idea what I'm doing right now. I'm just drawn to the beacon in the night. I don't know how I missed the new girl transferring here; she must have blended in with the arrival of the kids from Florentine's. It's a damn shame I'm only just seeing her now, but hopefully, she's not too disappointed in having to wait for my attention. I'm about to steamroll her and make up for it; I just need Dean to get his damn hands off her.

I was so enraptured in watching her dance that I was still staring at her as she drifted from the crowd and found a seat on the fallen tree. Her hair floated around her shoulders as she swayed to the music, lost in her own world, and that bubble she thrives in stayed wrapped around her. When she slipped over here, hiding from the sound of the party, I got an honest look at her.

Her hair, her eyes, her silky skin.

She reminds me of midnight, when the sky is at its darkest shade of blue-black, with the moon bright in the sky and the stars sparkling like a glimmer in the distance.

Her hair is the sky, her face the moon, and her eyes the stars.

I don't know where she came from, and I have no idea who she is, which is perfect for stumbling across her at a full moon party because any insignificant details don't matter. She doesn’t have to be a wolf; she doesn’t have to be anything but mine for the night.

Dean just needs to fuck off.

“Yeah, your bad, man. Now fuck off.”

His eyes widen, panic flickering across his face, and I bite back the grin threatening to transform my face as he rushes off into the crowd. The second he’s out of sight, I turn my attention to the spectacle beside me.

Dropping my hand from her shoulder, I skim my fingers around her waist, erasing the touch Dean left behind, and instead mark her for myself for the night. The touch has her eyes meeting mine, and even under the dark sky, the pink hues on her cheeks are noticeable, along with the dimples.

Fucking dimples.

She peers up at me, a hint of hesitation in her eyes as I grin.

"What's your name? Midnight?"

Her tongue sweeps across her bottom lip as she stares deep into my eyes. "Midnight?" she questions, her eyebrows gathering in confusion, and I shrug.

"Yeah." That's all I have to offer. I can decipher the meaning behind it later, but she never needs to know that. I expect her to push me for more, refusing to let it slide, but to my surprise, she shrugs, glancing away from me.

I can sense it. She's a deer caught in the headlights. She's clearly never felt the attention of Lincoln James before. That's all going to change tonight.

It's hard to get a read on her. I can't tell if she will come up with an excuse to take a step away, just like she did with Dean, or whether she'll lean into me, aware of the man she has in her grasp.

The seconds spread out so far that I'm considering another approach when she turns her attention back to me.

"Does my name matter at a full moon wolf party?"

My dick stirs to life at a simple question and my fingers press into her side. Hands down, that's the perfect response.

"No, I don't suppose it does," I say with a grin, bringing my other hand to her cheek as I shift us so we're standing face to face.

Her name doesn't matter anyway, not when I've already given her a nickname to last an eternity. Besides, everyone knows who I am. Forgetting her name come morning and having an awkward interaction tomorrow is foregone under these terms. Let's just hope she doesn't fall for my magical dick and expect anything more.

Tomorrow doesn't matter right now. All that matters is this moment. Introductions aren't necessary, but feeling her lips against mine is.

Running my thumb back and forth over her cheek, she locks onto my gaze like a warrior, ready for battle. There's a feisty side to her, one hiding behind the innocent vibe she's got going on, along with a hint of familiarity, but I have no clue how.

"Do you want to get out of here?" I ask, and once again, she rubs those pretty pink lips together as uncertainty wars inside of her.

"No."

My fingers tighten around her waist as my grip on her chin pulls her an inch closer. That's not what I expected, not even a little bit. That was clearly my first error.

"That's a shame," I breathe, and our noses touch as we move closer.

"Why?" Her breath blows across my face, teasing just how close she is, and the noise vibrating from the party dwindles to nothing more than a background whisper, dimming as she holds my attention captive.

"Because I want to get to know you better." My fingers curl under the hem of her silk shirt and she scoffs.

"You want to get to know *me* better, or my body?" she quizzes, and all I can do is grin because fuck, she's got me there.

Leaning in, I press my lips against her ear and she shivers at the contact before I've even uttered a word. "I want exactly what it seems your body wants, Midnight," I whisper, feeling the tremor run through her body even more intensely.

She tilts her head back, bringing her lips to my ear, and I can't deny that I'm enjoying this game we're playing.

"My body can't be trusted. It doesn't know

what's good for me," she states, and I have to bite back a groan as my dick presses against the zipper of my pants.

"Trust me. Let me help you figure it out."

It's an offer on the verge of a plea as her skin warms beneath my touch.

I feel the corner of her mouth tilt up in a silent grin, a snicker threatening to ripple from her throat. "Trusting you seems like the worst thing I could do."

"Low blow," I whisper, leaning back, and our noses touch as I position her face in front of mine again. But this time, I let go of her chin and place my hand on my chest. "Please, I'm a stand-up wolf. Besides, I've got a solid forty-five minutes before my wolf takes over and zero chance of any fun after that."

That's the downside to finding her at a full moon party, but it's just my luck to find a mystery in the night, and there's a time constraint on it.

She doesn't seem to understand the importance of that because she snickers for real this time. "You're insufferable."

I shrug. "Am I? Or do I just know what I want?" I retort, and she grins, her hands lifting to my chest, tugging me closer as I place both hands on her waist, blindly curling my fingers into the belt loops on her jeans. One small tug and we're hip to hip.

"And what's that?"

"You. What I want is you."

Her pupils dilate, but the grin is still playful. She's not just fighting me now; she's fighting herself. Her next words confirm my observation.

"Nice. Do those words work on everyone?"

"I'm a ladies' man with an ego to match. There's no use denying it," I say with a shrug. She'll see it for herself. Come tomorrow, and the day after, and the day after, this is just who I am.

Her lips purse a little as she assesses me, and I can't help but stare at them, eager to feel if they're as plump as they look and as soft as they promise.

Her fingers curl around the neckline of my t-shirt and my body tenses, excitement buzzing through my veins as I expect her to yank me closer and eliminate the remaining distance between us. I love a woman with control that promises to send me over the edge, but unfortunately for me, that's not what she offers.

"Unfortunately, I'm the opposite of what you're looking for." She moves to take a step back, but I stop her before she can move a single inch.

"I can't think of a single reason for that to be true," I insist, acutely aware that I'm pushing the same line that Dean just was. But she's not pushing me away like she did him. Not yet, at least.

She stiffens her shoulders, eyeballs glaring into mine as she tries to tell both herself and me at the same time. "I can tell you if you—"

Her words are cut short as I slam my mouth to hers, crushing our lips together, and I groan. Her lips are soft and full, just as I expected, but the stunned pause is not. Gently molding my lips to hers, I encourage a response, and just when I think she's not going to move, the slightest pressure pushes against my mouth, and the world around me ceases to exist.

Her fingernails claw into my neck, pulling me closer as I pry her lips open with my tongue, devouring every inch of her. She tastes just as delicious as I hoped, just as sweet, just as wicked, just…midnight.

Slipping my hands under the back of her shirt, her skin prickles even more intensely under my touch, goosebumps left in my wake as she battles for control, desperate for more. I need everything she has to offer. I yank back, lightheaded and dizzy, and stare deep into her eyes. She slowly flutters hers open.

"Tell me how you think this wouldn't be a

perfect end to the night?" I insist, and she sighs, the harsh sound becoming a scoff.

She runs her fingers down the side of my face as if she's committing me to memory. Something passes in her eyes, and I know whatever she's about to say is going to ruin me.

"Because it's experience you're looking for, and I'm a virgin."

18

POLARIS

His hold on me drops away like I just slapped him. His blue eyes are bright and wide, practically bulging out of his head as he rakes them over me from head to toe. He runs his fingers through his brown hair, failing to sweep it back off his face as an individual curl falls forward.

It's hard to hide the smirk as I watch his reaction, and for the first time tonight, I don't feel a single ounce of embarrassment. There's no burning in my cheeks, no desire for the ground to open up and swallow me whole, just a shimmering of glee and delight as I watch this man struggle to find any words.

I had a feeling the impending truth that hung in the air between us would shock him, but leaving him speechless was far greater than I could have hoped. Although, there's a tiny piece of me that regrets admitting it. Especially when the alternative is having his lips plastered against mine.

Damn.

I thought I had been kissed before, but nothing with T ever, *ever*, felt like that. This was something else entirely.

One moment, I am being mauled by some vampire who doesn't take no for an answer, and the next, I am letting this man do the exact same thing. The only difference is that I wanted him to.

I've been consumed by this man since the moment I got here. I've already seen him naked, felt his dick pressed against my thigh. I've already imagined the feel of his lips. But what remains abundantly clear is he doesn't know who I am.

I'm not the new girl with strikingly obvious silver hair who has been tainted by Florentine's.

I'm simply a mystery.

I'm Midnight.

A virgin.

It's the truth. It's not something I'm in denial over. I am a virgin. Although, the way he touched me made me wish I wasn't. Especially with the air of anonymity I seem to be wielding tonight.

Lincoln splutters, pressing his fingertips into his temples as he attempts to take a deep breath but fails miserably.

Rubbing my lips together nervously, I consider hightailing it out of here to avoid any further awkwardness as the silence stretches out between us, but as if sensing my thoughts, his eyes lock on mine.

"A virgin," he murmurs, repeating my words like a curse on his tongue, and I grin. But any response from me is paused as he shakes his head. "That's not possible."

I frown, tilting my head as I look at him. Even under the dim lights and shadows that cast over the party, his refusal to believe me is somewhat…cute. Yet I can't help but wonder how he's come to that conclusion. Who would lie about something like that?

Parting my lips, the question runs over my tongue, but before it can meet the air, he's suddenly in my face again. His hands grip my cheeks, curling under my chin as he tilts my face to the perfect angle for him to look down at me. He searches deep in my eyes, pupils blown as he runs his tongue over his bottom lip.

"So, does that usually work on other men? Do you lure them under your midnight spell and tease them with a forbidden fruit?" His words are raspy, sending a shiver down my spine as I gape at him.

"Forbidden fruit?" I repeat, finally finding the ability to speak again, and he snickers like he's in on some kind of joke I'm unaware of.

"A girl like you, who looks like this, is definitely not a virgin."

There's a righteous look in his eyes. A defiance he has no right to be wearing.

I can't believe I'm having to defend myself right now, especially not over my virginity.

"And what, exactly, do I look like?" I ask, adrenaline swirling through my limbs as I jut my chin, silently challenging him and his apparent assessment of me.

He huffs, his fingers tightening around my face as the corner of his mouth tips up in a grin.

"Hot."

The blush that creeps in this time sets my cheeks ablaze, sizzling even more as his breath blows over my face. "You say you're a virgin, but you kiss like—"

I snicker, bringing his observation to a halt as I watch him stare at my lips. "I didn't realize being a virgin meant I hadn't kissed someone before." Damn, my voice is raspy too.

"It doesn't," he grunts, eyes still tracking my lips.

"Good, then to clarify, I'm a virgin who has kissed. A lot," I reiterate, and his nostrils flare. I can't decide if there's a hint of irritation there, but it disappears quickly as his eyes find mine again.

They're like bright beacons in the night. My eyes are blue, but his are like crystal-clear waters floating through the land of freedom. Something I've always wanted to see up close and in person, but I never thought it would be in this form. Not when I didn't think I had a future.

"A virgin." He breathes the words in disbelief, uncertainty still lilting his tone as I offer a single nod.

"A virgin," I repeat for good measure, and it's like he hears me for the first time now. But to my surprise, he doesn't back away like he did before. He does, however, shake his head, disappointment rippling through him.

"I don't do virgins," he grunts, and I can't help but smile, a move that seems to confuse him.

"And you won't be doing this one. That's what I've been trying to say this whole time."

He blinks at me. Once, twice, three times, shuttering those crystal blues from my view before he tosses his head back with a laugh. His fingers remain planted against my skin as the hearty sound vibrates through me more prominently than the music filtering in from the party.

When his eyes finally meet mine again, there's a hint of wonder flickering behind them.

"That's a damn shame," he mutters, running his thumb across my bottom lip.

I'm torn between grinning joyfully at his words and crumbling at the distance threatening to part us.

"If you say so."

I'm acutely aware that we're not alone now and that revelation threatens to burst the bubble we've been in. But he moves closer so our noses touch once again. I can feel the heat rise around us, and this time, it's not from my burning cheeks but the sexual tension coiling between us.

It's like I can taste another kiss in the air. I just need to cut the remaining distance between us and take it.

Take it, Polaris. Take one more.

I feel light-headed and dizzy as we stare at each other. I blindly reach for the hem of his t-shirt, needing the support to remain steady on my feet—an ability that seems impossible as I watch his eyes darken to sapphires.

Another pass of his thumb over my bottom lip,

and I'm a goner as his words begin to breeze over my face again. "I could make an excep—"

A scream bites through the night air, jolting us back a step and out of each other's embrace.

I choke on the air I try to inhale into my lungs, startling at the shrill noise as panic coats my skin. Whipping my gaze around, I try to find the source of the sound, but it seems we're not the only ones caught off-guard by the cry that swept through the party louder than the music booming through the speakers.

Another pained cry rings out as the music grinds to a halt and my eyes latch onto a frantic girl in the center of the dance floor.

"Linc, help me!"

He doesn't think twice before he runs towards the plea, and for some reason, I find myself chasing after him.

I'm drowning in a sea of worry and a blizzard of panic from the body of students crowding the dance floor, but I shoulder my way through, slipping and sliding until I reach the center. The second I come to a stop, I wish I had stayed where I was; better yet, I wish I had run in the opposite direction.

Laying on the floor, blood trickling from her mouth with her eyes glazed over, is V.

Veronica.

I don't need anybody to say it. I can already tell. I can see it with my own eyes.

She's dead.

I fall to my knees, light-headed with panic this time, as the world blurs around me. All I can see is the girl who yelled for Lincoln's attention running her hands over Veronica's throat, searching for a pulse as she pleads under her breath for Lincoln to take control.

Again, without question, he does. If he's aware of the growing crowd watching in horror, he doesn't show it. His attention is fixated on Veronica's lifeless body.

His palm splays above her heart as he lowers his face to her parted lips, but the pull of his eyebrows shows that the breath he's searching for no longer exists.

"What the fuck is going on?" someone barks, and my gaze whips around toward a looming guy standing a few feet away.

A familiar one.

Wylder, that's what he said his name was. Gone is the calm and inviting guy from earlier, and in his place stands a tomb of strength, fury, and rage.

The panicked girl rises to her feet, swiping at

her cheeks with muddied hands as she turns to the brute statue. "Wylder, I-I don't know. I don't know. We were dancing. We…she just…she j-just dropped. She just dropped." Every word from her lips is filled with panic as tears brim in her eyes, trailing down her cheeks as she shakes her head in disbelief.

Lincoln rises to his feet, pulling her into the warm embrace that was mine mere moments ago. She curls into him, hiding her face in the crook of his neck.

"There's nothing more that can be done now," he says, the words like bullets to my heart as gasps ring throughout the gathered crowd.

"None of it makes sense, Linc. I don't understand what's going on," she says, and he looks around the sea of students, expecting the answer to reveal itself.

But nothing comes.

Everybody is staring, too scared to blink in case we miss something as my heart ricochets in my chest.

Rapid footsteps thunder along the ground, matching the beat of my heart, and my gaze spins to the approaching runner to find him heaving with every breath as he looms over Veronica's dead body on the ground.

"Oh, shit," he blurts, hands planted on his hips as he gapes with wide eyes.

"'Oh, shit' what, Asher?" Wylder grunts as he shakes his head, his arms limp at his sides and his chin falling flat against his chest.

"They were fighting," he rasps, pointing somewhere over his shoulder. "They were fighting, and he's dead. And now she…"

"Make sense, Asher. Make fucking sense," Lincoln growls, and the new arrival sighs, letting the weight of his words sink in before he shares them with the group.

"Dean is dead. Dean is dead, and now she's dead…because of her blood kin curse."

VERONICA IS DEAD.

Dead because of her blood.

Dean died first, and she wound up dead because she's cursed by blood that wields such pain she had no chance to fight it.

I feel like a fraud sitting here, Bryony at my side as we stare at Professor Whitmore taking center stage in the Grand Hall.

Gone is the party, the fun, and the liquor, along with the excitement and buzz everyone was riding moments ago, and in its place sits confusion, disaster, and tragedy. Gone is the mingling of the quads. Gone is the carefree atmosphere, and gone is a bubble of bliss that I had the slightest taste of before catastrophe struck.

Instead, I find myself consumed by desperation, dread, and a whole lot of separation. The witches are with the witches, wolves with wolves, vampires with vampires, and humans with humans.

I've heard the rumors already. I heard Asher speak them for myself in the black of night at the scene of the crime, but as I sit here, nestled in my luxurious seat, a deep bronze, just like everything else the witches touch, I hear the murmurs that swirl around the hall.

Dean was fighting with a wolf. Dean, the guy who was giving me the creeps not too long ago, is dead, and in dying, he took Veronica with him. For sure, he gave me ultimate sleazeball vibes, or as Bryony put it, cunt vibes, but the uncomfortable feeling that nestled in my gut didn't mean his death is something I would have wished for.

Professor Whitmore doesn't mention any of that, though, and he definitely doesn't mention what will happen to the wolf who did this. Instead, he stands solemn on the stage, spine straight as disappointment flashes in his eyes.

"I'm truly sorry we are gathered here tonight. The circumstances aren't at all what any of us would ever imagine. A tragedy has occurred on our very grounds. We have lost two lives tonight. The weight of the blood kin curse is prominent as we take every breath. This is not something I ever wish for my students to see. It's not something *I* ever want to experience myself, either. But alas, a curse is a curse. Pain is pain, and death is death. Life is a gift. One we must cherish more than those who don't suffer under the harrowing control of the blood kin curse."

My mind swirls, his words a vortex in my thoughts as I repeatedly recall Veronica's lifeless face on the ground. It's an undeniable realness, to the blood curse, the pain, and the weight behind it. We're not here for any reason other than survival. It's disastrous. A travesty waiting to happen. Well, I guess it already has.

Whispers ripple around the room and it's clear both the wolves and vampires are in a state of unrest. Both have lost one of their own, apparently at the hands of a wolf, but the finer details on the matter have yet to be revealed.

Unable to deny myself, I turn toward the wolves. My eyes find Lincoln through the sea of people now dividing us. The girl from earlier is right at his side, head on his shoulder as he drapes his arm around her, stroking his fingers languidly over her skin in comfort. She wipes at her cheeks and I quickly turn back around. It's impossible to ignore the feeling that I'm imposing on a vulnerable moment that has nothing to do with me. Right on cue, my face heats with embarrassment.

I try to fight the disappointment that takes hold inside of me, but I remind myself that it's for the best. After tonight's example of what this curse can do, I can't allow myself to be distracted, not by a single thing.

Professor Whitmore clears his throat as if he knows he has lost the room, pulling my attention back to him. "We will be investigating the entire situation, but for now, our priority is securing the remaining wolves on-site as the full moon is due to reach its peak. So, for all of my other quadrants, please return to your dorms, where you must stay for the rest of the night. Wolves, follow me."

At his order, the Grand Hall becomes a flurry of bodies, and I'm left seated in shock, with Bryony anchoring me in place.

"We should go," she says after a few moments, and I nod, yet my feet don't move. Neither do hers.

Tearing my gaze from the now-empty stage, Bryony captures my attention, shaking her head in disbelief as she tucks a loose blonde curl behind her ear.

"I can't believe I saw it with my own eyes," she murmurs, sadness creeping into her gaze as she looks back at me.

I nod, my tongue swooping over my bottom lip, but it does nothing to hydrate my parched skin. "It was the most horrifying thing I've ever seen," I admit, and she nods in agreement. Her bottom lip wobbles just enough for me to notice before she manages to swallow it down.

"How are we supposed to survive that?" she asks, the question as much for her as it is for me. It leaves a gaping hole in my chest as the same thought consumes me, but I don't have an answer. I don't have anything to offer, but the way she's looking at me communicates loud and clear that she needs something.

"I don't know, Bryony. I wish I did, but nothing can prepare us for that."

She clears her throat as she stands, gently shaking her head in a meek attempt to rid her mind of fear. She turns to me and offers me her hand, but the longer I stare at it, the more flustered she grows. Before I can react, she snatches my hand, squeezing tight as she stares deep into my eyes.

"No matter what, Polaris, we have to survive."

I nod, letting her pull me to my feet, and before I can take a single step toward the exit, she wraps me in her arms, pinning my chest against hers as she whispers in my ear. "I've seen the pain my siblings walk with every day. The reality of taking a life is that it's a dog-eat-dog world, and if we don't take theirs, they'll take ours. And after tonight. I know which I would rather. What about you?"

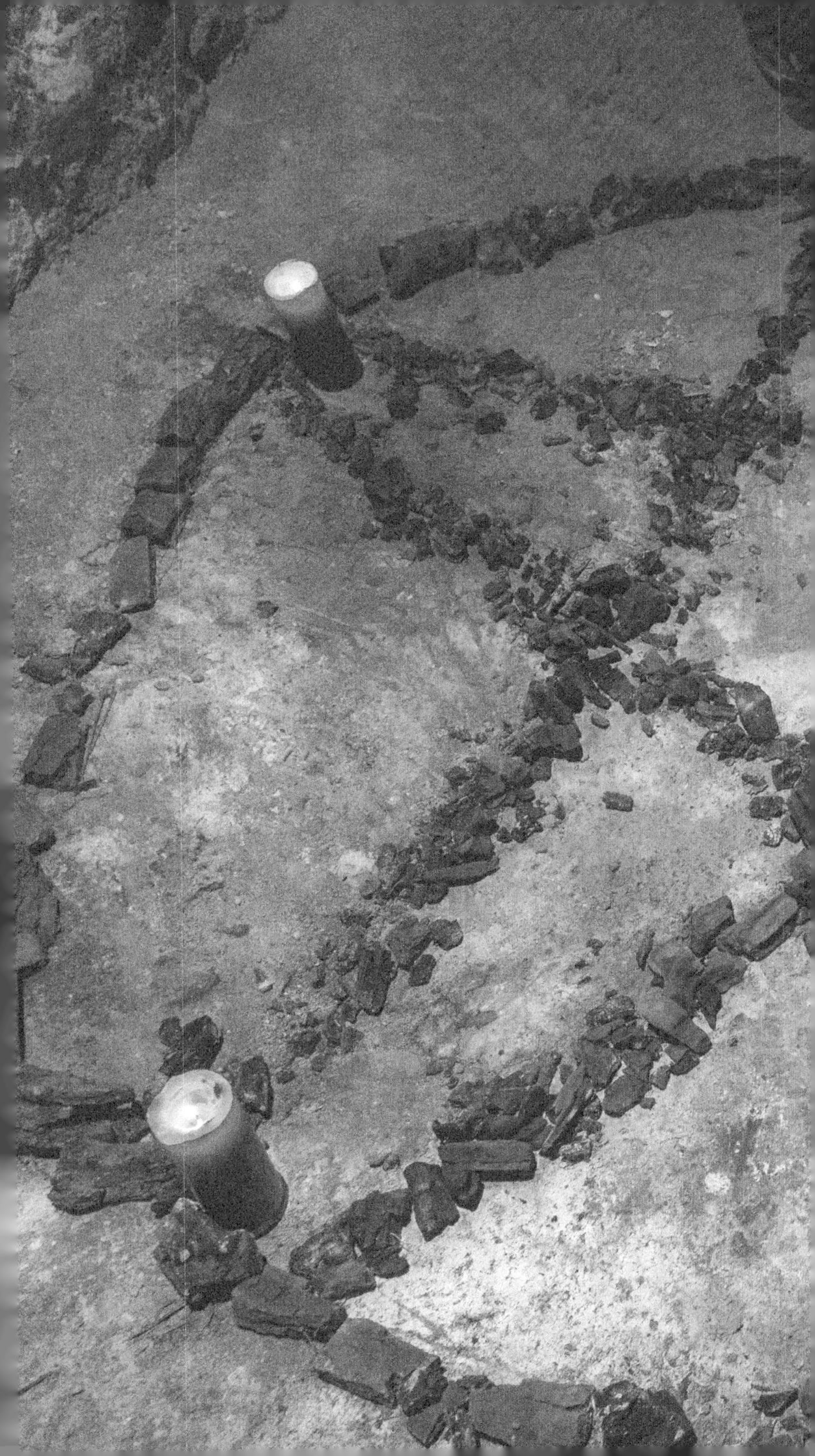

19

POLARIS

My alarm goes off, obnoxiously blaring through the air as I bolt upright in bed. My heart races from the sudden sound, but when my bedroom comes into focus, my panic calms a little as I take in the furnishings that are slowly becoming my new normal.

Brushing my hair back off my face, I adjust my pillow and lean back against the headboard. A sigh trickles through me, parting my lips as I accept the time. At least I managed to get two hours of sleep. Given the circumstances from last night, that seems to be a miracle in itself.

Now I have an extra issue to lie awake at night thinking about. On top of the new surroundings and lifestyle I've been given and the knowledge of all the lies that have been fed to me up to this point,

I now have the disastrous first few days here at Trinity Falls, along with the weight of Veronica's death, on my mind. Even the thought of her name makes the vision of last night flash along the back of my eyelids as I try to squeeze them shut tight, my fingers clenched, nails biting into my palms as I will the nausea churning inside of me to subside.

A fleeting thought of Lincoln comes to mind, along with a sprinkling of the cute guy behind the bar, and the nausea burns more fiercely. It's hard to remember that yesterday held more than just pain. Pressing my fingers to my lips, I replay the touch of Lincoln's lips against mine as I recall the kiss from the hot wolf. The wolf who didn't recognize me from the first time I met him. That single reminder should leave me disappointed, but it was somewhat…refreshing.

I kissed someone that wasn't Terence. I kissed someone because I really wanted to. I kissed someone, and I melted. My body felt things I didn't know were possible.

Stretching my arms over my head, I sigh again, the sound morphing into a yawn before I try to pep talk myself out of my sheets. Yesterday was yesterday, in all of its pain and glory, but now I need to get up and start getting ready for the day.

I exhale a withering breath, the tremble only

reinforcing the fact that I have no idea how I'm supposed to survive any of this. As if sensing my inner turmoil, a knock comes from the door. Pursing my lips, I consider my choices: to ignore or not to ignore. The next knock that rattles the door frame tells me I don't have a choice.

Swinging my legs over the side of the bed, I tiptoe across the distance between me and the banging, aware that I'm only in a t-shirt and panties, but there's not enough time for me to rectify that. I pry the door open just an inch to reveal Bryony on the other side, and I exhale with relief. She knocks the door open wider, bustling inside, leaving me at the threshold, gaping at her.

She takes over the space like a whirlwind as I shut the door behind her. We don't speak as I watch her pace back and forth across the width of my room a few times until she slams to a halt. With her hands on her hips and her head cocked to one side, she finally acknowledges my presence. In my own room.

"I wanted to check in on you after last night," she states, hiking her chin up an inch as she continues to assess me.

"Check in on me? I'm fine," I insist, trying to brush off the subject. I spent long enough lost to the turmoil last night; I was hoping to avoid it today.

Bryony, however, doesn't look that fine at all, and maybe that's why she's here. Although, the pointed look she's offering tells me she's aware of my bullshit.

I expect her to call me out on it, but instead, she scurries toward my bed, looking out the window as she folds her arms over her chest. She runs her tongue over her bottom lip before she glances back at me, and a frown takes over her face.

"I thought you liked your hair."

Confused, I scrunch my nose. "I do."

Her eyebrows only draw tighter. "Then why… I'm confused," she admits, rocking back on her heels as she continues to stare at me with a strange look in her eyes.

"Right back at you," I retort, completely bewildered by what's going on when she stomps towards me, unfolding her arms to grab my upper arm and tug me toward the armoire.

She forcefully swings the door open, leaving me to look at my reflection, and understanding quickly washes over me. Although I may understand her confusion, it doesn't mean I have the answer.

My gut clenches as I gape at the silver hair that frames my face.

Silver.

Not black.

The new version of myself that we created last night is long gone.

I'm just me: silver locks and all.

"I didn't touch it," I blurt, tentatively running my fingers through the ends to confirm what I see. When I'm sure it's not a figment of my imagination, my gaze whirls to Bryony. "How? How could this happen?"

Bryony shrugs, seemingly as lost as I am. "I don't know," she admits, rubbing her lips together as she stares at me. "Mine doesn't do that," she adds, fueling the confusion and irritation inside of me.

Turning away from the reflection to avoid the silver glaring back at me, I focus all of my attention on Bryony. "All I did was sleep. Well, mostly tossed and turned, but that's beside the point. I didn't do a single thing. I wouldn't have known how, even if I had wanted to." Lacing my fingers together, I look down at them with a hint of defeat burning in my gut. "I really liked it," I admit, my shoulders slumping with disappointment.

As Bryony stares at me, she mindlessly taps her fingertip against her lips. The smallest crinkle forms between her eyes, a flicker of uncertainty before she clears her throat. "It could be your magic," she breathes, and I freeze, feeling the color drain from my face as I turn to her.

"My magic? I don't have any, remember?" I lift my hands to gape at the bangles like she understands why they matter, but all she does is shrug.

"Maybe, but how else can you explain it?" she pushes, and I shake my head in disbelief.

"I can't." I shudder at the words. I can't explain it. The reality of that leaves me more overwhelmed than I care to admit. "It doesn't make sense."

She runs her hand down my arm comfortingly. "We can try and dye it again this weekend if you like?" she offers, and my face scrunches up.

"But what if it turns back to this again?" I grumble, irritating myself when I know for a fact there are much worse things going on right now around me. I fell in love with the mystery that came with the dark hair. Without it, my pain and discomfort rise to the surface.

"If it turns back, then it turns back, but at least we know it's not a random occurrence. That way we'll know it definitely has something to do with your magic," she insists, and I sigh. Her ability to see the positive side of the situation makes it impossible for me to dwell, a fact that's rather unsettling since I'm so good at it.

"I guess that's a good idea," I murmur, and she winks.

"I know it is. I'm full of them. Now let's go to breakfast so you can tell me all about last night," she states, and another shiver ripples through my body. This time, it's my turn to hide behind the barrier of my arms folded tightly across my chest as I will the horrors of last night to dissipate.

"I don't want to relive that terror ever again," I insist, and she smirks, waving me off as she heads toward the door.

"Not that part, silly, the Lincoln part."

RIGHT NOW ISN'T the time to remember. I shouldn't be remembering the taste of desire that flickered over my skin last night. I should be in mourning. We've suffered a significant loss of life. But as I look around the dining hall, it seems the rest of the academy is unfazed. Well, there's definitely a shift amongst the wolves today, but everyone else? No change at all.

The vampires don't seem even a little bit saddened by the loss of Dean. I run my eyes over their table, sitting parallel to ours in the dining hall, paying as close attention as possible, but my initial assessment seems correct.

I spy Sian and Terence down at the opposite end of the room, and there's not a morsel of sadness in their features. Maybe that's because we only just arrived? I don't know. I don't know how I would feel if it had been a witch, but what I do know is the fact that the wolf girl cried last night. She cried for a girl she barely knew. That's not the same vibe coming from the vampires.

Sian and Terence are in their own world, leaning close to Blaze as he talks with a gruff exterior, but to my surprise, whatever he says must be funny because a moment later, they toss their heads back with laughter. That seals it. They didn't lose someone they had known for years, just another stranger in another prison.

Staring down at the plate of food in front of me, the sadness that fills me when I acknowledge that people are dying and no one seems to care obliterates my desire to eat. As if sensing my inner turmoil, Bryony nudges my plate closer to me.

"Girl, we're not going to our first class until you catch me up to speed," she says.

It's not hard to read between the lines, understanding what she wants without outwardly saying it, but I'm guessing if I pretend to ignore it, she would push until she blurted it loud enough for everyone to hear, and I can't imagine anything worse.

My gaze darts across to where the wolves are, finding the man in question seated centrally at the huge table. The girl from last night is on his left, and Wylder, the guy from the bar, is on his right. I think the guy next to him is the one who delivered the awful news. Asher? I think. While the guy I was caught eavesdropping on sits beside the girl.

They all look tired and drained.

"The wolves are usually quiet the day after a full moon," Bryony explains, a fact that doesn't really make sense, so I shrug.

"Cool."

She clears her throat, rubbing her lips together as she nods in their direction. "You should go over there."

"I should not!" I exclaim, and she gapes at me. If it weren't for the twinkle in her eyes, I would believe her to be as naïve as she's acting.

"Why?"

I look down at my food again, planting my elbow on the table and resting my face in my hand. I feel completely under her scrutiny, and it makes me so uncomfortable that I consider picking up my fork again. However, the reminder of Veronica has me boycotting the quiet road.

Finding her gaze, I blurt the truth. "Because he didn't recognize me."

"He didn't recognize you," she repeats in confusion, and I roll my eyes at her.

"Are you a witch or a parrot?" I ask, acutely aware that I'm bad at repeating questions back to people, but I'm hoping to distract her from the topic at hand. I feel like I've already said enough.

Instead, she cocks her brow at me with an amused grin on her face. "Nice, but how could he not recognize you? And where would he recognize you from?"

I find the line of wolves once more, intrigued by the four men that gravitate toward one another, but jealousy sears through me at the sight of the girl in the mix. Shaking my head, I turn to face Bryony. There's no reason not to talk about it, I guess. It's not like anything more is ever going to happen. I've had my fleeting sliver of attention from a wolf. "I had the joy of meeting Lincoln during the first five minutes of arriving here from Florentines. Other than that, I haven't really seen him, but we've been in a few classes together."

Her eyebrows knit further together as she shakes

her head, confusion still morphing her features. "All we did was color your hair."

I snicker. "And do my makeup and make me look nothing like I do now," I add and she scoffs.

"Please, the makeup only enhanced the features you already have. He's dumb, but not blind."

I bite back a laugh, but she's not done assessing the situation. She leans forward, bracing her forearms on the table. "I was certain he was going to slip away with you deeper into the woods to have *S E X*," she stage-whispers, feeding her own grin, and I roll my eyes again.

"Oh, he was trying."

She leans back in shock, her hand pressed against her chest as she gapes at me with a mixture of bewilderment and horror. "And you said no?"

I can feel the familiar heat returning to my cheeks. "Well, technically not."

"You're gonna have to explain that, Polaris," she insists, nudging at my arm.

I press my lips together, unsure whether I should share, but there's a sense of comfort in her demeanor that, even though I can't decipher it, makes me feel safe. Besides, as much as it's personal, it was funny, and it still detracts from the sadness that clings to every fiber in my body.

"I told him I was a virgin."

"A virgin," she shouts, and I feel like my entire body is ablaze.

"Wow, Bryony, whisper much?" I grumble, refusing to lift my gaze from my plate as I plead for the ground to open beneath me.

"Sorry! Sorry. My brain is just so slow with all of this. There's too much information, I cannot keep up. I mean, I guess it makes sense since you had your first drink last night. But damn, that's not what I was expecting. How did he take the news?"

I shrug, continuing to avoid her gaze as I reach for my fork and push the eggs around my plate. Now that she's back to not shouting, I can think about it without worrying the embarrassment is going to kill me.

"He doesn't do virgins."

She scoffs again. "Of course not. He'll be worried about a stage five clinger," she insists. And I frown, finally peering at her from the corner of my eye. "Lincoln James is anything but the commitment type. I've honestly heard stories of him sharing women with his core pack," she whispers like that's a big secret. It's more of a secret than my virginity, but apparently, that's not something to be shy about, or yell about.

"Sharing?" I say with a gulp, the word heavy on my tongue, and she shrugs, nodding toward them.

"Yeah, core pack—him and his brothers—but apparently, you have to be a wolf for them to consider it," she insists, curling her fingers into air quotes.

Following her attention, I find my gaze latching back on them again, only this time, Lincoln is staring straight at me. My heart skips up into my throat, but he continues gazing around the room.

"Wow. He really is dumb. He had no acknowledgment of you then," Bryony murmurs in shock, and I shake my head, dropping my fork back to the plate as I lean back.

I'm too caught up on the sharing fact. Being overlooked doesn't even register in my brain. "It doesn't matter anyway. Last night was simply one of the distractions this place has to offer. I've been thinking about what you said non-stop, and as much as I don't want to kill someone, I don't want to die either, and if I don't want to die, I can't be distracted by the likes of Lincoln or feeble attempts at bullying from Blaze, or Wylder, for that matter."

"Wylder?" she interjects, eyebrows high as a blush creeps over my cheeks, and she winks at me. "He's friends with Lincoln, you know," she states, and I shrug.

"Good for him." I stand, done with my poor attempt at breakfast, but even more done with the hot distractions flaunted before me, yet it seems she's not done.

"You're really going to walk away from a chance at that?" she says, and my eyes meet hers.

I keep a straight face for all of five seconds before we both giggle. Flipping my hair over my shoulder, I put my back toward the wolves as I answer her honestly.

"There never was a chance to begin with."

20

WYLDER

I'm tired and cranky: two things I feel on a regular basis, but even more intensely today after the effects of the full moon last night. My wolf is more tired than I am if that's possible. Add to the fact that we lost one of our own last night, and everything is a wash. It definitely doesn't help that we're not given any leeway the day after a full moon. It's not like we *want* to shift into our wolves uncontrollably as the moon reaches its pinnacle in the sky. It's a euphoric feeling, for sure, but sitting here now, with the expectation to be ready for a day's worth of classes? No thanks.

I don't want to face anyone today after watching that poor girl last night.

Veronica.

She'd been here barely two days, and at the hands of the blood kin curse, her life was taken because of some dumb fight between a wolf and a vampire. Not her, though. No, that was all Dean and Declan. Declan has been detained and questioned, and no one is willing to offer us any further details, but that's beside the point.

Whatever comes next for Declan, we will have to take it in our stride. There's no excuse for killing a member of another quadrant, especially not over some girl, which is what Asher says they were yelling over. Declan should have sought refuge in his quad if he felt like he was getting out of control, but instead, he killed him—killed Dean—and, in doing so, killed Veronica too.

One of *his* own.

That doesn't matter right now. What we must do first is deal with the loss that has affected our pack. As if sensing my thoughts, Minnie looks my way.

"Have the arrangements been made for V?" she asks, her voice lacking the usual lilt that we're all familiar with.

"Yeah, everything is set for midnight," I answer, tempering the irritation I feel at the use of Veronica's nickname.

V.

From what I hear, at Florentine's, that's how they are addressed. A, B, C, D, all the way to Z. V is more than an initial. She'll die more than just an initial. She'll be appropriately remembered as Veronica, but I don't correct Minnie. I know she doesn't mean it. Besides, she seems to be feeling the loss the most.

"Fuck, we'll sleep when we're dead, right?" Lincoln grumbles, wiping a hand down his face, and I huff in agreement. The tendrils of sleep deprivation will wreak havoc on us all day.

"It's not good for my training. The fight is coming up and the lack of sleep doesn't help. Especially since the full moon wiped me out last night."

"Don't be so insensitive while there are condolences to be felt," Asher grumbles, giving me a pointed look, and I try not to roll my eyes.

"I'm not. I'm just trying not to sink in the madness that apparently is our lives," I retort, aware there's a bite to my words, but thankfully, no one calls me out on it.

Good.

I would have blamed it on the lack of sleep anyway.

"You're extra grouchy today, Wylder," Minnie says with the slightest hint of a smile at the corner of her lips, and I try my hardest not to glower at her. I can see the amusement on Lincoln's face, but I ignore him altogether, focusing entirely on Minnie.

The two of them always blow my mind: Lincoln and Minnie, his sister. Technically, they're twins, but they're not each other's blood kin because they weren't born at the exact same time. Even though they were born on the exact same day, minutes apart, their lives aren't intertwined under the blood curse.

Thank goodness, because the thought of losing one of them tears me apart.

While one is soft, one is hard. While one is sweet, one is bitter. Together, they are the yin and yang of the word wolf while also completing each other in ways I've never seen before.

Today is going to be a rough day for her. I can tell by the way she clings to Lincoln and the way he naturally holds her in his embrace. They bicker ninety-nine percent of the time, but in the rare moments of pain between them, they come together, solidifying their love for one another.

"How do you think Tatum is doing?" she asks,

lowering her voice as she glances at the guy sitting beside her as if he doesn't have heightened wolf hearing like the rest of us. But if he hears her, he doesn't react. Instead, he plays around with the food on his plate, deep in thought, a place he always seems to find himself.

"Not good," Lincoln states, concern storming in his eyes as he glances at Tatum before spinning back to me. "He might need to bunk with one of us for the next few nights," he admits, and I nod.

"We'll take it in turns," Asher says as Tatum's gaze lifts, and Minnie panics, desperately trying to steer the conversation in a different direction so she doesn't spook our closest friend.

"Anyway, what's this I heard about the Alpha Pack helping a witch out yesterday?" she asks, pressing her cheek into her palm as she leans against the table, eyeing each of us.

"It was nothing. Blaze was just being a dick, as always. She was new and scared. The least we could do is help," Asher states in his usual nonchalant way, while Minnie nods in understanding, a soft smile on her lips.

If anyone is ever going to help anyone, it is her. She's too kind, too sweet, and too innocent. Or, that's what Lincoln likes to think anyway.

"It was a girl from class, right? The one with the silver hair?"

"Yeah, it was her," Asher agrees in between stuffing food in his mouth, and my gaze darts across the room, acutely aware of where she is.

"Is someone catching feelings I need to be aware of?" Minnie asks, smirking at Asher, who scoffs.

"What? Of course not. Should we not be nice to people for the sake of it?" he pushes, and she waves him off, refusing to take on his grumbles.

"The Alpha Pack isn't nice to anyone," she insists, a teasing smile on her lips as she elbows her brother.

"Thanks for that," Lincoln grumbles, leaning back, feigning shock and disappointment, and she rolls her eyes.

"It's the truth. Besides, you seemed cozy enough with her last night," she states, turning to her brother, who frowns down at her.

"With who?"

"The girl."

Lincoln's frown darkens as he shakes his head. "Midnight? She had black hair, not silver."

"Midnight?" I repeat, eyeing him, confused, and he shakes his head.

"You wouldn't understand it."

Amusement churns in my gut. “Please, enlighten us,” I insist, finding it funny that he’s not aware that *Midnight* is the same girl we protected from Blaze yesterday.

Lincoln sighs like the conversation is irritating. “There's nothing to enlighten. She was a goddamn virgin, and I was not going there.”

Minnie looks at me, bewilderment written in her eyes, and I’m sure it reflects in mine, too.

This guy is dumb. How is he even pack alpha? Yes, her hair was black last night, and now it's silver again. However, it was clearly the same person beneath.

Polaris.

She said that was her name. I was mesmerized by how innocent she was to the world, eager to learn, and curious to understand. Flashing images consumed my thoughts all night as I saw her pressing the shot glass to her plump lips and watching the liquor pour down her throat. Her eyes were bright, her laugh soft.

It would be impossible to deny there is something about her that is enticing. There is definitely something about her that would entice Lincoln, that's for sure. But a virgin? Nothing screams a giant red stop sign like the word *virgin* to Lincoln.

Minnie peers at me, pointing slightly at her brother, but I shake my head.

We're not telling him.

He can figure that out for himself.

If he can't put one and one together to get two, that's not our problem. Besides, it'll be amusing to see when he realizes it.

"So, does Midnight have a name?" I ask, intrigued, and he shakes his head.

"Nope, just Midnight," he replies, taking a bite out of his breakfast.

"Are you feeling okay?" Minnie asks, leaning back so his arm drops off her shoulders, and he stares at her in confusion.

"I'm feeling fine. Why?"

She clears her throat. "No reason." She fails to hide her smirk as she glances across the room and then back to the table. When her eyes find mine, I know the subject has changed. "When's your next fight, Wylder?"

"Next weekend," I answer, already feeling the tremors of anticipation and adrenaline forming in my veins.

She nods. "We will be there to cheer you on, as always," she promises, and I grin.

"Thanks."

"Maybe Midnight could join us too?" she asks,

and I struggle to hold back the grin and laughter that threatens to burst from my lips.

Thankfully, the bell rings, cutting through the air and distracting Lincoln from the comment, but I can't deny that I like the thought of having Midnight or Polaris watch me in all of my glory.

21

POLARIS

"Good morning, students. I believe we have three new witches among us. Please, make yourselves known." The professor casts her gaze down the line of us waiting outside of her classroom, utterly oblivious to the other students hurrying to their next class. She makes eye contact with every single person before I have the strength to lift my hand.

D's hand is up first, quickly followed by H, leaving me to trail behind, which earns me a few side glances from the other students.

My heart ricochets in my chest from everyone's attention on us, but I focus on the new professor before us. Her long brown skirt reaches her ankles, and a white shirt tucked in and buttoned all the way up covers her to her neck. Her brown curly hair is pinned on top of her head, while her wide green eyes are framed by large circular glasses.

"Perfect, the three of you take your seats at the front of the class," she instructs, waving everyone inside, but it's impossible to move with the feeling of all eyes zoned in on me. Since I've been at Trinity Falls Academy, I've learned that nothing good ever comes from everyone's attention being focused on you, even in simple situations like this. So now I'm anticipating something even worse.

"Unlucky, my friend," Bryony says with a wince as she ushers me into the classroom, and a sickly feeling takes root in my throat.

How is this even my luck today?

D and H take the first two seats, leaving the chair closest to the door free for me, which almost feels like a blessing in disguise, assuaging a little of the discomfort that stirs inside of me.

The entire class gets seated, shuffling into the rows behind us as the professor seems to mindlessly rearrange the items on her desk for a moment. Thankfully, it gives me a chance to take in the space, which looks very similar to most of the other classrooms I've been in so far. There is dark wooden furniture and a soft coloring on the walls. In here, it's a pastel pink.

The walls are covered in shelves, with items

crammed in and spilling out of little drawers, while some space holds glass jars, each housing God-only-knows. It's weird and it's different, but somehow, a bubble of what I can only assume is excitement fizzles inside of me as I consider what the items are for.

Magic is the obvious answer, but beyond that, I have no idea. I guess I'm going to find out, though.

"Are we settled? Perfect," the professor says with a smile, not actually waiting for anyone to respond as she clasps her hands together. "To those that are new, my name is Professor Juniper. I come from a long line of witches, and I belong to the Serenity Coven." She says the words with such pride, I almost feel guilty that I have no idea what she's actually talking about. But she doesn't seem fazed as she casts her gaze over me. "It is with great importance that I spend this first lesson with our new pupils explaining the importance of magic and what it means to us as witches. Along with that comes the importance of how magic keeps balance within the supernatural world. You will learn more than ever about the differences between our quadrants, not just on campus but across the globe. Can anyone give a brief overview of the wolves?"

She finally turns her attention from me and

glances over the rest of the class, pointing at someone behind me.

"The wolves are very family-oriented. Bursting into their bubble is very difficult. They're almost impenetrable to anyone who is not a wolf," someone explains, and the professor nods eagerly.

"Excellent. Excellent. And vampires, anyone?"

I don't turn around, but I can practically hear the hands fly up for her attention before she chooses someone else.

"Vampires reign supreme, or they like to think they do, at least. However, they keep their friends close and their enemies even closer, politically speaking, of course. Once off campus, you don't tend to find vampires gathered together. Not for very long, anyway."

"That's right, and can we have an assumption on the humans?" The professor swiftly points at another student as I try my best to absorb the information being offered.

"Although there are many human warriors and hunters that come from the blood-cursed line, they are still often left at a disadvantage, and that's where we come in."

"That's exactly right," Juniper interjects before the person can say more. "Our magic can better anybody's chances, especially our own. That then leads me to the significance of witches. The importance of remaining unbiased is paramount. It's essential that we remain neutral among the other quads, not allowing our thoughts and opinions to waver under the lure of a vampire's compulsion or a wolf's heated desire come the full moon." She winks like it's a secret and my cheeks heat, forcing me to dip my head to hide my face. "Although, not in any official capacity, it is the job of the witches to maintain balance throughout each quadrant using the abilities we have in order to ensure an open playing field for all. Which simultaneously leads me to the importance of covens. A coven not only strengthens us as individuals as we connect with one another, but it also allows us to remain grounded. Leaning on one another is not a weakness for us. It is always our strength. Power in numbers, strength and abilities, and a handful of sand is exactly what a witch needs."

A chuckle ripples around the room at her mention of sand, and I can't help but feel the corner of my mouth tip up too. I manage to lift my head again as Juniper continues.

"My job is to give you everything you need to be as strong as you can, but nothing will be achievable until the three of you figure out how to remove your sigils."

The reminder of the barriers blocking my magic weighs heavy on my shoulders and I slump in my seat. My bangles are more prominent than ever on my wrists.

"If someone could help us with that bit, that would be great," D says, a sigh passing her lips, and I hum in agreement.

Juniper offers a tight smile. "You will get there. Above all else, I recommend that you focus on your sigil classes and continue to understand, embrace, and learn who you are." She clears her throat, her eyes dimming as she settles her gaze on me once again. "My sigil was removed when I found the strength to remember my mother's name."

I gasp, my heart pounding in my ears, reading between the lines of what she's not saying.

She was a Florentine.

She was a Florentine just like me, and now she stands here as a survivor and a professor, all because she found the strength to remember her mother's name. Such a key part of her past. Possibly insignificant to most, but life altering to us.

My gut lurches as the desire to know such a thing burns strong inside my soul.

If she senses me crumbling, she doesn't

acknowledge it. Instead, she waves a hand around the room, a soft, wistful smile on her face. "Today, we will focus on our more experienced witches, giving you examples of what we expect you to be able to achieve once you unlock your sigils. Three different sections fall under a witch's abilities, and they're broken down into potions, charms, and enchantments."

Three words that hold such meaning yet leave me slightly confused. I'm likely still reeling from her prior statement, but I try to shake it off because if there's one class I need to focus on, it's this. I want to gobble up every bit of information she has to offer, knowing she's a key piece to my success and survival.

"Please, Bryony, why don't you give an example to our new students of how we may use potions in a casual, fun way," Juniper states, pushing her glasses up the bridge of her nose before pointing for Bryony to join her at the front of the class.

For the first time, I glance back over my shoulder to find her. I avoid the rest of the witches, still uncomfortable under their silent scrutiny. Bryony smiles, sweeping her hair over her shoulder as she rises from her seat and all but skips to the front of the room. Her eyes cast around the edges of the class, eyeing all the items available before she quickly takes off doing a lap of the room. I watch in wonder as she gathers little items along the way, and as she nears the front of the room again, Professor Juniper murmurs under her breath before snapping her fingers, and I watch in awe as the floor opens up and a small cauldron rises.

Excitement buzzes through me as I watch Bryony line up what seem to be the ingredients she's pulled together. D and H to my left seem to be equally amazed, while the rest of the class watches on in amusement.

Slowly, she starts to mix the items together. "A sprinkling of strawberry seeds, a drop of potents snare, and a strand of hair clipped from a horse's mane," she explains as she goes, and my eyebrows furrow with every added item.

Those sound like some strange things to use, but I keep my opinions to myself and just watch instead of making any judgments too soon.

All too quickly, Bryony is using an empty vial to collect some of the potion.

"Please, Bryony, show the class what you have made."

Bryony smiles, pulling her hair forward, and drapes it over her left shoulder before she takes the vial and drops the liquid onto the ends. We all watch in awe as her blonde locks turn red—blood red.

She winks at me knowingly, and I grin, clapping with the other students as Bryony takes a dramatic bow.

"Wonderful Bryony. Thank you so much for sharing that with the class. Now, let's move on to a charm, shall we? And let's have Lucille. Lucille, please show our new students how we produce a charm."

Bryony retakes her seat, running her fingers through the red strands as I rub my lips together. I watch as another girl stands, beaming from ear to ear. Her face is alight with joy and her blonde hair falls in a sharp bob around her face, accentuating her soft features.

She already knows where she's heading, rushing around the room before she appears in front of the professor a few moments later.

"Charms don't hold for very long. They're said to last an hour at most. But with this little trinket here, I can use my words and this vial to create something magical." She holds out a cross pendant, one you would expect to find on a necklace. The bottle in her hand has something written on it, but it doesn't seem to be a language I can understand. Taking a drop of the liquid, she pours it onto the cross, and it's as if glitter coats the surface. Lucille shivers as if it affects her too, and she beams brightly. "Anyone with this pendant receives the gift of good luck for the next hour."

I gape at her as Juniper offers a small round of applause.

Good luck? No way. That's not possible, right?

"Wonderful, Lucille. I'll be taking that. I've got a meeting later on, and I need it to go well," the professor says with a wink, pocketing the pendant.

The second her hand slips into the pocket of her ankle-length skirt, I instinctively stuff my hand into my pocket too, blindly searching for the familiar weight of my coin.

I wasn't supposed to bring it out with me, but after last night, I couldn't bear to leave my room without it. Now, with the joker's face pressed into my palm, I take a deep breath and relish in the grounding sensation it gives me.

"And what would we say is a good example of an enchantment?" Juniper muses, tapping her chin as she looks around the room. "If we could have Foster step forward, please. Give us an example of an enchantment."

I peer over my shoulder, feeling more confident with every passing moment that a witch willingly offers us a sliver of knowledge. This time, a guy seated at the back of the class stands. His sharp nose and strong jawline make him look dark and dangerous, but he doesn't seem to have the confidence that comes with those features. He keeps his gaze downcast, avoiding everybody around him.

He steps to the front of the class and retrieves a bag of sand from behind the professor. She smiles at him proudly as he makes his way around the room, chanting under his breath as he lays the sand down. Once the sand encircles the entire room, he silently moves to the center. Ignoring the tables and people around him, he closes his eyes, holding his hands out softly in front of him. His words continue to repeat again and again until the air falls still around us.

My heart flutters in my chest as I wait for something to happen. It's only when his eyes blow wide and he drops his arms to his sides that he finally speaks.

"Protection is done."

He takes a seat as Professor Juniper applauds him, and everybody else falls in line. The noise echoes in the air, even though I have no idea what we're celebrating.

"Thank you so much, Foster. That, ladies and gentlemen, is what we call a protection spell. Anyone with any harmful intentions would never be able to step over the threshold unless a break in the sand occurs. No witch, vampire, wolf, or human will be able to penetrate this room if the magic senses ill intent on their behalf."

My mind is blown as I stare in wonder, completely shocked by such abilities, when the bell rings, cutting through the air and bringing the class to an end. I don't want to stand. I don't want to leave this spot. I want to continue devouring everything she has to offer—everything my peers have to offer, too, it seems.

Looking down at the bangles on my wrists, I plead for them to leave my skin, but it's futile. Until my sigil classes start, there's no way out of this. Even then, who knows how long it will take for me to figure it out?

"Thank you so much for attending my class today. To my three new students, I want to inform you that covens will consider the three of you, so be prepared to receive offers. What you may have to do to secure it ultimately depends on the coven itself." She smiles wide with pride, nodding at each of us before she glances toward the back of the class. "Bryony, please, could you help me tidy up the room?" Juniper asks, effectively dismissing everybody else, and I stand from my seat, making my way to the door before I peer back at Bryony.

As if sensing my concern, she offers me a soft smile. “Don't worry, Polaris. You go ahead. I'll catch up. Don't worry,” she repeats, and I nod.

My tongue runs over my bottom lip as nerves get the better of me, and I step out into the hall. The bustle of students is overwhelming, more so than usual, since I don’t have Bryony at my side. It also doesn’t help that I have no idea where I'm heading next. I've had the class before, offensive and defensive, but I'm still becoming familiar with my surroundings and I'm not sure where that is from here.

Spinning on the spot, I search for D and H, but they’re already gone. With my lips curled between my teeth, I keep myself pressed to the wall, heading in what I hope is the right direction. Another bell rings and the student body around me fizzles out to almost none. I'm sure I’ve made a wrong turn somewhere, as I don't remember any of the corridors I take, but I fight back the distress tingling at my fingertips.

As I turn to the left, I slam straight into a body and almost fall to the ground, but I'm saved from such a disastrous fall as I lock eyes with my savior.

I don't manage to speak a word before my world goes black.

22

POLARIS

My mind stirs awake, but all I can settle on is the back of my eyelids. Darkness floods my body and it feels like my head weighs one hundred pounds. There's an ache in my shoulders that lingers as I try to shake the stiffness from my body.

Confusion crawls through my veins as a subtle shake rattles my arm.

"Polaris? Polaris?"

My eyelids flicker at the sound of Bryony's voice, drawing me back to the present, and I slowly manage to lift my head and turn my attention to her. It takes an extra moment for my eyes to fully pry open, but the moment they do, the confusion and concern I see etched into her face is startling.

"Where have you been?" she asks, dropping down into the seat beside me with a heavy sigh.

Glancing around the room, the sudden onslaught of sound penetrates my ears as I find myself in the dining hall.

I…

What the…

"For real, Polaris. Where have you been?"

I gape at her, my mouth falling slack and slamming shut a few times before I shake my head in disbelief, disorientation getting the better of me. I can't make sense of…anything. My concern grows as I watch her eyebrows furrow together.

"What do you mean? You don't know?"

I wipe a hand down my face, willing my mind to give me an answer, but I come up empty. Maybe if I can walk through the last things I remember, it will help me understand what I'm missing.

"I left Professor Juniper's and headed toward where I thought our next class was, but once the next bell rang, I was completely lost. I remember turning left, hoping to find something familiar, and then…then I wound up here." I can hear the distress in my voice, the panic clawing at me, enhanced by the confusion rippling through my veins as I try to understand what the hell is going on.

I look back to Bryony, searching for answers I know she can't give, when I note her nostrils flaring in anger.

"What?"

"Nothing," she answers way too quickly for my liking. So I press on, grabbing her arm.

"Bryony," I plead, and she rubs her lips together, nervously avoiding my gaze as her eyes dart around the room. When she finally finds my stare, I feel like she might be relenting.

"Can I…"

Her eyes crinkle, but she doesn't finish her sentence. Desperate for anything, I push her along.

"Can you what?"

She clears her throat, lacing her fingers together in her lap as she tries again. "Can I look at your neck?"

"My neck?" I breathe, confused, but she seems to take that as a yes because she leans in close, tilting my chin back with the tip of her finger before she runs her gaze over my throat. Around the back and the front before she traces my skin with her fingers, following the same trail, but her brows continue to gather.

"Can I look at your arms?" she asks, and even though worry boils beneath the surface, I slip my arms out of my jacket one at a time so she can see my arms. I have no idea what she's looking for, but it doesn't seem like she's finding it. Once she's sure, she releases her hold on me and nods for me to put my jacket back on. "Are you hurting anywhere?"

It's impossible to hide the concern that she's building inside of me.

"No, but can you please tell me what's going on?" I beg as the rest of the dining hall continues with their life like mine isn't falling apart again.

"Do you usually forget periods of time, Polaris?" she asks, offering me a tight, reassuring smile as I shake my head.

"No. Well, not unless we're counting the two years at Florentine's that were erased from my memory and any parts of my life before that," I grumble, my head scrambling even as I press at my temples, willing the frustration away.

"That's sad," she says, tilting her head at me, her eyes crinkling from the emotion she speaks, but all I can do is shrug.

"We're getting off track. That's my fault. I'm sorry. Please keep your train of thought," I beg.

She sighs, her shoulders slumping. "Nothing, I just can't think of any other reason for you to black out like that unless you were attacked by a vampire," she admits, eyes peering in their direction at the next table along, and I follow her line of sight.

"A vampire?" I repeat, and she hums.

"Yeah, compulsion is a trait they love to use," she states, and a shudder runs down my spine.

Instinctively, I wrap my arms around myself, squeezing them tight, as if the barrier I'm creating will protect me from any further danger. I've heard that word before. I rack my brain and quickly recall it. Last night, with Dean, before he met his untimely death.

"Why would they do that?" I ask, already aware that she doesn't have the answer, but it doesn't hurt to try.

"I don't know, but more than that, who would want to?" she presses, her gaze peering down the line of vampires and back up again. My heart lurches as I find the familiar face of my apparent sworn vampire enemy at the far end of their table.

"He wouldn't," I breathe, wheezing internally.

"You're right, he wouldn't. I don't think. What about those two?" I cock a brow at her, confusion continuing to run through me. "The two you're familiar with," she clarifies, and I shake my head instinctively, but the movement slows as I consider how much has changed since we got here.

"No, well, they wouldn't have before, but now I

can't say for sure. Wait, they have sigils, like mine," I murmur and she hums.

She purses her lips, casting an intense glare around the room before she fixes her stare back on me. "We stick together from now on."

"You don't have to do that," I mutter, hating how much I seem to be relying on her after such a short time.

"I want to," she insists. "We're going to survive this together. We've promised each other that. That means if we have to be with each other to make sure no one's blacking out, then that's what we must do."

I smile at my friend.

My friend.

I have a freaking friend.

"Thank you, Bryony."

"No problem. If you happen to have any more blackouts, we'll get to the bottom of it, because nobody messes with my friend and gets away with it."

23

LINCOLN

I should have gotten her name.

I should have gotten her damn name.

No one has a clue who I mean when I refer to her as Midnight, like they didn't see that spectacular woman in the midst of the generic craziness that is a Trinity Falls moon party.

I like it and hate it all at once. I like the fact that it was just for me. I like that Midnight glistened right before my eyes, and I hate that there is nobody here to understand the loss I'm mourning. Not for the wolf we're here to celebrate, but the whisper of a woman I haven't seen since.

I should have gotten her name.

Tilting my head back, I look up at the moon, my wolf pumping beneath the surface. It's strong and unrelenting, as always. The sight of the moon shining down on us is always like a beacon in the dead of night, just like Midnight.

Fuck.

I need a distraction.

"Is everyone here?"

I turn to Asher, silently thanking him for pulling me from my thoughts before casting my gaze over the gathering just a few steps away. Here I am, lamenting the missed opportunity for pussy, even though I don't do virgins, when I should be focused on my pack and what they need from me.

Straightening my demeanor, I nod, but I'm sure it's more to myself than to him. "Yeah."

"Then let's go," he murmurs, as straight to the point as ever.

One day, Asher will have a story to tell. Someday, he'll talk about something that isn't a heaping of inconsequential shit that doesn't even matter. One day. Not today, though, not ever so far in his life. As a matter of fact, I don't think I've ever met anybody as blunt as him, but I like a man of few words.

When he does speak, his words hold weight and, in that, speak volumes.

I know what other word spoke volumes.

Virgin.

Fuck.

Rolling my shoulders back, I crack my neck from side to side and turn toward the gathering of wolves. "Thank you all for coming tonight," I state, hating that we're here at all, but we can't control that part. All we can control is what comes next. "I hate to address everybody under such difficult circumstances, but it's vital that we take time to recoup, not only as the wolves of this academy and for the strength of our pack, but for Veronica."

I spy Minnie standing shoulder to shoulder with Wylder, Tatum holding back a step, and my gut lurches. Between Tatum and Minnie, the loss of Veronica isn't going well. That's the thing with wolves; we grow an attachment. Even after a day, it seems.

"She was here for a matter of days, if I can even call it that much at all. And I can't begin to fathom what it is she experienced, torn from one hell hole to seemingly die at another. Not only did she lose her life, but we were reminded of the stark reality of this blood curse that holds *all* of us captive." I pause, making eye contact with every single person in the crowd, ensuring they understand the weight of my words. "Her life was lost and not because of her own choices. That same fact applies to all of us, each and every one of us. We don't know what tomorrow may bring, but we know that Veronica will be honored tonight."

Howls ripple through the air as the wolves promise her the send-off she deserves. Not only does it soothe my wolf, but it nestles deep within me too. I hate that tragedy is what bonds us all tighter, but we have to take strength from these moments unless we want to crumble under it all, and that's just not who we are.

"For a girl announced a wolf, yet unable to shift because of the sigil suppressing her other half, I feel it is only fitting that tonight we each take to the forest. We ride as one, and we ride for her." Cheers echo over the boom of my voice, transforming the solemn darkness into virtue and righteousness. "Veronica, we can't bring you back, we can't take the pain away, but we can honor you. Come morning, she will forever be in our hearts. Take to the night and make it so."

At my final words, the wolves need no further prompt as they dart toward the treeline. The group disperses, some shifting right in front of me, others inching closer to the forest before they let their wolves free. Minnie and Asher are right in the mix, but I'm acutely aware that Tatum is still standing ramrod straight in his original spot. His hands are stuffed in his pockets and his gaze is downcast as he makes no effort to join the crowd.

Wylder catches my eyes a few steps away, uncertainty warring in his stare as he tries to figure out how to help our friend, but I wave him off, nodding toward the treeline for him to join the others. He stutters a step, but it must be clear on my face because he shifts in the next breath, hightailing it toward the forest.

We all care, we always do. My pack is my life, but Minnie, Tatum, Asher, and Wylder? They're my family through and through. Tatum doesn't need all of us right now anyway. That would just overwhelm him.

Besides, they can run for the two of us until I pull him out of this funk.

I wait until everybody's gone, then turn toward my friend. It takes a handful of steps to cut the distance between us, and I match his stance, tucking my hands in my pockets and letting my shoulders relax in hopes of making him feel as calm as possible.

Closing the gap an inch more, I must distract him enough to pull him from his head because his eyes latch onto mine. His chin remains firmly pressed against his chest as he looks up at me through his lashes.

“I…this is all too much for me, Linc. I should just end it now,” he states, and I growl, the cool demeanor I was attempting completely obliterating in an instant.

“Over my dead fucking body.”

He shakes his head. “It's going to be someone's dead body, and I can't do that…”

His words trail off, his pain consuming the rest of his sentence as I try to shake my initial knee-jerk anger from my limbs.

I put my hands on his shoulders, squeezing in what I hope is comfort. “What happened to your parents was tragic, Tate, but this is different. Besides, harming yourself will only hurt someone else, then there are two unnecessary deaths that we don’t want,” I murmur, hoping to cut through the darkness that plagues him. I try to catch his eyes, but his stare remains down at his feet.

“Blood is blood, Linc. Death is death.” The defeat in his voice is enough to knock the air from my lungs. It doesn’t help that it was also the anniversary of his parents’ deaths yesterday. His emotions are already all over the place from that.

What pains me the most about Tatum, more than anything else in the whole entire world, is how he will never exist without that pain, the treachery and torture, how it will permanently taint his joy and tatter his life's journey.

"You're right. You're right, Tate, but we're going to figure it out this time." I finally earn his stare, but the pointed look is not what I had hoped for.

"We've been saying that for a long time."

He's right. There's no denying it.

"We're trying to do the impossible. It's going to take time."

His hand comes up to clamp on my arm, disappointment flickering across his features. "You said it yourself, Linc; it's impossible."

I can see the swirling torment in his eyes, and I can't bear it any longer. Yanking him toward me, I pull him into a tight hug, putting his chest against mine as I wrap my arms around him in a vice-like grip.

He trembles in my hold, but with every second that I squeeze, he seems to calm. Not completely, but enough to soften the worry fighting inside of me.

"We've got you, Tate. If I could kill your blood kin for you when we turn twenty-one, I would, but I can't. Instead, we're going to figure out how we make sure that day never comes for you."

Tatum nods, leaning back, and I reluctantly let go. His hands quickly make their way back into his pockets, but as he kicks his feet along the ground, he doesn't drop his gaze.

"We need a witch."

His statement is a swift punch to the gut.

"Like hell, we do," I grunt, and he gives me another one of those pointed looks that seems to work far too well on me.

"Be serious; we need someone willing and able to use magic, and that's not something we can do." His point is valid, but that doesn't mean I have to like it.

A witch. We thrive on not needing a witch. I don't even like witches. I don't even know a witch.

Unless…Midnight? What is she? A witch, a human, a vampire, a wolf?

I didn't ask. I didn't even get her goddamn name.

But…if she is a witch, could she—

I quickly shake my head, acutely aware of the fact that I'm pining over someone I can't have. Not only is she a virgin, but if she were a witch, that would just make me hate her more. We stick to our quadrants, and that's how we run, period.

"We'll figure it out, Tatum. We always figure it out, but for now, let's run. It will clear our thoughts."

"There's nothing to clear, Linc. I'm just stating the facts that you're not willing to face yet."

I look at him. *Really* look at him. This boy, this man, my brother. For as long as I can remember, since the day he watched his parents die, he has been my family, my pack. I love him just as much as I love Minnie. My parents must have known it, too; why else would they take him in and call him their own? From there, our pack began to grow with Wylder and Asher.

None of us are alike, apart from when it matters, apart from when it comes to caring for one another, then we're all exactly the same. And it's with that reminder that I bask in the promise I made a long time ago, watching as Tatum shifts, taking off toward the forest without a backward glance.

His brown marbled fur floats in the wind and I take a second in the silence to repeat it to myself once more.

I made a promise to my brother a long time ago. I won't go back on it. Not now, not ever.

I will find a way to end the blood kin curse.

Even if just for him.

Even at the cost of myself.

24

POLARIS

I'm not quite sure how, but I've made it to the end of the week with my memory still intact and my friendship with Bryony growing stronger. Since my blackout, I've managed to survive in my own little bubble, causing no ripples among the other students.

I just have to get through the rest of today, and then I will have the luxury of learning what it's like to spend the weekend alone. There are no classes on the weekend and I don't even know what I'm going to do with myself.

The first class of the day: Offensive and Defensive, again. Everyone filters into the room while I stand with my back pressed against the wall, trying to remain as invisible as possible while

Bryony chats with Professor Juniper at the end of the hall.

Sian and Terence appear from around the corner and I grimace. They both continue to act like I don't exist, turning to face away from me the second I'm close, just like now. With every day that passes, the desire for S and T to like me again dwindles.

My eyebrows gather as they slip by, entering the classroom as I consider the absence of one of our other Florentine friends. B—Benjamin. I haven't seen him since he was declared a human and we were all ushered out of the hall and to our quads. I haven't gone looking for him, though. Searching through the humans for the guy who dated your former friend seems dumb, but there's still a level of concern that I can't seem to shake.

Pressing my lips together, I try to eliminate anything related to Florentines from my thoughts, willing my mind to think positive.

I can stand on my own two feet without the fickle friendships I used to have.

If they can so easily leave me behind, they weren't my real friends anyways, and I don't need people like that in my life.

I scoff at myself. Maybe I am full of crap since I'm relying on Bryony so much. It's also impossible to rid my past from my thoughts so soon, despite how hard I try.

I left Florentine's five days ago. Five whole days, and it already feels like a distant memory. So much has happened since we arrived through those grand double doors that my head hurts from it all. I keep thinking about V—Veronica—wishing there was something I could have done to help her. Not so much with the dying part that was out of everyone's control, but more to do with the fact that I could have been her friend.

Maybe if she was still here I could have had a chance to be her friend. On the flipside, it's daunting how easily it could have been me in her place instead. We don't know who we're linked to. There's no heads up. Nothing. It's a blessing and a curse.

I could have been everybody's friend, but I chose to hide away at Florentine's in fear of the blood curse, and yet I watched it take somebody too soon.

The blood kin curse took Veronica without warning, without caution. Just…gone. It didn't care if she was friendly or mean, it didn't matter if she had friends or not, and it didn't even register that her sigil was still in place; it took her anyway.

It's surprising how much of an effect it's having on me.

The wolves seem to be at peace with it now or over it all together; either way, Bryony agrees they're back to normal after having lost one of their own. Apparently, they held a special moment for Veronica, but it was a private matter and by the time I learned of it, it was too late for me to find out if I could attend or not.

I do want to pay my respects, but if it's a wolf thing, I need to ask one of them, and the idea of that makes me uneasy. I can't bring myself to ask, not when it feels like the only wolves that might have the answers are the ones that surround Lincoln, and I'm not getting close to him. I'm not playing those games, not when he still doesn't know who I am.

The bell rings and my gaze darts to Bryony at the end of the hall. She's still huddled close to Juniper, so I decide to play it safe and wait for her inside. We've been together as much as possible. It's a foreign feeling to depend on someone, well, to depend on someone without pretending that I'm not.

As much as I appreciate her, I feel a sense of pride in myself for entering the class on my own, but I only make it two steps before I collide with a hard chest. Panic dulls me from the familiarity of the sensation and I brace for impact as if the floor is ready to rise and meet me. But instead, a hand wraps around my waist, holding me in place, and soft eyes find mine.

Wylder.

He looks every inch as handsome as he did at the party, but without the bar between us, it feels even more intimate than offering my first shot of liquor. His cropped blond hair makes my fingers tingle, fighting the desire to feel the texture, while his deep hazel eyes, a swirl of rich browns and emerald greens, hold me captive. His shoulders seem wider, and he somehow seems taller when I'm this close.

Hot damn.

The sound of someone clearing their throat startles me and I quickly remember myself. Forcing myself to stand unaided, I lurch from his hold, desperately aware that the distance I create between us is because he allows it. He could probably crush my skull with his bare hands.

A grin spreads across his face as he winks at me and I mutter my thanks, but as much as he releases his hold on me, he doesn't step back as I do; if anything, he inches closer.

"Anything for the girl who let me serve her her

first shot," he says, and I blush, hating how pink I know my cheeks are going to be right now. "I've got to say, though, this look definitely suits you better. The black is hot, but the silver is almost… whimsical," he says, tugging at a loose tendril of hair curling around my face, and my heart stills.

He knows.

He knows that the girl hiding beneath the silver hair is the same girl who was trying to reinvent herself with the jet-black hair. I didn't piece it together at first, with him mentioning my first drink, but he's making it clear he knows by pointing out my hair.

He doesn't seem confused by the fact that it's a different color, but I'm completely overcome with the need to explain myself. "The silver is an inconvenience. I dyed it black for a fresh start, for it to turn up like this again the following day," I admit, rambling to myself.

I have no idea why I'm sharing it with him. The need to make sure he understands is prominent and out of my control, it seems.

Dammit.

Where is Bryony? I need saving from this catastrophe before it unravels further.

My eyes widen, my throat drying as realization dawns on me; if he knows that the girl beneath the black hair is also the girl beneath the silver hair, then does Lincoln too?

"Hey, you made it on your own. I should be proud," Bryony says, interrupting my spiral. "I see you're getting reacquainted with the bartender," she adds with a chuckle, one that Wylder doesn't respond to. His eyes are still latched onto mine as if they're searching deep into my soul, desperate to understand what's beneath. I'm locked in a stare-off, one I can't seem to pull myself out of.

Bryony is acutely aware of the fact too, as she shakes my shoulder, drawing my attention toward her. "Are you free tonight?" she asks, and I roll my eyes, still aware that the guy is watching my every move.

"You're well aware that my after-school hours are always empty," I say, a mixture of a grumble and relief. If you had asked me back at Florentine's what I'd be doing if I had the opportunity to leave my room, I would tell you I would be everywhere. I would be free. But there's something comforting about my own space in a world I still don't understand, and I silently hate myself for not making a change.

"Good." Her shoulders lift as she beams at me, leaving an inkling of uncertainty tightening in my gut.

"Why?"

She shakes her head, offering no explanation, and my gaze flicks to Wylder, who presses his lips together in a thin line. I almost think he might know what she's not saying, but to my surprise, he offers me a wink before sauntering off.

I'm locked in place, watching him retreat, and it takes Bryony curling her fingers around my upper arm and tugging me to my seat to get me to move. I grumble under my breath when she plants her palms on my desk, looking deep into my eyes.

"Just be dressed to impress," she states, leaving me even more confused.

"Who am I impressing?" I push as she drops into her seat beside me. I expect her to leave me hanging, but instead, she does something even worse by answering.

"The coven."

I've been panicking on high alert all day, and all because of one word, five letters spoken by the girl I thought was my most genuine friend, yet she leaves me high and dry, strangled and stressed as the same word repeats over and over again in my head.

Coven.

Coven.

Coven.

She gave no inclination of what impressing them would look like, and as I stand in front of my armoire, feeling even more out of my depth than I have been since I got here, I begin to question her motives. Does she not realize that I spent so much of my life—the only part I can even remember—being forced to wear a uniform that itched?

I don't have a sense of style. I just wore what I was given, and even though clothes have been provided for me here, there's a sense of freedom with it that I've yet to latch onto. I don't know how to express myself. I just know how to feel comfortable in my own skin. But as much as I grumbled about what I should wear, she refused to give me any more details, swearing that she'd already said more than she should have.

I then had the pleasure of spending the rest of the day wondering whether it's better to know or not at this stage. With my blood pressure so high, I'm confident I would have been better not knowing. Especially since classes ended a few hours ago, and I haven't heard anything from her.

I've messaged her a few times, trying to make dinner plans, but I've had no reply. So it seems I'm going to dress to impress myself and eat alone.

Eyeing the clothes, I settle on a pair of black jeans with cargo pockets on the sides and a cute cropped t-shirt with puffed shoulders to go with my combat boots. I brush my fingers through my silver hair, letting it fall in waves around my face before I reach for my cell phone again. My fingers dance over the screen, growing more confident with the device as I tap out another message that I know will go unanswered.

Polaris: Help a girl out, Bryony. If not, can we grab food? I feel sick, but maybe dinner will help.

I press my lips together, staring at the screen like an answer will jump out at me. But just like the previous messages, this one remains unread.

Taking a deep breath, I head for the door, tucking my cell phone into my pocket along with my most prized possession: my coin. I feel a sudden burst of confidence. I can go to the dining hall and come home alone—safe and sound and all by myself.

I'll be fine.

The coven is clearly going to do something when I get back. Maybe make me wait until it's dark out. They're not going to jump me as I walk through the grounds on campus.

I hope…

Heading downstairs, I consider stopping on the first floor to use the bathroom, but a sense of eeriness suddenly surrounds me. The quietness feels unfamiliar, leaving me nervous and acutely aware that I'm alone in my own dorm, panicking.

Opting to find some form of life, be it anybody on campus at all, I decide to hurry down the final flight of stairs, only to grind to a halt at the bottom.

There are no sofas, coffee tables, or frames on the walls…

Nothing.

The lounge is gone. Every inch of furniture in the space is absent, and I gulp as I take in the seven figures dressed in deep purple robes that cover their bodies and faces, hidden beneath oversized hoods. A golden, thick rope wraps around each of their waists and all I can do is blink at them.

What in the heck is going on?

I don't move. I don't even breathe, yet one steps forward with an unfamiliar voice.

"Welcome to your initiation," they boom, leaving me to gape at them.

"Do I get a choice?" I blurt, tingles shimmering over my skin as my pulse wreaks havoc through my body.

"The Renegade coven is the most sought-after

coven, not only on campus, but in the world. It would be foolish to question us and even more abysmal for you to fail and prove we've chosen wrong. Now, are you ready?" they ask, and the words from class this week pass through my mind.

I have no idea where they may lead me or what it might entail, but the importance of a coven to not only my future as a witch but my magic, is paramount.

So, I ignore the grumble of my stomach and the desire for the bathroom and roll my shoulders back. Standing as tall and as proud as I can.

"I'm as ready as I'll ever be."

25

POLARIS

When I said I was ready, I didn't think that meant I was going to have a sack thrown over my head. I also didn't think they would literally kidnap me from the witches' dorm and take me to God only knows where. But even as I sit here now, with only the sound of dripping water to keep me company, I don't feel scared.

Maybe I should, but it seems I'm all too familiar with the darkness.

I'm too focused on the fact that coven initiation isn't as exciting as they first made it out to be, that's for sure.

My stomach grumbles, reminding me of the reason I left my room to begin with, and it makes me shift in my seat. The wooden chair is hard beneath me, the grooves pressed against my thighs and the air cool, almost damp, as I try not to fidget.

Drip. Drip. Drip.

The sound is impossible to escape. As the minutes stretch on around me, the uncertainty and fearful thoughts of the unknown make their presence known, and an unease threatens to trickle in. I clear my throat, swallowing down the gnawing emotions as I barely manage to keep it all at bay.

I remind myself I'm safe again and again. Bryony told me to dress to impress, to be ready; she wouldn't have said that if whatever was happening was an actual threat to my safety. Despite my mantra, my fingers itch in my lap. I'm desperate to feel the coin tucked into my pocket, but the fear of revealing a vulnerability keeps it firmly locked away.

I could probably tug at the sack and reveal my surroundings to my unknowing eyes. I'm not bound in any way, but something tells me the restraint I'm showing is what they're searching for. If that test is a part of the initiation, then bring it on; darkness is my best friend. I've spent a long time there; what's a little longer going to do?

The real issue is what comes with the darkness: the wandering thoughts. I don't like them. I'm powerless against them, and I like control—or the illusion of it, at least. My mind swirls with possibilities, as secrets and mysteries reveal themselves to me while I continue my adventure at Trinity Falls Academy.

When Professor Juniper mentioned coven initiations, I don't know what I expected, but it wasn't this. Despite my internal struggle, my breath remains steady, and just when I'm on the verge of throwing it all to hell, I feel the sack lift from my head.

I blink frantically, confusion clinging to me as I'm greeted with darkness, but then five figures come into view. My heart races and my breaths are shallow as the room floods with light, brought by flames that ignite around the exterior of the room. There must be one hundred of them, illuminating the space that holds me captive.

This is some theatrics.

Velvet robes shield all of them from view, keeping my audience a mystery to me.

My lips purse, nerves threading with a lick of excitement as one of them steps forward. Their head tilts, the hood moving with them as they assess me.

"You have been brought here to be considered for initiation into the Renegade coven." Their words carry around the room, booming with pride and strength. "As much as we are the highest regarded coven within the witching world, it doesn't matter when it comes down to our core values. The foundations of any coven, any witch, remain the same for everyone. It's a part of what makes us witches." I don't just listen to her words, but I try to focus on her voice. It's not Bryony, I know that much, but I don't think I recognize her voice at all.

"What you must understand before we proceed any further is what a coven stands for. We stand united as a found family, in a safety net that we call our home. We lean on each other while taking in each other's strength, and in doing so, we enhance our magic. Unfortunately, what comes along with that is the fact that there is no escaping us. Once you're in, you're in, and everyone knows everything that there is to know. To leave a coven would banish you from all covens. Luckily for you, here at the Renegade coven, we lost an elemental witch not too long ago, and if you prove to be the elemental witch we're looking for, you have a place among us."

I blink, trying to process the words she's firing at me.

A found family?

Safety?

Strength?

Enhanced magic?

How can they promise so much yet dangle it like a carrot before me?

What if I'm not who they're in search of?

What did they call it?

An elemental witch?

How am I supposed to know that?

"So, are you ready?" The woman asks, the four other witches standing in unison behind her. She doesn't seem to need an answer as she steps toward me, and I swiftly shake my head, instinctively rearing back as she draws closer.

"I'm going to need more information than that before I decide I'm ready," I blurt, halting her in her tracks as I sense the four spectators shift with uncertainty. "You want me to be a what witch?" I add for clarity, but the elongated silence that wraps around the room threatens to steal my breath.

Nobody moves, but I sense irritation flooding from the woman hiding beneath the hood in front of me as she clears her throat, sweeping her hands out at her sides.

"I am a mind witch, specializing in tarot. I stand as the central piece to the Renegade coven. I'm the focal point, if you will—like a wolf's Alpha. Every coven is made up of the same key elements. We currently have two elemental witches, a potions witch, and a charms witch. We need the third and final elemental witch to complete our coven. If you prove to be the elemental witch we're looking for, you have a home with us forever."

The room goes silent and I long for the sound of the dripping water to return, but it's lost to the flickering flames that heat the room.

All of this rests on an…if?

What if I'm not an elemental witch? And more than that, how am I supposed to know?

"I don't know what I am," I state feebly, shifting uncomfortably in my seat, nerves getting the better of me as my fingers twist together in my lap.

"That's not a problem. We can find out regardless."

My spine stiffens at the flippant way her words fall from her mouth, and the panic burning a trail up my spine makes its presence known.

"How?"

My fingers curl around the arms of the chair, nausea churning in my gut. I don't even know the answer yet, but something shifts inside of me.

Something is not right. I can feel it deep in my gut.

The hood moves slightly as the person beneath shakes their head. "It won't hurt…much."

There's almost a lingering hint of amusement to

their tone, and it's the wisp that I need to seal my fate.

"No."

I move to stand, but two witches step from behind the woman before me, knocking me back down into my chair with enough force that I feel the front two legs lift and my body tilts backward just enough that I brace for an impact that never comes.

"You can't find out my magic. I haven't released my sigil," I rush, panic clawing at me as I try to fight out of their hold, but it's futile. "My bangles are still in place," I insist, feeling the metal bite into my skin as they force my arms down on the chair.

"I told you, it won't take long. Just hold still," she orders, and the panic intensifies.

I glare at the witches holding me in place, panic turning to anger and hysteria as I try to tug my arms free from their hold, but I'm locked in place against my will.

"No. No! No," I plead, but it's as if the words go unheard as another witch steps forward, but the fifth witch, remaining at the back to my right, with one foot in front of the other, seems to falter at my terror.

They don't leap to my defense, though; they watch on in silence as fear consumes me, unraveling inside of me.

The apparent leader edges closer, her hand extended toward my face. Her fingers are curled and a glimmer seems to shift along her palm.

"I said no. Don't come near me," I shout, horror laced into every syllable as she ignores me.

If this is what it's like now, with them wondering if I fit their mold, what would it be like if I were indeed what they needed?

Would they listen to me then, or would I be ordered to fall in line?

I don't want to find out.

As her hand gets within an inch of my face, I sense a shift in the air, as if her magic is palpable, and the panic that consumes me morphs into a physical form, filling my chest as I push against the witches holding me in place.

"Make it stop," I scream, my throat burning as I yell. My head falls back, my breath stuttering in my lungs as I search deep inside for a strength I know I won't find, when a knot of pressure expands in my chest, curling deep in my gut, and I scream, releasing the taut tension.

The sound ricochets off the walls around me, and with a force like I've never felt before, I snap my wrists out of the witches' hold before pushing against their chests. The leader stumbles back in surprise, her hand still frozen in the air before her as the witches holding me in place fall to the floor.

The person at the back of the room remains frozen in place while the other idle witch edges toward me. My chest aches as I pant for breath, desperate to put as much distance between us as possible. I take a single step before I freeze, glancing down at the witch on the floor whose hood has fallen back to reveal a familiar face. My face screws up in disgust.

Foster. The guy who showed us the protection spell in class.

Asshat.

Snapping my gaze to my right, I see that the other witch on the floor is the girl from class who created the luck charm. Her name escapes me, and searing disappointment clings to my limbs. Nobody moves, and everyone seems as surprised by my outburst as I am.

I try to steady my breathing as I cast my gaze over everyone, settling on the person still hiding at the back of the room, and my gut tells me exactly who it is. I don't want to stick around to find out, though. My breathing isn't easing, it's not going to in here, and I need to think clearly. That's not going to happen with my heart pounding wildly in my chest, making it abundantly clear that I'm not as safe as I first thought.

With blurry eyes, I spin, looking beyond the witches to find a small space between the flickering flames around the room.

An exit.

Before I pass out and leave myself even more vulnerable to them, I make a run for it.

SICKNESS COILS IN MY VEINS. This time, it's not from hunger, but from despair.

I run from the room, relieved to find a set of stairs leading up to my freedom, and I climb them, two at a time, acutely aware that someone could overpower me at any moment. To my surprise, I barrel through the doors at the top into the early evening air without incident.

The building before me is familiar, but seeing the common room of the witches' dorm does not ease my concerns.

The basement?

They had me in the basement. We hadn't even left the building I'm supposed to call home.

Getting the hell out of there, I rush down the path, thankful that there are no other students around to see me crumble before I make a beeline for the trees. I don't know where I'm going or what I'm doing, but it seems my brain does when I come to the familiar spot in the forest outlining the hedge-high maze.

I drop to a heap on the ground, pressing my back into the earth, just like I did the first time I was here. This time, my terror feels amplified. Curling my fingers into the blades of grass, I try to take steady breaths, willing the panic to leave my body.

Should I have run? I don't know. I don't know what this means for me and my future in a coven, but all I know is I did not feel safe, and there was no reason for them to touch my body. They didn't deserve to pry the answer of what kind of witch I am from me. That is something I deserve to learn on my own. They were going to take it without care. They were going against my wishes and pleas, without my consent.

Deep down, I know I did the right thing running, yet there's a niggling part of me that is worried I've just made my life a hell of a lot more complicated than it needed to be.

"Polaris?" I still, unable to speak as my next breath lodges in my throat at the sound of Bryony's voice. "Polaris, are you here?"

I want to melt into the earth, hide beneath the

mud and the soil, and wait for her to pass. But more than that, I want her gone, and for that to happen, I need to get this over with as quickly as possible.

Pressing up onto my elbows, I lift just enough to see her over the hedges. The sun still lights up the sky in a mixture of pinks and oranges, offering a pretty background even when my world is burning in turmoil.

Her eyes widen when she spots me, and she hurries to cut the remaining distance. "Polaris, I—"

"You can stop right where you are," I interject, lifting my hand. To my surprise, there is a witch among the madness who hears what I'm saying. She pauses in place, but it doesn't stop the turmoil storming in her eyes.

"P—"

"Just don't come any closer," I insist, aware that I'm repeating myself, but I need the distance. I have to have the distance.

"I won't," she murmurs, nervously wrapping her arms around herself. "What happened back there?" she asks, and I scoff.

Is she for real right now?

"How about you tell me," I grumble, watching intently as she wipes a hand down her face. A robe no longer drapes over her body as she stands before me in a pair of skinny jeans and a tank top.

She unfolds her arms from around her waist, waving her hands at her side as she tries to find an explanation. Like she's going to find one that she thinks will make sense of whatever the hell that was. If she can find one that good, I'll be more than impressed because it's impossible, that I do know.

"We were just trying to…" Her words trail off, failing before they even really start, and I stand, glaring at her as I wipe my hands down my thighs.

"You were trying to do what? Make me do something against my will? Don't you think I've been through enough of that already? Don't you think I've lived at the hands of somebody else for long enough?"

The rage that coils inside me is unbounded as I release all the pent-up devastation I've endured this far.

"Polaris, I—"

"I was starting to trust you, Bryony. I was starting to *trust* you," I growl, more than aware that I'm not even letting her speak, but she had plenty of time to talk back there and said nothing.

Nothing.

My heart hammers in my chest as she takes a step toward me. I lift my hand more firmly, halting her again.

"You still can," she insists, and I cock my eyebrow.

"Can I? I said no, Bryony. I said stop, and my pleas went unheard. It was like I was in a room filled with…what did you call them? Cunts?"

Her head drops, her chin to her chest as she exhales heavily, silently admitting defeat. "Polaris, I'm sorry."

An apology, yet the desperation inside of me doesn't subside. I turn away from her, unable to look at the reminder of what just happened.

The silence stretches between us, growing more uncomfortable with every passing minute, and I hear her shuffling from foot to foot. "I don't want to leave you here," she says, and I scoff.

"And I don't want to be near you right now."

"We said we would stick together," she pushes, and I shake my head, finally turning back to her.

"That was before," I state, the emotion no longer clinging to my voice as defeat washes over me.

"Before what?" she asks, the sadness leaking into her tone, but I push on, letting the dejection take over me.

"Before I realized I'm safer being the loner I've always been."

26

POLARIS

Seconds turn into minutes, which morph into hours before my eyes as I focus on nothing and everything all at once. The sun sets, casting a quaint array of colors across the sky before the shadows really creep in.

It's funny how my heart slows as the moon rises and the murkiness of the night seeps in. If I were normal, I would have headed into one of the communal areas on campus, seeking strength in numbers from those around me, but I can't seem to lift my head.

I'm perfectly nestled in what I have now claimed as my spot. The hedge is a few inches above my head, shielding me from view while also providing an extra layer of warmth as the temperature slowly drops.

The only thing keeping me warm right now are the emotions weighing heavy in my veins. The anger has subsided, an all too familiar sense of numbness ridding the rage from my bones as I focus on the one thing that stands out to me: survival.

I would rather place all bets on myself than a group of people who overlooked my response to their actions. There is no strength in that, no safety like I hoped and they had promised. I don't remember my family; no matter how hard I try, it's impossible. However, my gut tells me that what this coven was trying to offer isn't what a family is about.

If it is, I want nothing to do with it. Count me out. I'll take this road solo. I know I can count on myself and that's all that matters.

Twirling my coin between my fingers, I hold it up to the muted light, embracing the comfort it always offers.

In the time I've been hiding here, contemplating my life, my next move, and my potential future, the main thing I have settled on is the fact that I *want* to be here. I *want* to advance and grow and be the best version of myself possible. Trinity Falls Academy is going to offer me everything I want, and things I don't, and I'm willing to embrace it all, positive or negative.

If I have to walk these halls every day as a witch without a coven, then so be it.

If I have to shuffle through campus with my head dipped to avoid any further drama from the vampires, or Blaze, more precisely, then I will.

If I have to see the hot wolves every day without ever doing anything about it, count me in.

Florentine's may have crippled me in comparison to most students here, but I can't let that same suffocating feeling follow me to Trinity Falls Academy as well.

A twig snaps, popping my peaceful bubble as goosebumps skim over my skin. Adrenaline floods my veins, my entire body on high alert as I strain my ears, waiting to hear another sound. I don't move, though. Not an inch. Fear locks me in place like it's a chain around my ankles and wrists, binding me to the earth beneath me.

My panic is in overdrive, making my breaths wheeze as the thumping of boots hitting the ground causes the earth beneath me to rumble. A shadow casts over where I lay, my next breath lodging in my throat as I watch a figure drop to the ground, ignoring my existence as they sigh.

Too scared to move or breathe, I watch, completely captivated by the man looming only a few feet away. He leans back in the opposite corner of the hedges, head tilted back as he squeezes the bridge of his nose. His free hand curls around something in his lap, and when he slumps farther into the corner, knees bent as he drops his hand from his face, I realize who it is.

I've been caught in this little maze on one other occasion in the short time I've been here, and it's just my luck that it's the same guy both times. His dark hair is pulled back off his face and coiled into a messy knot at the back of his head, but I find myself wondering what the cropped hairs along the sides would feel like under my fingertips.

I roll my eyes at myself, irritated with my train of thought the second my bubble pops, wavering my resolve.

One: I'm alone in the dark with a man I don't know. That's not safe. Far from it.

Two: the second I see one of the hot wolves, who I swore off mere minutes ago, has me questioning the most ridiculous things.

Three: I should be focusing on how I'm supposed to get myself out of this damn situation.

Running my tongue over my bottom lip, worry burns in my throat as I watch him.

He has no idea I'm here.

He hasn't lifted his gaze from his lap, staring at something, but his eyes don't seem focused.

Although, that could just be the shadows of the night playing tricks on me.

The scraping of paper jolts me, and I swiftly realize it's some kind of pad in his grasp, a pencil too. He hums gently, the sound almost swept away by the gentle breeze, but I hear it. There's something about it. It's light, airy, and…familiar? No, definitely not. I wouldn't have heard anything quite so charming at Florentine's.

Shaking my head, I focus on my predicament instead of a sweet tune that isn't going to help me survive.

He doesn't look like he's going to leave anytime soon, and as much as I could lie here forever, I don't think it's the best idea. Not when he could react badly. He seems calm enough now, and he didn't try to cause me any harm the last time I was here, but that doesn't mean I'm safe this time too…does it?

Before I can think of a better plan, I clear my throat. It's soft, almost nonexistent, but the reaction that erupts from the man before me is electric.

He launches to his feet, his pen and pad clattering to the ground as his fists coil at his sides and his eyes shine bright in the darkness. They zone in on me without a moment's pause as his chest heaves, watching my every move, or lack thereof, as I remain rooted to the spot.

"Sorry, I didn't mean to make you jump," I breathe, pressing my back further into the grass beneath me, trying to make myself appear as small as possible.

"Jump? I almost shifted into the afterlife," he blurts, staring down at me with wide eyes that soften just an inch. It's only when I note his hands relax that I know I'm safe, or hope I am, at least.

"That's…graphic?" I murmur, feeling my cheeks heat when I realize what I said, but he shrugs, relaxing a little more as his eyes dim.

"That's me."

He rolls his shoulders back, easing a little tension from his limbs before he drops back into the corner.

Pressing my lips together, I press my palms into the ground and sit up to lean back against the hedge behind me. I bend my legs, wrapping my arms around them nervously as I stare across the distance, waiting for…something, anything.

"I'm Polaris," I mutter, trying to soften the fact that I seem to be intruding on him even though I was here first.

His eyes meet mine, the corner of his mouth tilting up just an inch. "They missed a trick by not calling you Silver with the hair."

A soft smile lingers on my lips, a response I have

no control over. "Yeah, it's a shame I don't know who *they* are," I grumble, dropping my gaze as irritation claws through me.

Why did I say that?

"I'm Tatum, and I'm familiar with that," he states, drawing my attention back to him, but he's not looking at me; he's scratching away in his pad.

"With what?" I push, desperate for more.

"No parents."

"Florentine's?" I ask, positive I've never seen him before coming here, and he shakes his head.

"No."

Silence seeps into the little bubble that wraps around the both of us, but there's a burning desire deep in my gut that's desperate to know more. What the *more* is, I'm not sure, but I'm eager to find out.

"What are you doing?"

"Drawing," he mumbles, not lifting his gaze.

"Can I see?"

"No." His answer comes sharp and fast, drawing a thick line in the grass between us.

I should take it as a hint, but instead, I take it as a hurdle I can leap over.

"You're happy to share your pain but not your art?"

I really should have taken the hint. Instead, I'm

likely going to be taking my last breath if I don't shut the hell up.

"That's accurate," he replies, unfazed by my questions.

"That's…my level of sad," I admit, unwrapping my arms from around my knees as I cross my legs, getting more comfortable instead of leaving.

"There are levels to sad?" he asks, tearing his gaze from his pad to spy on me, and I shrug.

"It feels like it."

He nods, like my answer is enough for him to understand, even when I'm not entirely making sense of it myself.

"Are you going to tell me why you're outside so late?" he presses, putting the cap back on his pen as he gives me his full attention, and I shrug, nervously tucking a curl of hair behind my ear.

"I was in a panic, and before I realized it, I was here." I press my lips together, trying to halt the flood of words threatening to break the dam they're forming. He stares, eyes searching, but he doesn't push, and the air that lingers makes it clear there's more to be said. "I was taken to a coven initiation."

Dammit.

I press my teeth into my tongue, willing myself to shut up, but the way he looks at me, attentive, understanding, and patient, I can't stop the words from coming. "They…I…he…I didn't like it."

He nods, lacing his fingers together in his lap. "Did you complete the initiation?"

I shake my head. "They were…forceful."

Is that the right word? I don't know.

"Forceful? Are you hurt?" His eyebrows gather, concern dancing in his eyes as they shimmer with a little glow again.

"Oh, uh, no, I don't think so, I just…I panicked."

Shut up now, Polaris.

"Panicked?" he repeats, and I nod.

"Yeah. They didn't listen to me when I said no or wanted them to stop or even when I asked for more information. All that mattered was what *they* wanted."

The rock forms in my gut as visions threaten to consume my sight, reliving the moment again and again. I glance away from him. I have to; if I don't, I'll say more, and I've already said enough.

Embarrassed by my rambling, I rise to my feet, avoiding his stare as I clear my throat.

"I should go."

"You don't have to," he rushes out, scrubbing his chin as I peer at him from the corner of my eye.

"I know. Technically, I was here first, but I feel

like I'm imposing," I admit, and he climbs to his feet too.

"You're not," he insists, just as my stomach grumbles. He tilts his head, assessing me. "You're hungry. How long have you been out here?"

I wave him off. "I was, but then…I'll figure it out."

Gathering his pad and pen, he pulls a backpack from the other side of him, tucking them away before retrieving a small paper bag. He flicks open the top, aiming the opening in my direction, but I can't see from where I'm standing.

"How about we share this and head back to our quads?" When I don't immediately answer, he slips his hand inside to reveal a sandwich in his grasp. "Turkey and swiss?" He waves it teasingly, making it sound like it's something I should be salivating over, and truthfully, I'm so hungry, I could eat the slop back at Floretine's without complaint.

The smile on his face makes it even more impossible to say no, so I take a deep breath and eliminate some of the distance between us. Once I'm at arm's length, he hands me the sandwich before retrieving another from the bag, crumpling the paper, and stuffing it in his backpack before tossing it over his shoulder.

He takes the first step, and I follow. He takes the first bite, and I follow.

We eat in silence, the deliciousness consuming my every thought as we step out of the trees and follow the winding path toward the dorms. I take the last bite of my new favorite sandwich as we meet the fork in the road that leads to each dorm.

"Thank you for this, and for letting me talk your ear off," I murmur, stopping at the path to the witches.

I don't want to go back there, not really, but it's not like I have another choice.

"It's all good," he breathes, hiking his backpack higher up his shoulder before stepping onto the sand.

I gape at him in surprise, rushing after him. "You don't have to walk me all the way," I state, and he grimaces.

"I'm more concerned with what you might be walking into."

"Oh, I hadn't thought of that." I don't think I'll be walking into anything dangerous…will I?

"I thought that's why you were avoiding coming back." He looks from me to the witches' building and back again as my cheeks warm with another bout of embarrassment.

"No, I just, it's calm out there, and it feels... freeing," I admit, and he hums.

"Freeing? Florentine's, right?"

"Right," I confirm, ducking my head when the heat in my cheeks feels like I will ignite into real flames.

"I'm sorry about that."

My gaze darts right back to his. "Why would you be sorry?"

He shrugs, unable to give me an answer, but his words appease something inside me nonetheless.

As we reach the door, I twist the handle and peek through the gap. The living room is back to normal, and a few witches are lounging in the space. I exhale a breath I hadn't realized I was holding before turning my attention back to him.

His eyes are raking over me, making sure I'm okay, and I smile before placing my hand on his arm. He looks down at it, a little skittish as he tenses, but he doesn't step away.

"Thank you."

I'm trying to show my appreciation, but the words just aren't enough.

"I haven't done anything," he breathes, looking deep into my eyes.

"You did more than I can even begin to say," I

admit, the words still not doing him justice as I earn myself another soft smile on his full lips.

My body acts on its own accord as I eliminate the remaining distance between us, pushing up onto my tiptoes to press my lips against his cheek. It's a ghost of a touch, but the way my heart pounds manically in my chest is undeniable.

Desperate not to push my luck, I take a step back, smiling at him, acutely aware that the heat on my face has nothing to do with embarrassment this time.

"Goodnight, Tatum."

He lifts his hand to the exact spot my lips touched as he stares at me with a hint of wonder in his eyes.

"Goodnight, Polaris."

27

POLARIS

Breakfast alone isn't as scary as I initially thought. At this point, I've faced far worse than eating by myself. Especially when exhaustion clings to me like a second skin. It seems I now have another reason not to sleep, but it's not a priority I hold highly, not anymore.

After Veronica's death, there's only one thing I know for sure: I'll sleep when I'm dead, and that could be far sooner than I want if I don't focus.

Every time my eyelids closed, I heard a creak or a rustle in the distance, which sprung me back awake. I anticipated someone slipping into my room against my will, but no one came.

Not the Renegade coven. Not anyone.

Then, my mind would wander to the moment in the forest with Tatum.

I don't know what I expected of him, but he was nothing like I predicted.

He was kind, considerate, and…gentle, like he knew pain himself.

The chair beside me scrapes across the ground, pulling me from my thoughts. I tilt my head to find Bryony dropping down into the seat. Her gaze settles on mine as I drop my fork, my breakfast forgotten, and fold my arms over my chest.

Pressing my lips together, I bite back the surprise and snark as she has the audacity to give me a pointed look.

"How long are you going to be mad at me?"

How long? She's barely given me twelve hours. "I don't know, maybe forever," I grumble, my fingertips digging into my arms as I hold her stare, refusing to shy away like I desperately want to and usually would.

"Forever?" she scoffs, breaking eye contact to reach for a chocolate croissant before settling me with another stare that is infused with a hint of humor she doesn't deserve. "If you don't think I'm going to irritate you every day until you give in, then you haven't learned anything about me at all."

I purse my lips. "I think I've learned enough."

She shakes her head, taking a large bite of the

fresh pastry before she speaks. "No, you haven't, and we both know it."

I want to ask her a million questions, and I want to understand, yet I also want to give her the silent treatment and pretend she doesn't exist because maybe she doesn't deserve the opportunity to explain herself.

Looking away, I finally break her eye contact, only to latch onto a sneering vampire.

Blaze.

He stares at me, his eyes almost pitch-black, and I quickly avert my gaze.

"I'm your friend, Polaris."

It's my turn to scoff, cocking my brow at her as I turn to face her once again. "You're a part of the Renegade coven first."

"No, I'm a victim of the blood kin curse first."

Well, isn't that the truth for all of us.

"I didn't partake last night, Polaris. I—"

"You did nothing instead," I interject, noting the irritation that coils through me, which only grows with every passing second that I realize it's not all directed at her.

"I…I was their last recruit—a non-Florentine—and my initiation didn't entail any of that. If I had anticipated anything off-key, I wouldn't have gone there. I wouldn't have risked you like that." She slumps back in her seat with a sigh. "When Nessa died, we were all devastated, but the first thing they wanted to do was find a replacement. I was still sad and grieving, and then there was you. I trusted it to be you. Unfortunately, I didn't anticipate their actions, and I'm sorry for that."

Her words wash over me, offering me a dash of understanding. My gut twinges with a hint of sadness—not for myself, but for her. And as the silence stretches between us, I can't help but fixate on the defeat that nestles in her gaze.

"That sappy look isn't going to work on me," I grumble, clearing my throat, and she hums.

"I know." She nods, a disappointed smile curling her lips.

I don't know if I can truly trust her, the jury is still out on that one, but there's a burning question I can't deny. "They're not going to try and pull that kind of crap again, are they?"

She shakes her head fiercely. "No, you basically declined their offer. They won't reach out to you again. Even if they tried, I would make sure they didn't."

I scoff. "I declined their offer? I didn't let them force me, you mean."

"Yeah, that. I'm sorry about that," she insists, and I turn away.

"Yeah." I sigh, feeling the tendrils of defeat as she clears her throat.

"Turning down a coven, though, it won't look good for you among the rest of the witches. Not when it was the Renegades," she adds, and I shrug.

"I don't care. I have morals, standards, and boundaries. I was deprived of a life at Florentine's, yet I stood by those morals there, and I'll stand by them here. I don't want to be a part of a coven who is willing to take such drastic action to get what they want without asking permission. Not when I've finally been given a glance at freedom."

She nods, not saying anything else on the matter, as she finishes off her croissant and stands.

"Ready for class?" My eyebrows rise as I stare at her, and she offers me that familiar pointed look. "Are you going to spend the day getting lost on your own from one class to another, or would you lower your standards for five minutes at a time to stick by my side to survive another day?"

Damn, when she puts it like that…

Swiping a hand down my face, I sigh with reluctance. Survival comes first. That's precisely what I told myself all night. I can walk with her from class to class, but that doesn't mean I have to be her friend.

"Where are we going?" I ask, straightening my

jacket as I move away from the table, and she glances back over her shoulder at me.

"Combat."

As I STEP over the threshold into the combat classroom, I startle when I find the room morphing before my eyes, and by the time my foot presses against the floor, it's grass and dirt beneath my sneakers.

With wide eyes, I turn to Bryony, who frowns in response for a moment before understanding flashes over her features. "It's a hidden portal. It's set around the perimeter of the classroom door to lead you out to the far fields for training."

I nod like it makes total sense, but it definitely freaking doesn't. Stepping back, I notice a soft glow in the air, like a shimmer sprinkled around the small spot, when another student suddenly appears in front of it.

Another step back, another deep inhale, and I still sink into the overwhelming surroundings I find myself in. No one else cares, though; it is seemingly just me. Maybe I can do this.

Clearing my throat, I turn my attention to the rest of the class that gathers a few feet away. It takes half a second to acknowledge that the quadrants stand strong together out here too. The vampires are gathered at the far left, wolves beside them, followed by the humans, leaving the witches on the far right.

Remaining indifferent about the girl beside me, I wander along the outskirts of the group, bypassing the other quads as I move toward the witches. The second we round the wolves, my eyes snag on a familiar bun tied on the top of a ridiculously cute guy's head.

He spots me immediately, standing a little straighter as he offers me half a smirk and a slight lift of his chin in acknowledgment. I feel my cheeks heat as my lips curl of their own accord before I duck my head, tucking a loose silver curl behind my ear before I do something to embarrass myself.

Three steps. That's how many I manage before I glance in his direction again, and I find him still staring my way, only…Wylder is standing beside him, glancing between the both of us.

Scurrying away, I feel eyes on me, but thankfully, I'm saved by the professor who stands before everyone.

"We don't have time to waste this morning. We have assessments coming up soon and I need to see what I'm working with," she hollers, clapping her hands as her short blonde ponytail flaps in the breeze. "Once you're paired off, find a pitch to set up and get to it," she adds with a firm grumble, pointing at the squares that look to be spray-painted on the grass a few inches apart from one another. "Witches with—"

"How about we change it up today, Professor Drummond?"

Blaze's voice carries through the open air, sending a shiver down my spine as I turn my attention toward the vampires. The man in question stands dead center, a smug look on his face as he raises an eyebrow at me.

Me?

What the hell did I do?

I run my tongue over my bottom lip nervously as the professor follows my line of sight.

"You want me to allow different pairings?" she asks, planting her hands on her hips, eyeing each quadrant to see what they have to add.

"We're open to it," Lincoln hollers, snapping my attention their way to see him eyeing the vampires with a vengeance in his eyes that looks as though it will never be soothed.

"Humans?" Drummond hollers, and a few of them nod in response. I take a second to try and find B among the group, but he's nowhere to be seen. "Witches?" she adds, turning her attention our way, and I gulp.

I don't want to have to fight anyone if I don't have to, but survival is survival. I'll do what it takes.

"We're ready," a girl hollers from the front of the class, and I stiffen.

I know exactly who she is, a simple statement and flashbacks from last night flood my brain.

Tilting my face at Bryony, she looks dead ahead, but the slightest glimpse from the corner of her eyes tells me she knows. She just can't admit it.

"Okay then, may it be at your own peril. Remember: no permanent injuries, and when someone submits, you call it. Anyone seen breaking these rules will face Professor Whitmore."

I'm frozen in place for what feels like an eternity, listening to the professor read name after name off the list, waiting with bated breath for mine to be called.

"Bryony, witch, paired with Lincoln, wolf. Minnie, wolf, paired with Tatum, wolf. Asher wolf, paired with Blaze, vampire. Wylder, wolf, paired with Polaris, witch."

My gaze snaps to the wolves, landing on the cropped-blond beast of a man to find his eyes already taking me in. A wry smile transforms the anger from his face and I gulp.

He nods to his right, and with my lips pressed together nervously, I follow his silent order. I cut through the moving bodies, each finding their own marked square, until I'm standing in the same area as Wylder.

His eyes are set on me, but my nerves make it impossible for me to look at him right now. Instead, I peer over his shoulder, watching as a few wolves face off with some vampires. The animosity between them is palpable.

Eager to avoid the pent-up strain consuming the air, I finally relent and turn to Wylder. There's an amused grin on his face. "I—"

"Witch, right?"

The sudden appearance of Lincoln has us both surprised, but his pointed look is aimed at me. "Uh, yeah."

"Good. I'm looking for someone."

"Someone?" Wylder interjects, frowning at his friend, who nods.

"Yeah."

"I'm sure she might be able to help you, but a name would be a good start, Linc," he grumbles, rolling his shoulders back while Lincoln scrubs at the back of his neck nervously.

"Well, I don't have that."

He's looking for someone and doesn't know their name? I don't understand.

"Uh, I don't know how I can help you without it. Besides, I don't really know anyone's name to begin with," I add, and he shakes his head dismissively.

"Her name doesn't matter. She had midnight-black hair, bright blue eyes, and…and that's all that matters. Have you seen her in the witches' dorm? I've spoken to the rest of the quadrants, and no one has a clue, and I haven't seen her since the full moon party."

Holy crap.

He's talking about me. He's looking for me.

I search his eyes, waiting for the realization to hit him, but nothing comes.

Nothing.

Not even an iota.

Blinking at Wylder, who I know definitely knows, I find him hiding a grin behind his bear-like hand as he subtly shakes his head at me. I have no idea what he means by that, so I focus my attention back on Lincoln.

I just need to take a deep breath and tell him, blurt it out, and put his confusion to rest. Taking a deep breath, I stand tall, ready to explain, but as I go to take a step toward him, Wylder cuts me off.

With a single wink, he turns to his friend. "If she comes up with anything, she'll let you know. For now, let me get my fight on," he grumbles, making Lincoln sigh before he saunters off with a defeated air around him.

I instantly feel bad and move to step around the giant blocking me from his friend's path, but he stops me once again, this time with his hand locked around my arm. "I can't bear it any longer," I rasp as Wylder snickers.

"Please don't spoil my fun just yet," he pleads, looking down at me with wide eyes.

"Fun?"

"Yeah. I love him; he's my brother, my pack, my Alpha, but sometimes he's…dumb."

I scrunch my nose, unable to see the need to keep up the charade any longer, especially when it was done unintentionally.

"Don't pull cute faces at me," Wylder murmurs, a rasp to his voice that burns through my body as I meet his eyes.

"There's nothing cute—"

"I'll cut your tongue out if you say something mean about yourself," he interjects, steel in his words as his nostrils flare.

Wow.

Gulping, I shake my head, quickly retracting

whatever was about to part my lips. "I wasn't going to do that," I murmur feebly, and he rolls his eyes at me.

"Of course, you weren't."

His stare is unwavering, leaving me uncomfortable, so I take a step back, thankful when he drops his hold on me. Desperate to get on with the class and change the subject, I clear my throat and point at the ground. "Is it easier if I just lay down on the ground? I may as well get this over with quickly for you since I have no idea what I'm doing," I admit, and he frowns.

"No idea?" he clarifies, and I shake my head. His eyebrows somehow manage to pinch further as he takes a step toward me.

Without warning, he rears his arm back and swings it toward my face. My eyes pinch closed, bracing for impact, but I don't move, ready to face whatever he throws at me. It's only when a few moments pass that I realize nothing has touched me. I pry my eyes open to find a fist right in front of my face.

Why would he swing toward me but not hit me?

Anger vibrates from him, tainting the air between us as the rest of the class falls into the background. My lips part, ready to ask what's going on, but he beats me to it.

"Rule number one: closing your eyes isn't going to make the attack stop," he grunts, and I roll my eyes.

"Obviously," I mutter, looking down at my feet with embarrassment as he slowly lowers his hand.

"Rule number two: steeling yourself for the pain isn't the same as bracing yourself for an attack," he continues, and I peer through my lashes at him, nodding subtly as he proceeds. "Rule number three: I would never—*ever*—lay a hand on you."

"I didn't think—"

"The flinch says otherwise," he interjects again, and I sigh.

"In my defense, that's just instinct," I ramble, and he scoffs.

"Then I'll keep doing it until it's not instinct with me," he bites, and I feel my cheeks burn bright under his intense stare.

I can't bring myself to acknowledge his statement, so I clear my throat and try to return the topic back to the class. "So, am I making this easy for you or not?"

He grabs my shoulders with both hands, maneuvering me to the center of the square as he shakes his head.

"Hell no. I'm going to teach you everything you need to know."

28

POLARIS

"Let's try that again, but this time, you bring your elbow to here, just like that—yeah, just there. Your opponent will feel a lot more strength from you there." Wylder beams down at me, his eyes wide with encouragement.

His intense presence makes me feel…things. *A lot* of things.

Every time he redirects or maneuvers me into a new position, his body ends up draped all over mine—from head to toe—and the glassy look in his eyes tells me he knows exactly what he's doing.

Running my tongue over my bottom lip for what feels like the thousandth time, I nod in understanding as he stares down at me expectantly. At the same time, I'm also acutely aware that much of this information is unlikely to stick, given his proximity making it impossible to work on all cylinders.

The way the corner of his mouth twitches, just on the left side, makes me think he knows that too.

"Let's start wrapping things up, class; we have five minutes," the professor hollers, her voice like a razor through the tension thickening the air around me. It's like she pops a bubble I didn't realize I was in and the rest of the world comes back into focus.

I jolt, stepping out of Wylder's hold before I spin to face him.

"Play me through that sequence," he says encouragingly, and I gulp, frantically trying to piece it all together in my mind.

"I'm sure that's not necessary," I insist, glancing anywhere but at him. I'm startled by the number of people hitting the grass over and over again as they fight with more strength than I can fathom.

Dammit.

I'm not going to last more than five minutes. I shouldn't have lasted this long. I wouldn't have if Wylder hadn't taken it upon himself to try and help me. What a fat load of good that has done.

"Hey, focus on me, Polaris," he murmurs, his deep voice settling me as he cuts the little distance between us to grip my chin.

My breath is lodged in my throat as he uses his hold on my chin to make me nod in agreement.

The sound of someone clearing their throat breaks through our moment and I snap my gaze to the right to find Professor Drummond with her hands planted firmly on her hips.

"I can't declare a winner if neither of you hit the deck," she states, talking directly to Wylder as though I don't exist. I can read between the lines, though. She's encouraging him to drop me so she can call it. Rightfully so, I guess.

I attempt to step back, but Wylder locks his other hand around my wrist while his grip on my chin tightens, making it impossible. I frown at him, watching as his jaw tightens.

"Make the move, Polaris." The way his nostrils flare leaves no room for argument.

He's not going to quit it until I do; only now I have the added audience of Professor Drummond to make it even worse. I either get on with it or risk the audience growing even further.

Dammit, Wylder.

Flustered and desperate, I take a step back, only this time, he lets me go, aware that he has me under his control regardless. My shoulders rise and fall as I take a deep breath, silently going over the moves he's drilled into me for the past hour.

Any inkling of doubt or indecisiveness disappears when he takes two steps toward me, arms raised, ready to attack. He's moving quicker than before, exposing his purpose, and before I can come up with an excuse or slip to the side, I lift my hands, just as he taught me. My knees dip just an inch, giving into the motion as my left hand connects with his forearm, while my right hand presses against his neck, encouraged along by my right leg that crosses in front of me to wrap around the back of his leg.

Just as he promised, he topples over and hits the mat with a *thud*.

He grins up at me with wild eyes as I pant, disbelief coursing through my body as I stare down at him.

I did it.

I actually freaking did it.

"Impressive, Little Witch. Help me up," he says with a megawatt smile, and I tentatively offer him my hand. His palm is warm against mine, fueling the inferno that burns deep inside me as he uses me to haul himself back up. I don't offer anything but my hand, not even a tidbit of strength. I'm still gaping in awe. "You can declare it now, Professor," he adds, peering at Drummond, who is still assessing us.

She offers little more than a hum before she continues around the mats. When I turn my attention back to the dominating wolf that has consumed my morning, I find the smile on his face still burning bright.

"If anyone acknowledges that you took me down, I'll deny it," he states, his grin infectious as I nod, his palm still pressed against mine.

"Of course you will," I murmur a second before he yanks me close, pulling me into a half hug before he steps back and releases my hand.

"I just don't want a bad rep. Not when I have a fight this weekend," he adds, and my brows furrow in confusion.

"A fight?"

"Yeah, down at The Aurum," he explains, glancing around the open space, but when he turns back to me, he must notice the confusion on my face. "You've heard of the golden ring, right?"

My eyebrows rise, a slight wince crinkling the corners of my eyes as I shake my head. "Florentine, remember?"

"Right, shit, I forgot about that. Sorry."

"Don't apologize," I insist, but he doesn't acknowledge my words as he plants his hands on his hips, raking his eyes over me from head to toe three times before he settles on my face again.

"You're going to be there, right?"

"Be where?"

I can't focus on anything when he's looking at me like that.

"At the golden ring."

"Are we going to acknowledge the fact that I don't really have a clue what you're talking about?" I ask, and he rolls his eyes dramatically.

"What don't you know?"

The sound of Bryony's voice cuts through the air and I bristle. If either of them notice, none of them say a word.

"Perfect, your friend can be your chaperone," he explains, brushing a loose hair over my shoulder with a wink before he takes a step back and turns to Bryony. "I want Polaris at The Aurum, Friday night. I'm sure you know the drill." She nods, not questioning him further as the bell rings through the air, drawing an end to the class. "Excellent. Don't be late," he orders, wagging a finger at Bryony, who nods in understanding before he turns his attention back to me. "For all of my help today, maybe you could repay the favor and bring back the black hair for then too."

Without another word, he's gone, taking my fluttering heartbeat with him.

"What on Earth was that?" Bryony asks,

nudging her arm against mine, and I shake my head.

"Your guess is as good as mine."

Nerves ripple through me as I rock back on my heels, staring at the door before me like it's going to speak. I wonder if it could talk, what it would share.

I'm not the first to have a class on the other side of the threshold, I'm not the first to require knowledge on the sigil that binds my magic, and I certainly won't be the last. That being said, I still need to head in there and seek it. There's an invisible vice over me, holding me back from God only knows what, and if I want any chance of following through on my word to myself, then there's promise in those walls that is unattainable anywhere else.

The bell rings and students move around me, carrying on down the hallway or breaking away into the room in front of me.

Terence and Sian appear from my right, ignoring my presence as they slip into the room, and I somehow muster the strength to scurry in after them. There's no magic that washes over me as I step inside, no sudden epiphany, nothing. Just the view of a classroom, styled like all the rest, only this one has duck-egg-blue walls and beechwood furnishings outlining the space, but there are no desks or chairs. There's simply an aubergine-colored square rug in the center.

A dainty woman floats around the edges of the room, lighting candles and burning what looks like sage as she goes, while familiar students gather on the large rug, sitting cross-legged. I hover around the outskirts, everyone else from Florentine's with me.

Pressing my lips together, I peer to my left and see Sian standing with her head down, arms folded over her chest, and her gaze downcast. Terence is right beside her, and as the door clicks shut, B's absence is noticeable.

I consider keeping my mouth shut, but apparently, that's impossible as I take a small step toward my old…friend? Acquaintance?

"Go away, P," Sian mutters without lifting her head, and my nostrils flare, irritation itching under my skin.

"It's Polaris," I snap, the snarl to my tone making her gaze dart to mine, even with her head still tilted down. "Have you seen Benjamin?" I ask, getting straight to the point of why I was inching toward her to begin with.

"Why would I have seen him?" she grunts, frowning at me.

"He's your boyfriend, and I haven't seen him on campus since—"

"Boyfriend? He's not her boyfriend. Not anymore. Isn't that right, Sian?" Terence interjects, wrapping his arms around her as he steps up behind her.

It's intimate.

The way she stands tall at his closeness, the way he strokes his thumb over her stomach, resting his chin on her shoulder. She doesn't seem to lean into him, yet there's an air to her that pulls strength from him.

"Boyfriend or not, one of our friends hasn't been seen since he was announced as a human."

"That's really not our problem, P," Terence states, a slight grin on his mouth that I want to punch right off. Maybe I should have insisted Wylder teach me that instead. "We're vampires; well, Sian and I are, not you. You're lucky we're even talking to you, but a human?" He scoffs like the word is rancid on his tongue. "A human is none of our concern."

I snicker, no humor to the sound, as I glare at the asshole I wasted so much time kissing. Does it even count as kissing? Not in comparison to the little experience I've gained since being here, that's for sure.

"Are you forgetting that we were all at Florentine's being treated as humans, believing we were humans?" I grumble, and he rolls his eyes at me like my words are beneath him. "But don't you worry yourself over it, *T*," I grind out, forcing myself to take a step backward and outwardly using the initial to address him. "I'm sure there will come a time when it's *you* asking for help, and I'm going to take great pleasure in telling you to fuck off."

My cheeks warm with rage instead of the usual embarrassment as Sian gapes at me while Terence shakes his head in amusement. It's on the tip of my tongue to call him a cunt, since he fits Bryony's description so well, but the professor speaks, interrupting the foot-stomping tantrum that was about to unravel.

"Good afternoon, class. For those who are new, please take a seat. My name is Professor Sommers. My specialty is sigils—not only the ones holding you captive, but all sigils." She waves her hand toward the rug, encouraging everyone to take a seat. I find the closest inch of carpet and sit cross-legged, unsurprised when Sian and Terence opt to sit as far away from me as possible. "Now, let us swiftly make our way around the room. Each person, both new and old, please state your name and the item you believe to be binding your sigil," she commands gently, continuing to float around the room. Her worn denim overalls hang off one shoulder, rolled up over her ankles as she takes each step barefoot.

She points toward a girl a few spots away from me, who clears her throat. As she tilts her head to the side, I recognize her profile immediately. She must have left Florentine's the year before we did, which would make her twenty-one already.

I gulp, panic clawing at my chest.

Twenty-one and still bound by her sigil, yet still alive? Does she know who her blood kin is? How is she surviving right now?

"I'm Beth-Ann, and my anklet holds my sigil." She points at her ankle but doesn't lift her jeans to reveal the item mentioned.

The circle continues, quickly shifting to the newest arrivals, each listing their new-found names, and I quickly learn that D and H, the other witches from Florentine's, are indeed Danica and Helena. The former's sigil is a ring on her pinky finger, while the latter has a pair of earrings that are locked in place.

"My name is Sian, and my sigil is my pendant," she explains, tapping at her chest with a familiar heaviness.

Terence clears his throat and I opt to look anywhere but at him. “My name is Terence, I’m a vampire, and this damn bracelet is restricting my powers,” he grunts, lifting his hand to reveal a golden chain encasing his wrist.

All eyes turn my way as I glare at Terence and his insistence on stating what supernatural he is. I rub my lips together nervously for a second before I find my voice. “My name is Polaris, and my sigil is these bangles,” I state, lifting my hands just enough for the sleeves to roll down, revealing them both.

I want their presence to feel real in the room. I want the professor to feel their weight around my wrists. I want to hear the words from my lips. I want to be proud of them, but more than that, I want to be rid of them. Losing them from my wrists doesn’t mean I have to lose them altogether. They’re a representation of my past, and when all is said and done, I will keep them as a reminder of what I’ve faced.

Dropping my hands, my fingers twitch, and I give in to the urge to slip my hand into my pocket, feeling my coin. I take a deep breath, a real one. One that leaves me grounded and focused.

“Today is about understanding why your sigils were put in place,” Professor Sommers explains, finally rounding to a stop as she sits on the open window sill, legs crossed like the rest of us. "These sigils were placed on you to stop your abilities, making it easier to control you. To do so, they must use a piece of your past to impact your future. It is your job to unravel your past to unlock your future."

That sounds far easier said than done.

"The root of all of this, as with everything here, comes down to one thing and one thing only: the blood kin curse. A curse I'm sure you know little about."

I frown, her words hanging in the air.

"Of course we know about the blood kin curse. We're living with it," Danica grumbles, speaking my thoughts, and the soft, polite smile that Professor Sommers offers her is the kind of look I imagine you would give to a child who dropped their ice cream on the floor.

Pitiful.

"Think about it. Think about what you know other than the fact you're living with it. I'll give you a moment." Surprisingly, despite her words, her tone isn't as condescending as I expected, and instead of taking offense, I take her advice.

I think.

I think, and I think, and I think.

And…she's right.

Florentine's didn't teach us about the blood kin curse. They merely taught us to fear it. Rightfully so, I guess. Fearing it is the right action, but other than summarizing that fact, we know little else.

"I'm going to take your silence as an acknowledgment that there's more for you to know. Would you agree?" Sommers asks, and I nod, even though I wasn't the one to speak out to begin with. I'm not the only one, though. Almost everyone nods. All of us who are new, it seems. "The blood kin curse began almost four hundred years ago. The story goes that a witch who fell in love with a vampire, a wolf, and a human was left heartbroken when the quadrants denied their love among supernaturals. That love, uniting all, was tainted by the prejudice of others. She was so heartbroken when the war broke out, killing her men, that she tainted their ancestral lines for all of eternity. Witches included, because no quadrant offered her a sliver of grace. None but a few humans, but by the time she learned of this, it was too late."

I gape at her, as do the others, hanging on her every word as we learn where all of this began. It doesn't feel fair to be tangled in a blood curse because of someone else's views. Just because I have a blood connection to those who hurt her, whoever she actually was, doesn't mean I would have the same views as them…does it?

To love multiple men and have them love you back…what must that be like?

My cheeks heat as my heart races faster.

"How has a cure not been found after so many years?" Helena asks, and I hum in agreement, confused about how we're still here after so long.

Professor Sommers sighs like she feels the same confusion we do. "There is a whole faculty of witches, humans, vampires, and wolves dedicated to finding an answer. Why one hasn't been found yet is unknown, and all we can hope for is the answer to reveal itself one day soon. Until then, we have to figure out what part of your past you must recall to unlock the sigil from your body."

29

POLARIS

Days have passed since my first sigil class, but the bangles that render me powerless remain firmly in place. Sitting at the witches' table in the dining hall, the plush velvet cushioned seat beneath me, I will them to disappear from existence, yet the desire only seems to make them feel tighter against my flesh.

Crossing my hands, I run my fingertips across each one as my eyelids close. I take a moment to focus on my breathing as I rack my brain, desperate to remember something from my past that will help lead me to my future. But nothing jumps to the forefront of my mind, and when I pry my eyes back open again, the bangles haven't loosened an inch.

I sigh, sagging back in my seat with defeat as the

world around me continues while I internally combust.

"What's the matter, trash? Sad you're not a vampire?"

A shiver runs down my spine at the sound of the deep, booming voice. His presence oozes around me, making it impossible to escape.

I don't want to look, and I know I shouldn't, but even as I think those words, my gaze tilts to his as he leans against the dining table beside me. The sneer curling his lip is filled with venom as his eyes narrow, watching his words poison the space between us.

"Go away, Blaze," I mumble, instantly missing Bryony's presence today. She's been keeping her distance since I've barely said a word to her, but I can't deny the fact that I miss having her around in times like this. But if she were here now, all I would do is try and hide behind her, and that's not what I need. What I must do is learn to survive on my own and acknowledge that doesn't always entail hiding away or plastering myself against the wall to make myself invisible.

Trouble seems to be looking for me, and whether I like it or not, I need to start addressing things head-on. Or try, at least. Without getting myself killed. That's the most important part.

"Ah, so you have heard of me and my legacy," he states, folding his arms over his chest with an air and regalness that I've never witnessed before.

What the fuck? His legacy? This guy thinks way too highly of himself.

I try to sink my teeth into my tongue to keep my mouth shut, but it seems once I decide to stand my ground, there's no turning back. "If that's what you're calling it." I look away, acutely aware of my cheeks heating under his intense stare, but the longer I look at him, the more they threaten to heat for another reason.

It's not fair that someone so mean can simultaneously be so handsome. Imagine if his looks were tainted every time he was cruel. What would he look like then? I get the feeling he'd be unrecognizable.

"Look at me when I'm talking to you," he snaps, and before I can turn to glare at him, his fingers clench around my jaw, forcing my eyes to meet his.

I can practically feel his fingerprints burning into my skin as his eyes bore into mine. The piercing blue pools darken to an almost navy as his jaw ticks. I want to scream and cry and run for my life, but it's impossible with the hold he has on me.

Choking in a breath, I keep my gaze fixed on him as I speak. "Remove your hand from my face." The words are slow, precise, and stronger than I feel, but he doesn't relax his hold. All I see is his jaw clench tighter and his eyes ignite as he swipes his bottom lip along his teeth, making me gulp.

Maybe standing my ground was not the right thing to do.

Gulping, my skin tingles with panic, but I manage to keep my stare aimed at him until a voice booms from behind me.

"You can leave her alone now."

Tatum.

I'd know that voice anywhere after our night in the forest. I haven't really spoken to him since, but we've smiled in passing, each one reminding me of the moment we shared, the pain we unraveled.

"Ah, Tatum, I should have known two sad souls would find each other," Blaze says with a grunt, his amusement diabolical as my pulse thunders in my ears.

"I still don't see you leaving," Tatum states, not reacting to his statement, and to my surprise, Blaze releases his hold on my chin, dropping his hand to his side as he stands from the table.

The amusement that tainted his words lingers in

his eyes as he stares me down for a beat. "Catch you soon, P." He pops the *P* like his life depends on it and I cringe, a shiver running down my spine as he saunters off without a backward glance.

It's only when Tatum drops down into the chair beside me that I release a breath, only to inhale another as I take him in.

How have I gone from being consumed by one man to another in a completely different way? His long brown hair is braided back off his face before being secured in a bun today, and his brown eyes are wide, swirling with concern that I know is aimed my way, and I…like it.

I'm not saying he cares, but it almost feels like he might, and it's a foreign experience. I like it nonetheless.

"Are you okay?"

Clearing my throat, I settle my eyes on his. "You didn't have to do that, but thank you," I breathe, feeling the smile take over my features as he offers me one in return.

"No problem. That's what friends are for, right?" he states, tapping his fingers on the dining table as he assesses me.

"Is that what we are?" I ask, my breaths evening out with every pass as I find myself lost in his orbit.

He shrugs, his smile turning wry. "We're two sad souls; it's as if we *have* to be friends."

I snicker, dropping my gaze to my lap. "Yeah, two sad souls on an express train to an untimely death. How fitting," I muse, and he nods in agreement.

"Will I see you tonight?" he asks, lightening the conversation as I frown at him.

"Tonight?"

"At the fight," he explains, and I feel my cheeks heat instantly.

"Oh, Wylder invited me to that the other day, but..." My words trail off as he sits, patiently waiting for me to explain without pushing me for answers. It's refreshing to have someone wait for me to be ready. Clearing my throat, I try again. "Wylder invited me to watch him fight. I forget the name of the place, but he asked Bryony to take me, and she is my friend, or was, I guess. The one..."

"The member of the coven who made you sad," he finishes, finding the words I can't, and I've never been more thankful.

"Yeah," I say with a nod, my gaze turning glossy as I look at him.

He stares right back at me, rubbing his lips together as he thinks. "Can I give you some advice?"

"Sure," I murmur, unsure what he could possibly have to say.

"If I've learned anything, it's that deciding what is important to you is one of the rare freedoms we get in this life. What you have to ask yourself in regards to your friend, and anyone else for that matter, is, did she violate those morals, or was she a bystander? From there, you must decide if her being a bystander is just as disappointing as being the instigator. Plus, did she know your boundaries before she broke them? Once you've figured that part out, you can decide how hard you want to punish her and yourself for it, but don't stay hung up; that's not worth your time."

"That's a lot of words. I feel like they only complicate it more," I admit, my mind swirling, and he winks like he hasn't left me in internal turmoil.

"I'd say you're welcome, but we both know you're not thankful. That's generally the case when someone pushes you to think harder about a situation when all you want to do is bury your head in the sand," he states, the grin on his lips comforting before he glances at the table in front of me. "Now, are you finishing that?" he asks, pointing to the remainder of my lunch.

"No." There's no way I can eat now with all these questions floating around in my mind.

He takes the sandwich without another word, biting at the corner I had taken a nibble from as he rises from his seat. After a quick salute with the sandwich in hand, he smirks. "See you tonight, Polaris."

I gape at him in surprise. "I might not know how to get there," I state, and he gives me a pointed look as he steps back from the table.

"We both know you will," he says, a lot more confidently than I feel, before turning to leave me with my thoughts and an empty plate.

I LIFT MY HAND, panic, drop it to my side, and sigh. A set of motions I repeat three more times before I finally get a hold of myself and complete the final step: knocking. The noise thuds around me and I instantly regret it, stepping back in the hope of getting the hell out of here before the door opens, but it's too late.

A whoosh of air follows the click of a latch before the person on the other side appears.

"Hey," Bryony murmurs, linking her hands nervously in front of her as I blink, quickly remembering what I'm here for.

Clearing my throat, I stand tall, trying not to

rock back on my heels as I speak. "I don't like people trying to force me to do something… anything," I reiterate, and she nods.

"Okay?"

"I don't like people watching me suffer and doing nothing to help," I add, guilt clouding her eyes as she nods again.

"Understandable."

"And I don't like having to second guess someone's motives," I explain, and she offers me a tight smile.

"Agreed."

The silence stretches between us for a moment as I internally pat myself on the back for getting that off my chest. I also say a silent thank you to Tatum for giving me some important things to think about before I realize the hushed air between us is growing awkward because I'm stuck in my head.

"Those are my boundaries," I clarify, my fingers twitching at my sides as I fight the desire to stuff my hand in my pocket and grab my coin to feel grounded.

"Those are some pretty strong and understandable boundaries if you ask me," she replies, brushing her hair over her shoulder.

"They are in place for everyone," I confirm, and a sad twinge nips at her mouth.

"And I broke them."

"You did," I answer honestly with a nod, and her head dips in defeat.

"I'm sorry."

Has someone ever really apologized to me before? At Florentine's, they didn't care. You would follow their rules whether you like it or not, and the other students ignored me for the most part. Sian would be…Sian, and Terence…an ass, but an apology was never offered.

Was that because we didn't recall what an apology entailed? Or is remorse not something we're familiar with?

As products of our surroundings, were apologies hard to come by?

Maybe.

"There are no second chances after this. I might not have long left on this Earth with the blood kin curse in full force, and I don't want to waste my time having to deal with unnecessary cunts," I state, and she barks a laugh, shaking her head as humor dances in her eyes.

"I shouldn't have taught you that word," she mutters, making my cheeks burn as I try to hide my smile.

"You really shouldn't have," I admit, and she

stands taller, unlocking her fingers as she pushes her door open wider.

"So we're good?"

"As long as you respect my morals, then yeah."

"Good, because we need to leave for the fight soon," she says with a wide grin as she grabs my arm and tugs me inside.

"Wait," I call out as the door closes behind me, and she stares at me in confusion. "Do you have boundaries?" I ask, needing to make sure I show her the same respect.

Her frown crinkles between her eyebrows as she shrugs. "I don't know. Maybe? I haven't lived your life, Polaris. I don't know what I hate or don't, but if I figure any out, I'll let you know, okay?"

"Okay," I agree, and she's back to tugging me farther into her room.

I'm surprised to find that the layout is exactly the same as mine. I wondered if Florentine students received different treatment, but it seems that's not the case here. Her walls are a pastel pink, a floral bedspread matching the vibe, but she cuts past all of that to tug me toward the armoire, which is already open.

"So, let's pick out something cute since there's a wolf or two interested in my silver-haired bestie, yeah?" she asks, all but bouncing on the balls of her feet with excitement, and I pause, turning to face her head on.

"Uh, about that. How much time do we have?" I ask, running my fingers through the ends of my hair, and her smile turns cosmic as she excitedly releases a giggle.

"For you, all the time in the world."

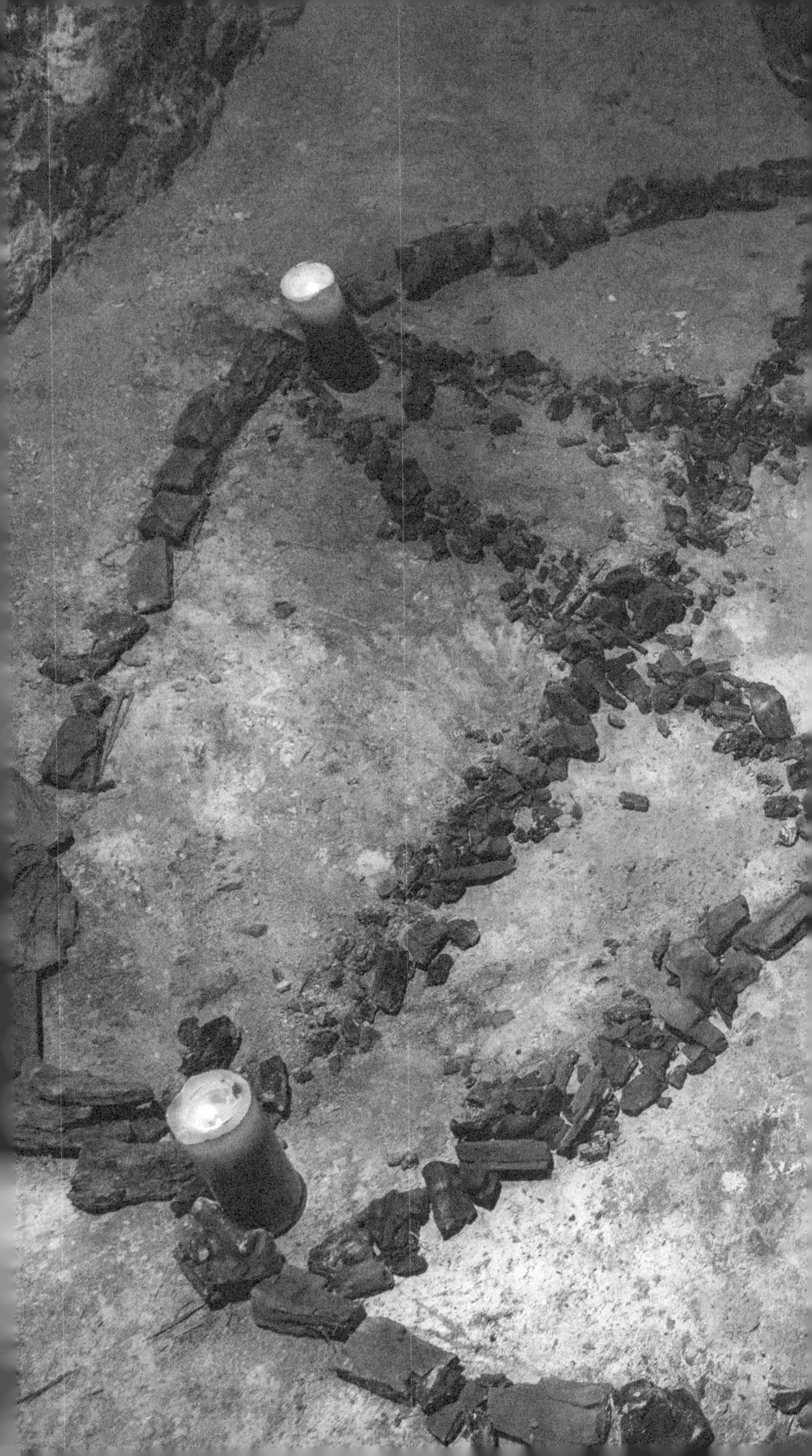

30

WYLDER

"Wylder, I don't recommend fighting without the tape."

I roll my eyes at the referee beside me.

I don't recommend needing a referee, but I keep my mouth shut. I'd much rather fight until someone passes out. Preferably not me. It's never been me, and I'm not concerned now.

The tape isn't going to make a difference. I like the bite of pain while it lasts, but as a wolf, it doesn't take long for me to heal once the fighting is done. The sting inflicted with every punch I throw fuels the adrenaline coursing through my veins. It's an electric life force, one that makes me feel alive yet grounds me all at once.

The ref clearly doesn't understand that. I don't mind; nobody seems to. Lincoln, Tatum, and Asher all nod eagerly along with Ref Collins's recommendations, but they don't fight, not like me. They don't understand that this is what I live for; it's what I breathe for. But it doesn't matter if they get it or not. They don't have to. They just have to let me be me.

"Anything else, Collins?" I ask when he doesn't take my silence as an answer, and he sighs, pinching the bridge of his nose with his ring-covered fingers.

"You're going to be the death of me, Son," he mutters, shaking his head and making his gray hair ruffle with the movement.

"As long as it's the death of you and not me, I'm good. And I'm not your son," I grunt, slapping my hand on his shoulder more harshly than necessary, but he doesn't grimace. He's built as broad and strong as me, but he likes to follow the rules while I…skirt them at best.

"One of these days, Wylder—"

"I'm going to regret the decisions I make. Yada, yada, yada. I get it, Collins. You can tell me you told me so over my dead body. Damn, you can etch it into my headstone if you want. But for now, do me a favor and fuck off. I'm trying to prep."

Thankfully, he takes the hint, stomping toward the locker room door without pause, but I don't miss the muttering under his breath as he goes.

Something about me being a godforsaken wolf with no damn brain cells, but I let it go over my head as I focus all of my attention on being ready for the real opponent I face tonight.

Dominic Turner.

He's been making a name for himself, that's for sure.

Not in my ring, though.

No, not in The Aurum.

Everywhere but my territory.

It's time I brought his reign to an end.

My distaste for him grows stronger with the knowledge that he's a vampire, but none of that matters when we step inside the ring. With our magic restricted, we're just two men relying on our strength and power to reach victory.

The locker room door swings open, the whoosh of air coating my skin as I turn to find Minnie.

"Are you ready? Your song is starting."

I roll my eyes again. I've told them a million times I don't want a damn song playing as I make my way to the ring, but the organizers insist on running this place like the humans do. The only humans in sight are those tainted by the blood kin curse; otherwise, they have no knowledge of our existence. I've heard of underground fighting in the human world; this is even deeper than that. Known only by the supernaturals invited.

"What the hell are you wearing?" Lincoln grunts, launching to his feet with his finger aimed in her direction.

I knew he was going to say something the second I laid eyes on her, and any other time, I would find it amusing. Right now, though, I don't have time for it.

"She's wearing a dress, Linc. It's short, but you've definitely seen shorter. Now back off and leave her alone," I grumble, earning a deathly glare from my friend, who swiftly turns his attention to Asher and Tatum sitting on the benches to my left.

"Help me out, guys," he grumbles, waving a hand blindly at his sister, but they both shrug, aware he's looming his overbearing tendencies over her again. "Whatever," he snaps, turning back to Minnie. "Don't think I'm letting you out of my sight dressed like that," he warns, and she scoffs, shaking her head dismissively.

"Please, you're going to get out there, catch some eye candy, and leave me in the dust," she states, her words facts. This man is always the same. She glances over his shoulder, meeting my stare, and her eyes glisten with a silent message that I instantly understand.

She's here.

What did he call her?

Midnight.

Damn.

I didn't realize how much I wanted her to show up until now, and my dick definitely likes it, but I can't be distracted. Not by rule sticklers like Collins, not by my brother getting unnecessarily protective, and definitely not by pussy. Even if it is virginal.

"Let's go," I order, sensing Asher and Tatum rising from their seats, and the five of us head for the door.

With my family around me, I storm through the short corridor, the bass of the music vibrating the ground as I step out into the walkway. The crowd is packed tight, but they're all a blur. My sights are set on the man already in the ring.

He cracks his neck from side to side, running his tongue over his teeth as he watches me approach. He lifts his hand, rubbing his jaw, and I see the tape firmly wrapped around his knuckles. A grin splits my face, but there's nothing nice about it. It's all menacing, just like my thoughts as I consider every way I can break this man in two.

I round to a stop at the foot of the steps, feeling a pat on the back from each of my three brothers before Minnie squeezes my shoulder. It's almost a ritual at this stage before they disperse into the crowd, leaving me to take the final steps to my damnation alone.

I plant my foot on the first step, and that's when I catch a flash of bright blue eyes, made only brighter by the darkness of her locks.

Fuck.

She's here.

Knowing it and seeing it for myself are two very different things. My muscles bunch and excitement gets the better of me, but I keep the vision of her in the corner of my eye instead of turning to give her my full attention.

She'll be my prize when I win. For now, I just have to make sure I put on a good show for her. She did dye her hair, after all. Maybe she deserves a prize of her own.

Quickly pushing the rest of that thought to the back of my mind, I climb the remaining steps, relishing in the cheers I finally allow past my senses.

She's not the only one who deserves a show. People come here to see me fight, and that's precisely what I'm going to give them.

The second I slip between the ropes, two guards approach and I hold my left arm out, ready. The bite of magic linked to the chain that cuts into my flesh sends my adrenaline haywire and I smirk in amusement as I spy my opponent hiss at the contact.

"I'm going to bring you down, Wylder. You're going to wish you never invited me here," Dom snarls, baring his teeth as I feel the blocker solidify between my magic and me.

"That's Mr. Aires to you, dick face. Only those who beat me get to call me Wylder," I grunt, and he scoffs.

"No one calls you Wylder inside the ring," one of the guards states, and I smirk.

"Precisely."

I settle my stare on my opponent, watching his every move. From the way he rolls his shoulders back to the half-step he makes with his right foot every time he sways from side to side. Taking him down is going to be easy, *too* easy, and with my prize waiting in the audience, I'm ready to wrap this up as quickly as possible.

"You both know the rules," Collins states, appearing between us with his hands raised like I can't play nice and might charge my opponent at any moment. "No death, no magic, no ignorance." What he really means is no ignoring him if he makes a call. I nod like always and Dominic follows suit. "Fight fair, fight clean, and don't get blood on my shirt," he adds with a smirk before the bell rings.

He steps back, creating a clear path between me and my target.

He's instantly bouncing on the balls of his feet. I heard he likes to try and tire his opponent out, but I'm not falling for that shit. I remain stoic, frozen in the center as he dances his adorable little fucking two-step around me. I don't move when he moves to my side, reaching my back, and it must confuse the fuck out of him because it takes him a whole two seconds to swing his fists in my direction.

I let the first hit fall. Nothing fuels me like the swift greeting of someone's knuckles against my flesh. Tingles run down my spine, the heat from the contact blossoming, and just as I hoped, he takes the victory of his first hit to come at me harder. Except the second punch doesn't connect as I spin, catching his wrist in the next breath.

Wide eyes collide with mine as I turn to face him, yanking him closer with my left hand as I swing with my right. The crush of my bare knuckles against his face earns a holler through the crowd and I grin at the crunch that erupts beneath the force of my blow.

I release his wrist, letting him cup the damaged area as blood drips down his chin.

"What the fuck?" he spits, glaring at me, and I

shrug, my grin growing wider as the crowd goes feral.

He clearly hasn't done any research on me; I've pulled this shit before. Too many times, really, but a man's ego is nothing to be messed with. It gets them every time.

Wiping the back of his hand across his face, he lifts his fists, finding the rhythm in his feet again. I regret not hitting him with my favorite double tap, so this would be over with already. But delayed gratification comes in many forms, and this is one of them.

He aims his fists in my direction, punching forward once, twice, three times with no luck before he starts swirling around me again. Unfortunately for him, I follow him this time, a fact that makes his nostrils flare as he stumbles over the little half-step he's been doing since he entered the ring.

I could do this all night, until I catch another glimpse of baby blues and jet-black locks over his shoulder. She doesn't know the influence she has on me. I sure as fuck don't either. I don't usually chase witches; I know my place as a wolf. Maybe I would venture at a full moon party, but not like this. Not outside of the night air and not as intensely as this.

I miss the trigger that warns me he's going to

swing and Dominic's fist collides with the side of my head.

Fuck. That.

The stained red hue falls over my eyes, like an infrared beacon in the night, honing in on one thing and one thing only…Dominic's face.

My muscles coil tight, the heat from his punch vibrating through my entire body as I swing with my right hand, making his defenses drop before I throw an uppercut with my left. I connect; the snap of his jaw slamming together is a euphoric sound in my ears, but nothing beats the way his eyes roll back, accompanying his fall.

He lands with a *thud* and Collins is standing over him instantly, hand raised in my direction to keep me back, but I know I'm done here. My pulse thrums in my ears, making it hard for the cheers to echo in my mind, but I hear them enough to feel the buzz it offers.

The crimson tint to my vision isn't gone, though.

No.

Now, it's directed elsewhere. I move an inch to the left, spying my new target immediately.

Someone grabs my wrist, lifting my hand in the air in victory, and the roars around the room turn insane, but I have no interest in basking in it. I'm over the rope and stomping through the crowd before they've even finished announcing my name.

Her eyes latch onto mine, wide with surprise as her jaw hangs loose.

Hot.

Hands pat at my arms and shoulders, murmurs of congratulations ring in the air, but none of it matters. I'm locked in, taking the stairs deeper into the crowd two at a time until I'm at her row. Thankfully, it's her friend in the end seat, and she's right beside her.

I consider holding my hand out, relishing the delight of feeling her skin against mine, but I'm not in the mood to take no for an answer right now. Especially when I know Lincoln is likely watching me. Especially when he will recognize her and want to claim her for himself.

Not tonight.

She's mine.

Wrapping my hand around her wrist, I tug her toward me, my free hand latching onto her waist as her chest lands against mine. She looks up at me through her lashes, her shoulders rising and falling with every breath, and it's intoxicating.

I take a step back and she instinctively takes one toward me.

Perfect.

Slipping my hand from her wrist to her palm, I lace our fingers, tugging her behind me as I move with purpose back down the stairs. Her digits are stiff in my grasp, but when I squeeze tighter, she relaxes or relents; either way, she curls her little fingers between mine and I move faster.

Lincoln appears in my periphery, but it's not me he's looking at, it's her, and there's no way in hell he's getting between me and my prize right now. I don't even care that the magic binder is still around my wrist. I just need to move.

Exiting the open space, the noise quiets as I drag her a step behind me down the small corridor before thrusting the locker room door open. It ricochets off the wall, barreling back toward me quicker than I expect, but we manage to slip inside before it closes. The second it shuts, I turn the latch, desperate for the privacy as my attention finally circles back to the woman before me.

Her teeth worry at her bottom lip as she rakes her eyes over me, chest heaving in time with mine as she struggles to catch up with what's happening.

Releasing her hand, I lift my fingers to the tips of her hair. "You went with the black," I breathe, and she nods, her eyes finding mine.

"That was…some fight," she states, a tremble running through her, and I grin.

“Yeah. Some might say it’s brutal, but I say it’s fucking glorious,” I rasp, taking a step toward her, but this time, she takes a step back.

She’s not scared. I would sense it if she were.

No.

It’s something else. I just don’t know what. I’m more than happy to put the work in to find out, though.

“What is it, Little Witch?” I whisper, and she shakes her head, continuing to retreat as I prowl toward her until her back presses against the cool stone wall.

She gasps, pupils blown as she blinks at me.

“Wylder.”

Fuck.

My name on her tongue is a sin.

I infiltrate her space until we’re chest to chest again, our breaths mingling between us as we drown in one another.

“I’ve got you, Polaris,” I murmur, watching her brows gather in confusion.

“Got me how?”

“Lincoln doesn’t do virgins, but I can help with that.”

31

POLARIS

"You want to…take my virginity so…your friend will fuck me too?" I rasp, blinking up at him in confusion.

I have no idea what's going on, but I'm caught under his spell, making it impossible to tear myself away even as he says something as crazy as that.

He rakes his teeth over his bottom lip, looking down at me with desire burning bright in his eyes. If he comes any closer, our lips will collide; they're only an inch away, and I can't deny how much I want to feel him press them against mine.

Watching him fight? Hot damn.

Watching him prowl through the crowd? Even *hotter* damn.

Watching him stomp away from his cheering audience with me in tow…scorching.

I was mesmerized watching him dominate in the ring so effortlessly. Hearing people cheer his name made my thighs clench, and seeing the sheer force behind his punches left me speechless. In combat class the other day, he could have snapped me in half and tossed me in the trash without a single stutter to his breath, yet he let me drop him to the floor in front of the professor. He *taught* me instead of treating me to the same outcome as his opponent.

Silently, I thank whoever is watching over me that he believes in teaching skills instead of demonstrating them. There's power in showing someone instead of raining dominance down upon them. Especially since I'm a powerless witch and he's…all wolf.

"I bet you make the prettiest circle with your lips when your whimpers fall from your mouth," he muses, pulling me from my thoughts. The blush on my cheeks grows more intense, burning like crazy as my blood pressure rises, leaving my entire body thrumming with every beat of my heart. "It's that blush, Little Witch. It makes you glow. I wonder if it would creep down your neck if I explore," he rasps, making me gulp as I remain still, with my back plastered against the wall and my palms flat against his chest.

He leans in closer, his lips ghosting over mine as he speaks. "I bet you taste sweet here too," he states, shifting his hands at my waist to press his thumbs against the apex of my thighs, and I gasp, the sound throatier than any noise I've ever made before. "Fuck, Little Witch. I know I'm right, but what I want to know is, has anyone ever found out?"

My eyelids fall closed as I dip my chin and shake my head. I'm not scared to tell him the truth; I'm just embarrassed at…I don't know. I never cared about my lack of experience until I got here. At Florentine's, I really didn't care. There was no way in hell I was letting somebody touch me out in the open with the professors watching. But here… there's privacy at every turn, opportunities to explore, and…men. Real men.

"Don't hide now, Polaris. Not unless you want this to stop," he mumbles against my cheek as he lifts one hand from my waist to tilt my chin up.

I sink my teeth into my bottom lip, nerves getting the better of me as I war with myself. I don't want it to stop, but I can't bring myself to open my eyes.

"Look at me." His command is soft, and before I can second guess myself, I pry my eyes open to find his swirling with a feral heat that only grows stronger by the second. "That's it. Good girl. Now, tell me which lips you think I should taste first."

His question hangs in the air like a guillotine, threatening to glide through me with unwavering strength as my cheeks burn brighter than ever.

Before I can summon an answer, he falls to his knees at my feet, letting my hands drop to my sides as he runs his fingers over my bare thighs, looking up at me through his lashes. "And you wore a skirt. Is it just for me, Little Witch, or was it for someone else?"

I'm too focused on the goosebumps rising at his touch as he inches his fingertips under the hem of the skirt I borrowed from Bryony. My jaw moves as I try to talk, but it takes a few attempts before the soft words slip off my tongue.

"I wore it for me."

A sinister grin spreads across his lips, his pupils blowing so wide I can barely tell the outline anymore.

"I like that answer. It suits you, Little Witch."

I want to put a stop to this new nickname he keeps using, but there's something about it that makes a burning sensation ripple in my chest.

"Now, give me confirmation, Polaris. I want a signal before I snap. Let me know if you want this, and I'll make it happen, but don't keep me waiting. I've waited long enough knowing you were watching me in the ring. You were a distraction out there, but in here, you're my prize. You just have to say yes."

My breath catches in my throat, my pulse pounding in my ears as I stare down at him.

I couldn't stop us now, even if I wanted to. I'm too far gone.

Tentatively, I reach out to run my fingers over his cropped hair, needing to feel the texture against my skin. He tilts his head back, leaning into my touch. My fingertips eventually stroke down the side of his face, cupping his chin.

I run my thumb across his bottom lip, with no real clue of what I'm doing, but the intensity in his stare tells me he likes it. "I've kissed people before, but I want the first time your lips are really on me to be…" My cheeks are nuclear now as the word falls short on my tongue.

"Say it, Little Witch. Say it, and I'll make it happen."

"Taste me."

"Taste you where?" he pushes, bunching up the skirt at my waist as he runs the pad of his finger over the lace of my panties.

Holy crap.

My eyes roll to the back of my head, a shudder rippling through my body as I whimper.

"Taste you where, Polaris?" he repeats, his breath warm against my core despite the fabric between us.

My hands retreat from his body, splaying flat against the wall beside me for purchase as the need and desire blossoming inside of me take control. Prying my eyes open, I settle my stare on him.

"My pussy," I manage, the words snapped up by the whoosh of air that parts his lips as he eliminates the remaining distance.

My panties dampen at the thick pad of his tongue as he rakes his teeth over my flesh, and I think I'm going to combust. He repeats the motion three times before I feel a tightness at my side, and the sound of tearing fabric rips through the air.

The lace separating us flutters to the floor, taking my innocence with it as he hooks my left leg over his shoulder and repeats the motion of his tongue against my pussy with nothing between us.

I tremble, the heat burning between us almost unbearable as he laps at my clit, making the tight nub tingle as my thighs clench, desperate for more.

With his lips still pressed against my exposed skin, he looks up at me with hooded eyes. "Have you ever…" His words trail off, his fingers taking ownership of the rest of his sentence as he teases the entrance to my core. I shake my head, watching as his eyes roll to the back of his head this time. "I think you might kill me, Little Witch. All these firsts, it's addicting," he breathes, his finger still swirling. "Eyes on me, don't look away," he orders before running his tongue over the seam of my pussy while he slowly sinks a finger inside me.

My mouth falls slack, my body on fire from head to toe as I clench around his singular digit. I can't breathe. I'm scared if I do, I'll shatter, but the sparkle in his eyes tells me that's exactly what he wants to happen.

"I'm going to make you come now, Polaris. Another first just for me, and your reward will be the euphoria that it gives you. Enjoy it, but don't worry too much; something tells me it's going to be the first of many."

I gulp, trying to keep myself stable, but my hands have nothing to grip onto, leaving me to put all of my trust in him.

He doesn't wait for me to speak this time. I'm sure my face says it all. He sucks my clit into his mouth in the next breath, retreating his finger from my core before thrusting it back in, swirling for good measure as he roots himself deep inside me.

Panting for breath, I can't stop the soft

whimpers tumbling from my lips as he elicits feelings inside me I've never even come close to feeling before. Just when I think I can't take it anymore, he presses an extra finger at my entrance, stretching me wider, at the same time he drags his teeth over my clit.

It's too much.

It's everything.

My breath.

My heartbeat.

My pulse.

All of it.

All of me.

I detonate inside, shaking as a cry pries my lips apart, and my hips jerk, riding his swirling fingers as my body spasms with the euphoria he promised.

Time passes in slow motion, the world shattering into a thousand pieces in his hazel eyes before they slowly reform, the colors new…brighter, deeper, more profound.

Only when the feelings subside inside of me does he retreat from my body, and I immediately feel the loss, another whimper tumbling from my mouth as he falls back on his ass, eyes still fixed on me.

Holy crap.

"Little Witch," he rasps, shaking his head in

disbelief, and I follow the movement with my own head, wholly enraptured by him.

I need to do something, anything, to have more of him. Before I can change my mind, I sink to my knees, peering at him with hungry eyes. "I can…" My gaze falls to the outline of his cock I can see through his shorts, and he scoffs.

"No, you fucking can't."

My body stiffens with embarrassment as I try to return to my feet, but his fingers wrap around my wrist before I get anywhere.

"It's bad enough your first climax is in a place like this, Polaris. You're not dirtying your knees in here. Next time, though. There will be no question. Besides, my adrenaline won't be fueling me, and it will be…better," he explains, making me gulp as I fixate on one part.

"Next time?"

"Yeah, next time." He rises to his feet, bringing me along with him, when a knock comes from the locker room door, reminding me exactly where we are. "I'm surprised the cavalry waited this long," he states, scrubbing a hand over his head as he looks from me to the door and back again. "Ready to party?" he asks, and I scoff at him, but the look on his face is way too genuine.

"Wait, I can barely walk, and you want me to

party?" I ask, and he nods, a smirk stretching across his lips as he leans down to grab something off the floor. I groan in horror when I realize it's my torn panties in his hand. He stuffs them in his pocket before I can grab them from him, leaving me to gape at him in disbelief. "I can't party without any panties," I grumble, trying to tug my hand from his, but his hold only grows tighter.

"Little Witch, I'm only just getting started with you. Partying with no panties is just the first step we're taking. My dick is going to be hard all night long, knowing there's nothing beneath your skirt. Besides, what do you have to lose? We might all be dead soon."

32

POLARIS

My cheeks heat the moment we exit the locker room, but there's no one waiting like I expect. I feel tingles zing up and down my spine, every inch of me on edge, ready to combust as if someone's waiting to scream and point in my direction, singing truths about my first orgasm.

First freaking orgasm.

I climaxed.

No failed attempt at my own hands like the few times I'd tried before.

No.

This was all him.

All him, and now there's a fire burning deep in my core that has never existed before.

If Wylder notices I'm falling apart, he doesn't say a single word as he tugs me down the short, narrow corridor to where the looming spectators await.

Instead of someone standing with an accusing finger aimed my way, our audience comes in the form of a packed-out space ready to greet us as we re-enter the room where the fight took place. Only now, the ring is gone, the lights are dim, and the music is vibrating through the floor. Bodies are everywhere, but the second Wylder makes an appearance, it's as if every set of eyes turns our way.

Another round of applause echoes around the room as we're bombarded by people congratulating him. I try to slip my hand from his and put as much distance between us as possible so I can slink into the background, but it's impossible when his hold tightens. He pins me to his side as he tries to make his way through the mass of people. I try to keep my head down, avoiding the attention as best as possible, but I still manage to spy a few familiar faces dispersed throughout the crowd.

The desire to lift my head is intense, but I tilt my face to the left, avoiding the vampires to see a flash of familiar brown-swept hair and wide blue eyes as he lifts his hand, stopping us in our tracks. Instead of looking at his friend as I expected, his eyes bore into mine.

"Midnight."

One word from his lips and my cheeks burn at the acknowledgment, and I shake my head, desperate to put an end to this now.

"Polaris," I murmur, my name barely audible over the music thumping through the room.

His eyebrows gather. "What?"

Clearing my throat, I muster whatever strength I have. "My name is Polaris." I'm louder this time, refusing to continue with this charade that Wylder instigated. He might have brought me to the peak of my desired sensations, but no more lying, even if it's just pretending.

Lincoln tilts his head to the side, staring deeper at me like he's waiting for something to pop up as some form of an explanation before he shakes his head. "Polaris, as in silver-haired witch, Polaris?"

I smile, shrugging as I pretend my cheeks aren't practically glowing. "One and the same," I admit, and his stare turns to a glare as his lips pinch.

"And you couldn't have told me that the other day?" he grunts, and Wylder plants a hand on his shoulder, his other hand still wrapped tightly around mine, squeezing in comfort as he takes a step forward, separating us.

He huffs a laugh, trying to alleviate the tension

growing. "That was my fault, asshole. Leave her alone."

Lincoln offers the same intense stare at his friend before turning back to me. His jaw ticks as he taps at his chin. "I need to talk to you," he states, but Wylder interjects before I can speak.

"Not now. I won. She's mine for the night. You can talk to her some other time," he insists, stepping around his friend as he pulls me along after him.

Torn about what I'm supposed to do, I automatically fall into step, surprised to find Lincoln right beside me as he grumbles under his breath with a sigh. "Whatever, everyone is waiting over here." He slips back in front, taking control of the situation as he forges a path through the crowd to where a wrought iron set of stairs rises against the far left wall. They lead up to a cordoned-off area with a security guy at the bottom, separating what seems to be the elite from the commoners.

Without a word, the security guard moves out of the way, dipping his head at Lincoln and Wylder as he lifts the rope, allowing Lincoln to pass while we follow quickly behind him. The stairs rattle as we make our way up to the top floor to find velvet drapes hanging around the upper level, shielding them from the rest of the party, while the wrought iron continues around the edge, offering a balcony to spectate the dance floor below.

Leather seats line the walls like large booths with circular tables dotted around the space, and a bar sits along the far edge. It's cute. It's relaxing, but it's not the wolves' Moon Party vibe. There's something different in the air. I just can't pinpoint what.

Lincoln guides us toward a table, and I'm relieved to see that Bryony is already sitting with them. She looks cute in her little matching skirt and shirt set that she insisted on wearing, which has an extra button missing and the collar sitting wide, revealing the valley between her breasts. Not that she's trying to get anyone's attention. It seems she's caught in a conversation with the girl I saw beside Lincoln the other day in the dining hall.

She's in a two-piece as well, except her top isn't as revealing. It's a sheer material with black lace over the top and see-through on the arms. With her smokey eye makeup, it has the same sultry effect as Bryony's outfit.

Beside her is Asher, wearing a pale-blue shirt with the top three buttons undone and the sleeves rolled up to his elbows. He's deep in his cell phone, paying no mind to anyone around him. I can't fight the soft smile that curls my lips as Tatum comes into view in a simple black fitted tee and matching fitted jeans.

He looks good; relaxed and calm. It suits him more than the darkness that seems to follow him like a second shadow.

Since I'm taking a moment to take everybody in, I give myself a second to stare at Lincoln now that the initial shock has worn off. It doesn't feel like a surprise to find him in a pair of fitted trousers and a white button-up shirt with wolf face cufflinks holding his sleeves in place.

Wylder, on the other hand, is in a pair of shorts and a white t-shirt, fresh from the shower he took after we had our…fun.

As if sensing his presence in my thoughts, Wylder squeezes my fingers once again before releasing my hand. I watch in awe as he makes his way around the table, accepting congratulations from his friends. The situation seems familiar to them. I use the moment to step over to the far side of the space toward the balcony so I can look down at the sea of people below.

The difference in the vibe becomes obvious from this vantage point.

It's noticeable not just in the air, but to the naked eye as well: no quadrants are mixing tonight. The vampires, the witches, the humans, and the wolves are all congregated among themselves… apart from us.

I gulp at the thought, uncertainty churning inside me at the expectation of being kicked back down to Earth at any moment. Not that I'd blame them, and not that I'd be sad about it, but the fear of embarrassment is an emotion I can't seem to let go of.

Maybe being up here isn't a good idea. Maybe everything that transpired in the locker room wasn't—

"Hey, Polaris, right?"

I tilt my face to find the girl who was with Lincoln at the dining hall the other day smiling wide at me. She clamps her hand on my shoulder. Weirdly, there's a comforting sensation and no animosity like I initially expect.

I nod and her smile only strengthens.

"Hi, I'm Minnie. Come and take a seat with us. Bryony was telling me all about you," she says with a wink, and my lips purse, unsure of what it is Bryony could possibly say, but the reassuring smile I get from both the girls fills me with a bit of confidence. It's with that I realize I'm making far too many assumptions about these people tonight, and as much as I need to be alert and safe, overanalyzing everything isn't what this evening is supposed to be about. "By the way, I'm

Lincoln's sister," she says as she links her arm through mine and drags me toward the table, but my steps falter at the information she offers.

"Sister?" I repeat. My question is soft among the music, but she still nods eagerly. There's a smile on her face, one filled with pride, as I take the seat between her and Bryony. I take a moment to glance back and forth between the siblings and the slice of jealousy I felt mere days ago disappears. Their eyes are the same bright blue and they hold themselves in the same way. It's a mixture of ready to go to war and an air of refusing to take anybody's shit that naturally exudes from their very beings.

I don't want to compliment Lincoln since he was a bit of an ass before. Although, he didn't take the news terribly, I guess, so I offer her a smile. "I don't know if I should apologize to you or something?" I say, earning a chuckle from her and a glare from her brother.

"He's nice for the most part," she states, a warm glow taking over her face as she looks at him. "I mean, he did save you from taking a football to the head on your first day, right?" she adds with a wink, making my cheeks heat to another level as Bryony frowns.

"He did what?" the latter pushes, giving me a

side glance as I internally die. The idea of recalling that moment is unbearable, and I regret skipping that part of our first interaction like the last time the topic came up between us. Still, I'm saved from being the one retelling the story as Minnie leans around me.

"It was hilarious. This poor girl had barely stepped on campus. God knows what she's just been told about us all because Florentines live a different life, right? And here she is, taking it all in when a football gets hurdled in her direction with meteoric force. Before anyone can react, Lincoln is off in wolf form, ready to save this girl before he collides with her, knocking her to the ground and shifting back into a human. A naked one at that. With his little penis pressed against her thigh."

She's cackling by the end of it, the sound infectious as Bryony clamps a hand over her mouth, and I look to the ceiling, praying for the blood kin curse to take me now.

"There is nothing little about my penis. Do not make me pull it out right now," Lincoln grumbles, swiping a hand down his face, irritation evident in his eyes.

My blush becomes unbearable as Minnie fake gags at her brother, who glares at her, but there's a softness to his eyes that isn't usually there when he aims a pointed stare your way.

There's love between them, that much is for sure.

Bryony can't catch her breath as she giggles along, her humor-filled eyes turning my way. "I think you missed that part," she says, and I roll my eyes.

"Maybe," I mutter, dipping my eyes to my lap as I try to conceal the embarrassment as best I can, but I think it's a little bit too late for that.

"What do you mean she missed that part? Have you been talking about me, Midnight?" he asks, and I lift my head to meet his eyes to find his eyebrow cocked in question. "Did you happen to tell them about the part where you were hiding from me?"

"I haven't been hiding from you," I reply, the words far more confident than I feel, but it's the truth. He must not feel the same, though. The scoff he gives confirms it.

"You didn't give me your name," he starts, pressing his fingertips together as he starts to count my apparent offenses off on his hand. "You hid your natural hair color, and you acted like you didn't know me when I spoke to you in combat."

My heart rate sparks even though his words are calm. I'm under fire, and as much as I want to run and hide away from it, I also feel like I deserve to explain myself.

Clearing my throat, I match his stance, fingers poised, ready to count off my responses back to him. "One, you're right. I didn't give you my name, but you were happy not to know it if I recall."

He shakes his head. "But you knew my name."

"Yes, I didn't realize I looked so different with my hair a darker color," I state, watching as he purses his lips, but I proceed. "Two, technically, I dyed my hair black to have a fresh start, but when I woke the next morning, it was silver again. That wasn't a choice, and I expect the same to happen tomorrow." He doesn't say anything to that, he just stares, his brows furrowing slightly. "And three, it's not my fault you didn't recognize me when everyone else did."

"*I* asked her not to tell you," Wylder adds, his hand suddenly on my shoulder as he stands beside me.

I lean back to peer up at him, and the second he has my attention, he winks as he leans down to speak with Minnie. "Is everything okay with Asher?" he asks, nodding toward the guy in question, who's still deep in his phone, while effectively cutting off Lincoln's tirade.

Asher's jaw is clenched tight, his eyes crinkled with a mixture of concern and frustration.

Minnie shrugs and shakes her head. "It's his uncle again," she says, and that must mean something to Wylder because he hums in agreement. I run my tongue along my bottom lip as I take him in, trying to understand what they know and I don't, but I don't dare ask. It's not my place.

Instead, I accept the shot placed before me at Wylder's direction to a waiter, and the amusement on his face tells me it's tequila. Again. I don't even need to taste it to know. He reaches for my hand, running his tongue over my finger, and I shiver at the contact, but he's quickly gone, scattering a small line of salt in his wake. I'm left gaping at him as he places a wedge of lime down in front of me before reaching for his own shot glass. My words are lodged in my throat, so I do the only thing I can do, which is clink my glass. I copy his movement, sweeping my tongue over the salt before tossing the liquor back, feeling the familiar burn. It's not as bad this time. It's not amazing, but I'm sure it's still better than the beer everyone keeps warning me about. The second I place my glass down, he reaches for the lime, and I follow suit, biting into the tangy citric fruit with a hiss as the juices coat my tongue.

The song changes in the background. I only notice because it seems to turn up a notch before a squeal comes from Minnie, and she's on her feet, darting toward Lincoln as the first word is sung. As if anticipating her approach, he spins to catch her just in time and the pair of them start to dance. They shake their asses, they laugh, they do some kind of synchronized moves that are a little bit concerning, yet hilarious to watch.

I catch his stare a few times. He offers me nothing but a pinched expression followed by a shake of his head before he looks away. Again, and again, and again. It's only when Wylder takes Minnie's seat beside me with a chuckle on his lips that I'm aware Lincoln's questionable behavior is noticeable to everyone.

"I think I'm visibly watching him get hot for you, then remind himself you're a virgin," Wylder whispers against my ear as he squeezes his hand against my thigh, and I grimace. Not from his touch, but from his acknowledgment of Lincoln's little show.

"You caught that?" I grumble, dipping my face, but he catches my chin and chuckles.

"When it comes to you, it seems I catch everything, Little Witch."

His words turn me into lava, reminding me of

the state he left me in earlier and what he was able to do to my body, and I bite back a groan.

The air shifts slightly when Asher lifts his cell phone to his ear, muttering something into the device before tucking it away in his pocket.

"We need to get ready to leave," he grumbles, rising from his seat without looking at everyone.

Nobody seems to argue, though. They just stop what they're doing and start following his order.

Even though I'm slightly disappointed that there's nothing left of the day, I'm barely standing after the opportunities I've had the chance to experience.

"I'll walk you back," Wylder says, reaching for my hand and tugging me to my feet. Then Tatum suddenly appears in my peripheral vision.

"That's my job."

It's as if the music has been muted and everyone turns to look our way. I can feel their eyes dart back and forth between Tatum and me as Wylder's fingers flex against mine.

"Your job?" Wylder asks as I sense Minnie and Lincoln edge closer. Asher remains on the fringe of the group in his own little world, but Tatum's eyes remain set on mine, and I can't look away.

A shiver runs down my spine as he takes a small, almost nervous step toward me.

"It's my job, right?"

I sink my teeth into my bottom lip, feeling my cheeks burn even brighter than they ever have at this stage in my life. I'm pretty sure my cheeks will forever be burning. I don't recall the general sensation of them not being on fire since arriving at Trinity Falls.

Despite the audience we've garnered, everything that unraveled tonight with Wylder, and the conversation with Lincoln, I find myself nodding as my heart ricochets against my ribcage.

"It's your job," I breathe, expecting to self-combust, but it's worth it to see the smile curl the corner of his lip.

I don't know why I agree, or even how, but the moment the words leave my lips I believe in them.

He nods, pleased with himself. He doesn't offer me his hand, just waves for me to follow him, and to my surprise, Wylder relaxes his hold on my fingers and I finally manage to look up at him. He nods toward Tatum, his lips clamped shut, and before I can second guess myself, I'm up and at his side before anyone else seems to move.

Tatum doesn't hesitate as he leads the way downstairs, making sure I'm right behind him. We cut through the crowd and head toward a side exit, and a few moments later, we're out in the night air.

I take a deep breath, appreciating the change in temperature, hoping it will kill the heat in my cheeks and the rest of my body as I walk side by side with the mysterious boy who continues to make his presence known.

"You look different with the dark hair," he states, and I nervously tuck a loose curl behind my ear, worried that he doesn't like it. Not that it should matter, but it seems I'm eager to please under their scrutiny. I don't know how or why I feel enticed by them, but it's undeniable. "In a good way I mean," he adds, and I fail to bite back the smile turning the corners of my lips.

"Thanks. I've been trying something new, even if it's only for a few hours."

His eyes narrow, and there is a hint of confusion in his deep stare, but he shrugs it off as we head up the path I took to get here. It's only a ten-minute walk, and I know we'll be back at the quadrants soon enough.

A comfortable silence washes over both of us and I glance over my shoulder to see everybody else is only a few steps behind. Bryony included. Weirdly, nobody tries to walk with us. I start to worry that I've done something wrong, but when I turn back to Tatum, it's to find a smile spread across his face.

"What?" I ask, and he shakes his head. Concern threatens to get the better of me, and I ask again, "What?"

He looks at me and I'm certain there's a hint of pink on his cheeks.

"I can hear them."

"Hear them?" I ask, and he taps his ear.

"Wolf senses," he states as if that's explanation enough, nodding his head behind to where the rest of the group trail behind.

"Apparently, I might need educating on that," I say, still confused, and the smile on his face softens.

"I can teach you whatever you want to know."

I tilt my head, taking him in, and decide now is not the time to learn every single thing about a wolf. Instead, I point my thumb over my shoulder.

"What are they saying?"

He glances back, following the direction of my thumb, before turning back to the front with his eyes downcast.

"Nothing," he insists, but the smile he's failing to hide from his face is something different.

Attempting my best pointed look, I wait for him to turn to face me, and by the time he does, it's in full strength. Instead of faltering at the look on my face, his grin spreads wider.

"Does that stare get you everything you want?" he asks, and I shrug.

"I don't know. This is my first time trying it," I admit truthfully, and the smile on his face turns into a bubble of laughter.

"He's laughing," Minnie giggles from behind, and I glance back.

"Even I heard that," I state, and he laughs again, the sound raspy as it swirls around us.

Neither of us says a word and a comfortable air settles around us again. I don't know what it is, but it feels like there's an understanding between us that feels…safe.

Safe.

A word I don't use very often, if at all. Yet, in these moments where there's not even a single breath between us, I feel it.

Following the winding path, the quadrants come into view, and a hint of sadness creeps into my bones at the fact that the night is over, although I'm sure I'll lie awake in bed analyzing everything that's happened tonight.

"I'm sad a lot," he blurts, his eyes clouding with an emotion I can't quite place under the moonlit sky.

I hum, keeping my stare dead ahead. "I'm lost a

lot," I admit, feeling his raw fact deserves one from me too.

"There's something in you I find in myself," he admits as we approach the fork in the road leading to the different quads.

"I'm glad," I breathe as he stops to face me properly.

"To the door?" he asks, and I bite back a smile.

"To the door," I agree, stepping onto the sandy path that leads to the witches' dorm.

No words are said. Nothing is needed. And despite the fact that Wylder has done things to my body tonight, on a level of intimacy I've never felt before in my life, I somehow feel just as close to Tatum in this moment. It's another thing for me to analyze instead of sleeping tonight.

He stops by the door and I turn to face him, noting the rest of his friends and Bryony a few feet away, watching us like a movie unraveling before their very eyes.

"Thank you. You really didn't have to," I insist, and he smiles, the air thickening in just a way that I know a repeat of last time is in order. Ignoring our audience, I cut the distance between us, placing my hand on his shoulder as I rise onto my tiptoes and press my lips against his cheek. "Goodnight,

Tatum," I murmur, stepping back, and his smile imprints in my mind as he breathes.

"Goodnight. Polaris."

33

POLARIS

The weekend passed by in a blur. I didn't leave the comfort of my room as I spent an embarrassing amount of time beneath my sheets trying to replicate what Wylder did to me.

It's impossible.

That man is no wolf; he's a wizard. One that twists me in knots only to unravel me in the most unbelievable way possible.

I didn't see any of them in the dining hall over the weekend, and Bryony said she was busy, probably with her coven, but it was nice to soak in the familiar comfort of my own company again. It's definitely not as good as the company I kept on Friday night, but it was nice all the same.

Terence and Sian continue to ignore me, a fact I've accepted now that it's become our new norm.

However, B's absence still concerns me. I'm sure if anything had happened to him, we would have been told about it, and something would have happened to someone else, too, since we're all fighting the blood kin curse here.

The sound of someone clearing their throat pulls me from my thoughts and I quickly focus on the present. Professor Juniper quirks a brow at me and I sit up straighter in my seat.

Daydreaming in my witch classes isn't the best idea when I've got a lot to learn, but ever since I walked through the door, she's been pretending I don't exist. She speaks while looking right through me. Even when addressing the other Florentines, I'm seemingly not here.

Until now.

There's a weird air, one that leaves a sickly feeling in the pit of my stomach.

"Must I repeat myself, Polaris?" Professor Juniper asks, and I gulp, acutely aware everyone is staring at me.

"Please," I breathe, curling my fingers on my lap as I bite back the tingle of humiliation.

She sighs, her lips pursing, and I can't help but wonder what it is I've done wrong. Her soft demeanor from last time is gone, and in its place is a rigid woman inconvenienced by my presence.

"Why is sand so important to witches?"

I blink at her. I have no clue. If she just told us, I definitely wasn't paying attention.

My jaw hangs loose as I scramble to say something.

"Not only does it represent the unconscious mind, but it enhances our abilities, allowing us to protect ourselves and others where necessary," Bryony answers for me. I spin to meet her stare and silently thank her.

"Thank you, Bryony, but I recall asking Polaris," Juniper says, turning toward the board at the front of the class as she pushes her glasses up the bridge of her nose.

The thick air stretches around the room as Bryony remains as quiet as I do.

Dammit.

I don't want her to get the cold shoulder for trying to help me. I need to say something, anything, but before I can figure out a single word, Juniper proceeds. "Sand is one of the most used ingredients in any spell, potion, or enchantment. It is recommended that a witch always carries a small pouch wherever they go. Who here holds one?"

Her gaze rakes over the room and I glance behind me to watch every other student lift a small velvet pouch, each a varying color. The only people not holding a pouch are the three of us seated up front.

She offers a reassuring smile to Danica and Helena, but it drops off as her eyes meet mine. Leaning back in my seat, I feel even more out of my depth than usual. This has become a hostile and tense environment, one I haven't created. It almost feels like I'm clambering to safety, but every step comes with a slip on the uneven terrain and I find myself right back at the starting line.

Wordlessly, she moves behind her desk, retrieving three small purple pouches, offering us one each as she breezes past.

"Keep them on you at all times. I haven't been made aware that any of you have lifted your sigils, but it's important to follow certain practices immediately so you can make it a habit for when the time comes."

Is that it? Is that why she's mad? Because of the sigil?

That can't be the case; Danica and Helena are as magicless as I am.

I roll the small pouch in my hand, warmth spreading down my fingertips. I squeeze them tight around my first witchy talisman, something that indicates who I am meant to be, and I pray it will offer me a glimmer of what my future holds. The flex of my hand has my other hand diving into my pocket, pressing the familiar metal against my palm until I can feel the outline of the entire face against my skin.

I take a deep breath and try to ignore my worries just as the bell rings, bringing the class to an end.

Chairs scrape against the floor as Juniper dismisses everyone, and I rise from my seat, only to feel a hand press against my shoulder a moment later.

"Stay behind, Polaris," Professor Juniper advises, releasing her hold as she circles around her desk, watching everyone leave. Bryony hovers by the door, her eyebrows gathered with concern, but I shake my head, encouraging her to go on without me. She's already received backlash over my inadequacy; she doesn't need to make it worse.

The air is palpable as the final person leaves. She mutters a string of words under her breath and flicks her hand, making the door click shut behind them before she drops into her seat, lacing her fingers together as she stares at me. A second ticks into another, and another, until minutes extend in the air as I brace for the impending doom she's ready to throw at me.

"I believe you declined your invite from the Renegade coven."

Ah, there it is.

The second I understand is the exact moment I find my backbone.

"You believe correct." My voice is firmer than I expect, but I lean into it, taking strength from myself.

"Please help me understand why you would turn down such a prestigious offer." She sighs, leaning back in her seat as her hands fall lax in her lap.

"Was it an offer, or was it a forced invasion of my privacy to see if I would suit them?" I ask, and she cocks a brow at me.

When I know what I'm defending myself for, I won't back down. Not even now.

"The Renegade coven is the most—"

"I know what they are. I also know what they're willing to do to complete their coven. It's not something I'm interested in, and if that's how other covens operate, I won't be joining them either."

She scoffs. "You turned down the Renegades. Who do you think is going to invite you now?"

Her words are pained with a hint of despair, but I shrug.

"You're forgetting that there was once a time

you didn't know about this life. All I know is how I have been treated, and being overlooked and my words dismissed is not something I take lightly. Not when it's expected that I commit myself to them for as long as I live. Not when that could be a mere few months or all of eternity. I will not lower my standards for anyone, not even the most elite."

Her eyes bore into mine, searching for answers she's unwilling to ask questions about.

"You're going to regret this, Polaris."

"I'm not," I state firmly, shaking my head. "I would regret allowing someone else power over me when they wanted to take it without my consent."

"You may not have been the witch they were looking for," she offers, pushing her glasses up the bridge of her nose again, and it's my turn to scoff.

"That's beside the point," I grumble, leaning forward to plant my hands on her desk as I level my stare at hers. "Ask me. Ask me what happened."

She shakes her head instantly, a slight pinch to her lips, one coiled with fear. "It's not my place to question another coven, especially not the Renegades," she insists, and I huff.

"Then it's not your place to question me either." I push off the desk and step back, desperate to put some much-needed space between us. For a Florentine, she has no idea what I'm talking about.

The need to be free, the desire to be my own person, and the fight for the puppet strings to be forever removed from my limbs.

Now, she's fully embraced in this new world, where other witches matter more than yourself based on a hierarchy I don't understand, and no one seems willing to explain.

"Is there anything else, Professor?" I ask, hoping to draw the conversation to an end, and she sighs, shaking her head. I take it as my cue to get the hell out of here, darting for the door before she can change her mind.

I suck in a huge breath as I step out into the hallway, but it's still stiff and rigid out here. Maybe I need to head outside for a second. I don't see Bryony anywhere. She must have gone to the next class already, but I think I know which direction I'm going in now.

Hurrying outside, I let the cooler air wash over me, and I calm a little.

"Hey, fancy seeing you here."

I spin to find Minnie bounding toward me. Her smile is as infectious as ever, and despite my racing pulse, I manage to smile back.

"Hey."

"Are you okay?" she asks, and I nod, waving my hand dismissively. Her eyes crinkle a little as she assesses me but she doesn't push any further. "Do you want to hang out tonight?"

I stare at her, her question catching me off guard. "Hang out?"

"Yeah, you know, watch a movie, have a picnic, people watch, gossip; all of the fun things," she offers, and I nod along like it all makes sense.

"Sure?" It definitely comes out as a question, one word that does nothing to summarize the thoughts swirling in my head, but she doesn't seem to mind.

"Perfect, I'll meet you by the main building steps around seven, yeah?"

I nod, but she's already squeezing my arm and darting off before I can respond.

She's even more of a whirlwind than her brother, but the excitement at having some kind of plans tonight is enough to put a spring in my step and push the worries from moments earlier to the back of my mind.

There's a soft smile on my face as I turn to re-enter the academy building, but a hand lands on my shoulder, the feel of someone's breath breezes past my ear, and the world goes dark.

My nose crinkles at the trickling of water on my face. It takes me a moment to lift my hand, wiping away the trail down my cheek to no avail because another quickly replaces it. Frowning, I pry my eyes open, only to be greeted by darkness.

Darkness and rain.

The sound of the water hitting the ground around me is the only noise as I try to focus my eyes and figure out where I am. Running my tongue over my damp lip, I notice the hard ground beneath me and the stone wall behind me.

I'm propped up against the academy building, the forest off to my right, which has me assuming the quads are on the opposite side of me. Not that it really matters, though. What matters is *why* I'm here…I don't understand.

Looking down the length of myself, I'm drenched from head to toe, the rain unrelenting as I scramble to my feet. I don't know how long I've been out here, but it's dark now, only the moon up high in the sky to guide me.

Wiping a hand down my face, I sigh before quickly recalling what Bryony said the last time this happened to me. I run my fingers over my neck, feeling nothing out of the ordinary before I turn my attention to my arms, but there's nothing there either.

I slip my hands into my pockets, retrieving my cell phone from one and feeling the usual bite of my coin in the other. My eyes widen when I realize it's almost eight thirty at night.

Holy crap. I've really lost a lot of time.

My stomach grumbles, reminding me that I've missed both lunch and dinner, but more than that, I was supposed to meet Minnie over an hour ago.

Rushing around the perimeter of the building, I confirm my whereabouts as the steps where I was supposed to meet her come into view. She's not there though, not that I would expect her to be.

Drenched to the bone, I stare at the double doors leading inside as I consider what I'm supposed to do next. If she's in there, and I storm in like this, it will only add to my embarrassment, but if I don't try to explain myself, I fear it may make me feel even worse.

My face falls into my hands as I try to shake the rest of the fog that clouds my thoughts while the rain continues to pound down on me.

"Ah, so the wicked witch of Florentine's isn't dead then." My gaze snaps to find Lincoln standing on the top step, glaring at me from his dry perch. My mouth falls open, an explanation on my tongue, but I don't get a chance to breathe a word before he's in my face. "She waited for you. She waited for you, and you didn't come. Is this a joke to you? Is my sister a pawn for you to play with? Is that what you think? Because let me set one thing straight: I will make sure you regret mistreating her, and I'll enjoy doing it."

"I didn't—"

"Save it. I should have known letting her trust someone like you was the wrong thing to do," he snaps, unfazed by the rain pouring down on him, too. I want to defend myself, explain what happened, but I'm transfixed on the droplets of rain that fall from the tip of his hair hanging over his eyes.

Damn.

I want to tell him what's going on, that I'm scared, confused, and questioning everything, but right now, he's rightfully defending his sister, and anything I say is pointless in comparison.

Instead, I settle on two simple words. "I'm sorry."

He sneers, a scoff curling his lips further. "It's not me you should be apologizing to. I don't even want you to apologize to her, but she deserves an explanation, and you're going to give her one."

I nod, desperate for the chance, and he takes a step back, finally allowing me a second to breathe.

"She's inside. Wait at the doors. I'll have her

come to you. We don't need you causing a scene in the dining hall," he grunts before effectively dismissing me and storming inside.

I follow after him, appreciating the reprieve from the rain. The hallways are mostly quiet, but I earn a few confused stares from the students passing by, so I press my back against the wall in the far corner and do my best to hide away.

"Polaris, what an earth?" Minnie turns the corner, eyes scanning me from head to toe, and I try my best not to think about how ridiculous I look.

My teeth start to chatter, and I can't decide if it's from the cold of the rain or the nerves building inside of me. I fold my arms over my chest, offering a weak smile. "I'm sorry."

She waves her hand as she stops in front of me. "Screw that, what happened to you?"

Shaking my head, I force myself to keep my head high and my eyes locked on hers. "It doesn't matter. I shouldn't have—"

"Polaris, cut the shit. What's going on? I knew you wouldn't just leave me hanging like that. Tatum and Wylder agreed with me. I'm not sure what Lincoln said, but ignore him. Whatever is going on here is more important."

"It's not," I rasp, her whirlwind vibe almost bringing me to my knees.

"You can tell me, or you can tell all of us," she warns, and I gulp, acutely aware that there's no way out of this.

Clearing my throat, I decide on the former.

"I honestly don't know. I don't remember anything after leaving you earlier."

Her brows gather in confusion, making it abundantly clear that I'm not making sense, but it doesn't make sense to me either.

"This is not the first time it's happened. Bryony mentioned possibly the vampires, but I don't know…I have no clue."

I swipe my hair back off my face, defeated in every sense of the word, and in the next breath, she's bundling me in her arms, offering me a tight hug.

"You're okay, Polaris. You're safe." Her words nestle deep in my gut, and as much as I take strength from them, I'm scared they're not real. "Do you need help?"

I shake my head as she steps back. "No, I'm good. I just needed you to understand."

"We can help with this, Polaris," she insists, and I shake my head more firmly.

"Please, Minnie, please don't mention this to anyone. I appear weak enough as it is." Her smile is dipped in sadness, but she nods all the same.

I tuck a wet lock of hair behind my ear and she grins. "The silver came back, huh?"

"Sadly," I mumble, and she rolls her eyes at me.

"The silver suits you."

"Thanks."

Clearing her throat, she tilts her head at me. "Any luck with your sigil?"

"No," I admit, aware that I'm a one-word robot right now, but my brain isn't running on all cylinders.

She nibbles at her bottom lip before taking a deep breath. "I thought it could have something to do with your hair."

"My hair?" I repeat, confused, and she nods eagerly.

"Yes, the fact that it changes back."

"I have no idea why," I explain, completely deflated, but she bounces on the balls of her feet.

"Maybe that's what we need to find out. That way, we won't have to tell anyone about what's happening, but we can finally let you have your magic and handle the situation accordingly."

"I don't know where to begin. I—"

"I can help."

"But you're a wolf," I blurt, and she rears back, almost offended.

"And…?"

Dammit. "It's not a bad thing; it's just…it seems a wolf and a witch aren't meant to be friends."

"Says who?"

"Says everyone I've spoken to since I got here."

"Did *I* say it?" she asks, and I give her a pointed look. We both know she didn't. "Perfect, then you'll come with me tomorrow."

"With you?" I repeat, struggling to keep up with her.

"Yeah, you can bring Bryony too. She's cute."

"Where?"

"For some fun," she states, her smile back to full beam.

"I don't understand what that has to do with my hair," I mutter lamely, and she shrugs.

"It doesn't, but I want to get to know you before I trust you."

"That's…fair."

"I know, so what do you say?"

I'm scared to say anything because I messed it up last time.

Biting back the worry, I take a deep breath and nod. "I want to learn more about you too."

"Then we're on," she declares, stepping back as she winks. "Don't be late this time."

34

POLARIS

"I don't think it's safe for you to go in there alone," Bryony murmurs, and I offer her a tight smile. I don't want to step in there on my own either, but it's literally the only class she's not with me. I should be able to handle that. I *have* to.

Her concern is appreciated. She's been all hawk-eyes on me since I told her everything that unraveled yesterday. When I hadn't shown up at our next class, she assumed Juniper had kept me behind longer, and by the time the end of the day rolled around, she was summoned by her coven leader.

The guilt is etched into her eyebrows now as she glances between the classroom before us and me. It's not her fault, though. It seems I'm the subject of some sick game, and as much as I don't like it, I can't hide from it.

"I'll be okay. Nobody in here could be doing it. None of us have access to our magic," I state, and although her lips are pressed in a firm line, she nods in agreement.

"Don't leave here without me. Understand?" Her glare leaves no room for questioning so I nod as she squeezes my arm before pushing me over the threshold of the classroom entryway and hurrying to her next class.

My sudden burst through the door earns me a few questioning looks from the others in the room. However, it seems my weirdness is no different from how it was at Florentine's because everybody from there doesn't even bother to roll their eyes at me.

Professor Sommers stands in the far corner of the room, hands clasped together as she stares at me with wide eyes. She rocks back on her heels, waiting for my outburst to continue, but when I drop to the carpet in the middle of the room, hoping to become invisible, she claps, garnering everyone's attention.

"Gather around everyone; there's no time to waste. We have sigils to break and magic to learn. The quicker you master what's holding you back, the quicker you see the back of me," she declares, a soft giggle vibrating through the room. "Has anyone broken their sigil without me knowing?" she adds, casting her gaze around the room, only earning everyone's disappointment before she proceeds. "Okay. Well, those who have been with me longer, please, make use of the books in the corner. My newest Florentines, please, follow me."

Scrambling to my feet, I run my hands down my jeans nervously as I follow behind Sian and Terence to where Sommers guides us. There's a large table set up with just enough seats for us, and I opt to take a chair on the opposite side of the table from the vampires, who think I'm beneath them now. Helena and Danica get comfortable on my left, and it's clear that B still isn't here.

Would he need to be if he's a human?

I don't know, but it's still concerning.

"Okay, it's important for us to learn a little more about you. I don't have much, but I have very limited documents that specify your last name and the place that name originated. By some miracle, it may trigger your sigil, but the chances are slim. However, from there it's possible to begin searching for lineage in the right places that may offer the smallest sliver of knowledge that is the true key to your sigil."

My heart pounds in my chest, shocked by her words, as I try to take a calming breath. She needs to prepare me for groundbreaking information like this. I'm not ready.

"I'll start at random in whatever order the documentation is filed in, and then you can join the others searching through the research files we have. Any questions?" she asks, taking the free seat at the head of the table, only waiting a beat for anyone to respond before she proceeds. "First up, Helena Davenport," she states, glancing around the table, and Helena lifts her hand nervously beside me. "Davenport is your family name that trails back centuries, a strong line of witches from Buttercup Roe, which is confirmed from the knowledge we have stored. When researching, focus on the bloodline Davenport and any connection to Buttercup Roe," she explains, waving her hand for Helena to join the others.

"Thank you," she breathes, twisting her hands nervously in front of her as she slowly rises and scurries away without a backward glance.

It's as simple as that: Helena now has something to go on. I'm almost irritated that this information wasn't provided in our last lesson, but I guess it was already information overload, and we can't learn everything all at once.

"Sian Gloom. Gloom…Gloom…" Professor Sommers repeats her last name a few times, tapping at her chin as if she's deep in thought. Then her eyes draw wide and her face seems to pale.

"What is it?" Terence asks, planting a hand on Sian's shoulder as she rolls her lips together nervously.

"Oh, it's just…I believe the Gloom line of vampires leads back to those initially impacted by the curse." Her words grow soft with every new one that parts her lips, unaware that she's stolen everyone's breath at the table as we wait for her to proceed.

"As in the blood kin curse?" Sian clarifies, eyes sparkling with awe as the professor nods. "You're telling me I'm linked to those loved by the witch?" Her voice is almost whimsical, like there's a sense of pride in what she's hearing, but the way Sommers's lips draw thin as she looks down at the table tells a different story.

"Actually," the professor states, offering a tight smile Sian's way. "I believe the Gloom lineage is linked to those banished for treason."

"What does that mean?" she asks, balking at the accusation as if it affects her personally.

"Well, it means your ancestors were some of the first cursed because of their prejudice."

"My ancestors were…bad?" Her bottom lip wobbles and Terence drapes an arm around her shoulders in comfort. It's weird seeing them like this, but it doesn't seem to stoke any feelings inside of me.

"Bad is subjective; I guess it depends whose side you stand on," Sommers explains, scanning the document in her hand again. "Right now, what you need to focus on is your ancestors and their connection to…the Marshlands."

"I have banished ancestors and you want me to focus on something other than that fact?" Sian grumbles, her face heating with agitation as Sommers sighs.

"Unless that fact alone will lift your sigil, then yes."

As if triggered by her words, Sian's hand clamps on her chest, a scream rippling through the air as she tosses her head back. Terence leaps back, eyes bugging out as we all gape at her. The cry of pain seems to stretch on for an eternity before she falls silent and limp in her seat.

"What the—"

"Quiet, Terence," Sommers snaps, seemingly unaware that panic flickers through all of us until Sian slowly tilts her face. She slips her fingers beneath the neckline of her t-shirt, her frown growing tighter and tighter with every passing second as she slowly retrieves a golden pendant from around her neck. Only…it's as if it's been burned right down the middle and the chain is no longer hanging as one.

"My sigil," she whispers, disbelief morphing her voice as she holds out the necklace.

"Your sigil is free, Miss Gloom."

"Oh my gosh!" she cries, knocking her chair backward as she rushes to her feet. "I'm free. I'm really free."

"Well, freedom is also subjective, Sian. You now will fall prisoner to your lineage. You will now feel both the pros and cons of being a vampire."

"Which means I no longer need this class, right?" She's too busy staring at the necklace hanging from her fingertips to even look at Sommers, and the second the professor speaks her agreement, Sian's out of the door, leaving all of us behind.

"Good riddance," Danica mutters under her breath, but it's clear everyone at the table hears her, and she quickly finds herself on the end of a deathly glare from Terence.

"Watch your tongue, witch," he snaps, and Danica cackles, her head falling back with glee as she mocks him.

"Watch *my* tongue. Maybe you should watch

your tongue because last I recall, you don't know what to do with it."

I gape in a mixture of horror and disbelief before a laugh bubbles in my stomach, impossible to hold down as it parts my lips, and I clap a hand over my mouth. My cheeks heat as others chuckle too, while Sommers and Terence both splutter to redirect the conversation. Terence's eyes find mine, a snarl on his lips, but it only amuses me more.

Apparently, Danica is more fun than I thought. I'd love to tell her who I *know* is excellent with his tongue, but I would never want her to find out for herself.

"Let's remain focused, shall we?" Sommers calls out, drenching the space in silence. "Polaris Beauchamp," she calls out, and I freeze, feeling all eyes at the table swing my way. "It shows here that you're linked to the Marshlands as well. Use your last name and the location to begin your research," she orders, waving her hand dismissively, and I rise with a sigh.

She could have delivered such news a little gentler, but it seems that's not her priority, I guess. Her job is to give us the tools needed to remove the sigil, and I'm more than ready to break these bands around my wrists.

Rising from my seat, I take the slip of paper

from her hand and head toward the corner where everyone else is gathered, face buried in a book as they desperately read through page after page, hoping for something.

The bookcase behind them is lined with so many books I don't know where to begin, but starting somewhere is better than starting nowhere, so I head for the top left corner and decide I'll make that my beginning.

Running my finger down the spine, I note the title of the book, *Witches and Their Bloodlines*.

It seems like a good enough place to start.

With my heavy book in hand, I find an empty seat and open it to the first page. I only make it five pages deep before the bell rings, pulling me from the sheets of finely typed information.

"Whatever book you are holding, take it with you. Your assignment for the week is to complete it," Professor Sommers explains, twisting her hair into a messy bun on top of her head as she addresses us.

With the leather-bound book pressed against my chest, I head for the exit, looking left and right before I step out into the hall. Keeping my back pressed against the wall as I exit, I regret not knowing exactly which direction Bryony is in so I can head toward her.

"Are you heading to the dining hall?" Danica asks, and it takes me a second to realize she's talking to me.

Gulping nervously, I nod, and she rolls her eyes as she tilts her head to the right. "You can walk with us if you want to meet your friend there," she offers, already walking away. It takes me a split second to make a decision before I relent, hurrying after her and Helena, who don't offer up any conversation as we head toward the dining hall.

I balance my new book with one hand as I slip the other into my pocket to retrieve my cell phone, tapping out a message to Bryony as I try to keep up with them.

Polaris: Meet you at the dining hall.

Polaris: Don't worry, I'm not alone. Danica and Helena are here.

The little dots appear on the screen immediately, followed swiftly by a message.

Bryony: Who?

I roll my eyes at her but quickly tap out an answer before I slip the device away.

> Polaris: The two other new witches from Florentine's. I just learned that Danica is quite funny, so if I die, hopefully I'll have a laugh along the way.

I'm sure I'll pay for that. It's probably not a subject to make fun of, but it's amusing nonetheless.

The dining hall quickly comes into view and the two seem to speed up to grab their preferred seats. They don't bother to glance back to see if I'm still here, but I almost appreciate it. I don't need to try to understand their motives right now, either.

As soon as the vampire table comes into view, I bolt to the left, avoiding it the best I can, only to pay more attention to the humans' table instead. As I make my way up the walkway between the witches' and the humans' table, I nibble at my bottom lip, considering whether to approach someone or not.

I fight with myself all the way up to the far end, and just when I'm about to forget about it and take a seat, a girl from the human table lifts her gaze. Before I can even think about what I'm actually doing, I cut the distance between us, rounding to a stop an inch or two way too close to her.

"Hi."

Her eyebrows pinch together as she leans back slightly. "Uh, hi?"

"I'm so sorry, I just…I'm new, from Florentine's, actually. I don't know if you've heard of that or not, it's just—"

"I have," she interjects, and I blink at her. "Heard of Florentine's, I mean," she explains, and I'm acutely aware that I was rambling like Minnie. I need to rein myself in.

"Good. That's great. I actually came here with a friend, a few of them, and well…he was announced as a human when we did the whole hands in the water thing, but honestly, I haven't seen him since we got here. I was wondering if you have?"

There, I finally got to the damn point.

"What's his name?" she asks, and I smile, the curl genuine on my lips as I beam at her.

"B, uh, Benjamin. His name is Benjamin."

I hold my breath, but the moment she purses her lips and shakes her head I know the words she's going to say before her mouth opens.

"I haven't heard of him, sorry."

Damn.

She spins back around to face her table, effectively dismissing me as I stand frozen in place, letting the defeat settle in before I slink away to my own table. I don't know why I'm so bothered by it. It might be related to the loss of Veronica. I can't think too much about it right now, though. I need to focus on my surroundings.

Dropping down into an open seat, with an empty spot beside me for Bryony, I rake my gaze over the food on offer. Steamed salmon, vegetable gratin, burgers, hot dogs, lasagna. There's too much to choose from. I don't know what to settle on, so I opt for the closest option and load my plate with some lasagna and garlic bread on the side.

Snatching up my cutlery, I poise my hands, ready to dig in, when I sense someone taking the seat beside me. Relieved to have Bryony at my side again, I spin to face her, only to find someone else entirely.

She's stunning. Brunette waves fall around her face perfectly, her green eyes bright, and the natural glow that enhances her features is undeniable. I haven't seen her before, though, and the way she glares at me tells me I wish I weren't seeing her now, either.

"Do you really think you can take my place at the head of the Alpha Pack?" she bites, sitting straighter in her seat so her breasts are almost in my face.

"I'm sorry?" I mumble, gaping at her as she bares her teeth.

"Don't play dumb. It's unbecoming," she snaps, rolling her eyes at me.

Clearing my throat, I lower my cutlery, silently saying goodbye to my food as I tilt myself to face her better.

"Do I know you?"

She scoffs. "You should." She leans closer, her eyes locked on mine as she presses her palm on the table. "Minnie is my friend, Lincoln is mine, and Wylder is mine too," she reads off, and horror sinks into my gut.

Oh, God.

Her eyes widen as she takes note of my reaction. "So something *did* happen between you and them?"

I stutter, scrambling to make my brain work, but it seems something is broken up there, and she's going to kill me for it. Literally.

"Bianca."

She stills, peering to her right at the sound of her name, and I follow her line of sight to find Asher glaring down at her.

"Asher," she snipes, her lips twisting in distaste. "We were just talking," she adds, tilting her head back just enough to look down her nose at me.

"Fuck off," Asher snaps, tucking his hands into his pockets as he glares at her.

She presses her hand against her chest, drawing more attention to the swell of her breasts, which are now on full display. "Don't be rude," she grinds out, and Asher scoffs.

"Then don't be you."

Whatever this is, I want nothing to do with it.

It seems Bianca feels the same way because a moment later, she launches to her feet and storms off without a backward glance.

"Sorry about that," Asher murmurs, cocking a brow at me, and I shake my head in disbelief.

"I don't really know what *that* was."

"She's an omega," he offers, but all I can do is blink at him too. "It's a ranking within the wolves," he adds like that makes sense, and I nod slowly, hoping to appease him, but I think he sees right through me.

"Hey, miss me?" Bryony hollers, filling the seat Bianca just vacated, and I nod as she glances between the two of us. I consider catching her up to speed, but I'd rather do it without Asher listening. But something comes to mind and I snap my gaze back to Asher.

"She mentioned the Alpha Pack. That's who helped me the first day with Blaze..." I breathe, my pulse thundering in my ears as he nods slowly, like he's worried about spooking me.

"That was me."

That was me?

He says it so casually.

"Why?" I ask, and he shrugs, stepping back, and I sense whatever chance I may have had of learning something from him went away the moment Bryony took her seat.

He shrugs again as if confirming my thought, taking another step back to seal it. Just before he disappears, he nods at me. "Don't be late. Minnie is always a stickler for punctuality."

Just as quickly as he arrived, he's gone, and I'm no wiser to what the hell is going on here.

35

LINCOLN

"Remind me why we're doing this again?" I grumble, irritation thick in my throat as Minnie rolls her eyes at me.

The living room in the wolves' quad is sparse, and the five of us are alone, spread from one end to the other, and I just so happened to get the short straw of dealing with my sister. Which is really no feat at all, but she's driving me insane right now.

"Because she made Tatum laugh and I want to feel her out before we let her get any closer," she explains, and I sigh. The second she mentions Tatum, I know there's no chance in hell we're getting out of this.

Midnight had me locked in a trance. Polaris, on the other hand…there was something about her I couldn't put my finger on. I don't like it, not even a bit, but I think that has more to do with the fact that it does nothing to deter my attraction to her.

"That's pretty feral," I mutter, smirking at my sister. There's no use fighting her on the matter; she always wins. Besides, it's a good idea. I'm not the only one she seems to have under her spell, and not just Tatum, but Wylder too. At least I can restrain myself.

"You're welcome," she preens with a grin, her eyes darting across the room to where the man in question sits hunched over in his seat. "Just don't tell him; he'll be sad," she adds, and I frown.

"Then don't do it," I blurt, not wanting to cause one of my closest friends pain.

"Tell me I'm wrong," she challenges, doubling down on her point as she turns her attention to Wylder, who happens to be seated beside me on the sofa.

"Don't ask him. He's playing with my new toy," I blurt, aiming my thumb at my friend while earning a glare from the brute beside me.

"She's not a damn toy. Besides, you don't want to play with her because she's a virgin," he snarks back, stirring my dick to life at the mention of that little tidbit. It should put me off, as it usually does, but with her, it seems everything is different.

"Is that still the case?" I ask, quirking a brow at

him while internally cursing myself out for revealing that it's even still a thought to me.

"Would it matter if she wasn't?" He leans back in his seat, draping his arm along the back of the sofa as he stares me down, baiting me.

"Wylder," I snarl, my nostrils flaring to life as my gaze narrows.

"Don't push him, Wylder. That's the last thing we need when it seems he's already wound tight," Minnie murmurs, but there's a teasing in her tone that I'm all too familiar with.

Wylder leans toward me until there's only an inch or two between us. The sparkle in his eyes is the only warning I get before he speaks. "She tastes like Heaven." His words are nothing more than a breath of air.

"Fuck. You," I grind out, jealousy burning through my veins, but it's not lost on me that his words don't confirm he took her virginity.

My thoughts are interrupted by a knock coming from the door.

Minnie bounds to her feet, aiming a deadly stare at me and Wylder. "Thank goodness she's not a wolf with the ability to hear the crap coming from you two," she gripes, and Wylder scoffs.

"Yeah, or a vampire," he adds, and the sneer that curls my lip deepens.

"If she were one of them, we definitely wouldn't be in this situation right now," I correct. Still, neither of them offers me any acknowledgment as Minnie swings the door open to reveal my silver-haired distraction with her friend beside her.

I notice how my sister rakes her eyes over the friend; the friend also glances over my sister. Hmm. That's a heartache waiting to happen, but I refuse to get involved. My sister still hasn't let me live it down the last time I tried to intervene. So I'll remain silent and be here when she needs me when the downfall inevitably happens.

"Ready to go?" Minnie beams, and Polaris nods nervously, nipping at her bottom lip, and my dick stirs at the sight.

"Where are we going?"

"To have some fun, remember?" Minnie insists, waving her off as I take a second to drink her in.

I'm still mad at her for leaving my sister waiting, even though Minnie insists she had a good reason; not that she shared it with me. Regardless, I'll be mad until I say I'm not. Even if she stands before me in a pleated skirt and cropped white-collared shirt that reveals the tiniest sliver of her stomach.

I wonder if her skin is as soft as it looks.

Fuck.

I need to get my head out of the gutter. What I should be considering is the point Tatum made the other night about needing a witch.

Is she trustworthy?

There's only one way to find out. Either way, something tells me that, in her presence, we're all fucking doomed.

36

POLARIS

Bryony squeals, clapping her hands excitedly as we stare up at the colossal sign ahead. "How are we even here?"

I have no idea where *here* actually is, but it's practically buzzing.

Crowds of people bustle around us, some squealing as excitedly as Bryony while others take pictures, leaving a few to grumble that we've stopped in their way. But most don't seem to care. Me included. I'm too enamored with the vibrant lights, soft music playing, and the attractions that lead off in every direction.

"It's a family business," Minnie explains, beaming from ear to ear, and I blink at her.

A family business for what exactly?

As if sensing my confusion, Bryony links her

arm through mine. "It's a theme park, Polaris."

"Which means…" My words hang in the air as the wolves around us finally realize I'm way out of my depth.

"You've never been to a theme park before?" Asher confirms, eyebrows raised, and I dip my gaze. Bryony must sense my discomfort because her grip tightens.

"I don't think they offered field trips at Florentine's," she states, and I force myself to lift my head to find all six of them gaping at me.

"What about before that?" Minnie asks, and I shrug.

"They take all our memories and wipe them clean when we enter Florentine's."

"What the fuck?" she blurts, horror dancing in her eyes. "Why?"

I shrug again, my shoulders falling heavier this time. "Who knows? Probably to keep us at a disadvantage. That was the whole point of me being there, right? The sigil keeps my magic dormant, and I'm already drenched in ignorance and isolated. It's all part of their plan."

"Well, we're here to have fun," Minnie insists, linking my other arm so I'm sandwiched between them both.

"Fun?"

"Yes," she insists, tugging me to walk under the huge sign and down the brightly lit walkway along with everyone else. "This entire place is for us to have fun. That's why everyone is here, and we're going to join in with them."

I nod along, the pretty lights and sweet music luring me in as I opt not to put up a fight. There's a sense of magic and excitement in the air, but one thing is for sure: there are no other supernaturals among the sea of people.

It's almost overwhelming, walking alongside people like I'm…normal. I'm in a world, a brief pocket of time where I'm just Polaris.

No academy.

No blood kin curse.

No impending death.

It may only be a small piece of time, but I vow to make the most of it.

After everything, I think I deserve a break, especially when I have to acknowledge that I'm learning not just the life of a supernatural being, but also the life of an everyday human.

"What are we going on first?" Bryony asks, and Minnie tugs us toward the left, the music changing to a softer melody as I grind to a halt, watching a ride sprint past lightning fast with people screaming as it goes. I can't tell if the noise is laced with fear or glee, but as Bryony and Minnie encourage me closer, I understand their intentions.

Glancing back over my shoulder, considering whether I should make a run for it, I find Wylder, Tatum, Lincoln, and Asher a step behind, effectively trapping me in. Wylder winks at me, making me blush, and I quickly turn back around, accepting my fate.

I watch the ride pass by one more time, the screams not exactly filling me with hope, before Minnie drags me down a lane for VIPs.

"I don't know if this is a good idea," I explain, trying to slip from between them, but it's impossible as we're led down a path that narrows right to where the entrance to the ride is.

Minnie takes over, talking with the staff, and a moment later, I'm being pulled onto the ride. The seats are paired in twos. Minnie is beside me, Bryony and Asher behind, followed by Tatum and Lincoln, while Wylder sits alone at the back.

"I'm scared," I mutter, my heart thumping wildly in my chest, and Minnie giggles.

"It's going to be worth it, I swear," she promises as a bar is pushed down onto my lap, locking me in place.

"Minnie," I plead, my face heating with the

increase in my blood pressure. She doesn't answer me as a small bell rings and we start to move.

Panicked, I grab the handle before me, holding on for dear life as we lean back in our seats, the cart aiming for the sky. Clenching my eyes shut, I feel my breaths grow shallow as the ride levels out again, but the reprieve is short-lived as we tip down, barreling toward the ground, picking up speed with every second.

I scream.

The sound is one of fear laced with adrenaline as we dip and weave, up and down, round and round, as I keep my eyes firmly shut. I don't want to let go of the bar, but I force my right hand to my hip, finding the tiny pocket in my even smaller skirt to feel the familiar press of my coin. It's a mixture of fear of losing it and needing the strength it offers as the ride goes faster and faster.

My fingers curl around the coin, taking the invisible strength, and after a beat, I manage to pry my eyes open, watching the world swirl before me. I have no idea how much time passes before we come to a stop and Minnie pats me on the thigh.

"How was it?" she asks as the bar fixed against my lap eases.

Minnie smiles excitedly as I try to find my

words. Shaking my head in disbelief, I answer her truthfully.

"That was amazing."

She cackles, climbing out of the cart to the left and waving for me to follow her. The second I'm back at her side, she tugs me toward the exit, still laughing.

"How do you know it was amazing if your eyes were closed?" I hide my face behind my hands, embarrassed, but it only makes her laugh more as she pulls at my arm and drags me away from the ride. "The real question is, are you doing another one?"

I fix my stare on hers, nodding excitedly. I need that hit again; it almost gave me the same tingles as Wylder did, and if his option isn't available, I'll take this instead.

ONE RIDE LEADS TO ANOTHER, and another, and another. I feel sick from all the sweets. Cotton candy is apparently my favorite, while the smell of buttered popcorn makes me gag.

Who knew you could learn so much about yourself in a place like this?

I've worried about losing my coin more than

once, but there have been some calmer rides that haven't left my heart at the peak of a drop that steals my breath.

Tatum appears in front of me, pulling me from my thoughts as he holds a weird food item in front of me. He nods for me to take it, but I eye it with concern.

"What is it?"

He bites back a smile, shaking his head at me. "It's a corndog, and I promise you, it's good," he insists, and I slowly take the stick from his grasp.

"I'm going to hold you to that statement," I muse, and his grin widens.

"If you don't like it, I'll join the parade," he declares, pointing toward the celebration parade, slowly passing in a wave of music, dance, and joy.

"And if I do like it?" I ask, and his eyes bore into mine.

"If you like it, then you get to sit with me on the Ferris wheel," he explains, pointing to the giant wheel slowly spinning in the distance.

I can't deny that I like the sound of his offer. I've been passed back and forth between Bryony and Minnie, but I've seen the way they're looking at each other. They could sit together on the Ferris wheel if I like the corndog.

Desperate to like it, I take a big bite, groaning the second the flavors hit my tongue.

"I'll take that sound as a success," he murmurs, leaning closer so I can hear him over the music, and my cheeks return to the permanent pink hue they take on in their proximity.

"You owe me a ride on the Ferris wheel," I mutter in response as he leans back enough for me to see his pupils dilate.

Damn.

"Fuck," Asher grunts, garnering everyone's attention as he stands, glaring down at his cell phone like there isn't a glow of magic playing before him.

"Is he okay?" I ask, peering up at Tatum, who places his hand on my back, keeping me close.

"Yeah, he just…Lincoln is our Alpha, but Asher has a lot to deal with. Especially from his uncle."

"His uncle," I repeat, frowning in confusion.

"Yeah, he's a member of The Imperium." He must see that I have no idea what that means because he explains a little further, keeping his voice as low as possible. "The Imperium is the authority over the supernatural world. More specifically, the wolves, but it comes with responsibility in each quadrant. Which I'm sure is great, but Asher doesn't like him or the deals he makes."

I try to absorb his words, blinking slowly when Asher curses again.

"Are we ready for the Ferris wheel? I need to make some calls," he states, looking to Lincoln for confirmation, and we all wordlessly follow after them toward the next ride. Bryony and Minnie giggle between themselves as we join the VIP line again, and no one complains when I board with Tatum.

The bench is small as I take a seat, my thigh pressing against his as he gets comfortable beside me. The door closes behind him, forming the perfect bubble around us as we slowly lift in the air. We don't get far before the ride stops for the rest of the group to get on.

We are enveloped in a comfortable silence as we look out over the night, watching the lights dance beneath us.

"It's magical," I murmur, looking at Tatum, who offers me a soft, wistful smile.

"I forgot how magical this place could be until I got the pleasure of seeing it through your eyes. Clearly, I've been taking it for granted for too long."

Thankfully, it's dimmer in here so I don't have to worry about my pink cheeks appearing again. Especially when he makes it clear he's paying attention to me.

His gaze is locked on mine, making it impossible to look away, even as the ride takes off high into the air at a slow pace.

"Polaris," he breathes, turning to face me with his arm braced along the back of the seat, and I gulp.

My heart races, knowing precisely what he's saying without uttering another word, and I nod. Desperate.

He closes the gap between us until there's only an inch remaining. I steel my spine and inhale the best I can before I eliminate the last of the space between us.

Instead of my lips being pressed against his cheek this time, they're firmly against his. His touch is soft, delicate, and wistful. He lifts his hand to cup my face, deepening our connection as our lips meld together again and again.

We kiss, and we kiss, and we kiss.

I don't think I could ever tire of his mouth on mine. Everything is slow, making the sensations he creates bubble beneath my skin. There's a desperation beneath the surface of our touch, but it's injected with a lack of urgency that makes it even more intimate.

"When you're done, we're waiting."

Minnie's voice cuts through the air, jolting us

apart, and for this first time, I don't blush. Or maybe I'm already blushing, and that's why I don't feel the heat. I see it, though, in Tatum's eyes.

Damn.

"That was..." Tatum's sentence trails off as he reluctantly stands, and I nod, not knowing what word fits his statement, but I feel it nonetheless.

The second he steps off the ride, I know our moment has passed, but before I can climb out, a hand is offered for me to take. The second I place my palm against theirs, I know it's Wylder I'll find at the end of it.

"How do we get to ride with the guest of honor?" he asks, tugging me into his side and draping an arm over my shoulder.

I shake my head at him playfully, but when I meet his stare, he gives me a pointed look, confirming he's not playing around.

"Where to next?" I ask, and Lincoln chimes in for the first time all night. "We've got about thirty minutes before the fireworks happen."

"Maybe the log flume, then?" Minnie asks, but it's an order more than anything. One that Lincoln doesn't argue with as he rolls his eyes at her.

"I get you on the log flume, right?" Wylder asks, and I nod, earning a smile from him as the group heads off toward the final ride.

Once again, the wait time barely exists as we cut the masses and head down the VIP line instead. Wylder holds me back, letting everyone else take the two-seated flumes before us before finally letting me climb into the next one. "Give us a five-row barrier, man," he says to the worker, who nods eagerly to please him before Wylder takes a seat beside me.

We barely make it around the first corner, the boat rocking beneath us, before he leans in to press his lips against my ear. "I saw you kissing Tatum."

Oh crap.

My eyes blow wide as I lean back, trying to read his expression, but all I find is a heated stare.

"I…uh, I—"

"I'm not mad, Little Witch. I'm hard," he states as he grabs my hand from my lap and presses it against the apex of his thighs, where I feel the outline of his dick.

I shiver, flexing my fingers, and he groans, tossing his head back, leaving me to gape in wonder at him.

"That's enough of that, Polaris. I want you wet," he grunts, dropping his hand to my thigh. Wordlessly, he drags his fingertips higher, lifting the hem of my skirt to trace over the silk panties beneath. "Damn, that's hot," he breathes, running his fingertips back and forth until they dampen beneath his touch. Then he tugs at the side and the fabric snaps at my waist, just like last time.

"Wylder," I whisper-yell, staring at him with wide eyes as the boat rocks back, taking the incline slowly, but he pays me no mind as he runs his fingers through my folds with nothing between us. "Oh, God."

"That's it, Little Witch. Say a prayer," he rasps, shifting slightly in his seat so he can tease at my entrance while his thumb rubs over my clit.

"Wylder, I can't get off the ride if you do this. My skirt will be damp, and I'll never be able to make sure I don't expose myself." My plea is weak I want it just as badly as last time, but I'm aware there will be repercussions once the ride ends.

"It's a water ride. You're going to get wet either way. This way is just better," he states at the same time he thrusts a finger into my pussy. "Just don't make a sound. Otherwise, you're going to gain an audience," he murmurs, nodding ahead to the rest of the group.

I sink my teeth into my bottom lip, biting back a groan as he runs his lips over my neck, leaving goosebumps in his wake. My hips tilt, desperate for him to go deeper as he stretches me with a second finger. I feel his lips curl against my skin.

"That's it, Little Witch, ride my hand."

I don't think, I just move. My mind is still latched onto the fact that he was turned on by Tatum kissing me, and I'm eager to please him if I wind up with the same result as last time.

He claims my lips in the next breath and I curl my fingers around his neck with one hand while I hold onto the handlebar with the other, letting my hips take over as the ride disappears into the background.

I rock back and forth against his hand, his fingers filling me as his thumb grazes my needy nub repeatedly. With his lips on mine, dominating me, combined with the public setting, it's impossible to hold back the desire that burns through my veins. I'm familiar with the tingles that shoot up my legs this time, and I crush my lips harder against his as I fall apart.

Wave after wave of euphoria claims me as I press my nails into his flesh, but he doesn't seem to mind since he leans back, forcing me to look at him as my body stops convulsing around him.

"So fucking hot, Polaris. I've made you come with black hair and silver hair now. Let's find out if you taste just as sweet," he rasps, pulling his hand from my core to run his tongue over his soaked fingers.

I groan again, but the sound is snapped from

the air as we suddenly start barreling forward, hitting the shimmering water at the bottom of the ride with a splash. Wylder laughs immediately while I splutter to catch my breath, realizing just how drenched I am, but the water does nothing to dampen the heat rising between us.

"I want to repay the favor, Wylder," I breathe, sinking my teeth into my bottom lip as I stare at the outline of his cock, and he grins.

"Soon. Real fucking soon, Little Witch."

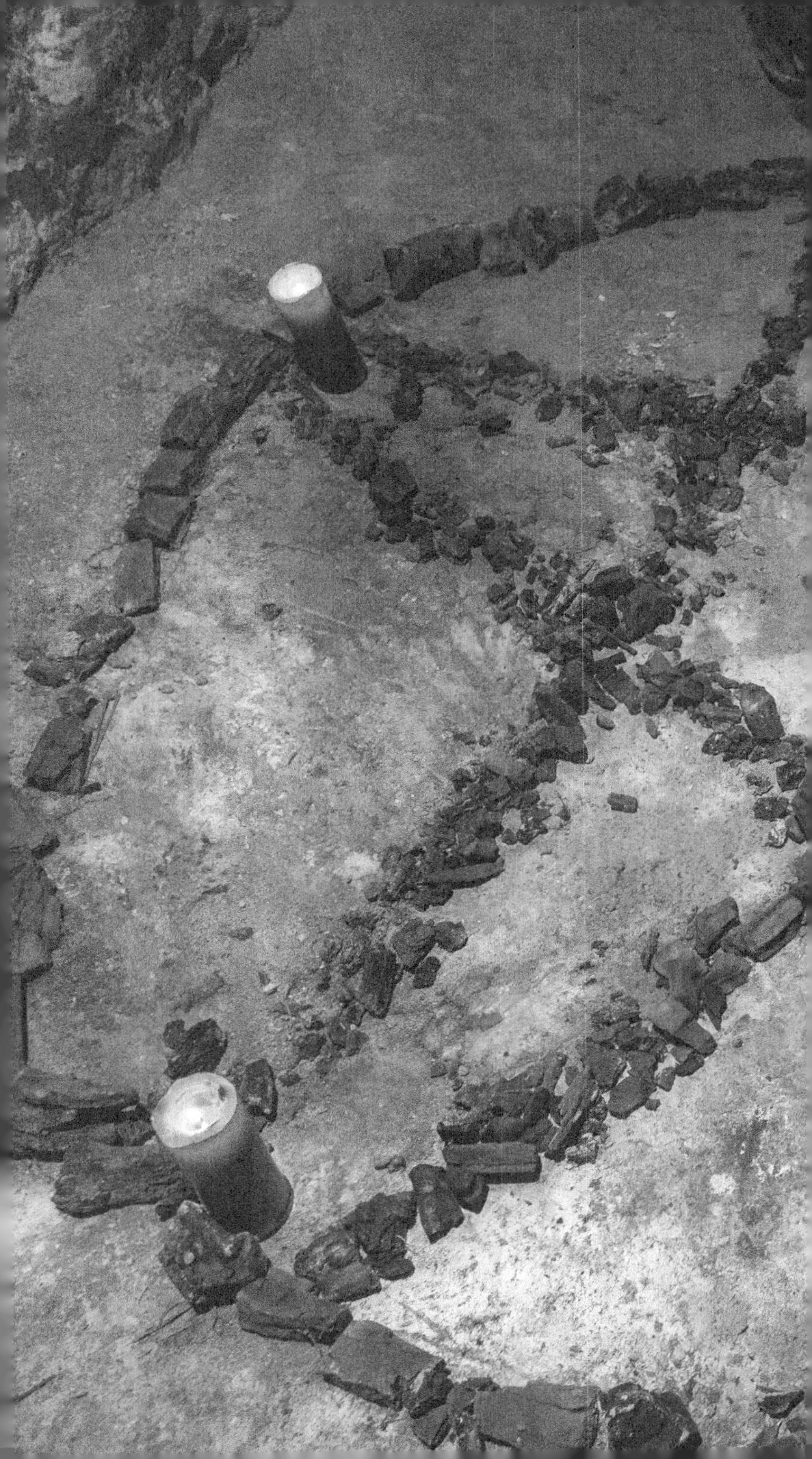

37

LINCOLN

She walks like a virgin, and she tells me she's a virgin, yet the shit-eating grin on Wylder's face tells a different story. I watch as they climb off the log flume together. Her cheeks are more flushed than usual, and she's nervously toying with the hem of her skirt. But it's not that sliver of information that holds me captive; it's the little show Wylder makes of licking his fingers one by one when he thinks no one else is looking.

That motherfucker.

The sound of a snicker from my right pulls my attention away to find Bryony grinning at me.

"You're not subtle in watching her, you know," she muses, and I scoff.

"And you're not subtle about watching my sister," I retort, enjoying how her eyes widen in surprise. She neither confirms nor denies my accusation, and truthfully, I like the silence.

"Hurry, there's not much time before the fireworks," Minnie hollers, leading the way to the private two-story platform our family has toward the back of the park. It offers the best view of the fireworks, and secretly, it's my favorite part of the whole day.

My parents inherited ownership from my paternal grandparents, a family lineage in the human world, which allows us to ensure our continued understanding of the non-supernatural world. We've been coming here for as long as I can remember. Whenever we submit requests to leave campus, it's almost always to come here.

It's a slice of peace away from our reality, but I hate the hustle and bustle of it all. That's why the balcony is my favorite part, because we can soak it all in without having to deal with anyone else.

I keep my head down as we wind our way through the crowd, bypassing the security blocking off our private area before taking the stairs two at a time. When I reach the top, I opt to head toward the bathroom. I need to clear my head. I'm supposed to be mad at her, at Polaris, yet she consumes me.

Fuck.

I avoid staring at myself in the mirror as I splash water on my face, acutely aware that I'm already damp from the last ride. I need to get through the fireworks, then we can get the hell out of here and I no longer have to participate in whatever Minnie is trying to accomplish with the trip.

I step out of the men's room at the exact same time the women's door opens, and just my luck, it's the one woman I'm trying to avoid.

Polaris.

Midnight.

Fuck.

Her silver hair is dripping at the ends, damp from the log flume, and the water marks on her top expose the outline of her taut nipples.

Double fuck.

She offers me a soft, nervous smile before tucking her head down and moving to walk around me, and I almost let her go.

Almost.

I would have, I really fucking would have, if I hadn't caught her scent.

Her fucking scent.

Reaching out, I grab her arm, stopping her in her tracks as my pulse thrums through my entire body.

“Who touched you?” I grind out, already aware of the answer. I know how to put two and two together, but I want to hear her say it.

“I don’t know what you mean,” she murmurs, looking up through her lashes at me, and I scoff, my grip on her arm growing tighter.

“Don’t,” I growl, stepping closer so we’re chest to chest, trying to keep my feral wolf at bay. “Don’t you dare fucking lie to me. I can smell you.”

She cringes, her face scrunching up in a mixture of disbelief and embarrassment, but she doesn’t deny it.

Spinning us, she moves effortlessly in my arms as I pin her back to the wall. She doesn’t shy away like I expect; if anything, her nipples look sharper.

I hold still for a beat, and when she doesn’t move, my body does. Slipping a hand beneath her skirt, I hiss at the bare contact with her pussy.

Her. Damp. Bare. Pussy.

“You’re still wet,” I croak, my fingers gliding with ease through her folds as she gasps, but she doesn’t try to push me away.

I watch as her chest rises and falls sharply, my own breaths following the same pattern as I swirl a finger around her clit before throwing all of my cares away and plunging a single finger into her core.

She moans, and I groan, the sounds melding together between us as my eyes widen.

She's so tight. So damn tight.

Her hands lift to my arms, holding on instead of pushing me away.

"I'm still a virgin, Lincoln," she whispers, her jaw slack as she stares at me with a need I know reflects in my own eyes.

"What?"

"A virgin," she repeats, attempting to bring me back to Earth, but it's too late for that. Not with her essence in the air and her sweet, wet pussy in my grasp

It's all too fucking late.

Later, I can figure out where it all went wrong, but now is the time for exploring.

Laughter echoes in the distance, reminding me that my family and her friend are outside on the first-floor balcony, and before I can change my mind, I grab her hand and dart for the stairs. She stumbles after me without complaint, our pace only slowing when we step out onto the second-floor balcony, with views of the park beneath us.

I don't look at her as I pull her toward the edge, the railing separating us from the guests below as they all wait for the firework show to draw the night to an end. They're not the only fireworks I'm chasing, though; I want hers too.

Maneuvering her so she's braced against the railing, with both hands holding onto the steel barrier, I crowd her from behind, pressing my chest to her back. She shivers, making my cock strain against the waistband of my pants.

"Are you forgetting the virgin part?" she repeats, like I'm the only one who might regret this at the end of the night, but I push that thought aside and run my hands over her waist where a sliver of delicate skin is exposed.

"Is that what you want?"

"I don't understand," she breathes, tilting her face to look back at me, but I quickly angle her back toward the park.

"Do you want to leave here a virgin?"

My words hang in the air, draping us with the desire flowing thick between us.

A second passes, then another, and another, before she shakes her head.

Maybe I should demand verbal consent. Perhaps I should ask again, be extra sure, but fuck it all to hell, I don't want her to change her mind.

"Watch the sky," I order, and she tries to glance back again.

"Why?"

I shake my head as I pinch her jaw gently and turn her back around again. "You ask too many questions, Midnight."

Thankfully, she doesn't try to move out of position again, and the questions stop as I drop to my knees behind her, skimming my fingers over the hem of her skirt that barely covers her bare pussy. Moving higher, I palm the globes of her ass, enjoying the way she leans farther into the fence, perching herself out to me for better access.

If she's a virgin now, she must have been a sex goddess in another life because she's writhing already.

With the new angle, I lean forward, swiping my tongue along her exposed core, and she whimpers, a sound that will forever be etched into my memory.

She's sweet. So fucking sweet, just like Wylder promised.

I tease her a few more times, but it's clear Wylder has already made her come, so she's ready for me, and I want to time this perfectly with the fireworks. As if sensing my thoughts, the lights below grow dim in preparation and I quickly rise to my feet, undoing the button of my pants before I line up my cock with her entrance.

It's on the tip of my tongue to offer her a final

out, but she rises up on her tiptoes, tilting her hips at the perfect angle as I sheath a condom down my length.

"Bite my arm," I rasp, and she glances back at me in confusion as I extend my arm around her neck, grabbing onto the opposite shoulder.

"What?" she asks, but I'm done talking. Instead, I push past the final veil of resistance between us, relishing at the feel of her teeth sinking into my arm as I fill her completely.

The moment I'm all the way in, I freeze. Maybe for her, but definitely for me.

She's too fucking tight. I will come without moving another inch if I don't give myself a second.

Her muted whimpers against my flesh are almost diminished by the first whistles of the multi-colored fireworks popping off in the distance, but I still hear them.

Resting my head between her shoulder blades, I try to count to ten, but she's wiggling before I reach five. "I'm trying to go easy on you," I rasp against her skin, and she shivers.

"If I wanted easy, I wouldn't be giving it to you," she mutters back, her lips moving along my skin.

Fuck.

Flexing my other hand on her waist, I slowly pull my cock all the way out, noting a few spots of red on the condom.

Holy fuck.

One glance at the blood and everything turns red in my vision. I grow more feral with every second, and the strength needed to keep myself at bay becomes harder to control.

"Please move," she begs, making my eyes roll to the back of my head.

"I can't."

"Please, Linc."

"If I move an inch right now, I'm going to fuck you without restraint, and you deserve at least a little of it," I bite, and she glances back over her shoulder again, ignoring the fireworks before us as her eyes do all the talking.

I'm definitely going to hell for this, but with the glimmer in her eyes, she'll be right there with me. I slam back into her with the same force as the first stroke and her teeth bite down on my flesh again. The world disappears around us as I fuck her. Really fuck her, just like she wants.

She matches every thrust of my cock head-on, crying out against my arm as I feel her core tense and her release flood our connection.

I tighten my hold, keeping her upright as her

body goes lax, and just when I think she's done, she spasms around me again, leaving me no choice but to fall over the cliff with her.

Ecstasy burns through my veins as my movements become staggered, claiming every inch of her orgasm along with my own. The fireworks reach their crescendo in the distance as we lean on one another, letting the weight of the sizzling tension ease.

I don't want to move. If anything, I want to go again, but even if I am able to convince her, I know a new condom would be needed. Pulling out, we both tremble at the loss, and I release my hold on her to discard the condom.

Stepping back, a hint of gold flashes on the ground, pausing my movement as I blink at it.

The desire that coursed through me moments ago dissolves into nothing as I slowly reach down to grab it. Standing to full height, she turns to face me, spying the item in my hand. Her eyes grow wide with panic, and she pats at the pockets of her skirt. Realization washes over her and she tries to grab it from my hand, but I close my fingers around it before she can make contact.

Taking a step back, I level her with a pointed glare.

"How do you have this?"

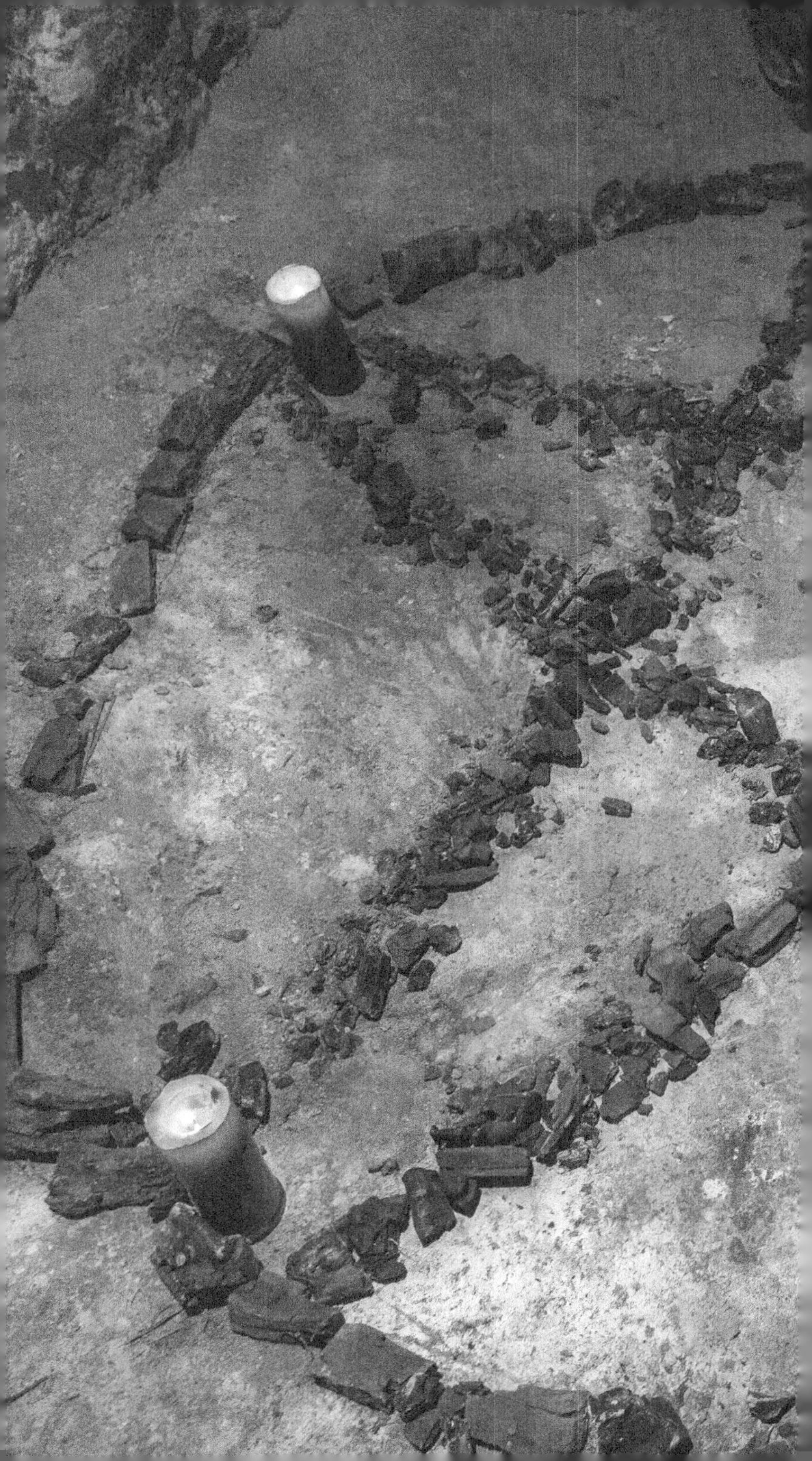

38

POLARIS

My heart thunders in my chest, stealing my breath as I try to grab at his hand again, but he moves farther back. Desperation claws at me as he points a finger in my direction.

"Stay where you are," he bites, using his spare hand to remove the blood-stained condom from his dick before zipping his pants back up.

"Give that back," I murmur, trying to remain as calm as possible, but it's harder than I expect.

He scoffs, shaking his head at me. "Give it back? You're going to tell me why you stole it."

I gape at him in disbelief. "I didn't steal it," I insist, but he doesn't hear me.

"What's going on?"

I die when the question comes from behind Lincoln. We've got a whole audience now.

Wylder, Tatum, Asher, Minnie, and Bryony.

Lincoln seems more than pleased to have reinforcements, though. Turning to his sister, he flings an arm in my direction as everyone draws closer. “We let her in, and for what? To steal from us,” he snarls before turning back to face me. “Are you even a Florentine?” he growls, and I try to calm my despair as I gape at him in horror.

“Are you joking right now?”

“Lincoln, what’s going on?” Wylder asks, frowning between us, but he doesn’t take the final step toward me. He stays right at his friend’s side.

Lincoln opens his hand to reveal the coin. Not just any coin, *my* coin.

“Where did you get that?” Tatum asks, frowning at the gold in the night air, and I shake my head.

“I don’t know,” I breathe as Minnie inches closer, folding her arms over her chest as she looks at me.

“You’re not helping your case right now.”

Pressing my face into my hands, I force two deep breaths into my lungs before I look at her again. “I’ve always had it, but I don’t know how because I don’t recall anything before Florentine’s. Now, give it back,” I plead, turning to Lincoln, who scoffs at me.

“Like fuck,” he snaps, and my knees buckle

beneath me. I manage to grab the railing behind me to keep my balance, but the nausea that churns in my gut doesn't waiver.

"I think she's telling the truth," Bryony states, moving around the wolves to come to my side. She offers me a tight smile, but there's little she can do here. This is all on me.

"Of course you would say that; you're a witch as well. You were probably in on it," Lincoln snarls while Asher remains frozen in place, cell phone in hand, as he stares at us intently.

"I think she's telling the truth too," Tatum adds, making my heart ache as he looks over me from head to toe. "She's bleeding," he mutters, pointing at my leg, and I look down the length of my body to see what he means, only to be overcome with mortification.

Understanding washes over Wylder's face. He, along with everyone else, knows what just happened here, and now it's all a damn mess.

"Let me help you," Bryony murmurs, offering me her hand, but I can't go anywhere, not without that coin.

I shake my head as I step back, tears burning the back of my eyes as I turn to face Lincoln.

"Give it back," I demand, my words firm as my nostrils flare.

"It's not yours," he growls, and I stand taller despite the ache between my thighs, leveling him with a deadly stare.

"Give. It. Back," I repeat, aware I'm trembling from head to toe, when Asher finally edges closer. He takes the coin from Lincoln, who doesn't stop him as distress coils through my bones.

"Only five of these exist in the whole world, and you're telling me you have one of them?" he asks, holding the coin between us, and I shake my head, confused and scared.

"It's just a coin, it's just—"

"That's the face of The Joker. Do you not know what that means?" he interjects, his voice harsh as he narrows his eyes at me.

"Obviously not, asshole," Bryony snarls, coming to my defense.

The trembling grows stronger as I silently plead with him to give it back.

"It's the symbol of the original ancestors. It's linked to those the first witch loved," Asher explains.

I gape at him, eyes wide at the information he just dropped, but I don't understand. "It's just a coin, it's just a…Ahh—"

A burning sensation claws at my wrists, tearing a strangled scream from my lungs as I collapse to my knees, the pain unbearable as my head snaps back, eyes peering up at the sky. It feels like an eternity before the sensation subsides when a clanging rings through the air, drawing my attention to the ground…where my bangles lie broken before me.

PREORDER the next book in The Savage Six series here.

OR CONTINUE READING for a glimpse at a completed dark academia series.

AFTERWORD

I can't even explain to you how much fun I have had so far with this series!

For the first time, the woman isn't already a strong badass queen. I have to make her one, and I think this reflects me a lot right now. Things aren't always easy, and sometimes there's no reason why, but as I build Polaris up, I'm building myself back up too.

I hope you don't relate to her, but if you do, I hope I'm doing her justice for you.

Let's get ready for the ride, it's going to be a good one.

See you on the other side, queens!

ACKNOWLEDGMENTS

Michael. Michael. Michael.
The husband. The wonder that is.
Thank you for everything, especially the moments where I'm struggling and you blow dry my hair for me. It's in those moments I feel the strongest, and it's because of you.
I love you.

My angels, I love you so much. Keep being awesome. I don't know how I became so blessed to have two cool-ass kids like you guys, but I'm thankful every day. Even when you use my own sass back on me.

Nicole and Jeni. The Alpha Queens. I don't know what I would do without your encouraging words. You help make all of this possible, thank you!

Kirsty, my fam, you're a G. Thank you for keeping this ship afloat. It means so much!

My beta readers, you are so freaking awesome, your constant support and cheer gives me life.

David, when you make me work for it, I hate you. When it's done, you're awesome, haha. Thank you.

Sarah, as always, my queen. You're 10/10 forever!

ABOUT THE AUTHOR

KC Kean began her writing journey in 2020 amidst the pandemic and homeschooling… yay! After reading all of the steam, from fade to black, to steamy reads, MM, and reverse harem, she decided to immerse herself in her own worlds too.

When KC isn't hiding away in the writing cave, she is playing Dreamlight Valley, enjoying the limited UK sunshine with her husband, children, and furbabies, or collecting vinyls like it's a competition.

Come and join me over at my Aceholes Reader Group, follow my author's Facebook page, and enjoy Instagram with me on the links below.

ALSO BY KC KEAN - CONTEMPORARY

All of the below series are based in the same world and cross overs of characters may happen throughout.

FEATHERSTONE ACADEMY

My Bloodline

Your Bloodline

Our Bloodline

Red

Freedom

Redemption

ALLSTARS SERIES

Toxic Creek

Tainted Creek

Twisted Creek

BETHANY & RYAN'S STORY

Burn to Ash

EMERSON U SERIES

Watch Me Fall

Watch Me Rise

Watch Me Reign

RUTHLESS BROTHERS MC

Ruthless Rage

Ruthless Rebel

Ruthless Riot

ALSO BY KC KEAN - FANTASY/PARANORMAL

Each series listed below takes place in their own worlds and there is no cross connections.

SAINTS ACADEMY

Reckless Souls

Damaged Souls

Vicious Souls

Fearless Souls

Heartless Souls

SILVERCREST ACADEMY

Falling Shadows

Destined Shadows

Cursed Shadows

Unchained Shadows

HEIR ACADEMY

Kingdom of Ruin

Reign of Blood

Hunt of Night

Fate of Eternity

Court of Truth

THE SAVAGE SIX SERIES

Savage Hope

Savage Desire - coming April 2025

Savage Torment - coming June 2025

Savage Sacrifice - coming August 2025

Made in the USA
Las Vegas, NV
20 March 2026

43968911R00308